Island Song

Madeleine Bunting

GRANTA

Granta Publications, 12 Addison Avenue, London W11 4QR
First published in Great Britain by Granta Books, 2019
This paperback edition published by Granta Books, 2020

A CIP catalogue record for this book
is available from the British Library.

1 3 5 7 9 10 8 6 4 2

ISBN 978 1 78378 463 9
eISBN 978 1 78378 462 2

Typeset by Avon DataSet Ltd, Bidford-on-Avon, Warwickshire

Printed and bound by CPI Group (UK) Ltd, Croydon, CR0 4YY

www.granta.com

For my mother, Romola,
who painted a vivid picture of her wartime childhood
on our country walks and thus introduced me to
storytelling and history.

The sea awoke at midnight from its sleep,
And round the pebbly beaches far and wide
I heard the first wave of the rising tide
Rush onward with uninterrupted sweep;
A voice out of the silence of the deep,
A sound mysteriously multiplied
As of a cataract from the mountain's side,
Or roar of winds upon a wooded steep.
So comes to us at times, from the unknown
And inaccessible solitudes of being,
The rushing of the sea-tides of the soul;
And inspirations, that we deem our own,
Are some divine of foreshadowing and foreseeing
Of things beyond our reason or control.

From *The Sound of the Sea*,
Henry Wadsworth Longfellow

Prologue

1994

Helene was sleeping, her shallow breaths barely audible over the whirr and beep of the machines. Each breath was hesitant, like a wave that appears to stand still at the crest before it breaks. From time to time, Roz followed the whispered intake and exhalation, wondering if there would be another. Her mother was holding on longer than the doctors had expected.

Her soft white hair was awry. Roz found it easier to focus on her hands, which still described the character of her life: elegant, but worn. Long fingers with two rings – the engagement ring with the large single diamond, and the band of gold, which had thinned over the half century of use. Nails short and never polished. Gardener's hands, and rougher than you would expect.

Helene's eyes opened and fell on Roz, sitting beside the bed.

'You're back,' she said, her voice surprisingly steady. 'The funniest thing. I dreamed we were on the clifftops, that time in Devon when the three of us went away together after . . . and do you remember? It was so hot – not a breath of wind. We sunbathed.'

Roz did remember. It had been about ten years ago, shortly after her marriage had ended. Helene and Justin, Roz's father, had been walking through the woods ahead of her, and once they came out on top of the cliffs they sat down to wait. As Roz arrived, Helene stripped off her shirt and lay back on the turf in her black bra, luxuriating in the sun's warmth on her skin. Her sunglasses were pushed to the top of her head, her eyes were closed and a smile hovered around her mouth. Roz caught Justin's eye briefly as they shared their appreciation of the indomitable woman between them. Roz flopped on the ground and Justin put his arm around her shoulder. She leaned against him, and felt a familiar comfort as he kissed her hair. That was the moment when life started for her again – when she was able to feel happy once more.

'You were so sad at that time, after Nick. It broke our hearts. The sunshine brought us all back to life,' said Helene.

Roz closed her eyes and thought of the Devon cliffs, the sound of the sea on the rocks and the sweet smell of earth and grass baking in the heat.

'I was happy then,' murmured Helene.

Roz knew what her mother was not saying: that the moment had been rare, and that happiness had often appeared to be just out of Helene's reach. Roz had never understood: a loving husband, a busy family, a cherished home – many would regard Helene's as an enviable life. Roz had instinctively withdrawn from Helene's unease, as if it had been contagious.

Through the hospital window Roz watched the summer rain ease and a bar of soft yellow light unexpectedly open up on the horizon. Roz liked resting her eye on that point where the city petered out south of Crystal Palace, and the chalk rose up to form the downs of Kent on its way to the coast. Roz gathered up her bag to leave.

Helene reached out for Roz's hand. 'I was never going to let you go,' she said. 'I managed that at least.'

'Sorry, Mother,' said Roz, confused. 'I'll be back tomorrow. Same time.'

Helene held fast to her hand. 'Thank you, dear Rosamund.'

Roz bent over and smoothed a strand of Helene's hair across her forehead, before kissing her cheek, as her mother had done for her as a child. And then – so softly that Roz wasn't sure she had heard right – Helene added, 'I was so proud of you. Of your courage. You and me together, we came a long way.'

Later, in her flat, Roz thought of Helene on the cliffs and was pleased that the memory had found its way into her mother's dreams. She liked the image of her as a woman who had taken life in both hands, even in her sixties, rather than as a fragile body battered by illness.

This business of dying was disorganizing her thoughts. That evening she was trying to catch up with some work on a case, the papers spread over the dining table, when another memory interrupted her. The detail was vague, but she knew she was in the garden at home in London. She must have been about eight or so, because she was carrying Jim, and he was wriggling to be put down. She remembered clearly the weight of him on her hip as she tried to imitate how her mother held the plump baby. Helene was wearing a pretty smock dress, and in the sunshine the pale fabric stood out against the dark green foliage behind. Her face was unfamiliar, flushed and full with the weight of two pregnancies in almost as many years. Edward was sitting on Justin's lap. A blue tablecloth, a vase of flowers. Perhaps they were having lunch in the garden. Helene handed Justin a plate of food and was telling him something.

Abruptly, Helene stopped talking, and jumped to her feet. The colour drained from her face and her eyes widened with panic. Justin put Edward on a chair and moved swiftly to put his arms around her. She began to sob and was clinging to him. Roz stumbled to comfort her mother, still carrying Jim, who was slipping from her grasp. She buried her face in the folds of her mother's dress, breathing in her sweet, soapy smell, feeling the bone of her hip, and her mother's body shuddering. Jim broke free and dropped to the ground, howling.

A plane was roaring overhead, low over the roofs. Justin was saying, 'It's the Queen's birthday parade.' The next moment, the nanny scooped up the boys and pulled Roz by the hand into the kitchen.

Roz couldn't remember any other occasion when she had seen her mother cry, let alone with that kind of hysteria. Perhaps she had misremembered it. She would ask her in the morning.

Early the next day, the telephone woke her. Helene had died peacefully in the night. The tears slid down Roz's cheeks as she dialled Jim's number in France.

'She was on her own at the end?' Jim's voice was thick.

Roz nodded silently.

PART 1

I

Helene unpinned her hat and laid it on the stone bench of the handsome Victorian shelter before leaning back against the rough wall, feeling the cool damp of the Guernsey granite through her cotton dress. After the heat of the town and the weight of her shopping bags, it was a relief to wait for the others here in the shade. She could hear the pigeons in the wooded hillside behind her, and, from the sea, the sound of waves on the headland. The green seawater lapped gently at the steps of the old curved pool, built into the rocks.

It looked very inviting. She unbuttoned her shoes and unclipped her stockings, rolling them down to her ankles before carefully slipping them off. It was a relief to feel the dark stone slabs on the soles of her bare feet. Stockings seemed too grown up, but Aunt Lily had been firm: she must remember she was no longer a girl, but a married woman. Helene tucked her dress up and tiptoed over to the steps. First one foot, then the other, paddling in the chilly water amidst the glossy brown seaweed. She raised a hand to shield her eyes from the brightness of the sea and looked over to Castle Cornet, glowing a creamy yellow in the bay. In the distance, she could see the pale contours of the islands of Jethou and Herm, hazy in the late-June sun.

It was hard to remember that this was war. She thought back to the strange tone of her father's voice that morning on the telephone. The door to his study had been ajar, and she had hesitated with her hand on the door handle. High-pitched, strained; she had never heard him speak like that . . .

'Going to be cut, you say? Good God.'

Then, 'The telephone cable to the mainland? So we are on our own? – This is it? – It's goodbye? – We are sure the Germans have been notified of the demilitarization? – Well, that's something.'

There was a long pause. Helene held her breath. She thought of the Germans in Paris, across the water in Normandy.

'We are in the hands of the Lord now,' her father said quietly. 'Goodbye.'

She heard the quiet click as her father replaced the receiver. They were on their own.

Now she pushed the thought away. The girls were coming – she could hear their voices. Felicity and Annie were unusually subdued; both had been told by their parents to come home early from St Peter Port. They pulled off their dresses and folded them on the stone bench in the shelter, leaning against the old granite pillars as they tugged on their costumes. Finally they piled their hair up onto their heads and put on swimming hats, fastened under the chin.

They swam in the big pool, diving into the glassy water with arms outstretched as they had been taught. As usual, they raced each other – crawl and then breaststroke – for several circuits. Before the war, the three of them had been in the swimming team and at the annual tournament spectators had crowded along the edge of this pool and perched on the rocks above to cheer them. Now just the seagulls and pigeons witnessed their efforts. Helene won, as usual, her long limbs slicing cleanly through the fresh seawater, refilled by the recent tide.

Afterwards, they floated on their backs as the water stilled. Helene stared up into the pale blue sky and watched the scraps of cloud to find shapes. This was once a familiar pleasure but now nothing soothed her nagging anxieties. Her husband gone within days of their marriage, her brother on the same boat, and then, worst of all, Lily. All of them across the Channel in England.

The girls climbed out and lay on the rocks in the sun, licking the salt off their lips, and feeling their skin tighten as the seawater dried. They dressed in a few minutes, and helped each other to tuck up their damp hair, and pin on their hats. Helene's long, wavy hair was the most troublesome; there was too much to neatly fit under a hat. Annie and Felicity offered to help carry Helene's bags back to the stop to catch the last bus home to Torteval. They were heavy – she had been lucky to find flour and sugar. The sun was dipping behind the woods and the pools were now in shade. Only Castle Cornet still caught the sun, ruddy red. As the girls walked back towards the South Esplanade, a mother was packing up her deckchair on the sands of Havelet Bay, and gathering her children's buckets and spades. They had built a castle.

Annie told them that she had heard another boat was due to take passengers to England any day. Helene knew it was unlikely now France had fallen. She would remember later how the mother was calling to her boy, who was running in and out of the waves, when three black dots appeared above the horizon. She watched them coming nearer, half listening to Annie's talk of the carnations and freesias being dug up and the glasshouses replanted with vegetables – they would need food not flowers in this war.

The dots became planes. They were flying low and straight towards them. Annie and Felicity followed Helene's gaze and all three girls stopped to stare.

'It's the Germans,' cried Annie, panicking.

'We can't tell yet,' replied Helene, her voice thin. If they waited until they could see the markings, would it be too late? Did they need to take shelter? Were the planes heading to the airport?

'Come on – we've got to hide,' Annie screamed. She was pulling them both back. Only Helene resisted, paralysed by fear and indecision. When she turned round, the other girls were running across the esplanade towards the doorway of a café. It was closed, but they hammered on the door. She caught up with them. Now she could hear the juddering of the planes' engines, so low they must be planning to land. Annie was right – they needed to get off the seafront. The door suddenly opened and all three stumbled into the café. Mr Duquemin was in an apron. He had been mopping the floor after closing up. The chairs were stacked on top of the tables. He looked over the girls out to sea.

'Quick, in the back,' he muttered.

Several other people were now behind them, jostling to get in. More were running across the esplanade towards the café. Helene briefly glanced back and glimpsed two planes, low over the harbour. They were dropping what looked like black packages – then she realized, with a start, that they were bombs. She heard the first crump of an explosion and saw a plume of smoke rise over the quayside, where the tomato lorries had been waiting. Then she heard the sharp rap of machine-gun bullets bouncing off the road and roofs, and glass shattering. People were crowding to the back of the café, where a door led to the kitchens.

'On the floor, everyone, take cover, take cover,' someone shouted hoarsely, again and again.

Helene and Felicity pushed through and ducked under a long table. They clutched their knees and buried their heads. The building shook with each explosion. Glass smashed – the café windows must have gone. At one point the sound of the planes faded, and Helene raised her head. People were still pushing in and some were trying to make their way through to a door down to the cellar. Others were crouching or sitting on the floor. After a few breathless moments, the planes flew back for another round.

Felicity's plump body squeezed against her, flinching at each thump. Helene grabbed her clammy hand and held it tightly. Annie must be in the basement.

Another girl crawled in beside them. She was gasping for breath and had blood running down the side of her face. She pressed close to Helene.

'Are you all right?' asked Helene, in a pause between explosions.

'It's glass,' said the girl, sobbing between half-caught breaths.

Helene could see how the blood was matted in her hair. She had been cut in several places.

'I'm all right – b-but there are bodies in the harbour – men under the lorries,' she stammered.

Helene took hold of her hand and held it as tightly as Felicity's. It was the only comfort she could offer as the explosions and machine-gun fire continued. Every time the planes' engines grew more distant, Helene hoped it was ending, only for the sound to come round again, and she would brace her body once more. The brief quiet gaps between explosions were the most terrifying. Would the next bomb hit them?

When the noise of engines and gunfire fell away completely, Helene listened intently. Was it finally over? The fire-engine sirens sounded the all clear. Later, when Helene was told the raid had lasted about an hour, she was incredulous. It had been the longest hour of her life.

The girl Helene had befriended was hysterical. A woman was dabbing at her cuts with a handkerchief to dislodge the fragments of glass. Helene and Felicity stumbled back into the dining area of the café. The floor was covered with broken glass. Amongst the white faces emerging from the cellar, Helene spotted Annie's. It was a short moment of intense relief. Ahead, through what had been the window, they could see fires in the harbour. Thick acrid smoke filled the sky. Helene tasted grit and her eyes began to smart.

The girls hesitated – where to go, what to do? In front of them the body of a woman lay on the ground. One man, then another, came running up to the prostrate figure. In the distance, an ambulance siren sounded. Helene looked across the beach, where an hour before she had watched the boy playing in the waves. To her horror, she could see the small dark form of a body sprawled on the sand.

The girls stumbled along the esplanade, dazed. They had a vague sense that they needed to help. In the harbour, they glimpsed through the smoke the wreck of bombed warehouses and lorries, and they could hear the furious crackling and snapping of flames. A policeman ran past the girls, his face red, his breathing hoarse. Some of the smoke had begun to clear. Here was the bus stop where Helene had been about to wait for her bus home. Nearby, a lorry was overturned, its crates scattered on the ground. Tomatoes had spilled across the road and been crushed in the melee of running feet. Helene stared at the red stains and, with a start, saw blood had mingled with the tomato juice.

'Get back! Get back!' An air-raid warden, a band on his arm, was pushing them roughly. He leaned over and shouted in their frightened faces. 'Go home. Now.'

★

In the days that followed, Helene could not speak beyond a brief whisper. Nanna made her herbal teas and insisted she stay near her, sitting in the kitchen of The Vicarage by the warmth of the stove. The presence of each was a comfort to the other. For several hours after the bombing, Helene had not been able to get word home that she was safe. In Torteval, on the other side of the island, her old nanny and Father had listened in horror to the bombing raid on St Peter Port. Thirty-three had been killed.

Helene repeatedly saw in her mind the images of blood spreading over the granite cobbles. One body lying beside a bombed lorry had been twisted at an awkward angle. Scattered around him were carnations, their buds still tightly closed. Even worse was the memory of the boy playing in the waves. What kind of men were these Germans, who could strafe a child playing on a beach? It wasn't only the bombing which had swallowed her words. She was choking on the disturbing feeling that the world was unsteady – that nothing was holding, and that the fragments seemed to presage horror to come. Nanna stroked her hair as if she were a little girl again.

★

It felt a lifetime since Tom and Edward had left on the boat back in April yet it was only ten weeks. Helene had been proud of her new husband and her brother as they mingled with the other young recruits on the quay. Children were waving Union Jacks and Guernsey flags, bought from the kiosk on the South Esplanade. But for the tears, the atmosphere was akin to a carnival. Helene had been unnerved by the furtive tears of the nervous youths and worried fathers, and the sobbing mothers. They knew something. Tom had hugged her tight, and she put her arms around his neck, feeling the roughness of his new uniform. She was elated at the ring on her finger, and the memory of the last few days – their wedding and brief honeymoon in the hotel over in Cobo. Later, Tom and Edward had stood on deck, waving and grinning. They looked so young – Tom was only twenty and Edward just eighteen. She couldn't imagine them fighting. They weren't soldiers.

Then, Lily had changed her mind suddenly and decided to leave, taking Helene with her – Father had agreed, believing she would be safer in England. More mother than aunt, Lily had left two weeks ago, after waiting in the queue for days. It was chaos in the harbour. Helene got the message late that Lily had tickets, and reached the quayside just as they were pulling up the gangplank. People were crowded onto the decks for the dangerous crossing. Lily was at the railing, gesturing to her, but Helene couldn't catch her words. She shouted that she would follow on the next boat. Three days in a row Helene went to the harbour, and waited amongst the crowd of anxious islanders, but no more boats arrived to take them.

And then France signed an armistice. Hitler attended a victory parade in Paris. On the island, there was an odd calm, as if everyone was waiting. The cushions of thrift on the cliffs were dotted with flower heads fading to rust, and the gorse bloomed brilliant yellow. Occasionally, planes flew high overhead in the clear summer skies, and Helene's heart would thud heavily and fear would constrict her throat. As they flew on to England, she couldn't feel relief: they were carrying bombs which might kill Tom, Edward or Lily.

The steady accumulation of fear was disorientating: everything Helene had always taken for granted was shifting. Like overhearing the women on the bus, on the way to St Peter Port the day of the bombing. The sentences reverberated in her mind.

'Helped themselves, so I gather – they'd been neighbours for years.'

'That's how they knew what they wanted. Took the best china, so I'm told.'

This was not the Guernsey she knew, where islanders prided themselves on never needing a door key. Looting? What was happening to people?

Father had assured Helene and Nanna that the Germans would leave the islands alone – like in the last war. A lifetime in the pulpit had given him the ability to sound persuasive, Helene realized, as his certainty was proved wrong, several times, in these strange days.

Nanna's nephew came by for a cup of tea, and described how he had been over to Alderney to clear the livestock. Everyone had been evacuated. He had had to shoot the starving dogs and cats that roamed around. Plates of food had been left half eaten on the tables. From the cliffs, he had seen German troops on the French coast through his binoculars. He had come back to Guernsey with a boatload of half-starved refugees – French women and children who had been lost at sea for a week.

Three days after the bombing, Helene, still shaky, was helping Nanna with the baking. Father came into the kitchen, his eyes fierce and his voice an urgent whisper. The women listened in silence, their hands covered with flour. A detachment of German troops had landed at the airport. The German command had taken over a hotel in St Peter Port as its headquarters. The island government had announced that they were cooperating with the German forces, and that it would be a 'model occupation'. He was ashen white. Nanna took a sharp breath and sat down heavily in a chair. Helene saw them glancing at her meaningfully as they exchanged looks of horrified helplessness.

II

Roz wanted a house full of flowers for the funeral tea. She took
a pair of secateurs and her mother's old trug from the outhouse
and wandered into the garden in the cool summer evening. In
the trees overhead there was birdsong, in the distance the steady
hum of London traffic. With a sharp stab of grief, she could hear
her mother's voice instructing her on which flowers to cut and
which to leave. There was no longer any reason to obey, and the
house would be sold before long. She cut large bunches of white
roses, lilies and the precious blue delphiniums of which her
mother had been so proud. She carried them into the kitchen and
laid them on the table ready to arrange in the vases she had found
in the cupboard. The largest vase was for the drawing room, and
she slid in a long branch of copper beech with its dark leaves; in
the smaller jugs she added stems of pittosporum to the blue and
white. After the last few days of meetings at the undertaker's and
the solicitor's, it was pleasurable work.

Roz wasn't sure she had brought much comfort to her mother
in the months before she died, and that made her treasure the
memory of her murmured *thank you*. In the weeks when she
was still at home, Helene's distress had been evident: her hand
had clutched and pawed at the blanket. In hospital, she had
been calmer but in pain. It had been a relief when she died. Now,
Roz wanted – needed – these abundant displays of mourning as
testimony to her mother's vibrant strength.

The phone rang, abrupt and insistent, breaking the silence of
the house. Roz's first instinct was to leave it. She wasn't sure she

could announce her mother's death to another of Helene's friends. But it rang on, it's old-fashioned ring reverberating on the stone flags.

It was Robert, the family solicitor. He wanted to know if she could come to his office on Monday.

'Of course,' said Roz. 'Have you asked Edward and Jim as well?'

'That won't be necessary. I need to give you something. Just you.'

'Right,' said Roz. She was puzzled. Everything was to be shared equally between the three siblings.

'I'm following instructions. It must be Monday. Shall we say nine o'clock?'

Roz agreed, and Robert rang off. Roz stood in the hall, thinking. She and her brothers had seen Robert already for the reading of the will. He must have forgotten some detail that she, as executor, needed to deal with. Dismissing the matter, she checked the dining room and glanced around the drawing room to ensure it was ready for the following day. She counted again the teacups and saucers, the piles of plates and napkins. The sandwiches would arrive in the morning. Everything was in place.

They were rooms full of the memory of her parents and her grandparents. Much of the furniture and china had been inherited from her father's family and bore the imprint of an exotic history of empire and travel: the Chinese vase which her grandfather had brought back; the embroideries and tiles her grandmother had collected in India. Little had changed in this room since she was a child.

★

With loud goodbyes, the front door banged shut again. A few people lingered in the drawing room, and Ed had found them some wine in the cellar. Roz put her head round the door.

'Come and join us,' said Jim, looking up. His eyes were red. Roz had noticed the tears rolling down his cheeks throughout the short service at the crematorium. It had moved her. Jim had a gentle soul.

'I'm going to clear up the dining room with Meg. Try and straighten things a bit.'

In the dining room, the table was covered with the remains of the sandwiches, scrunched-up napkins and used teacups. Meg helped Roz stack the plates. Meg had cared for Helene for several months before her admission to hospital, and had asked to come to the funeral. They chatted while they worked, commenting on the people that had filled the house to bursting. The crush had made it hard to squeeze through the hall or find a space in the drawing room to sit. People had introduced themselves to Roz, explaining how they had come to know Helene. Roz had always marvelled at the way her mother made acquaintances – at the post office or the doctor's surgery – and invited them to tea. Some graduated to regular visits, the ritual of teacups and saucers laid out on a tray, perhaps with a home-baked cake. Helene had never been much of a conversationalist, nor was she a good listener. She wasn't curious about people, but Roz knew well the power of her old-fashioned graciousness. As she looked into the faces of the tall middle-aged man with his teenage daughter, the young woman with her toddler, and the distinguished elderly lady, she realized they had valued their times with Helene. The front door shut again as Jim ushered out the last guests.

Roz looked at the garden. June had unleashed one of its un-expected downpours, but, despite the rain, people had wandered into the garden to escape the crowded drawing room. At intervals, Roz had noticed with a sort of detached horror how guests trampled mud back into the drawing room across the gold-yellow carpet. This inconsequential detail was a sharp reminder that Helene was dead. It would never have happened when she presided over the house, with her combination of distant charm and authority. She inspired in her guests a genteel politeness. Even her children, now in middle age, had rarely dared challenge her. Roz could recollect only one moment when she had tried – and failed – to face Helene down. After Justin's memorial, Roz had been keen to get home, but Helene wanted her to stay for supper. Roz was in the hall with her coat on when Helene drew herself up and fixed her with a glare. Even as Roz protested, Helene had overruled her, raising her walking stick for added emphasis – a magnificently defiant performance. Roz had stayed, balancing a plate at the corner of the table, squeezed between two other guests.

She smiled and straightened her shoulders with a sigh. It was all over, and soon the house, which had seen a century of her father's family history, would have to be sorted, boxed and dispersed. She had grown up with her father's memories of the place. The sitting room upstairs was still called the nursery. Bunk beds remained in the cellar, where the family had slept during the Blitz. The attic stored boxes of photographs and letters belonging to her uncles who died in the First World War. The front door slammed again. Dogs barking and children squabbling. It must be Edward. He and his three children had taken the dogs for a walk.

'How is it going?' Ed came in, picking up a stray biscuit to nibble. 'Can I help finish off?'

Ed had a way of making offers he was unlikely to fulfil, but he made a token gesture of piling up some bowls and taking them to the kitchen. Roz went to join Jim by the fire. It was cheering on this chilly summer day.

'The pictures will go probably midweek,' said Roz as she and Jim sat on the sofa watching the flames. The two most valuable paintings had been left to museums, as arranged by Justin before his death six years ago. These striking images – the only ones which had remained after the catastrophe of the trial –

had borne witness to their family life, adding their own silent, powerful contribution to this room. Perhaps some of Helene's acquaintances had come to sit with them as much as with her, reflected Roz.

'We need to put stickers on the furniture and pictures we have chosen,' said Roz as Ed came back in.

'It should be straightforward,' said Ed. 'The house will be on the market from tomorrow.'

Roz was shocked, but Edward was not one to waste time. He had a brusque energy which jarred on her. He had been Helene's favourite – Helene had always found the boys easier. Roz felt a rush of sympathy for them both, for she had discovered that losing a mother was more difficult than she had expected. A wise friend had likened bereavement to a table with one leg slightly short. She was out of balance, liable to burst into tears, which had proved embarrassing several times already. It was not proving, as Ed put it, 'straightforward'.

She left her brothers by the fire with their wine. Ed's wife had taken the children home, and Jim's wife had found a television upstairs for their girls to watch while she fed the baby. The rain had at last eased, and Roz went outside. She would miss the garden, its mulberry tree sprawled drunkenly across the width of the lawn, one of its branches propped up. Every year, she had gathered the berries for stewing. They were impossible to pick and eat without the juice staining fingers and mouth as their fragile skins burst. The house might be sold before this year's harvest, she realized. Drops of water landed on her head from the foliage overhead. One thing was niggling her: Robert's tone of voice on the phone had been unusually emphatic. A mild-mannered man, rather timid in his way, he had meticulously maintained the family's affairs all his life, and there wasn't much he didn't know about them. The will had been simple, and exactly as Justin had explained a decade ago, several years before he died. The money from the sale of the house would be helpful for Jim – he never had much – and, well, Ed would know how to spend it. The house was in disrepair, but it was Georgian and Hampstead, which would ensure a decent price.

Roz had always loved its generous character. The gentle curve of its bay windows overlooking the front lawn, the handsome stone steps up to the front door, with its cast-iron grate for wiping feet. Here, London became no more than a murmur. World crises came and went, but the house had changed so little that it slowed time down. Just being here allowed memories to bloom as vivid as the present moment – even more so, at times.

The grass was long in the orchard – there had been no one to organize the cutting for the last month. They had been too busy with Helene as she went in and out of hospital. The flower beds were unkempt and the roses needed deadheading. It unnerved her. This house had always been so orderly, the pattern of habit and season well established: the pile of logs in the side passage for the fire; the leaves gathered and burned in autumn bonfires; the stewed mulberries and quince jelly from the trees in the orchard; the rose on the front of the house which needed pruning twice a year.

★

Roz arrived at Robert's office in the city with her usual punctuality, and he greeted her warmly.

'I know this must seem a little strange. Tea? Coffee?' He gestured her to a seat opposite him, and sat down himself.

In front of him was an envelope. Roz could see that it was addressed to her in Justin's handwriting.

'I have one last set of instructions to carry out for your parents,' said Robert slowly. 'The arrangements for this conversation were agreed with Justin and Helene ten years ago, in 1984. Helene added further stipulations that this letter should not be given to you until after the funeral.

'This will be a surprise for you, Roz, and I am sorry that I'm the bearer of some very difficult information –' He broke off while an assistant placed a coffee in front of Roz, and waited until she had left the room. 'Justin was very concerned that you should know. It troubled him greatly in the last few years of his life, but Helene insisted that this information should not be divulged until after her death.'

He paused and Roz took a mouthful of coffee, feeling apprehensive.

He pushed the envelope across the desk. It was bulky. A large A4 brown envelope addressed to 'Rosie' with Justin's distinctive handwriting in ink. His pet name for her.

'I was instructed by them to inform you briefly of its contents before you read it.'

He took a deep breath and began, his voice softer.

'Roz, Justin was not your father. He adopted you when you were a small child. You were nearly three when he first met you.'

He cleared his throat.

'He has never known who your father was and Helene refused to say. Justin knew this could cause you pain, but believed you had the right to know. He wanted to tell you many times. He wanted me to assure you that he always loved you as his daughter.'

Roz saw the kindliness of Robert's eyes, the wrinkles gathered at the corners, and his thinning hair. She heard what he was saying, but couldn't grasp its implications. She looked past him at a picture on the wall, a splash of red paint and a circle of blue. Its randomness seemed appropriate for this moment.

'Yes, of course,' said Roz, glancing at her watch automatically to check that she wouldn't be too late for work. She had a meeting in an hour.

'I see,' she added vaguely.

She cast her mind back to her earliest memory of Justin. It might have been one of those bonfires in the orchard. Helping him rake leaves. Maybe she was seven or so. She thought she remembered earlier occasions: a trip to a fair and a gift of candy floss, a visit to Kenwood to look at the pink Gainsborough lady, as she used to call the portrait.

'My mother said they'd lost an album after the war,' said Roz slowly, recalling a conversation about why there were no photos of her as a baby. There had been plenty of the boys, as babies sitting on her Justin's lap, beaming, or with Helene pushing the pram, or as toddlers. She searched her memory; she remembered a small photo of herself in a sailor suit, aged perhaps four. That was the earliest photo she could recall.

'Your parentage has not affected anything relating to the will. Its impact is simply personal, there are no material issues arising from this letter,' he concluded. 'I hope it does not prove too challenging. In due course, I'm sure you will come to terms with this.'

He was looking at her, Roz felt, as one sensible lawyer to another. They knew how to tidy up and manage these odd details of people's lives. He shuffled some papers and sat forward in his chair, his fingertips touching, almost as if in prayer.

'On a personal note, I would add that I saw, over the course of decades, Justin's deep affection for you, and it seems to me that that would be the most significant issue to keep in mind over the coming months as you adjust to this information. As for your mother's reluctance to let Justin tell you —'

He broke off and took some coffee before resuming, his voice stronger. 'It remains more mysterious. But the war was difficult for many people, and I think those of us who have lived in easier times can give them that understanding at least.'

He waited a few moments and then stood up, stretching out his hand to shake hers. Roz gathered up her bag. He placed his other hand over hers. There was sympathy in his eyes.

Roz wondered if he had read Justin's letter. She held it tightly against her chest as she left his office.

*

Roz was sensible – all who knew her agreed on that, and it was a characteristic on which she prided herself. Her brothers had always relied on her diplomatic steadiness. As she left Robert's offices and stepped out into the street, she told herself she would cope with this announcement. For a moment, she had felt lost, even abandoned, but the odd feeling had passed swiftly. She gathered herself together. She realized with a start that she had always called her father Justin – but they all had. The announcement was disconcerting but, Robert was right, she knew Justin had loved her and that she had loved him. He had been a gentle and attentive father, and their relationship had been full of shared enthusiasms.

She hailed a cab. She would be in the office in twenty minutes. She refused to let herself dwell on the matter and pulled out some papers in the taxi as it manoeuvred through traffic.

Later, during her meeting, she found her mind wandering after the first quarter of an hour. She looked over her colleagues' shoulders out of the window at the building opposite and watched another group of people gathered around a table in a meeting. One of those odd, unbidden memories came back to her. She and Helene had gone to see Justin's body, laid out in the hospital chapel. Her father was lying on a bier; he looked calm but painfully still. Helene had leaned over the body to kiss his cold forehead, and as she straightened, she turned to Roz and said with unnecessary emphasis, 'I loved your father. I really did.' She sounded defensive.

'Of course.'

It was the only moment that her mother's reserve had slipped after her father's death. At the funeral, she had followed the coffin dry-eyed, alone and, as ever, elegant.

'Roz?'

Startled, she realized all her colleagues were looking at her.

'I'm sorry.' She forced a quick laugh. 'I was distracted – what was that?'

A colleague gave her a brief summary; they needed her opinion. Roz normally kept everyone else on their toes. As they were leaving the meeting, her boss asked Roz if she needed some time off.

'I'm fine. It was just a busy weekend, organizing the service, clearing up. Solicitors – that kind of thing.'

She got back to her own office and opened up some files on her computer, but her mind strayed to her bag under the desk and the envelope. She hesitated. Should she read it now? Or slip out for an early lunch? Head home? She tried a couple of times to bring her attention back to the case she was working on, but the words were dancing on the screen in front of her. She decided on an early lunch break. She picked up her bag and threw her raincoat on, trying to think of somewhere quiet to read the letter, somewhere she wouldn't be disturbed. A park bench would be too busy at this time of year in the sunshine. A church might be a better option. There was one round the corner where she had once attended a lunchtime concert.

A few minutes' walk weaving past office workers also heading for an early lunch, and she was at the gateway. As she walked down the path, the sounds of traffic receded. St Bartholomew's was dwarfed by new office blocks. It was well dug in, the path more than a metre below the level of its graveyard. A large plane tree offered a canopy of green to shelter the place from its overbearing neighbours. The centuries were accumulating around it, an island for the ancient rites that had worn hollows and curves in its steps and stone-flagged floors.

The heavy door swung shut behind her and the smell of incense and the thick silence were comforting. She wandered down the aisle, uncertain where to sit. She could hear a small child and its mother murmuring on the other side of the church; otherwise the place was empty. At the turn of the apse, she found a chair. In front of her was a row of squat pillars, holding up the weight of the storeys above. They had the force and strength of a military fort, built to withstand all comers.

She ripped open the envelope and took out a bundle of typed papers. On the top in Justin's handwriting was a letter addressed to her. She felt her heart heave. He had been dead six years, and she missed him. And now, here they were in another kind of conversation, only this one, the last, was a monologue.

12th April 1984
My dear Rosie,

Over the last few years I have repeatedly had a sense that I must put things in order. Above all, that meant bringing myself to account to you for how we met. On one or two occasions, I tried to speak but failed, either in the courage or the words, to explain what has lain on my heart for the best part of forty years. I apologize.

I have asked myself many times if the truth has to be told. Some think that truth is like bubbles in a fine champagne – they cannot but rise to the surface. I have learned that this is not always so. Truth has been a rare property in my life. For years, I have tried to fill the gaps where basic details were missing. Twenty years ago, some of those details emerged, but since then I have colluded in the misrepresentations which took the place of truth.

Much of this story belongs to your mother, not to me. I had hoped for many years that she would tell both of us more of it, but she always refused. She has insisted that you should not know until after her death.

In the pages which accompany this letter, I have tried to recall with as much precision as possible the details of how and when your mother and I met. There were no outright lies between us, only omissions and misunderstandings, developed with subtlety by both your mother and myself. She did not want to explain, and I chose not to press her. I loved her. I will leave you with a mystery, and I fear that if you want to resolve it, you will need the skills of a detective and an historian. In some ways, it was the fact that I had so little to say that made me reticent. What was the point of telling you I was not your father, and that we first met when you were nearly three, when I couldn't offer you any explanation of who your father was? But in the end, I felt I had a duty to give you that opportunity.

My love for your mother has carried a heavy price in my career and reputation, as you know. I have asked myself all my life what secrets she has hidden from me, and I have always feared that if I knew them, I might not be able to forgive her. So I chose to accept the silences. None of this alters the more important truth which has sustained my life since I met you both – which is that I have loved you both.

Your loving father – if you will allow me, I will still describe myself as such,

Justin

Roz looked up at the pillars in front of her, and past them into the nave, where a group of tourists were gathered around a guide. The stones were marked by their age, splashes and streaks of pale grey, but a shaft of sunshine brought out a suggestion of faded yellow. Poor Justin. She had felt in him a loss buried deep. She had attributed it to his time fighting in the war and the deaths of his brothers, but perhaps it had been this secret of Helene's. She could not answer him now, or assure him that he was still, and always would be, her father.

She turned the page.

28th March 1981
The clocks have gone forward, Rosie, and you are due this

afternoon for tea. I have some time ahead of me to write. I am sitting at the desk in the nursery overlooking the garden. I can see the roses are beginning to sprout new leaves of a shiny dark red, a promise of spring. The daffodils are out and their yellow, I think, is painfully brave in the bleakness of this cold English spring.

I first met Helene in 1946. It must have been October. I had just started working at Berkin and Upton's. My uncle ran the business then and had given me a job after I was demobilized. He died when you were still small. I was trying to persuade him to open a modern prints and drawings department. I was young – only thirty-four – and impatient. The passion of my years studying in Paris in the 1930s was with me still. But Berkin and Upton was a very old-fashioned place in those days; we were still in the Mayfair offices and mostly dealing with old masters.

I have a very vivid memory of that meeting. It was sunny but cold. There was little coal that winter, so the grate would have been empty. My first impression was of Helene's slightness. Her delicacy was accentuated by the over-large, frequently mended tweed coat she was wearing. Her blonde hair was tied back. She had very pale, smooth skin which emphasized the curve of her cheekbones, her full lips and the darkness of her long eyelashes – which you all inherited from your mother. But it was her eyes, as you know well, which I found compelling. Everyone does. Their translucent, pale blue.

She wore no make-up and no jewellery except a wedding ring. She was wearing stout boys' shoes, and I noticed the laces had been broken and knotted together repeatedly. She was very nervous, and I sensed that she was making an enormous effort to contain herself and restrain the impulse to run away. The tension of it was tangible.

She told me that she had some prints she wanted to sell. She had an accent I couldn't place. Her voice was very quiet and urgent. She barely looked at me as she spoke. She passed a

*battered cardboard folder over the desk. I was more interested in
her than in its contents. Inside were three drawings wrapped in
yellowed tissue paper. She said she didn't know the artist.*

*The cheap paper was covered in small, hasty sketches. The
thick charcoal and pastel strokes were flamboyant. They were little
outline portraits. Mostly they were of young women. Several were
smoking or drinking, and there were details of lace, pouting red
lips, feathers and elegant ankles. The last sheet was better quality
paper, and was a much more careful reworking of one of the
smaller sketches on the previous sheet. I didn't need the signature
on the last sheet to know what I was looking at. The confidence
and vivacity of these café-society characters was unmistakeable. The
arrogant, sprawling 'Degas' signature was simply confirmation.*

*Her remark seemed disingenuous. Surely she had looked at
the drawings and had read that signature? But when I glanced
up at her – she wouldn't sit down – she looked wary, and I
didn't comment.*

*As you can imagine, it worried me immediately as to how these
drawings had come into the possession of this shabbily dressed
young woman. At the time, I presumed that she was a refugee
who had fled with a few family heirlooms, but lurking at the back
of my mind was the possibility that she had come by them by some
more circuitous and less honourable route. I was aware of the
implications of what I was about to do. Rumours of illicit traffic
were circulating amongst dealers in London. We had heard that
the war had broken up some of Europe's biggest collections,
scattering them all over the world. The Nazis had raided
collections, taking the spoils back to Germany; individual
Germans had picked up what they could. Paintings and drawings
had been hidden, lost and misappropriated in the chaos. Treasures
had 'disappeared'; some were destroyed, others sold at huge illegal
profits to American collectors. You were not in England at the time
of my trial, but perhaps you read the coverage.*

I told her I would need to know the drawings' provenance. She was silent and I remember she stared straight at me. It was a contest of wills. She began to fold the tissue back around the drawings. There were many thoughts chasing through my head, but the most powerful was that I did not want to lose her. I did not want her to walk out of the door and out onto London's crowded streets, where I might never find her.

She had the folder under her arm and her hand was on the doorknob when I made an impulsive decision, which was to have such devastating consequences for me nearly twenty years later. At that precise moment, my only thought was that if I bought the drawings, I would need to take her address. I wouldn't lose her. I offered to buy them. For the first and only time in my life, I embarked on a gamble, which, as you know, ended up destroying my career. After the trial, you were very angry with me and wanted to know more, but I couldn't talk about it. It was bound up with how Helene and you appeared in my life.

The art collection had been Helene's. That was astonishing. It was Helene who had sold it to Justin, not the Hungarian refugee whom he had gone to such lengths to describe in his statement at the trial. And Justin, stupidly devoted, had taken the blame.

She understood why Justin was giving her such detail. Having lied for so long, he had to convince her of this new story, at odds with everything she had always believed of her mother. A few hours ago, she had been told that Justin was not her father, and now, the woman she believed her mother to have been was exposed as a delicate fabrication. She took a deep breath, and smelled the musty stone, wood polish and candlewax. She was sensible and she would manage.

Roz thought of Justin sitting at the desk in the nursery on a cold spring day. There had been many weekends when she would visit after walking on the Heath. Often Helene would be out visiting a friend, and Roz would make the tea and carry it upstairs. She and Justin would sit by the fire and discuss exhibitions they had seen, or a book one of them was reading. He had never let slip a word of this letter. She flicked through the pages. There was much more. With characteristic attention to detail, Justin was trying to give her something – a sense of it all as it happened.

She stared at the gravestones on the floor, with their inscriptions of those who had 'departed this life' centuries ago, and she thought of how, for a period towards the end, her mother had been very agitated at night, disturbed by nightmares. One night, Meg had been sitting with her, and when Roz had come to the door of her mother's room, Meg had urged her to go back to bed. She heard her mother calling out, 'No, no, please, no.' Then she heard moaning through the wall – an eerie sound she would never have associated with Helene. In the morning, Roz had taken over the task of sitting with her mother, and she had been more peaceful. After Helene died, Meg had said something puzzling about Helene having suffered terrible tragedy in her life – that Helene's distressed ramblings had moved her to tears. It had taken Roz aback. She had imagined Helene's life as uneventful, apart from the trial. She turned back to the letter.

She was clearly relieved at my decision. I suggested a price, apologizing that it was not more, and explained that the market was depressed, flooded with work. I even suggested that she would do better to wait until the economic situation was better, perhaps in five or ten years, when she would be able to command a very respectable price. She didn't seem to be listening and unhesitatingly accepted my offer. I asked her to write down the name and address to which I should send the payment. For the first time, something like engagement registered in her face. She looked alarmed and asked if I could pay her immediately. When I explained that our normal procedure was to pay by post, she almost pleaded with me for a cash payment. I had to go downstairs to the cashiers to find the money. She got the cash, and I did not get her address. When I asked if she had more drawings, she was non-committal.

I kept them in my desk drawer for a couple of months after her first visit. I took them out almost daily to admire the fluency of the strokes and the vivid characterization. Part of my delight in them was the sense of proximity to their strange, previous owner. Fingering the edges of the paper and unwrapping the tissue brought back those inscrutable blue eyes.

20th April
Re-reading what I wrote almost a month ago, I think you might ask why Helene had such an extraordinary and immediate effect on me. There had been few women in my life, partly through lack of opportunity but, more importantly, because of a combination of intense shyness and fastidiousness. I poured myself into my studies at university and in Paris, and left women well alone. The hurried, desperate dalliances with women during the war appalled me.

Helene's second visit was as unexpected as the first, and as brief. It must have been about February of that awful winter of 1946/47. The long cold evenings with little fuel or light had taken a toll on all of us; passers-by on the street had the dogged, head-down appearance of people who have suffered one calamity after another. Hope had faded of an end to rationing and the shabby mend-and-make-do of the war years. It must be hard for you to imagine the relentlessness of that scarcity now. I longed for a cup of good coffee or a decent piece of chocolate.

I knew Helene would come back. It was absurd, but I refused to accept that someone could have such a dramatic effect on me and not return. Besides, if she had three Degas drawings, she might have more, though probably of lower quality. If she was in need of

*money (which the urgent request for cash had suggested), she
would have sold her best first. When she returned, she looked a
little better than she did the first time. She was wearing the same
absurd coat, but at least she was wearing women's shoes. There
was even a touch of colour on her cheeks and it made her look less
drawn and pale. She smiled shyly when I greeted her warmly.
This time, I was astonished when she brought out several prints by
Picasso. One was of a boy with a sleeping woman. It had been
produced for the art dealer Ambroise Clément. Another was a very
striking etching and aquatint of a mother kissing her child. At her
feet was a basket of mending. It was after a painting from Picasso's
Blue Period. It was called* La mère. *In the deep blue, you could
see the artist's fingerprints. There was also a lithograph – the
image of a woman. She had a long straight nose, a smile playing
on her lips and narrow eyes. It was beautiful and not unlike
Helene. I even wondered if she could have been a model for
Picasso in Paris. The signature on all these works was
unmistakeable. The strong vertical line for P, and the flamboyant
underlining. They were hand-signed.*

*I knew that Clément had died in 1939 and part of his collection
had recently appeared in Canada. Rumours had circulated that
another part of the collection had been hidden in a duck hide in
the marshes of Chantilly. I asked her if she knew Paris well.
She vigorously shook her head. Again, she asked for payment
in cash. The whole transaction could not have taken more than
fifteen minutes.*

*It was not until the third visit that Helene relaxed a little. She
had begun to trust me. She was in less of a hurry to leave and
when I offered her tea, she accepted. She unbuttoned her coat,
although she declined my offer to hang it up for her.*

*I had rehearsed this first proper conversation many times, but it
seemed as if any topic, other than the weather and the shortages,
risked her falling silent. Questions about the war might be seen as*

prying into the sensitive subject of how she had chanced on the works. Inevitably I blundered. I had thought an inquiry about where she came from was innocent enough, but it prompted her to drain her teacup, do up her coat, and leave.

During the course of that year, she would appear in my office every few months. Each time, she had one or two exquisite drawings or prints. It was an extraordinary collection of recent modernist work: Léger, Klee, Braque and Miró. Each work was of excellent quality. Her nervousness led me to the unavoidable conclusion that she could not have come by the collection through innocent means. I continued to suspect that they were from Clément's collection. More likely than not, I was handling stolen property. I could have spent time working out their likely provenance; I could have asked around and talked to dealers in Paris. Miriam Rothschild's collection had apparently been lost after being buried in sand dunes near Dieppe. But I didn't ask or tell anyone anything.

It took me some time to find a buyer. I wanted someone I could trust and who would be discreet about the provenance. I had one or two leads from clients who had hinted delicately that they would be interested in acquiring modern art that had reached London in the course of the war. About six months after Helene's first visit, one of our most loyal American clients had come in. Harry was a buyer for various collectors. He was also enchanted by her collection, and bought it immediately; he said he understood the situation, and knew of a collector in Ohio who would fit the bill. I told him that there might be more. The chain was Helene, myself, Harry, and the unnamed Ohio collector.

Sometimes, when I mulled over the strange turn of events, I was astonished at how a fleeting encounter with a woman had tipped me from meticulous respect for the law into outright illegality. I had lightly tossed aside decades of family tradition and personal principle on an impulse.

Hiding these transactions in the books was not difficult. My uncle was a superb dealer with a web of contacts around the world, a genuine love of art, and all the necessary character traits – charm, love of company and enthusiasm – but he had the English middle-class disdain for money. Accountants were bespectacled creatures from Bromley, and he left them to sort out the ledgers. He was delighted with the profits I was turning in for the company, and he never dreamed of inquiring more closely where they came from. He knew the value of discretion for a dealer and respected my circumspect answers.

22nd April
By the spring of 1948, I had not managed to find out any more about Helene. I didn't know whether her husband was alive, where she lived or where her unfamiliar accent came from. I had, of course, imagined hundreds of different answers to all these questions. Her accent sounded like clumsy French at times, but I noticed that it was gradually disappearing. She was making a great effort to change the way she spoke. She appeared to come from an educated family, but she wasn't particularly interested in the work she brought me, and did not share my enthusiasm. In fact, I noticed that she was bemused by my delight in them. 'They look like a child's scribbles,' she said once of a Miró print. I began to assume that her husband must have died; there was an air of self-reliance about her. If she had had a husband, surely he would have brought the drawings to me, rather than leaving his young wife to conduct the delicate negotiations.

That gave me a mad hope. About eighteen months after our first meeting, she brought an exquisite Picasso pastel – dating from the early 1930s – a portrait of a young woman. It was the first drawing for which she had shown any liking. We were leaning over it together, and our shoulders brushed. She quickly pulled back and sat down.

She asked me for a cigarette. She held it delicately in her childlike fingers and she put a question to me for the first time. Had I fought in the war? When I said I had, she replied that the war had 'scarred us all' and, by way of explanation, said that her husband had been killed in Italy when she was pregnant. She delivered the statements one after the other, with a short pause between each. I didn't want to scare her with a misplaced interjection, so I waited, alert for every fragment she revealed of her life. She told me she had a small daughter, but no other family. She had arrived in London shortly before she first came to see me. I knew some of this could be untrue, but all that mattered to me was that she did not have a husband. There were many women with children in London whose husbands were shadowy, fictional creatures. She looked uncomfortable, and drew deeply on her cigarette. She was like a teenager smoking for the first time. Her nails were bitten to the quick. She smoked with the affectation of someone who has watched more films than smoked cigarettes. I watched her as she looked out of the window at the plane tree.

As she got up to go, I said, with all the casualness I could muster, that I had two tickets for a piano recital at the Wigmore Hall. Would she care to come? To my delighted amazement, she agreed. She did not know the Wigmore Hall, and so I drew an elaborate little map, with tiny sketches of the prominent landmarks. The map enchanted her and, for the first time, something of her smile reached those tense eyes. As she left, she shook my hand and I was struck by their roughness. She worked with her hands, or had done in the war.

She was late for the concert. She arrived, out of breath, her cheeks flushed with running. She was full of apologies; her child had been fretful at being left with a friend, she explained. But the concert was a success. It was Chopin, and she loved it. More importantly, she couldn't suppress her amusement at a contretemps in the row in front between two stout ladies over umbrellas. She agreed to supper before hurrying home.

Over the autumn of 1948, we met every fortnight or so. By now, she had given me an address in a modest part of Clapham. I had learned that her daughter was two and half, and that Helene had an aunt living in Devon. She told me she was twenty-eight. I lapped up these details about her life with gratitude. Then, one day, she brought you. We were to have tea after a visit to the National Gallery, if I remember rightly. You were very quiet and you held Helene's hand tightly throughout. I was taken by your solemn blue eyes and their steady scrutiny of me. At one point, Helene had to leave the table to take you to the lavatory, and she left her handbag at our table. As I waited, it occurred to me that it might contain identity papers which could give more information about Helene's past. I'm afraid, to my shame, I surreptitiously put my hand inside and fumbled amongst the contents until I felt a slim canvas purse. It contained a zipped pocket for coins and, tucked in the back, a passport. Underneath the table I flicked through the pages, glancing up to check the door through which she would emerge at any moment.

She was born in 1920, so she had not lied about her age. But it was her place of birth which surprised me: she was born in Guernsey, in the Channel Islands. Her surname sounded French – Le Lacheur. I had no time to see more because Helene appeared at that moment and I replaced the purse in the handbag. Had she lived there, or had she just been born there? I didn't see the date the passport had been issued. That was when my curiosity ceased. I didn't want to know any more. My infatuation was so intense that, just as it had led me into illegal dealing, it stopped me from jeopardizing our love affair. Looking back, I think some half-conscious premonition warned me from searching any further. In the following months, Helene sensed that I had abandoned my attempts to know more of her background. We were very happy.

It was a genteel courtship conducted in galleries, museums and parks. There were few concerts, because she could only occasionally find a babysitter. During the day, she always brought you, and I slowly adjusted to the fragmented conversation caused by a child's need for attention.

I began to take an interest in this little girl with her sad eyes. I hadn't had any experience of children, and it was an unexpected joy to discover that I could elicit a shy smile with some small kindness, and that doing so was an increasingly important source of pleasure in my meetings with Helene. We married in the March of 1949 in Hampstead registry office. Helene wanted a very quiet wedding, and in the end only my parents and brother came as witnesses. They were led to believe that I was regularizing an earlier wartime liaison and that you were my natural daughter. They accepted this without question. She told me she had no close family in the country — I understood the aunt who lived in Devon had moved to the Far East and she told me that her parents were dead. We celebrated here afterwards with a tea of rare cream cakes and champagne — there was still rationing.

13th June

I'm sorry that we have lied to you. You quickly became like a daughter to me, and I have loved you, I believe, just as I would have loved my own. When Helene and I married, I adopted you, and since Helene insisted she had lost your birth certificate, the replacement named me as your father. It was not entirely legal, but it meant that the paperwork never exposed the truth. I wanted to tell you when you were twenty-one, but Helene forbade it. She said it might disrupt your studies. When you came back from university so full of your new life, it seemed cruel to destabilize you with this revelation when we were all struggling to cope with the aftermath of the trial. I always hoped there would be a suitable time in our lives. I was weak to give in to Helene. As the years went by, it became harder to reveal the truth. I was afraid you would be angry with us. Just before you married, I again suggested to Helene that we tell you, but she was adamant. Each time she had a different and plausible explanation.

17th June
All that remains is to explain the sad chapter in our family history with which you are already familiar. You will remember the crisis which brought my career to an end. You were studying in America at that time, and rather preoccupied with your own life. Your studies and your boyfriends were taking up your attention. I remember writing one or two letters explaining a little of what was going on, but it must have been quite a shock when you came home for good in 1968 and realized everything that had happened: your father's reputation shattered and his career over. Fortunately, you were more interested in settling back into England, taking up your legal studies and marrying Nick. It was only later that you asked questions. I didn't know how I could tell one part of the story without another, so I never gave you a proper explanation. You learned that, like so many aspects of our family life, this was forbidden territory.

To explain fully, I will have to return to 1949. The years after Helene and I married were the happiest of my life. Let no one say happiness cannot be based on an illusion. We moved into this house in late March 1950 after my mother had bought a flat. She wanted the next generation to grow up in the family home. The birth of the boys was a great delight to her after the losses she had experienced over two wars. When she visited, she told us she loved to hear the sound of children playing here. The house was dilapidated, but it had a mature magnolia tree in front and a delicately scented wisteria clambered over the balcony. In late summer, we gathered the mulberries and quince from the back garden. Helene loved the garden, and I finally discovered why her hands were so rough. She was a very knowledgeable and skilled gardener, as you well know.

The day we moved in, the deep pink cups of magnolia blossom blazed in front of the peeling white stucco façade, and you ran around the lawn, gathering the fallen waxy petals, and laughing with delight. Helene fell in love with this house. Over the years, it has brought her a peace and happiness I could not entirely fathom; there was an intense emotional identification with it. I think she came to love me for it – and I was glad of that, because I knew that, in truth, she did not love me when we married.

By now, the story is familiar to you. Your two brothers arrived, and during those years I think she was happy. She took huge pleasure in transforming the back garden, which had been abandoned for over a decade, and was full of buddleia. She designed it with the pond, the twisting path and hidden benches. In summer, it was a blaze of colour, a cool oasis and refuge from the city. Helene was a model wife. She looked after the house and cooked careful meals. She planned a small vegetable garden and I marvelled at her skill with every kind of plant. There was a deep mutual respect between us, but there was also a distance that saddened me. I would never describe us as close. But I knew that she would never leave me. There was no restlessness in her to meet another man or to explore the world outside our home. I respected her privacy, and that meant asking no questions about where she had lived, where the art collection had come from, where her family was and who your father was. From time to time, she received letters with Guernsey stamps, and sometimes I gathered that there were visitors to the house when I was out. There were even short trips away. She would ask for some money, and I gave it without questioning her about where she was going.

Much to our delight – and Helene's surprise – you excelled at school. We read together every night and I enjoyed your precocious intelligence. You were a serious little girl, and didn't make friends easily, until you won your scholarship to America. At university there, you came out of yourself and learned to laugh. Laughter was a rare thing in our house, but I regarded myself as happy. My work flourished; I became well known and my opinion was sought by curators and collectors all over the world. I produced some monographs, which were well received, particularly one on Picasso's prints, and then, in 1960, my biography on Miró came out, and was the standard work for a while, until a bitter period when young art historians delighted in attacking it.

In the late 1950s, I had received a letter asking me to serve on an international committee which had been set up to investigate the fate of various major collections during the war. I declined, pleading volume of work, but I knew it was likely to be only a matter of time before the issue caught up with me. In the two years before our marriage, I had sold thirty-four prints and drawings, and I understood Helene had lived off the proceeds. When we moved here, she had brought a trunk which she put in the attic. I had forgotten about it. I never knew what it contained and, stupidly, I had never thought to ask.

Then in 1963, I heard that the Ohio collector who had bought the bulk of Helene's drawings had died, leaving his vast art collection to a gallery. A conscientious curator had already begun to make inquiries to establish the provenance of the drawings and prints; the trail would quickly lead back to me. I couldn't see a way to prevent it; I believed I could protect Helene by fabricating a story of how I came by the collection, but I couldn't save myself or my reputation. I did nothing but wait with a growing sense of dread.

On 23rd August 1964 three police detectives came round to the house with a search warrant. It was a hot afternoon, and I had been sitting in the garden in a deckchair, reading. Helene was pruning and deadheading roses. I let them in and called to her to explain that the detectives wanted to search the house. She stood

there and nodded, her face drawn but utterly composed. Upstairs,
from the nursery, I watched Helene as the detectives rifled through
papers. She continued calmly and methodically grasping the small
bunches of dry, brown petals, snipping the stems and dropping
them into a basket at her feet. When the police saw the attic hatch,
they became insistent. We had to fetch a ladder, and two of the
men climbed up. They brought down the old trunk belonging to
Helene. I was later told that the trunk had a false bottom that
contained a selection of drawings. The policemen's manner had
changed; they were more confident and there was an aggressive
edge to their self-importance. They took some details from me and
asked for our passports; they told Helene and me to come to the
station for questioning the following morning.

After they had gone, I returned to the garden. I stared at my
straw hat and the book I had flung on the grass when I had
heard the doorbell. I found Helene right at the end of the garden,
next to the pond. She was sitting on a step with her arms wrapped
tight around her legs, her knees hunched up under her chin.
She was staring at the ground. Neither of us said a word. I can
hardly bear to bring to mind that long, warm evening. It grew
dark, but Helene and I stayed where we were; she barely
altered her position.

She spoke that evening like someone who knew that one day
she would be caught out, and was surprised that it had not been
earlier. She had nothing to be ashamed of over your conception,
she kept repeating, with uncharacteristic passion and defiance. The
rest of that night I slept fitfully on a couch in my study, listening
to the birds at dawn.

Somehow the papers got hold of the story. On our return from
the police station, there were reporters at the front door. I held a
minor honorary post as adviser to the Queen on modern art
acquisitions, so I suppose there was some news value in the story
of a royal art historian found with a stash of stolen Picassos in his

attic. The embarrassment was the worst part. I lost my job at the Courtauld, and my position at the Tate. We hired excellent lawyers, who were cripplingly expensive, as you know, but they managed to prevent Helene's role emerging. The court case, in the end, resulted in a suspended jail sentence and fines. We had to sell the cottage in Devon, but we managed to hang on – just – to this house. The most painful part was selling most of my collection.

Since that time, I have done what I could to allay Helene's guilt. It was my decision. I do not blame her, and neither, I hope, will you. My love for her is what has given my life meaning.

Justin's papers had come to an abrupt end. Roz realized she had cramp, she had been sitting still for so long. She stood up and put the pages back in the envelope. She remembered the confusing events of those two years from 1964 to 1966 and those strange transatlantic phone calls. Helene had always changed the subject, and Justin had been uncharacteristically terse. He was right: she had been too preoccupied with her own life to persist with her questions. When Roz got back to England, she had turned her anger on Justin, accusing him of a foolishness which had cost the family dear. She had loved the Devon cottage's views over the sea and the old fir trees. With her memories of their own family holidays, she had assumed she would take her own children there one day. It had taken her a long time to forgive him. His distress had been manifest in the last twenty years of his life, and he seemed to crumple into a shadow of his old self.

The memory was suddenly sharply painful, and she felt over-whelmed with guilt. She had been so critical and judgemental, and all the while, he was protecting Helene. She had never wanted so badly to speak to him. Just one conversation, even one brief word would suffice: sorry. But the dead couldn't hear.

'Can I help?'

A young man in a full-length black cassock was standing beside her. She turned to look at him, confused.

'Rather poignant, I think,' he said hesitantly, gesturing to the memorial in front of Roz.

Roz realized she had been staring vacantly at the wall.

'Edward Cook, a philosopher. Only thirty-nine years old. 1652,' he read out, adding half apologetically, 'Just after the Civil War – I find myself imagining his story.'

Roz looked at the marble bust of the earnest man with a book in his hands. She murmured a non-committal reply. The curate read the inscription quietly:

> *'Unsluice yo' briny floods, what can yee keepe*
> *Yo' eyes from teares, and see the marble weepe*
> *Burst out for shame: or if yee find noe vent*
> *For teares, yet stay and see the stones relent.'*

Roz was baffled. She didn't know what to say, but he turned to her and, smiling, offered a summary: 'Sometimes tears are needed.'

She gave a polite smile and got up to walk down the aisle to the front door, and he fell in step beside her.

'You have been here a long time.' He made it sound like a question.

He looked painfully young, almost young enough to be her son. Roz nodded.

'I'm just on my way out,' she said, and she put the envelope back in her bag. But he was still standing there, waiting.

'I received a letter from my father today. He died six years ago. It was held back until my mother's death,' Roz found herself blurting out to this stranger. She looked up to the vaulted ceiling to blink back tears. 'It turns out he wasn't my father after all.'

She listened to herself, and found the sound of the words and her brittle voice shocking. 'I don't know who my father was.'

The curate looked at her. She could see panic – or was it curiosity? – in his face. Over his shoulder she noticed the beautiful calligraphy of a framed prayer hanging on a pillar. A phrase caught her eye:

His eyes shall be open and His ears intending on this House, Day and Night, that he who askes may have, he who seekes may find . . .

What a magnificent, absurd consolation, she thought, and pulled her attention back to the eager face in front of her. His eyes behind his thick glasses were full of professional concern.

'Does it matter?' she asked him suddenly. 'Do you think it *matters* if I don't know?'

Very gravely and with all his youthful certainty, he replied, 'It matters, yes. Now you will have to look for your father.'

She suddenly wondered if he meant a human or a divine father. Fortunately, they were at the church door. He held out his hand and she shook it, offering a tight smile.

III

'For what we are about to receive, may the Lord make us truly thankful.'

Helene didn't need to open her eyes to see her father's face in prayer. She knew it well: the head slightly tilted back to face the Almighty in his heaven, the eyelids heavy and veined, and the brow creased with the concentration of emotion required for that final word. She opened her eyes to stare at the tablecloth and the meagre meal which awaited them. Her stomach rumbled loudly.

'Amen,' Helene and Nanna murmured in reply.

Most of their meals were now conducted in silence. Each was absorbed by their own anxieties. Helene ate quickly. She usually found herself waiting for her father to finish his portion of cabbage stew before Nanna cleared away the plates. Her gaze shifted out of the window and she noticed the fine Atlantic rain billowing up the valley. The sodden ground would make digging hard this afternoon.

It was over eighteen months since the boys had left, but it felt much longer. The only contact with the mainland was the brief Red Cross messages, and they were rare. Helene missed Lily, and longed for a letter from Tom, with his passionate protestations of love. It was almost a year since she had heard from him and she needed to know that he hadn't forgotten her. She had a packet of his letters from before the Occupation by her bed. The folds of the paper were wearing thin from her re-readings of his accounts of the training camp.

Her father was scraping his bowl of the last drops, and the sound fuelled a cold fury of impatience inside Helene. She fiddled with the turned-up sleeve of the jumper she was wearing. It was one of Edward's, and she was wearing his trousers too. Nanna had taken the trousers in around the waist. She had suggested that in the house and garden, Helene should use old clothes, saving anything respectable for the rare occasions when she was out. It made sense, but she almost never left the house and garden these days. German soldiers were everywhere. The clothes she had worn before the war now hung, unused, in her wardrobe, waiting. For what? The end of the war seemed unimaginably distant. She hadn't been to St Peter Port for several months. Even if Father agreed to her walking that far, there was no point. He had had to cut her allowance, so she had little money to spend. Besides, there was nothing to buy, and the cinema showed German films. If she did meet a friend, the conversation was dominated by recipes and rations. Everyone had the same pre-occupation with food: where the next meal was coming from and how to make it more palatable.

She noticed mud wedged thick under each fingernail. While she waited for Father to finish, she tried to clean them, but her nails were half broken. She remembered how she used to compare nails with Felicity and Annie when they were schoolgirls. She had begun to bite them to keep them short. Her palms and fingertips were ingrained with soil from the garden. The last few bars of soap were kept for 'special occasions', such as Sunday church, and the rare days when they saw people. At night, she went to bed with the faint but unmistakeable smell of horse manure on her hands, no matter how much she scrubbed them with cold water. Mucking out Sandy's stable and spreading the manure on the vegetable plot had fallen to her. George couldn't do everything, her father had told her when she had protested. She saw his point, and over the last year had come to find the garden a source of solace. She was learning from George. It kept her busy.

'Pudding' was a slice of heavy rough bread thinly spread with butter and a small portion of raspberry jam. They had restricted the jam to Wednesdays and Sundays to eke out the last of their stock. Without sugar, they couldn't make any more.

As Helene tried to swallow her bread, she reflected that she couldn't remember a year when she hadn't helped Nanna make jam – until the war. Since she was small, she had loved the sense of occasion. Mother would announce it was time. George would pick baskets of strawberries and line them up along the dresser. She would help Nanna top and cut the berries, and the fruit would fill the big kitchen bowls before being poured into the largest saucepans. All day the house would be full of the sweet smell of stewing strawberries. As the pans simmered, Nanna would write out the labels in her old-fashioned handwriting using her best ink pen: 'Strawberry Jam, The Vicarage' and the date. Then she would ladle the syrup into each jar. Helene's job was to add the disc of greaseproof paper, wipe the jar for stray sticky drops and tie the string around the paper cap.

A month later, the process would begin again for the raspberries, then the plums and the damsons. Sometimes they even made a final batch of jelly with the crab apples, or with the blackberries that Helene gathered from the hedgerows in September. The quantities exceeded the household's needs but Nanna and Mother had given the jars of jam as presents – small tokens of cheer for bereaved or ailing parishioners. Since Mother's death, the larder shelves had emptied more slowly, but Nanna had kept up the tradition. Now, they were working their way through the plenty of past summers. Another blessing, Nanna might say. Both Nanna and Father frequently repeated how blessed they were to have a big garden and a glasshouse. They were right, but there were many times when Helene was overwhelmed by fierce exasperation at this determination to be grateful. Afterwards she felt a dull ache of shame.

When he had finished eating, Father pulled over the small Bible which sat on the table beside him, and opened it at the red tasselled marker, Psalm 49. He had read a psalm aloud after lunch ever since Edward had left. There had been no announcement or explanation, simply an expectation that Helene and Nanna would not leave the table until he had finished. Helene did not listen. 'Like sheep they are laid in the grave; death shall feed on them; and the upright shall have dominion over them in the morning; and their beauty shall consume in the grave from their dwelling,' he recited. Helene's mind shifted to the tasks awaiting her in the garden.

The forbidding verses seemed to ease briefly her father's impotent rage at another war. When he fell silent, Helene got up to leave, still feeling hungry.

'One moment, Helene,' said her father, in the tone which presaged a serious discussion. Nanna tactfully left the room.

Father pushed back his chair and rubbed his wrinkled forehead. He turned to face Helene.

'You have to find good cheer to endure. The Occupation could go on for a considerable while.' With careful emphasis, he added, 'There are a lot of people much worse off than us.'

The war was ageing him. Wrinkles were deepening around his reddened eyes. She knew he struggled to sleep. He was worried about Edward, and waited impatiently for the Red Cross messages. He was at a loss as to how to look after a daughter under the Occupation. Always an austere man, he didn't seem to mind their limited diet; only the electricity shortages bothered him. The long dark evenings when he couldn't read or write made him restless. Many times, Helene heard him pacing the floor of his study in the dark. She preferred to tire herself out in the vegetable garden and the glasshouse so that there were only a few hours of dark before her head fell gratefully onto her pillow.

'Helene, nobody finds this time easy. We are all suffering in many ways, but your situation is preferable to that of many others. Go to some of the cottages up the road where the children are close to starving. Or into St Peter Port and visit homes where they have no fuel for heat or cooking. You have no idea how blessed you are.'

He was drumming his fingers on the cover of his Bible.

'You need a job. You need to see more of what is going on around us. I had thought the garden and the house would be enough work for you – and safer – but you need your eyes opening to see how others are managing to keep cheerful against bigger odds than us.'

Then his voice softened, as if he were beseeching her.

'It's no good fretting about Tom or dreaming of parties and fancy dresses. We have to commit our young men to the mercy of God. Peace will come in time. London is sure to liberate the islands. It may be only a few more months, but right now we have to concentrate on keeping people alive and in good spirit.'

Helene stared at the carpet.

'I've spoken to Mr Le Prevost at the school in St Peter's, and he says he could do with an extra hand in the infants'.'

Now he had his daughter's attention. She was alarmed.

'I can't teach. I was terrible at school and I've no idea how to look after children. I'd be hopeless.'

'They need help. I can't force you – you are twenty-one, a grown woman – but you have a duty, as we all do, to help our island through this dreadful time.'

Helene listened to the rain on the window pane. Reluctantly, she nodded.

'You'll start a week on Monday,' said her father, getting up to go to his study. 'I think you will come to enjoy it in time. Please make an effort.'

'Father, please,' protested Helene, but her father was already leaving the room.

Teaching, thought Helene ruefully. She remembered her failures for her School Certificate. She had hated algebra. Nor did she like the idea of being cooped up inside; her only pleasure was being out in the wind, rain and sun, either riding Sandy or working in the garden.

Most of the time, her father took little notice of her. Either he was out at meetings in St Peter Port, discussing how to increase food production, or he was buried in his study with his reports, and his visitors. She could remember a gentler man, one who had taught her the names of the wildflowers as they walked along the lanes, visiting his parishioners. He used to take her to the vestry when she was small. She would creep in amongst the hanging vestments in the big wardrobe while he talked about the collection and cleaning rotas with the churchwardens. She had liked the musty smell, and had imagined that this was the smell of God. Sometimes they brought a big basket of flowers, which George or her mother had picked from the conservatory and the garden for the church. Together, she and her father would fill the brass pots with water and arrange the crimson gladioli and cream lilies which her mother thought appropriate. Father would chuckle as he complimented her on a 'woman's touch'. Mother visited the church on Sundays, though often not even then.

But after Mother died in 1936, grief made him silent and withdrawn. In the years before the war, he had spent much of his time in his study, only emerging for meals. He struggled to accept that his beautiful wife, so much younger than him, had been taken so swiftly and brutally. Helene watched him in church as he stood in the pulpit delivering his sermon, his restless eyes searching the congregation, and at the altar, where, his back bowed over the altar table, he mumbled the prayers which Helene no longer believed in. Not after Mother died. Helene was not yet sixteen.

She felt the pity of the congregation in the rows behind her; their sorrowful eyes on her when she came back from Communion; their murmured platitudes at the church door afterwards. She hated the repressed emotion of their earnest inquiries.

At the back door, she pulled on thick socks and a pair of Edward's boots. She was furious. She took down the old coat of her father's she used in the garden. Nanna called from the kitchen, where she was sitting darning. Nanna had taken to wearing a coat and fingerless mittens indoors to fend off the damp cold – they saved their wood supply for the late afternoon. Would Helene go over to Felicity's in the Forest later that afternoon and fetch some eggs which her mother had promised? asked Nanna. Helene agreed and bent to kiss her. Nanna's anxious face showed that she had heard Helene's brief altercation with her father.

'He's worn out. He doesn't mean to sound harsh, dear. He is a man without a wife, and now there's no news of Edward – nor much prospect of it. And he worries himself sick about you here.'

She patted Helene's arm, her wrinkled hands reddened with eczema.

'Oh, Nanna, your poor hands,' exclaimed Helene, and held one open to look at the palm. The creases were red and her skin was peeling.

'It's nothing,' Nanna insisted, pulling her hand away. 'Felicity's father might have a package for me.'

She buttoned up Helene's coat as if she were still a child. 'You'd better get on if you're to do anything in the garden before you go, and be back before dark.'

There were a lot of people for Helene to worry about – Tom, Edward, Lily, Father – but Nanna was the one who most pre-occupied her. She had been with the family for almost fifty years, nanny to Mother and then to Helene and Edward, and now housekeeper. She was too old and frail for the deprivations of Occupation, and she depended on the packages which their doctor, Felicity's father, gave her to treat her diabetes. Helene didn't know of all Nanna's ailments, because she never spoke about them, but there were times when Helene chanced upon her in the kitchen or in the pantry, her face convulsed with pain, her hand on her waist to ease her back.

Outside, low clouds threatened more rain, but the wind was mild. It was the kind of weather Helene liked: a soft, grey wetness which left every blade and leaf heavy with moisture, so that drops of water fell from each twig that she brushed. She made her way to the tool shed to pick out a fork and spade. George was there, sitting by the window, rubbing the arthritic joints in his hands, but he was in no mood for talking. Helene had learned to avoid his bad temper.

The evenings were closing in now, and most of the leaves had come down in the recent gales. She remembered the harsh cold of last winter. She had spent many hours over the last six months gathering every branch she could find in the copses and hedge-rows for fuel. Not only had she scoured their own parish of Torteval, but she had gone over to St Saviour's and as far as St Andrew's. She stayed off the main roads.

She had dug up half the croquet lawn already. It was hard work breaking the sods and digging into the earth compacted over the years by all the games her family and their friends had played. It was a melancholy task which sent her mind back to the summer days of 1935, when she was fifteen and the whole family had played croquet together in the long warm evenings. Lily, so much younger than Mother, would bring her boyfriend, and would shriek with delight at a good shot. Even Mother was happy then, laughing with the guests and sipping a drink sitting on the bench between turns. Helene straightened her back, her hand on the spade handle, and looked up at the bench between the windows where her mother used to sit. In her mind's eye, she could clearly see her in one of her beautiful dresses, a splash of vibrant colour against the grey granite wall of the old house. Helene remembered one occasion when Edward was sitting next to Mother. She had put her arm around his shoulders. He was still young enough to enjoy the affection, but embarrassed in front of the guests. A gawky fourteen-year-old, all legs and arms, Edward was at Elizabeth College. She recalled his sunburned face and how Mother had ruffled his blond hair. For a moment, they both seemed so real that she wondered whether they could see her. She imagined their shock at her over-large clothes and big boots in the mud of their former croquet lawn.

Enough of the daydreams and the ghosts, she told herself, setting herself to work on the remainder of the lawn. She cut the turf with the spade and peeled it back before loosening the soil beneath with the fork. She found her progress maddeningly slow, but she didn't have the strength to break up the compacted earth as quickly as a labourer, and her meagre diet was affecting her energy. Sometimes she felt so dizzy she had to stop and wait for a few minutes. She heaved the turfs into a wheelbarrow. She could see a new row of freshly turned earth slowly emerging behind her. She was warm with the physical exertion and her face was flushed with the effort. An hour or so later, she stopped. She would need to leave for Felicity's if she was to be home in time. The nights were drawing in and she had to be back well before curfew. She would take the path along the cliffs to avoid the road. She had no wish to bump into any soldiers.

It was several weeks since she had seen the sea properly. Down here in the valley, they were sheltered from the fierce winter gales, and she could only catch a glimpse of the sea from the house or from the top of Sandy's field. Before the war she had been out on the clifftops most days, but her favourite places had been cut off by barbed wire. The Germans were laying mines along the coast at Rocquaine and L'Erée. The rumour was that they would mine Petit Bot Bay and Saints Bay. It was already impossible to reach their favourite beaches, where she and Edward used to swim, at Le Jaonnet and La Bette.

That had been one of the worst blows for Helene. When she'd heard the news from George, something had snapped. It struck her as a gratuitous act of cruelty; there was no road access to either Le Jaonnet or La Bette, so they could hardly be used for a British assault. If the Germans wanted the cooperation and the well-being of the islanders, as the *Guernsey Evening Press* claimed, then they shouldn't cut them off from their sea. It was the commando raids dreamed up in England that were to blame. A friend of Tom's, Hubert Nicolle, had been sent to the island twice on reconnaissance missions in the summer of 1940. He ended up being captured. She knew Father dreaded Edward or Tom being recruited for some foolhardy mission. England's exploits brought a bitter price for the islanders.

George's son, Jack, wasn't even allowed a licence to fish, and had had to hand over his boat. It was insufferable that a gentle, quiet man couldn't get on with the business of feeding his numerous children because of a whim of German bureaucracy. The German official in the Feldkommandantur had claimed there were no licences left by the time Jack applied. The poor man was now working in the kitchens at the German officers' mess, and he hated it. Helene knew how much he longed for the open sea, a crisp sea breeze and the weight of fish in his hold, instead of the greasy fug of a kitchen and the slops of dirty water.

The island's Bailiff had issued repeated reassurances since the Germans invaded that there was no cause for concern, providing people complied with all the regulations of this 'model occupation'. Father had impressed on Helene the importance of avoiding all contact with the soldiers. On a few occasions in town, she had observed their pompous manner and stilted English. Once or twice in the lanes around Torteval she had been asked for directions; on one occasion the same motorbike had passed Helene several times in the space of a quarter of an hour. More unpleasant was the sound of marching soldiers singing Nazi songs up on the main road. They rarely ventured down the back lanes because they were too narrow for their vehicles – and it was so easy to get lost. With some care, she usually managed to duck behind hedges or into side roads at the first sound of a vehicle. The one time soldiers came to the house to speak to her father, he asked her to stay in her bedroom. It was as if he wanted to hide his daughter for the whole war. There was only one time when she ignored his advice. Nanna had run out of insulin and George said that Arthur Brown, the caretaker at Dieu Donne, had talked about a German doctor billeted at the house. She had stood on the doorstep shaking with fear. He had been curt in his refusal to help; embarrassed, she had blushed deep red and left quickly, almost running down the drive.

Helene slipped out of the garden by the back gate under the trees and took a path up the valley to cross the road, before heading across the fields to the cliffs. She liked the taste of salt on her lips as the rain blew into her face. At least Edward's boots kept her feet dry in the long, wet grass. She noticed that several fields, which had been pasture for cows, had recently been ploughed. They were probably destined to produce vegetables for German dinner plates. She'd heard the gossip from George of farmers who were selling their crops to the Germans, leaving little for the islanders to buy.

They were inordinately greedy, Helene reflected bitterly. Whatever the Germans saw, they wanted: cars, houses, boats. They had requisitioned Dieu Donne, Tom's family's house, and within a few days of the soldiers moving in, she heard that they were breaking up the furniture for firewood. They had even ripped off the skirting boards. Mr Brown lived up there in the caretaker's cottage, and he told George that they had made a terrible mess, until a senior officer had taken the matter in hand.

It wasn't enough for them to live in the biggest country in Europe, it wasn't enough to invade Austria and Czechoslovakia and then Poland, but they had to occupy all of Europe, even tiny islands like Guernsey and Jersey, which could be of no imaginable use to them.

She edged through the rolls of barbed wire at the point where George had shown her. He had cut the wire and then carefully covered the small gap with dead bracken. Out on top of the cliffs, she took a deep breath of the fresh Atlantic breeze. The sea was a dark grey, and the wind was beginning to whip up white crests. It eased the bitterness of her thoughts. Up here, she could look down on the seagulls wheeling below, their wings outstretched as they turned and turned about, before alighting on the clefts and ledges of the cliffs, where they would build their nests in the spring. Their greediness, their noise and their self-importance were comparable to the Germans', she thought wryly. One bird settled on a rocky outcrop not far from where she stood. Despite Edward's keen interest in ornithology, she couldn't remember the names of the different gulls. This one eyed her beadily as it shuffled from one scaly foot to another, before taking off again, wings beating heavily to gain height. She could hear the creak of bone, muscle and feather, as the tensed strength of the plump body leveraged itself against the air to rise into the sky.

She set off along the path skirting this part of the cliffs, and the wind tugged her thick hair free. Further along was the granite outcrop she and Edward used to visit. They would clamber down the cliff, clinging to the stiff roots of the bracken, until they reached the uneven platform of the outcrop. There, they could lie in the sun, with the sky overhead and the flat sea stretched out below. They would watch the small boats heading to the moorings at Saints Bay further along the coast. They never used to talk much. Helene daydreamed and Edward watched birds through his binoculars in companionable silence.

The freedom of those days seemed almost magical, thought Helene, realizing that the hem of her overcoat was wet from brushing through the dead bracken and long grass. Nanna would fret about how to dry it. The old cotton bag she had brought for the eggs was also sodden from swinging it to and fro as she walked. The paths were overgrown for lack of use: there hadn't been any English visitors for more than two years.

She was in a dip in the cliffs, slightly protected from the wind by the wizened blackthorn and hawthorn which almost formed a tunnel, bent by the Atlantic's rough winter winds. The contour of the cliffs sheltered her from the roar of the waves breaking on the rocks below. At first she presumed the figure heading up the path towards her, with his head down, was an islander. She had not expected to see anyone out here. She hesitated, and at that moment the man glanced up and saw her. He paused and straightened; he was as surprised to see her as she was to see him. He was not an islander, Helene realized with a start. He was wearing a full-length black rubber cape, and, underneath the hood, Helene caught sight of an officer's peaked cap. She looked around her but the brushwood was too dense for her to leave the path. She had no option but to continue walking, her head down, her mouth dry with fear. As he came closer, she stepped to one side, to let him pass on the narrow path, her heart pounding. She stared down at her mud-spattered boots. He stopped just a few feet below her.

'Curious day to choose for a walk.' He spoke English with barely a trace of accent. Helene didn't dare look up. She said nothing.

She moved to pass him, but he was blocking her path. He pulled out a silver cigarette case and took out a cigarette, which he tapped on the case before lighting. Then, as an afterthought, he offered the open case to Helene. Her eyes still lowered, she shook her head vigorously. He pulled on his cigarette, fingering the case in his other hand. He was in no hurry.

Helene stood there miserably, a thorn scratching the back of her neck, drops of rain from an overhead branch falling on her head.

'Where are you from?'

His tone was conversational, but Helene wasn't sure if this was the start of an interrogation. Islanders were banned from the cliffs.

'The Vicarage in Torteval.'

He nodded.

'I'm lost,' he said calmly. 'Can you take me back to the main road?'

Was that an order or a request? thought Helene. She didn't believe he was lost. She nodded silently and turned to lead him back up the cliff. She was searching her mind for a ruse to avoid showing him the gap in the barbed wire, and to get away from him. For about a quarter of an hour, they walked without a word.

She could smell his cigarette behind her. It was nearly a year since she had smelled the real thing; George had taken to making cigarettes from herbs, but this was a strong French brand, similar to those Edward had smoked in the evenings in the orchard with his friends.

She was walking as quickly as she dared, and at the top of a sharp climb he called to her to wait. When he caught up, he paused to catch his breath. They stood in the shelter of a clump of pine trees, and he seemed to be listening to how they whispered in the wind. She held herself rigid, still trying to devise a plan. He moved away to look down at the sea, throwing back the hood of his cape now that the rain had stopped, and took off his cap.

Helene glanced at his profile. He was old, probably thirty, and his black hair was cut very short and neatly combed. His eyes were deep-set beneath thick eyebrows, and his lips were thin, pursed with preoccupation. He looked tense and his forehead was creased. Something was worrying him. He turned back to her and caught her eye. He gave her a brief smile, and his eyes lightened momentarily before she quickly looked away.

'We have trees like these at home in Berlin,' he said. His tone was matter-of-fact, hard to read. Was he homesick? Was he trying to start a conversation?

Helene stared at his boots, thick with mud. They had nearly reached Les Tielles, where the path led back to the road, and were only a few metres from the gap in the wire, but she couldn't think of an alternative. When she showed him the cut wire, he made no comment. She pointed to the lane across the field. Now he seemed in a hurry. He held out his hand and Helene offered hers before she knew what she was doing, and he shook it. He made as if to raise his cap, and as he turned to leave Helene saw that his lips were compressed in a smile.

She headed back along the cliff path, retracing her steps once more. She needed to walk fast to get to Felicity's in the Forest and back home. He could report her. She held out her hand and her muddy fingers were trembling with fear.

IV

The hall was full of boxes. Ed had selected what he wanted and the removals van was due any moment. Roz made her way through to the sitting room. The carpet was strewn with belongings for friends and relatives to pick through. What was left would end up with the house-clearance company: picture frames, a bicycle wheel, a pram, piles of old, neatly darned linen. Helene had been very good at sewing, reflected Roz ruefully, one of many domestic skills she had not inherited from her mother. Someone had brought in trays of empty Kilner jars from the larder, the last remnant of her mother's jam-making days. No one seemed interested in taking them.

Empty spaces on the wall showed where Ed had lifted down the pictures he had chosen. Roz looked around, shocked at how the house, once so meticulously arranged, was unravelling so swiftly. It looked very shabby. Patches of damp showed on the walls and the carpet was threadbare.

One more bookcase needed sorting out in the drawing room. Roz was working her way through every book in the house, shaking their pages out in the hope of a scrap of paper, an old envelope or letter, anything that might offer a clue to her mother's history. She wasn't sure she wanted to find anything, but nor did she want to lose anything she might regret at a later date. The obsessive searching of the last few weeks was for her future peace of mind, so she could rest easy that information about her mother had not slipped through her fingers.

Helene had long since cleared out the desk. Above its worn

writing surface, several small drawers and shelves contained old address books, a few faded postcards and letters, but there was no stray note or envelopes with an unfamiliar address. It was as if Helene had foreseen Roz's curiosity. In the main drawers were household bills, old cuttings with recipes or gardening tips. Roz had then turned to the nursery cupboards and the bedside chests of drawers, but these only contained piles of neatly folded underwear, interleaved with Helene's distinctive lavender bags. The soft sweet smell of home-grown lavender was a powerful reminder of childhood. Roz remembered those evenings when, as a girl, she would stoop to kiss Helene's upturned cheek as she sat in the drawing room, sewing. Helene's skin had always felt smooth, cool and lightly scented.

Roz spent one long Saturday in the basement, working through a near century of discarded belongings which Helene's tidying up had not touched. Roz found old cricket bats, tennis rackets, a pair of antique roller skates, and boxes of old magazines and newspapers dating from the 1950s. She found folders of her father's teaching notes, an old typewriter, and a couple of record players and speakers. Amongst the unloved junk were beguiling mementos: a trunk covered with stickers of travels from the 1920s and, inside, a box of beautifully embroidered Chinese collars wrapped in tissue paper. Nothing revealed where her mother had come from, or those mysterious connections to which her father had referred in the letter – the visitors to the house, the trips she had taken.

'You're rummaging through the house as if you're looking for something,' called Jim from the landing. He was supposed to be helping to clear the house but he kept getting distracted.

Roz had started work on the attic. She looked down through the hatch at her brother, who was standing at the bottom of the ladder with two cups of coffee. She climbed down and gratefully took one.

'I suppose I am,' she said. She sat down on a box on the landing, cup in hand.

She hadn't told either of her brothers about Justin's letter. It was best to start with Jim. She took a deep breath and steeled herself.

'Jim, I need to tell you something.'

Alert to the shift of tone, Jim looked closely at her and waited.

'Justin was not my father. He wrote a letter to me. Robert gave it to me a fortnight ago.'

He raised his eyebrows. He was stunned. 'So who was?'

'He never knew. Helene wouldn't tell him. She said I couldn't have the letter until after her death. And it was Mother who sold him the stolen art collection.'

'Blimey,' he said, and there was a long pause. He rubbed his forehead. 'That's a lot to take in.'

'That's how they met. She came to the dealers where he worked with a Picasso in her battered suitcase – that sort of thing. It was just after the war.'

'How odd . . . Where did she get it from?'

'The problem is, Jim, everything Justin wrote in his long letter – which you can read if you want – only begs dozens more questions.'

'Do you want to find your real father?'

'*Real*? I don't even like the question,' she said softly.

'You're right. You were always a daddy's girl. You and Justin were so close. He adored you. That's real.' There was a pause. 'Are you sure it was Helene who stopped him from explaining?'

Roz shrugged her shoulders.

That rubbing of the forehead, his mouth twisted to the side. Roz knew that expression. He was confused. Like her. They sat drinking their coffee.

Suddenly, Jim slammed his hand down on the floor and exclaimed, 'So the pictures business was all to do with Mother.

She wasn't even interested in art. Father covered up for her and lost everything.'

Roz involuntarily let out a groan. 'I feel so disorientated – and angry, with both of them.'

Jim reached out to put an arm around her shoulder, and tears came to her eyes. 'Poor Roz.'

'How could Mother let Justin carry the blame for the pictures? She saw our anger towards him at the time, and did nothing. That seems the worst. She lied all her life to everyone. As for my biological father – she wouldn't let Justin tell me until it was too late to find anything out.' Roz wiped her tears with the back of her sleeve and sniffed loudly.

Jim handed her his handkerchief and smiled. 'You've dust on your cheek.'

They sat side by side, and in the hall the clock struck the quarter-hour.

'It feels like I've lost both parents twice over: Justin again, and now Helene. She's died, and it turns out she was not the mother I thought she was. She has – or rather had – some murky past which she never let anyone know about.'

'And Justin protected her from it – from our questions. There was always something rather distant about her,' mused Jim. 'Didn't we meet an aunt or something once? But there was no other family – they couldn't all have died, surely? Can we really believe her – did her brother really die in the war? Did her mother die when she was young? And was her father dead before we were born? There was so little of a past to go on. She never talked much about her childhood, apart from all that horse riding. You couldn't really know her,' he concluded.

'No, I didn't see it like that at all. I was sure, absolutely sure, I knew her. It turns out I was wrong. Meg told me something. She said she had been reduced to tears by things Mother had told her one night before she went into hospital. Meg said she had just sat on the floor, leaning against the wall, with tears running down her face.'

'That's strange. Did Meg give any more details? Were there any names?'

'She told me this after we took Mother to hospital. I raised it with her when we were clearing up after the funeral, but she brushed it off. I think she had decided to protect Helene, and I didn't press it.'

'Are you going to try and find out more? Hire a private detective?' Jim joked.

She shook her head slowly.

'What's the point? I'm not sure it matters any more. They're both dead.'

She sighed heavily and when she spoke again, her voice was steadier.

'I would have liked to have known twenty years ago. It might have been helpful then. I might even have managed to trace him – this father, I mean.'

'Your father?'

'He's not mine,' she said quickly. 'I had a father – Justin.'

After a moment Roz added, 'She was born in Guernsey, Justin said in the letter. He looked at her passport shortly after they met. Her maiden name was Le Lacheur – French.'

'Strange,' said Jim. 'We always thought she was born in Devon.' Then he changed tack. 'Justin must have loved her a lot to forgive her for destroying his career, and to take the blame.'

'In his letter, he's clear: he doesn't blame her. He said he knew what he was doing when he bought them.'

'But she had more drawings hidden. Why? What for? In case she ever wanted to leave him and might need the money?'

'Oh, Jim, don't be ridiculous. Mother would never have left. Maybe she didn't know what to do with them. She didn't need the money any more, and she didn't even tell Father she had them. She might have been embarrassed about the whole thing.'

Roz stood up, brushing dust off her jeans. 'I've been thinking it over. I think she must have lied about all kinds of things. That family home in Devon? How come we never went to visit it if it was so beautiful and she loved it so much? She said it would be too painful. Even if her parents and brother were dead – and perhaps that was a lie too – there must have been other relatives. Not just one aunt in the Far East.' Roz remembered visiting the great-aunt for tea once in Devon when she was about eight. 'Why didn't we ever see her again?'

Jim rubbed his forehead. 'We didn't ask questions. She was good at keeping things vague – so good, that she managed to make it look completely normal. She would shift the attention back to Father's family, and there were so many of them, we stopped noticing the gap.'

'That's what has really thrown me. It wasn't that she didn't answer questions, it's that we never thought to ask them: how did she manage that?'

Roz started to climb the ladder back up to the attic. She turned and looked down at Jim, and burst out, 'It's disturbing, Jim. Guernsey was occupied by the Germans in the Second World War. I bought a guidebook after I got the letter.'

Jim was startled by Roz's tone of voice. She was always the calm one.

'Hang on, Roz. Slow down. She may have been born there, but she could have still grown up in Devon. I believe her on that. There will have been a love affair at the end of the war that she didn't want to talk about. He was probably married or something.'

Jim wasn't usually this definite. Roz found it reassuring.

'I'll come with you to Guernsey one day if you are that interested. We could ask around. It's not a big place and on those kinds of islands, everyone knows everyone else's business.

Someone might know something, and I'd be curious to see where Mother was born. Only don't get ahead of yourself – don't start imagining some kind of Second World War film plot. That's not like you, Roz.'

'Of course,' she agreed quickly. She climbed to the top of the ladder.

'Funny how you and Ed were the ones who looked alike. I'm the different one. No one would have guessed,' Jim mused, as he gathered the mugs to take back to the kitchen.

'No, and no one did.' Roz tucked a strand of hair behind her ear. 'I forgot my car keys in a coffee shop yesterday. I never do that kind of thing. And then I missed a meeting. Stupid little things, but I don't recognize myself. I need to pull myself together.'

*

Roz took boxes of her favourite things home as the house was dismantled. After a few days, she saw that the few ornaments she had chosen – a dove carved from alabaster, a framed mirror – had been broken a long time ago. She hadn't noticed. The dove had had its tail clumsily glued back on; an awkward wooden pin was meant to fix it to the base, but it kept coming apart. The frame had a piece missing, and another bit fell off soon after she had taken it back to her flat. When the things had been in her parents' house, the damage had not been apparent – as if everything had been held in suspense, subject to her mother's steely will. Now the disrepair was evident at every turn. The curtains in the spare room disintegrated as Roz took them down, the silk threads fraying to dust in her hands. The rug in the drawing room concealed a stained patch of carpet. The beauty of the old house masked two decades of genteel poverty, which both Helene and Justin had been too proud to admit. The upstairs spare bedroom, locked for the last ten years or so, had a rotting window frame which they had simply boarded up. Roz had not thought to ask why the door had always been shut. She had never asked about their financial affairs; she had assumed they had had enough. Now she'd seen the will, she understood why the house had been so cold. They had claimed they preferred it the way they had both been brought up – sitting by the wood fire in the nursery, an icy chill in the rest of the house, and the drawing room shrouded in dust sheets for the winter. But now she understood they had been trying to make their savings last. They could have asked her to help – or Ed. It was painful. She was glad that she had finally stepped in to insist on paying for Meg.

Roz had broached Justin's letter with Ed one morning as they sorted piles of bills and legal documents. He wasn't interested in Roz's news.

'Forget it,' he told her. 'It's history. Jim's probably right about a wartime love affair. I'm not sure what's served by digging into it. They were good parents, best leave it at that.'

Of course it's history, she thought, irritated by his nonchalance. *My* history.

Ed had brought in a gardener to dig up two camellias from the garden. Their conversation was cut short by her shouts for directions. Edward helped her carry the big pots out to the waiting van. Roz watched from the front window; her mother had loved her camellias. Roz had no room on her balcony for them.

The three siblings had one last supper – more like a picnic – sitting in the empty dining room one late-August evening. They ate what was left in the fridge – eggs and cheese – and some salad. They drank the last bottle of red wine from Justin's once-handsome cellar. They toasted the family.

★

Roz woke with a start, confused. She didn't recognize the patterned wallpaper or the heavy wardrobe. Brilliant sunshine burst through a crack between the heavy curtains. She could hear the intense song of birds and the distant cry of seagulls. She rolled over in the crisp white sheets. She was in Guernsey.

The previous evening's flight and her late arrival at the hotel came back to her. She flicked on the radio on the bedside table, and lay listening to the morning news: in the early hours, a fishing boat had been towed to safety by St Sampson's lifeboat service; a new parking scheme in St Peter Port would get the go-ahead next week. Roz felt a vague sense of unease at the tightly knit parochialism of the island. She was an outsider, and she didn't really know why she was here. She had said to herself repeatedly over the last six months that she didn't want to dig into her mother's past.

She drew the curtains and sunlight poured into the room. She shaded her eyes to take in the magnificent view of lawns curving down to a line of trees and a soft blue sea beyond. There were palm trees and the camellia bushes were already in bloom. She had left London steeped in a bitter January grey. Here, the flowers blazed a deep pink and brilliant white against the shiny dark green leaves.

At breakfast, she sat in a dining room whose windows looked out on to the same view. She ate her poached eggs with a guide-book propped against the teapot in front of her, and she occasionally looked up at the bright colours outside. A large single camellia had been picked for the vase on her table. The petals were a delicate pale pink and, flamboyant in the centre, hung heavy, pale yellow stamens.

Roz's eye slid from the flower back to her guidebook:

. . . a network of underground tunnels excavated out of solid rock by some of the 16,000 Organisation Todt labourers brought from all over Occupied Europe to work on Inselwahn, Hitler's island madness – his obsession to secure his one piece of British territory, in the Channel

Islands. A total of 484,000 cubic metres of concrete was poured into fortifications which dot the islands, a fatal diversion which weakened the Normandy defences and ultimately enabled the Allied victory on D-Day.

She flicked through a few pages, looking for something unconnected to the Occupation. Victor Hugo had fled here from French repression and installed both his wife and his mistress in St Peter Port, to the horror of the respectable islanders. Granite menhirs and extensive prehistoric remains recorded centuries of human habitation on this fertile island. Each of the Channel Islands had its own system of government. Guernsey's parliament was called the States. She was bemused: the islands could not be described as part of the United Kingdom; they were known as a Crown Dependency. They weren't part of the European Union. She had never even heard of other Channel Islands such as Herm and Jethou, or the island of Sark, which prided itself on its feudalism. She beckoned to the waitress for more tea.

In the months since Helene had died, Roz had put aside the matter of Justin's letter. She had been busy with a big case at work and with Helene's probate, now almost completed. Then, in the dreary days of early January, by pure coincidence a friend had mentioned a recent visit to Guernsey. She had an aunt living in Alderney, and she suggested that Roz might enjoy the sea air and, if she was lucky, some winter sunshine.

On the flight last night, Roz had argued with herself that she could just as easily be visiting the Isle of Wight or the Scilly Isles. But she wasn't being honest: she was intensely curious. When she'd got to her room in the hotel, she immediately started looking through the telephone directory for entries under Le Lacheur. She found one, and dialled the number. A young man answered and Roz struggled to keep her voice calm as she asked for Edith Le Lacheur. He said his grandmother was too ill to come to the phone. She asked him to see if his grandmother knew of a Helene Le Lacheur. The man sounded irritated, but agreed to take Roz's number in London. Frustrated, she'd gone down to dinner and ordered a large glass of white wine. She was here to rest and relax, she had reminded herself, not to rummage for family secrets.

Now she drained her coffee cup and put the guidebook back in her bag: a walk on the beach would clear the stale air of London. She studied the map she had brought and chose a wide sweeping bay on the west of the island, marked as Vazon Bay.

She buttoned up her coat as she left the hotel. It was chilly, despite the sunshine. Last night she had seen nothing on her arrival; now she was curious to get her bearings. The hotel was a handsome old house of grey granite. Rows of windows, their frames freshly painted, punctured the thick walls. She admired the neatly trimmed verge in the centre of the nearby village, St Peter's, and the curve of the wall above the old church. The low winter sunlight caught the moss on the walls. Narcissi were coming into bloom in the churchyard and, in the gardens, camellia bushes spilled over the walls, studded with flowers and fat buds promising more to come. Everything seemed to be brimming with the promise of an imminent spring. It was delightful. Her friend had been right.

Vazon Bay was a short drive away. The lanes were narrow and twisted round sharp corners between banked-up verges, but within a few minutes, she had arrived at the coast. The place was tiny, a miniature English county surrounded by the Atlantic. As she got out of the car, she pulled up her hood and put on her gloves, braced for the January wind. She had spotted a network of paths around a promontory marked as Fort Hommet on the map. The sea was translucent, a deep turquoise green. The waves rolled in calmly and then roared as they broke against the rocks, frothing white spume and throwing spray high into the air. There was a history on this headland of violent seas smashing the Guernsey granite into a scattering of sharp serrations and jagged outcrops. It looked like the aftermath of a battle scene, each year accounting for new wounds and boulders thrown high up the headland. A recent rockfall had exposed fresh rock the colour of smoked salmon. Once weathered by the sea, it darkened to rust, and higher on the shore, it was iced pale grey with lichen.

Roz clambered over the rocks down onto the wet sand left behind by the receding tide. The gulls circling above made little noise. At the water's edge the waves broke and then bustled, racing over the sand to reach her. The expanse of blue sky soared above her and the green sea spread out across the horizon, beyond which lay nothing but this heaving body of water for thousands of miles. She walked back along the top of the sea wall past the rows of small cottages. In summer, the place must be busy with tourists, but at this time of year there were only a few people walking their dogs.

Back in the car, trying to warm her frozen fingers, she chose a route on the map which would take her round the north of the island back to her hotel for lunch. The road curved along the bays on the west coast – Cobo, Saline, Portinfer – before reaching the beaches of Grand Havre and L'Ancresse. She drove slowly past rows of bungalows with names such as Spindrift, Bon Repos, Querida and Esperanza. It was an island of retreat and comfortable prosperity, thought Roz. Verges were neatly cut, hedges trimmed and early daffodils lined drives and roads. Walls were freshly painted and windows were sparkling clean. Some bungalows boasted extravagant flights of fancy: a cherub standing over a pond, a sculpture of a prancing stallion by a driveway, stone lions with bared teeth guarding a gateway. Guernsey's financial services were funding some lavish home improvements, she thought. Occasionally, there was a rough whitewashed wall, hinting at an older Guernsey, from before the tourists and the inventions of plate glass. A past when the islanders had picked a modest living from the land and sea, and learned to knit their seamen's jumpers. The old farmhouses hunkered down into folds between the fields, shielded from the gales and the sea spray up on the clifftops, where the hedges of hawthorn and blackthorn were whipped into twisted forms. The islanders had taken their character from this granite outcrop facing out over the Atlantic to Newfoundland, Roz concluded. Steadfast – or stubborn, depending on your point of view. Standing by the British monarchy, staying out of the European Union, setting the island up as a financial centre. A plucky little vessel, bravely riding out the waves which an unforgiving ocean regularly sent crashing against the cliffs and over the sea walls, leaving a scattering of beach pebbles and scraps of seaweed. Roz had noticed the debris of a storm still lying in places on the road. Between the fishing, milking and knitting, they had prayed and sung hymns to warm their hearts in the plain Methodist chapels and old parish churches. The bungalows and cherubs came much later, Guernsey's proud reply to an urban, industrial age.

The lane wound round so many corners that Roz lost her bearings. There didn't seem to be any signposts, only names carved into the granite at waist height, but by the time she had spotted their discreet lettering, she had invariably taken the wrong turning. The roads had been built on top of farm tracks evolved for the plod of carthorse hoof, not for the motor car, let alone the ungainly four-wheel-drive vehicles which the islanders seemed to favour. Roz squeezed past yet another wide-bellied vehicle and the wing mirror tickled the wall. Glimpses of the sea helped her find her way, but by the time she had returned to the hotel for lunch, the exhilaration of the beach walk had evaporated and she felt exasperated. She began to feel hemmed in by the cosy fussiness – too much pampas grass, she said to herself wryly. Over lunch, the feeling intensified. She was ushered to a seated area by the bar to inspect the menu. Her eye fell on the group dining at the next-door table. In their early seventies, they were enjoying a prosperous retirement; the men slapped their thighs with loud good humour. She stared at them, wondering what their war had been, and whether there were memories which interrupted their sleep.

Roz had given up studying history at fourteen. She'd told her history teacher that she couldn't see the point. Miss Wraysford had tried to persuade her brightest pupil to continue, but Roz had been very sure. 'A keenly logical and clear-cut mind,' read her end-of-term report, and she had opted instead for economics, geography and biology. Both Helene and Justin were apt to wonder where she had come from; she smiled now as she remembered those comments. She had wanted to know the mechanics of things: money, tax, rivers, plants and blood and cells. At university, law had suited her; she liked the order of it. She'd ended up in family law partly because the company had assumed that, as a woman, she would be more adept at dealing with the procession of emotionally distressed clients and their divorces. Her matter-of-fact approach seemed to work. In the middle of a personal crisis, a client needed someone with their head firmly screwed on, attending to the detail.

She liked her tidy life. It had taken an effort to reorder things after Nick left – divide the finances, share out the friends, the record collection and the pictures. She had discovered an affair and he told her it was 'perfectly rational to fall out of love'. It was such an odd comment that she was speechless. Did loyalty and commitment for twelve years mean nothing? It appeared not, and Nick moved into his new life effortlessly, or so it seemed to Roz. She was very glad that they hadn't had kids. It had made things much simpler. She had never been sure she wanted any, and she had been uncomfortable with Nick's desire for a large family. He left her the flat. She focused on her career, unencumbered by the struggles she witnessed in colleagues with children. For a long time she had missed him badly, but she hadn't seen him now for many years. She had heard he had children. Since then, she had had a few affairs, but no one had persuaded her to give up her cherished independence. As the chance of a child receded, she was philosophical; she was godmother to several of her friends' children, and she had nieces and nephews, who arrived at regular intervals as her brothers' families grew. She batted away her mother's questions firmly. She was not going to be a mother. She could be a good friend, sister, daughter, and aunt instead. There were many roles in life left, she told herself – and anyone brave enough to ask.

She regularly borrowed a small cottage in Dorset from an old friend, and loved her weekends there, either alone or with friends and their families. She had inherited her mother's love of gardens and her father's love of art – she visited exhibitions, collected paintings, and she gardened at the cottage. She enjoyed her expensive holidays. It was a comfortable life, and that was how she liked it.

Roz had even begun to agree with Ed: Justin's letter didn't matter. Helene and Justin had had a complicated marriage, as many do. Helene had not wished them to know more for a reason. It was best left that way.

Then a new client, Francesca, had appeared in her office, with a mind as sharp as a razor and a sassy assertiveness.

'I want to find out who my father was,' she said, sizing up Roz, dressed in her expensive blue suit and discreet gold jewellery. 'I've studied genetics for two years at university, and I want to know what became of my father, given our shared DNA. Did our nucleotides send him round the twist, or is he some hugely successful businessman? Or even a rock star? I need to know.'

Francesca couldn't be more than twenty-one, thought Roz. She was still studying.

'You've tried asking your mother, I presume.'

'Yip – knows nothing. Artificial insemination in a Harley Street clinic. That's where I began. In a syringe. No love affair, not even a passionate one-night stand. My parents never even met each other. He signed a form and handed over a test tube. The clinic can't give me his name. Donors were guaranteed anonymity. Not exactly romantic, is it?' She leaned forward and put her elbows on the table, propping up her strong chin. Her nose was pierced and her hair was streaked with pink.

Roz inwardly flinched at the directness of this young woman, but she took on the case, intrigued by the possibility of pursuing it through the European Court. Could the case come under the Convention's right to family life? She was spending a bit of time on it – Francesca was not short of money. She found the case preyed on her mind because of the obvious questions it provoked about her own father. Roz had become distinctly uncomfortable at the realization that she knew very little, if anything, of either of her parents' backgrounds or their life together. She had this odd sensation of the ground falling away beneath her. Dizzy spells had prompted her to visit the doctor, but he had little to offer. He suggested bereavement counselling, which she had dismissed outright. But she was troubled by persistent questions: how could she pretend her life was so orderly when she knew so little about what lay in her own past? It was in the midst of this unease that her friend had suggested the winter break in Guernsey. Despite her reservations, she booked a flight. She reasoned that a dose of fresh sea air would do her good. Here she was, nearly twenty-four hours after landing, and she still couldn't make up her mind about her real motive for coming.

As she was finishing her lunch, one of the hotel staff came to her table with a note. Jim had rung and asked her to call him. She had turned down his half-hearted offer to accompany her. She headed back to her room to call him.

His voice was excited. 'Listen, I've got something. It's not much, but you might be able to use it. You know Mother's desk? It's here now, in my sitting room. I pulled out the lining paper this morning, and a newspaper cutting slipped out. It was a sale notice of a house called Les Bois Verts. There's handwriting down the margin.'

'Can you see a date?'

'It's torn, but I think it's 1978. The handwritten comment says: "Sold again. Thought you might be interested. L". There's a photo. It's very bad quality, but it's a large stone house surrounded by trees. There is a handsome stone arch over the front door and a big garden. It's a beautiful house. Funny – it's just occurred to me – it looks like there is a fanlight over the door similar to home in London.'

'Is there any mention of where it is on the island?'

'Something about Torteval.'

'That's a parish, I think. No street or road name?'

'I'm afraid not. I think it's important, Roz. You need to find this house. I've a sense that this was where Helene was born. That arch is unusual. It can't be hard to trace in a small village.'

'Maybe . . . I wonder who L was.' Roz was distracted. She had pulled out the map and spread it over the bed. 'I can see Torteval. But there are dozens of small lanes. The house could be anywhere.' She folded the map. 'I'm on holiday. I want to do some walking. Rest. Visit some gardens. I doubt there will be time to bother with this. It's too vague, Jim. Could be just a friend's house.'

'It doesn't give us much to go on, I agree,' apologized Jim. 'I'm sorry I'm not there to help.'

Roz rang off. Jim had his painting, a patient wife and three children. There was little money or spare time.

*

A coach was disgorging its contents at the entrance to the

museum. Roz was swept along with a group of German tourists. They fell silent as they entered the tunnel in the cliff. Light from a naked bulb illuminated the damp walls, and the dummies in Wehrmacht uniforms with staring eyes and stiff limbs. A tape recording of German martial songs reverberated in the space, which was hung with Swastika flags, helmets and guns. Cases displayed wartime newspapers and German medals. Roz looked at the maps of elaborate fortifications, and the black-and-white photographs of German troops marching down the narrow, cobbled streets of St Peter Port.

She paused by the photos, wondering if, by some astonishing coincidence, she might see her mother in one of them. Was she amongst the islanders crowded on the quaysides to catch the last evacuation boats to England? Or was she one of those happy faces greeting the British soldiers in 1945? Perhaps Helene might be the young woman reaching up to kiss a British soldier, and, who knows, maybe that was her father. Had she been conceived in a fit of patriotic fervour on the night of Liberation? Was she the result of Helene's thank-you embrace, ecstatic after the monotony and fear of five years of Occupation, delirious at the first taste of whisky and tea? But none of these buxom, ruddy-cheeked tomato workers and flower pickers bore any resemblance to her mother.

The tunnel bore into the solid rock of the hillside. A weight of earth and rock pressed down above her head. Water had seeped through in several of the rooms, leaving long streaks of mould on the painted concrete walls. One part of the network of tunnels had not been finished, and tools were scattered amongst the rubble, the wet rock rough where the painful task of hacking at its surface had been interrupted. There was a close dampness, as if walking through thick fog, which she could feel in her nostrils and chest. The rock gleamed in the dim light. A crude soundtrack played of workers digging the tunnels, the crashing, smashing and banging blurred into a roar. Then for a brief moment, as the tape rewound, it was quiet but for the trickle of water, and the cries of children in another part of the museum.

Roz retraced her steps to the exit with relief. Once outside, she took a big breath of sea air and wandered back along the rocky foreshore towards St Peter Port's harbour. A shabby café was perched on the edge of the sea, its windows steamed up with condensation. It looked temptingly warm. Inside, the tables were covered with checked plastic tablecloths, and Roz found the clatter of crockery and tea-making comforting. She bought a cup of tea and sat down with her guidebook. But it lay on the table unopened. She couldn't bear to read any more of this history. She looked out at the small beach of Havelet Bay. Further along there were pools cut into the rock. In the summer, this spot would offer a pretty view of the houses of St Peter Port climbing the hill and of Castle Cornet sitting in the middle of the bay.

'Sorry, love, time to close up.' A waitress, a cheerful woman in her early sixties, was standing by her table.

Roz looked up and smiled. She gathered her bag and book, but the woman didn't move.

'Over for a holiday?' She looked at her with frank curiosity. 'Having nice weather, aren't you? Cold but clear. First time here?'

Roz nodded.

'We like it. Some say it's quiet, but I think it's a lovely place to bring up children. Never need to worry about locking doors or cars. No crime here to worry about. Not like London. I went there once, and it was a bit busy for me. Everyone rushing around. We like a slower pace of life here.'

Roz smiled in reply.

'Interested in the Occupation?' asked the woman, twisting her head to see the guidebook.

'I didn't know anything about it before I came.'

'That's what a lot of the tourists say. They didn't know that a bit of British territory was occupied by the Nazis. Then they start asking questions –' she paused for a breath – 'about what we did in the war. They want to know why we *collaborated*.'

She spat out the last word.

'I'd like to have known what they would have done. All so self-righteous about their bombing raids and munitions factories back in Birmingham. Quite a different matter when you've got to live with Germans and keep your family fed. It's getting easier now. Those who lived through the war are too old to come and visit. The younger ones don't care.'

'Were you here in the Occupation?' asked Roz.

'Yes, but I was young. I can't say I remember a lot – other than my dad coming home in 1946.'

Roz took a breath, nervous. 'I'm doing a bit of family history research. I think my grandparents may have lived here once.'

The woman looked at her closely, with more interest.

'Research? We've had a few of those before, and then they turn out to be journalists looking for the German bastards who were born to the jerrybags.'

Roz looked puzzled.

'That was the name for the girls who carried on with Germans. But can you blame them? Very few British men about, and plenty of handsome Germans – well, that's what I was told,' she said, laughing.

'No, not that sort of thing at all,' Roz interjected quickly. 'My mother was married to an Englishman.'

'A woman used to work here who retired a year or two ago. She might be able to help,' said the woman doubtfully. 'Maev knows everybody on the island. She lives at the end of the left turn past where the bank used to be in St Sampson. Number fifteen. A whitewashed old cottage opposite the garage.'

She spoke as if everyone knew the island as well as she did.

Roz took down the name and what she had understood of the directions. The woman moved on with a cheery goodbye and resumed wiping the tables, scattering the crumbs in a wide arc onto the floor.

★

Roz had booked a trip to Alderney the following day. It only took twenty minutes by plane to reach the neighbouring island, and her friend, Sally, had insisted Roz would like her aunt and find Alderney fascinating. The aunt had retired to Alderney after a distinguished career as an architect, and when Roz had looked up the island in the guidebook in London, she had been intrigued by the pocket size of the place. She took up Sally's suggestion and when she rang, the aunt promptly offered a tour. It was too good a day trip to miss.

It was another cold but sunny day. Roz no longer felt blinded by the brightness. Her eyes had adjusted to the island sharpness of this clean ocean light. As she walked across the airstrip to the tiny plane, her heart lifted. She was enjoying this. She loved flying. As the engines started up, the roar was too intense for anything but sign language from the air steward. The whole vehicle creaked uncannily as it gathered momentum; it seemed a frail construction to generate such a volume of noise. Suddenly, with a jerk, it was airborne, climbing steeply into the sky. Down below, the pebble-dash bungalows fell away, with their granite walls, lanes and gardens dotted with shrubs. The plane pulled north across a crumpled patchwork of small green fields scattered with glass-houses glinting in the sun. Roz craned her neck to see the last of Guernsey as they wheeled over the rocky coast interspersed with sandy bays. The waves foamed white, and from a headland traces of spume trailed across the sea. Then there was only the silvery surface of the water, like beaten metal, and one boat, no bigger than a speck, on a similar course towards Alderney.

In the distance, beyond the airplane wing, Roz glimpsed the coast of France, and, to the south, the island of Jersey. They seemed to have been in the air only a few moments when they began to lose height again. Alderney was beneath them. The steep cliffs were clothed in the orange-brown of dead bracken. The ocean crashed onto the rocks at their base. The island seemed barely fit for human habitation, little more than a treeless rock cast adrift. Then she saw a small harbour, a scattering of houses and the square tower of a church, like a child's toy town. They were landing.

When she emerged from the plane, a tall woman in her seventies came bounding over to greet her. Now Roz understood why Sally had been so insistent: Penny was brimming with enthusiasm, and Roz knew she was going to like her; there was a directness to her manner and a keen intelligence which she instantly appreciated as they walked back to her car.

'I had no idea I would end up in Alderney,' she laughed as she put the key in the ignition. 'I inherited the house from an uncle, and after I retired, I found myself spending more and more time here. It suited me. I liked having the sea all around, but I was never a sailor, so it seemed a good solution.'

She had used her retirement to learn about the place – its flora, fauna and its wars – and her curiosity was infectious. They followed the small lanes in the old car, heavy with rust from the salt-laden air, on a tour of the island. Roz learned of the nesting patterns of puffins and gannets, terns and flocks of migrating birds on their way south to Africa from Iceland, and of the rare species of flowers which survive the salt-laden gales to multiply on the exposed cliffs. She heard of how successive generations of British and French had fought each other over this tiny scrap of rock, each century leaving behind another set of fortifications, piled up in layers, one on top of the other.

'Married? Children?' asked Penny. 'No, well, these things

don't always work out. I only ever managed the first, and it didn't last. But I've discovered I rather like being an aunt. Now I have lots of great-nieces and -nephews. They come in the summer to visit.'

Roz was relieved. So many conversations with older women required explanations of why she had not had children. None of that was necessary with Penny. They had swiftly established a shared understanding.

'Being an aunt is very interesting, with none of the responsibility,' she laughed.

It was true; Roz loved her visits to Jim's noisy household of three little girls, yet there was always a sense of relief as she left. The two women chatted about Penny's career as an architect as they drew up in front of her bungalow.

On the dining table, Penny had spread out huge maps with meticulous scale drawings of Alderney's German fortifications, the most complex and extensive of those built on all the islands. They studied the drawings, and Penny pointed out instances of the Germans' technical prowess and their engineering skill. She'd made a plate of sandwiches. After they had eaten them and had examined the maps, she said there was something else.

'I'll show you my masterpiece!' she declared. 'I've always loved model-building. We did some of it at college when we were training.'

She led Roz outside and down the path to the garage. Inside, across the floor, the island of Alderney had been recreated as it was at the peak of the German Occupation. Tiny rolls of barbed wire ran along the tiny beaches. Bunkers dotted the hillsides, with the gun batteries on the cliffs and the little narrow-gauge railway running to the town. There were tiny German soldiers marching in columns down the road to the harbour, where ships were unloading at the quayside. All that was missing from this perfect miniature, Roz noticed, were the slave labourers who had built it. When she queried this point, Penny was uncharacteristically absent-minded.

It was nearly four, the winter sun was dipping to the horizon, and the conversation had begun to ebb. Penny suggested one last visit before getting back to the airport for the return flight to Guernsey. She drove them to a patch of wasteland covered in brambles and bracken, and bordered by the high wire fence surrounding the airstrip. They parked and picked their way across the puddles. They were on high ground, and all around them the sea stretched out, reflecting the sinking sun's light. Roz paused to admire the beautiful drama, changing every second, but Penny was calling to her. She was standing beside a concrete pillar concealed in brambles. Here and there amidst the bracken could be glimpsed a concrete platform and rubble.

'This is all that's left of the SS camp the Germans built, SS Sylt. They brought here French Jews, German criminals and Eastern Europeans, and worked them to death,' said Penny quietly.

She led the way along a narrow muddy path. After about ten minutes, they came to a slope which opened out towards the sea. Another large rectangular concrete platform was visible here, broken in places by weeds.

'This was the site of the bungalow of the SS commandant. A view of the sea, but sheltered from the winds up on the top.'

A vast fiery red ball was now hanging just above the horizon and the sea had turned a smoky blue. The setting sun cast a path made up of splinters of golden light. The bungalow would have witnessed such sunsets while men discussed the running of the camp, supplies and rations. The German soldiers would have worried about bombing raids at home and waited for letters from loved ones as they sat on this rock in the Atlantic, a distant outpost of the Führer's Reich. They would have listened to his shrill-voiced speeches on crackly wirelesses, stirring them on to fight, just as their comrades did in Belorussia, on sunny Greek islands, and in the deserts of North Africa. Then, with little else to do on a winter afternoon, perhaps they had turned to stare at a setting sun like this, watching the same magnificent spectacle. Roz found the thought chilling. Up above them on that exposed spot by the airstrip, the prisoners would have been hungry and cold in the Atlantic storms.

The quietness of the winter afternoon was suddenly full of the shadows of thousands of men, prisoners and imprisoners; some had died and been buried on this island, and some had taken their memories home with them. There must still be men, frail with age, living in Germany, Poland, Ukraine, Russia and Belorussia, who remembered this sun and sea. Memories of shame and self-hatred, as well as fear. Did their nightmares wake them in the early hours, leaving them fretful as they lay beside their sleeping wives? Roz shivered.

Subdued, the two women walked back to the car. At the airport, Roz offered Penny profuse thanks for her hospitality, but as she went to the departure gate, she felt unnerved by her visit. The beauty of the place jarred with its disturbing history. The island which Penny enjoyed in her busy retirement must have once induced despair in those prisoners thousands of miles from home.

Half an hour later, Roz watched as Alderney's cliffs, glowing in the last light of the setting sun, slipped away. The plane was pulling up into a sky fast fading to lemon and peppermint green in the wake of the sun's fiery finale. The first lights of Guernsey were winking in the gloom ahead. Tomorrow she would look for Maev, she decided.

*

Roz was muffled up in a big scarf and hat, and, after half an hour of walking on the beach, her cheeks were red and her eyes were smarting with the cold. But the morning walk served its purpose of clearing the mind after a disturbed night's sleep. The sunshine had gone, leaving grey skies, a bitter wind, and the sea a dark turquoise. She found a café, which was almost empty. The woman behind the counter produced a cup of coffee, and Roz sat beside a big window looking out over the beach. She wrapped her hands around the cup to warm them. During the night, she had lain awake, thinking of the slave labourers on the treeless rock, Alderney. Perhaps she had had enough for one weekend. It was not the weather for wandering around lanes looking for a house with an arch. No, she would try and find Maev, and then head for the airport. She was beginning to think of being back in London this evening and the office in the morning.

To Roz's surprise, the absurd directions to Maev's home – who uses a non-existent bank as a landmark? – proved easier to follow than she had expected. As she drove, she wondered at a shared sense of change and history which allowed someone to refer so offhandedly to places which no longer existed. Heavy rain was drumming on the windscreen as she found the white-washed cottage. She parked and got out of the car, opened the wrought-iron gate and had walked up the path before she had worked out what she was going to say. Shells were stuck in the pebble-dash around the door. She pressed the doorbell and a woman opened the frosted-glass door.

'I'm sorry to disturb you. I was at the museum on Saturday and a lady in the tearoom said someone called Maev might be able to help me.'

Roz looked at the woman's expectant face, and plunged on. 'Are you Maev?

The woman nodded.

'I'm trying to find out about my mother, Helene Le Lacheur. She used to live on Guernsey a long time ago.'

Maev looked quizzically at Roz, but her expression was kindly.

'Would you be so kind as to answer a few questions?'

Roz had pulled her hood up in the heavy rain.

'You'd better come in,' said Maev, opening the door wide.

Roz followed her into a small sitting room.

'It's very kind of you. I have some family history connected to the island which I'm trying to understand a little more. I'm from London.' She felt nervous.

'You look very cold and a bit wet. Let me make you a cup of coffee to warm you up. Have a seat.'

Maev disappeared down a corridor. On the mantelpiece, a brass clock chimed noon. Just as it finished, a Swiss cuckoo clock on the other side of the room began its noonday performance. A cat stirred from its sleep in front of an artificial coal fire.

'Here's the coffee, and here's a copy of my memoirs,' said Maev proudly, producing a pamphlet. 'I was a child during the Occupation.'

Roz took her cue.

'Thank you, let me give you the money.' She rummaged in her bag for her purse. 'Actually, it's not the Occupation I'm interested in. My mother was born here. She died last year. She never talked about Guernsey. I don't know when she left, but it must have been before the war. I wondered if anyone might have heard of her.'

'I'm so sorry to hear of your mother passing away.' Maev fussed over the cat, who had jumped into her lap.

'She was born in 1920, I think. I don't really know how to trace any details, such as where she lived or whether there is any distant family still living here.'

'What was she called again, love?'

'Helene Le Lacheur,' said Roz.

'Well, I do remember the Le Lacheur family. Do you know which parish she lived in?'

Roz shook her head.

'There was the Le Lacheur boy. Tom, I think. I can't remember what happened to him. I don't remember a girl.' Maev put her head to one side, thinking. She patted her hair.

'I was young at the time, only twelve at the end of the Occupation,' she said, and then brightened. 'Why don't we ask my mother? Her mind wanders a bit, but she's better on things that happened a long time ago than she is about anything that went on yesterday. She's just next door. We could pop round this afternoon if you like.'

'You've been very kind, but I'm flying back to London this afternoon.'

'Listen, I'll go round now, and have a word. I don't like springing things on old people, but if I can persuade her, I'll come back to get you.'

She put a coat around her shoulders, and picked up an umbrella from a stand. A few minutes later, she reappeared.

'Come on, love, my mother says it's all right.'

In the cottage next door, Maev's elderly mother was sitting with a knitted blanket across her knees. Maev introduced Roz to Mrs Blampied.

'This is the lady from London, Mum.'

Mrs Blampied went straight to the point. 'You are wanting to know about the Le Lacheur family? Was your mother one of those at Dieu Donne, the big house in Torteval?' she demanded. She leaned forward to stare at Roz.

'I'm afraid I don't know.'

'Did your mother never talk about Guernsey?' interjected Maev.

'Oh, Maev, girl, don't interrupt,' said Mrs Blampied impatiently. 'What was her first name again?'

'Helene.'

'Ah, now that rings a bell. Helene Le Lacheur,' she repeated. 'I'm sure I remember something about a girl called Helene at the end of the Occupation, but I don't think she was a Le Lacheur.

88

Are you sure that was her surname? Was she one of them up at Torteval, Maev?'

Maev suddenly looked very anxious. 'Didn't your mother leave any papers behind that could help you?' she asked.

Roz shook her head. She saw Maev look meaningfully at her mother, but the elderly lady ignored her.

Mrs Blampied was still looking at her intently. Her stare was unnerving Roz.

'Yes, yes. I'm sure the girl up at the Torteval vicarage was called Helene. I knew of her father, the vicar. I see a family likeness.'

Mrs Blampied looked down at her hands. Her voice was more hesitant. 'Definitely a likeness. Same blonde hair, same slightness.'

'When would this have been? Was the vicar here in the war?' asked Roz, a tone of urgency creeping into her voice.

'Well, if my memory serves me right, the girl left not long after the war. It was just gossip that she'd gone, mind. We didn't know when she left, because we didn't see her about town after the war. Didn't see her about town during the war, for that matter, but we heard something of what went on.'

She paused.

'There was plenty of gossip about that girl. People like Arthur Brown. Always telling tales about people. What he didn't know, he would make up, and he was no one to point fingers. He did well enough out of the war. He spread plenty of gossip about what went on over in Torteval. She was too pretty for her own good,' said the mother, leaning back in her chair, adding, 'though I never saw it, mind. A slip of a thing . . .'

'But that was only gossip, Mum,' remonstrated Maev, and she turned to Roz. 'I don't think any of it was true. You couldn't believe the likes of Mr Brown.'

Roz suddenly realized that Maev had suspected this outcome

all along. Going to her mother had been a way to divert the responsibility.

'Of course, gossip always exaggerates,' Roz forced herself to say, and she even managed a short laugh as she tried to put both women at their ease. They looked anxious. She felt her hands were slightly clammy.

'Wasn't there rumours that she had hidden a Russian?' Maev asked her mother. 'That's what I heard after the war.'

'A Russian?' said Roz, bewildered.

'One of the foreign workers that the Germans brought over to build the fortifications,' explained Maev. 'A few islanders took pity on them. Some workers were very badly treated – they got sick and beaten. Some escaped, and islanders gave them food and shelter. You probably don't remember much more, do you, Mum? She couldn't have played a big part in looking after Russians or she would have got a watch, like the others,' added Maev. 'The Soviet government gave out several watches, thanking people for looking after the workers. I don't think your mother ever got one.'

'No, she didn't get a watch, and that got people's tongues wagging. They said it had been made up to cover up for other things,' said Mrs Blampied. 'And then after the Liberation – that was awful . . . One thing for sure, that Helene didn't stick around for long after the war. She disappeared – after . . .'

Mrs Blampied's voice petered out. She smoothed the blanket with her hand. 'That was awful,' she concluded quietly.

For a moment, neither mother nor daughter knew what to say. Then Maev, her voice strained, repeated, 'It was all gossip. I'm sure too many people had nothing to do during the Occupation but talk.'

She recounted an anecdote about how, as an act of sabotage, she and her brother had put sand in the petrol tank of a German lorry. She didn't pause before offering another tale of how she milked the cows in the field at night to supplement her family's rations.

'Well, I'd better go. I'm late already,' said Roz.

'Yes, yes, of course,' said Maev, jumping up. 'I'm talking too much.'

'Perhaps I might be able to contact you again to see if any other memories of my mother come back to you?' Roz asked the old lady as she said goodbye.

'I doubt very much that my mother will remember anything else. She gets names muddled up all the time,' Maev replied firmly, looking at her mother.

Her mother, cowed, mumbled her goodbye.

On the doorstep, it occurred to Roz. 'Have you heard of a house called Les Bois Verts?' she asked Maev.

'Oh, yes, I think that used to be The Vicarage. It's up in Torteval. It was renamed back in the 1970s when the old vicar left and the church sold it off.'

Roz said her goodbyes and headed back to the car. The whole encounter had lasted no more than three quarters of an hour, but her mind was in turmoil. She sat in the car, the rain drumming on the roof. She had an hour until her flight left, but she couldn't move. The rain was coming down so hard it was bouncing on the road. Her mother had been here, on the island, during the Occupation. She knew now where Helene had lived. Perhaps she could piece her mother's life together after all. She felt a deep sense of unease: what had been awful?

V

Helene was the first to see them. She was sitting with a group of children, reading, and one of her pupils was stumbling their way through a page of a battered copy of *The Water Babies*. As his grubby finger traced the words and he slowly sounded them out, she heard an unusual noise. The engine of a car. Immediately she was on edge. There were few civilian cars on the road these days. She stood up and saw the vehicle had stopped in the lane outside the school. Then another drew up. The chromework sparkled in the sun. She recognized one of the cars – it used to belong to the bank manager in St Peter Port. It now had a small insignia flying from the bonnet.

Several Germans were getting out. She saw the peaked caps of two officers. A soldier held the door open and saluted. Helene could feel her heart thump with fear. She called across to Mrs Duquemin and pointed to the window. The Germans had opened the school gate and were crossing the playground. Mrs Duquemin came over and looked out of the window.

'Go and tell Miss Tostevin – now,' she said in a hoarse whisper in Helene's ear. Her voice was unsteady.

Next door, Miss Tostevin's class of ten-year-olds were chorusing their five times table.

'Nine times five is forty-five, ten times five is fifty . . .' they chanted. But their voices were beginning to trail away. These farm children found it hard to concentrate at the best of times, but it was especially hard in the June heat and at the end of the morning, when they were hungry. Many of them were up at dawn for chores before school. Helene stood by the door, trying to catch Miss Tostevin's attention.

She was ignoring Helene, intent on her task.

'German officers are here,' Helene burst out.

The children stopped their chant and stared at Helene, immediately anxious. Miss Tostevin put her hand on her chest. The colour drained from her face.

'Quick, quick, children . . . quick . . .' The children waited nervously for her instructions as she fussed with the papers on her desk. Finally, she found what she was looking for and stood up, smoothing her hair and straightening her skirt.

'Now, children. Put away your books and fold your arms. Sit up straight. And not a word . . . not a word from any of you. Remember, *Guten Tag* for "good morning".'

Her voice was quavering as she started reading out some German verbs from a sheet. She stumbled over the unfamiliar words. There was no knock on the school door, only the sound of their boots in the tiled corridor outside. The class was eerily silent as the normally restless children sat still, their eyes fixed on the classroom door. Two Germans entered. Helene kept her eyes lowered, as her father had instructed; she stared at their boots.

Miss Tostevin came down off the podium and, her face wreathed in nervous smiles, ushered them to her seat. She beckoned to one of the older boys to bring another chair.

'We would like to hear the children learning the German lesson with the books we have provided,' said one of the officers in English. 'We are showing the commandant the excellent progress we have made in establishing the Führer's Reich here on your beautiful island.'

He had light sandy hair and looked very young, perhaps in his early twenties. He had a small moustache. He inclined his head towards Miss Tostevin. She looked terrified. The children's eyes flickered from adult to adult.

'Sir, I'm very sorry, we are learning your wonderful language from this sheet. Some of the children only speak Guernsey dialect, their English is not good, but we make progress with German. But we do not have German books – they have not yet arrived . . . they are on order, I assure you, but . . .' Miss Tostevin was babbling in her hurry to offer excuses. 'Finances are short and we have been t-told they are out of p-print,' she stammered.

A frown appeared on the older man's plump face. He must be the commandant, thought Helene. She had heard about him. Miss Tostevin was fiddling with her handkerchief, twisting it around her fingers as she looked up at the faces of the two men seated on the podium.

'The school day is very short, but we do German lessons three times a week,' she added.

The young officer began making notes.

'This is not satisfactory. All the schools on the island have been issued with the correct books. The commandant has been most particular in wanting to see children in the country parishes using the books.'

'Of course, any day now, we have been assured . . . only last week, we called the printers. They promised.'

There was an awkward pause, with only the sound of the officer's pen scratching on his notebook. The children barely seemed to be breathing.

'This will have to be taken up with the island authorities at the earliest possible time. We will investigate the delay we have seen here, Miss . . . er . . . Tostevin. Your address?'

Miss Tostevin was close to tears as she gave her address.

'And this young lady? Is she a member of your staff? Your name and address, please?'

Helene whispered her name. Miss Tostevin gave her address.

The commandant stood up, spoke to the officer, and then

launched into a speech in German, which the younger man translated.

'I am most disappointed. These are the kinds of lazy behaviours that are displeasing to the Führer. He is justly proud of this little island. He admires your country and has no quarrel with the English. We are two peoples, like brother and sister. We will care for you, as a brother cares for his little sister. We will show the world, here, on this little island. But the sister must do what the brother tells her to do, for her own safety.'

His voice had risen, and the children's eyes widened with alarm.

At that point, another officer slipped into the room. He seemed to be of a more senior rank than the young sandy-haired officer, who made way for him. He whispered something in the commandant's ear, and, although the commandant looked as if he was warming up for a longer speech, he broke off and gathered his gloves and cap. The new arrival, a dark-haired man, turned to the class.

'Thank you, children, for your attention. That will be all for today. We wish you well in your studies and are delighted you are doing well in your German.'

His English was excellent and his voice quiet.

'*Heil Hitler!*' he shouted with unexpected force, and saluted along with the other officers. '*Heil Hitler,*' the children replied, their arms held high as they had been taught. Miss Tostevin and Helene awkwardly followed suit.

As the two officers followed the commandant out, Helene saw how the dark-haired one spoke rapidly in German to the younger officer, who then ripped out the pages of his notebook on which he had scribbled the addresses, and gave them to him.

This officer fell behind. He turned and spoke quietly to Miss Tostevin.

'I do hope we have not caused any inconvenience. I shall enter a report that we are satisfied with the progress at your institution, and that you were honoured, indeed delighted, to have had a visit from the commandant and to have had the benefit of a fine speech . . . Miss . . .' He looked down at the notes. 'Miss Tostevin – and Miss Le Lacheur?'

'*Mrs* Le Lacheur,' replied Helene shakily. The voice was familiar.

'Mrs Le Lacheur.' He inclined his head politely, folded the pieces of notepaper and put them in his breast pocket. His manner was brisk and formal.

The door closed behind him. Car doors slammed and the engines started up. There was a thick silence. Miss Tostevin sat down heavily.

'Children, you can take a break early today,' she said, strained. 'Helene, could you fetch me some water?'

That voice, thought Helene as she filled a glass at the tap. That perfect English. Where had she heard it before?

Over the last two years, she had met few German soldiers. In town, on her rare visits, one or two had raised their hats to her, and tried to engage her in conversation, but she averted her eyes to avoid contact. One recent incident had left her shaken: she had been riding Sandy along the lane early one evening. A truck had careered around a corner, forcing the horse tight into the bank. She had just managed to keep him calm. With a screeching of brakes, the truck had stopped and two Germans jumped out, ordering her to dismount and demanding her identity papers. Thankfully, she had them; it was one piece of Nanna's advice she had taken seriously. She had no wish to be asked to attend the Feldkommandantur in St Peter's Port over identity papers. It had seemed like an age while they examined her papers and matched the photo, scrutinizing her face, and then walked around her, looking her up and down. She had felt naked, their eyes taking in her open-necked shirt and jodhpurs. One man had just put his hand out to touch her arm when they heard the sound of a vehicle coming down the lane, and he quickly drew back. Fortunately, it had been Felicity's father on his rounds; he slowed his car and rolled down the window to ask if she needed help. It had been a very lucky escape. The Germans sauntered back to their truck, whistling. Sandy seemed to have sensed the tension and flared his nostrils, stamping his feet impatiently.

A few days after the school visit, it came back to Helene. The voice was that of the German officer on the cliffs that rainy November day. In the seven months since then, she hadn't taken the cliff path. She had been too frightened that she might meet him again, and for several months she was terrified that he might have reported her. She wasn't certain it was him, because she couldn't remember his face well, but how many of the Germans were able to speak such fluent English?

They had built a watchtower on the cliffs now. Helene had seen the lorries transporting the building materials, and she had been riding down the back lane once when a column of slave labourers had marched past. She had been appalled by their ragged clothes and thin faces. Their boots were falling apart and were stuffed with straw. After that she avoided the area, and only rode Sandy in the fields near the house.

For years after, the first flush of early summer heat would bring back the day of the school inspection: the gripping fear, her parched throat, the hollow sensation in her legs as the terror subsided, not once, but twice – first in the classroom, and again, later in the afternoon. For years, Helene marvelled at the coincidence of the two encounters on the same day. Even at the time, she saw it as some kind of omen.

School closed early, because Miss Tostevin said she had a bad attack of nerves and needed to rest. Helene usually walked home with a group of children who lived on the edge of the parish; parents had become anxious about their children, so she accompanied them back to one of the farms and, in return, they gave her a glass of milk.

The hot sun beat down with a flat brightness from a pale sky. Helene squinted at the whiteness of the grit on the road, and she could feel the sweat between her breasts and running down the inside of her legs under her skirt. Several times, she paused and took off her hat to wipe her forehead on her sleeve while the children searched the verge for wild strawberries and picked ragged bunches of purple vetch, mauve field scabious and fat yellow buttercups. The cow parsley had shot up, spilling over into the lane, unchecked by traffic. There were so few cars these days that the weeds were recapturing the road, breaking through the surface in an uneven line down the middle, and many of the trees hadn't been cut back for two years, because of the shortage of farmworkers. Helene feared these unkempt roads presaged the chaos that lay ahead for the island. She was haunted by a future in which the island was pockmarked by smoking craters and strewn with dead bodies, as she had seen in the bombing two years before. She had gone back to praying. It was a short, simple prayer every night before she went to sleep: 'Please God, don't let England try to liberate us. Please let England forget about us.'

She drank the thick, creamy milk at the farm in one gulp. It was still cool from the stone cellar where it was stored. The farmers' children were thriving on the war. They had plenty of food and were growing plump on the profits from selling the rich yellow butter that the Germans had developed such a liking for. On the last stretch of the walk home across the fields she was alone. She preferred to avoid the road, even if she did get scratched, and sometimes stung by nettles, when she climbed over the old bank which divided the fields. She arrived by the barn and walked along its length to the garden gate. The granite was warm under her hand in the heat of the afternoon sun. Suddenly, she heard a whimpering. She paused, and the sound stopped. She slowly took a few steps and it started again. She walked as softly as she could through the tall grass. From a small opening above her head, she thought she heard a suppressed sob. She quickened her pace, the sound receded behind her, and she reached the vegetable garden, where George was tending the raspberry canes.

Together, they headed back to the barn, George, with his bad leg, limping behind Helene. The heavy door was ajar. Inside, it took a while for their eyes to adjust to the gloom. Everything seemed in order: the heap of hay, tackle hanging on the wall, the pile of neatly folded sacks. They listened, but heard nothing.

'You must have been imagining it,' said George with irritation, and he turned to leave. 'There's nothing here.'

He had hardly uttered the words when they heard a sharp intake of breath from the far corner. George picked up a pitchfork, and Helene fell back behind him. They saw the whites of his eyes first, staring out of the darkness. His face was dirty and he was very thin. He had curled into a corner, lying half under some hay, which he had tried clumsily to pull across his body. Only his leg was fully exposed, jerked out at an awkward angle. George grabbed him by the scruff of his clothing and pulled him roughly into the light from the doorway, cursing him. The whimpering turned to a sharp cry of pain. Helene laid a hand on George's arm.

'Careful, I think he's hurt.'

'Come on, lad, speak. What's the matter with you? What are you doing?' George's voice was rough, suspicious that the boy was a thief.

Helene pushed the barn door wide open to give them more light. Only then could they see the terrible state the boy was in. His twisted leg was caked in blood and dirt. One side of his face was a mass of cuts, gummy with blood and pus. His clothing was spattered with blood and wretchedly torn, revealing a skinny body covered in sores and dirt. The smell of him made Helene retch. His hair was matted with filth and bits of twigs; his eyes flicked from side to side; his expression was feral.

Helene crouched down and tried to coax him into telling her where he had come from, but he shrank from her touch and shook his head vigorously. With his better hand, he gestured that he needed water. She filled an old tin cup from the standpipe for him. He drank it greedily, the water slopping down his chin onto his clothes. His hand shook as he held the cup.

Helene looked up at George. 'He needs a doctor. These cuts need to be cleaned.'

'But he's one of the Russians. One of those criminals the Nazis have brought.'

They were both silent.

'What do we do?' she asked. She felt as if she was going to vomit.

'Leave him here, he'll move on again. He's on the run.'

This boy can barely move, thought Helene.

'We can't touch him,' hissed George. 'He's trouble.'

'We can't just leave him here. We'll still get into trouble.'

George shrugged his shoulders. Then the boy moved, and held out his hands in a gesture of prayer to Helene, his eyes pleading. She quickly looked away.

'We'll have to help him get better and then tell him to move on,' Helene said finally, but with a firmness that surprised even herself. George nodded, still doubtful.

They made a rough bed for him of hay covered with an old horse blanket. Helene fetched a bowl of warm water from the kitchen and an old sheet. She ripped it into narrow strips. George watched her. She hesitantly tried to clean some of the dirt and blood from the wounds, trying not to gag. The old man knelt down awkwardly beside the boy and began to work on the leg. The boy winced with pain. His eyes moved from one face to the other, searching for the eye contact which both of them avoided. Helene watched George's surprising skill as he bound the leg with strips of sheet.

Helene fetched some old crusts which she soaked in a little milk mixed with water. She put the bowl beside him, and sat back to watch, but she realized he was too weak even to raise himself onto an elbow to feed. She propped him up against her arm and picked up a spoonful of the mashed crust. It dribbled down his chin, but at least she got some past his teeth, now chattering with the first signs of a fever.

'It's his leg I'm worried about,' said George gruffly. 'He should really have a doctor to set it properly with a splint.'

Helene knew that beneath George's irritability he had a good heart.

'He's not safe here. I'll move him into my back room. He'll be more comfortable there. I'll do it after it's dark, we don't want no snooping.'

For the next few days, the boy drifted in and out of a fever. Sometimes he slept for hours, his breathing so quiet that Helene and George thought he might have died. Other times he raved in his language, clutching at Helene's sleeve or hand, holding it so tight that she couldn't loosen his fingers. They took turns to spend time sitting with him, wiping his forehead of the beads of sweat in the close air of the room. His raving was so loud they didn't dare to open the window. Nor could they risk getting the doctor; it was unlikely Felicity's father would agree to treat the boy anyway. He had an important and delicate relationship to maintain with the Germans. They agreed that they wouldn't tell Nanna or Father for the time being. It would only cause them more worry. George's rooms next to the barn were far enough away from the house for them not to hear anything. The only difficulty was how to extricate the small quantities of food – scraps of bread and some milk – from the pantry, which was under Nanna's close management. In the end, Helene used the excuse of a hungry child at school. It wasn't completely a lie.

After a couple of days, George said he would set the boy's leg himself. He found the handle of an old hoe for the splint, and they used torn-up sheets which Helene smuggled out of the house. It was a rough job, George said, and would probably leave him with a limp. They cut his clothes off him. Helene was embarrassed at the festering sores around the boy's genitals and horrified at how every rib was sharply delineated through his thin skin; his limbs were little more than bones. Moving him seemed to cause huge pain.

His arrival changed things. Helene found it harder to sleep. She lay awake at night, straining for the sound of a vehicle, tense with fear. When she was working in the garden, bent over weeding, she was still listening. If a truck went past in the lane, she held herself rigid and alert. After the engine noise receded, she would sit on the bench for a few moments to recover. As she helped Nanna with the washing-up in the evenings, she was preoccupied. She imagined the arrest, the questioning, the trial, the imprisonment, even the terrifying thought of deportation. She had heard of a friend's mother who had been sent to prison in France just for having a wireless. That was six months ago and she was still not back. As George said, the hope was that the boy would move on as soon as he was stronger, but she worried he had nowhere to go, and that she would have to live with this fear for weeks, maybe even months, to come.

About three weeks after the boy's arrival, Helene, back from school, was in the kitchen shelling peas for supper when she heard a car in the lane. Then the sound of boots on the stone path, and a ring at the front door. She slipped out the back and made her way to the furthest end of the vegetable garden. She knelt down to pick a lettuce and crouched there, waiting. Hiding. She heard her father call from the terrace. Her hands were shaking as she walked towards him.

'Some German officers want to check the identity papers of everyone in the house,' said her father, on edge. 'Can you get George? They are looking over the house as a possible billet.'

This was what her father had dreaded ever since the Germans arrived on Guernsey. The distance of the parish from St Peter Port had, up to now, protected them. Even if they didn't take the whole house, they might billet men on them. The empty Le Lacheur house, Dieu Donne, on the other side of the parish, had been requisitioned almost immediately, as Tom's family had left for England before the invasion in 1940. Helene had sometimes caught a snatch of gramophone music carried on the breeze on summer evenings, and the sound of car engines in the middle of the night after the Germans' parties. She had heard rumours of what went on. She gave the place a wide berth when she was out on Sandy.

Helene found George in the glasshouse. She jumbled her words in her haste to explain.

'They're not searching the outbuildings, they're just looking over the house. Keep quiet, don't say anything,' hissed George in her ear.

When she got back to the house, they were in the drawing room with Father, standing amongst the shrouded furniture. One officer had his back to the room and was looking out of the window down the garden, where Helene had left her trug of lettuce and tomatoes. The other two were checking identity papers.

'Rooms? How many?' one barked at her father. 'Bathrooms?' He wrote down her father's answers on a form. Finally, he looked up and his voice was more polite.

'This property would be highly suitable. There are three officers in need of comfortable accommodation and they require the best rooms. They have breakfast and, occasionally, dinner. Your staff are responsible for the laundry and the cleaning of the rooms. We need everything to be ready for a week on Thursday, when they will arrive.' He added, 'You will be paid.'

Helene's father began to speak, but the German held up his hand.

'This is a war, Mr Le Marchant, and I understand you are a minister, but we have orders. You can continue to live here – with your family.' He nodded to Helene and George. 'Any questions of a *practical* nature?'

Her father was flustered, his hands remonstrating uselessly. Helene was aghast. Finally, he asked, 'But food? Where are we to get the food?'

'You have plenty of food. A beautiful vegetable garden, and a magnificent glasshouse,' said the officer by the window, speaking for the first time. 'We can share your food,' he concluded, as he turned round to face them, smiling.

Helene looked at him. It was the same accent. The officer from the school inspection. He caught her eye. 'Ah, Mrs Le Lacheur, if I remember rightly?'

Her father looked from the officer to Helene with astonishment. She blushed a deep red.

'How are the German lessons coming on, Mrs Le Lacheur?' he said as he moved across the room. He stood in front of her and seemed to be enjoying her embarrassment. She kept her eyes on the floor.

'V-very well, thank you,' she stammered.

'Good, good. Well, we had better be going. We have more houses to visit in the neighbourhood. Thank you, Mr Le Marchant, for your time.'

From an upstairs window, Helene watched, hidden by the curtain, as the Germans left the house accompanied by her father. The officer dropped back behind the others, and spoke to her father for a few moments. He even placed a hand briefly on her father's arm before shaking his hand. Then he surveyed the front of the house, before getting in the car.

'He wants to come to lunch with us on Sunday,' said her father flatly as he came back into the hall and Helene came down the stairs. He was frowning. He looked at her briefly. He hadn't known how to say no. They both knew what the other was thinking: they had been lucky to avoid this for so long. Back in the earliest days of the Occupation, the States had announced a law making it illegal to jeopardize good relations with the Germans. People had been sent to prison for even trivial acts deemed to be lacking in the appropriate respect. Every islander's interaction with the Germans since had been laden with fear. She saw the panic in his eyes, and it made her feel cold with fear.

On Saturday, a large joint of beef arrived. It was wrapped in brown paper and tied with string. The blood had seeped through the wrapping. One of the Le Poidevin boys had brought it over from a farm in St Saviour's; it had been ordered by a Captain Schulze and came with a note from the captain giving instructions on how to cook it: the beef should be lightly done, with plenty of fresh garlic. When Father read out the note to Nanna, she said nothing, but her eyebrows were arched with suppressed indignation. It would be the first meat they had eaten in over a year.

After several heated discussions, George and Helene felt they had no choice but to keep the Russian boy where he was. Moving him would be more dangerous. Now that his raving had subsided, they could keep him hidden from one German for a few hours, Helene reasoned. The boy was making a good recovery. He could feed himself, propped up on the pillows, and the wounds on his face were healing. Only the leg still caused them anxiety. George worried it was going gangrenous; he remembered such things from the Boer War. They changed the bandages every day.

On the Sunday morning when Helene took him some porridge, the boy spoke for the first time.

'Alexei,' he said, gesturing to his chest, and then he pointed at her.

'Helene,' she replied.

'Hel . . . ene,' he stumbled, and smiled. Two of his teeth had been smashed, but the gap-toothed smile created deep creases in his thin face, with its sprinkling of fair wispy hairs. She smiled back. A few moments later, George came in, and Alexei repeated his gestures. 'George . . .' he repeated, and then understanding lit up his eyes. 'Georgi . . . Georgi,' he said with excitement, and George and Helene nodded.

*

Father gave Helene precise advice for the lunch. She was not to engage in conversation with the officer; she was to come to the table at the last moment and she was to leave at the earliest opportunity. She was to help Nanna serve the meal.

'He is a guest, a guest in strange circumstances, but a guest all the same. We will show him British hospitality,' he told a furious Nanna.

Helene was tense with worry as she gathered the beans and potatoes from the garden and laid the table; she tried not to think of the man who was about to arrive, nor let her mind stray to the thought of Alexei lying on the bed in George's back room. The house filled with the unfamiliar smell of roasting meat. Helene's mouth watered at the prospect of the richly flavoured beef. It brought back childhood memories of family Sunday lunch. She hoped there would be some broth she could feed to Alexei.

Just after noon, Father hurried in from church, still in his cassock, and shortly after, a car stopped at the gate. The gate clicked and the captain walked down the path to the front door. From the kitchen, Helene heard the murmur of the two men's voices in the hall, and then her father's study door closed behind them. At one o'clock, as agreed, the men took their seats, and when she could not leave it any longer, she joined them.

She kept her eyes on her plate while her father and the captain talked. They discussed the history of the island and the nearby French coast. They discovered they knew some of the same places in Normandy. They talked about German poetry and philosophy. The captain was polite with her father and expressed his appreciation of the meal. Helene gave monosyllabic answers to the few questions addressed directly to her. She didn't listen to what the two men were talking about until her father asked why Captain Schulze spoke such good English.

'I was at Oxford before the war. My parents admired the English educational system, so they sent me to study in England. My grandmother is English.'

Helene's father couldn't help himself. He beamed with surprise and delight.

'Trinity, myself. I matriculated in 1901,' he said.

The captain smiled. 'You read theology?'

Father nodded. 'And you?'

'Philosophy.'

'Did you row?' asked her father eagerly.

'For the college, yes. My grandmother came from Devon, so I spent summer holidays there, when we were not on the Baltic coast.'

'And your grandmother now? She is in Germany?' Helene asked, unable to contain her curiosity.

'No, she died before the war —' the captain hesitated — 'fortunately. It would have been very difficult for her. Our family has had to make clear our complete loyalty to the Führer and the Fatherland. No one can question that now — one brother has fallen already on the Eastern Front. Two of us remain, serving Germany.'

His face was closed off, thought Helene, looking at him for a moment for the first time. Impossible to read. He sounded like a Nazi, but she knew he broke the regulations. At that moment, Nanna came in from the scullery to clear the plates – she had refused to eat with them – and Father stiffened again. Helene was getting up to leave when the captain asked if he could see more of the garden before he returned to town.

'Perhaps your daughter would be so kind as to show me?'

'I will,' said her father quickly.

'All of us, then,' the captain responded smoothly.

Father led the way out to the garden. Helene pointed out some of the plants blooming in the beds against the wall of the house; in one corner were the lilies her mother had planted. The captain leaned over to smell their heavy perfume. He wanted to see the greenhouses, and asked the names of the different varieties of tomato George had taught her to grow. She knew Alexei was a few feet away, and that the two men were separated only by the thick stone wall against which the glasshouse leaned. There was a small ventilation grill above their heads, and Alexei would be able to hear their voices.

'May I pick a few of the lilies for my room?' asked the captain as they left the glasshouse.

She nodded, unable to trust her own voice, and picked up some secateurs lying on a ledge. As she leaned over the flower bed to cut the stems, her hands were unsteady. He held out his hand.

'Let me.'

He took the secateurs, and cut several. He offered one to Helene in a gesture so quick that it escaped her father's eye.

After he had finally left, Helene sat out on the bench. It was a warm afternoon and full of the scent of blossom. She was twenty-two years old and had never felt so lonely. She longed for Lily's reassuring good sense. She remembered her way of turning difficulties into laughter when they used to meet in St Peter Port during her lunch hour, or when she came to visit in her red motor car. Helene admired her elegance, but most of all she had loved her aunt's faith that the twists and turns of life, however challenging or painful, were shaped to some greater good. Despite her grief at her sister's death, and a troubled love life which meant she had married late, her optimism had been unshakeable. But that was before the war. Perhaps not even Lily would know how to live in these fear-filled days, when one's fate lay in the hands of inscrutable strangers. And where one's actions – whatever the motive – could bring catastrophe down on innocent heads. She had seen the fear in her father's eyes, and yet he knew only the half of it, unaware of Alexei, helpless and totally dependent on her and George.

Now there was another fear, far more disturbing – inchoate and overwhelming – provoked by this German captain. His self-assurance and blithe indifference to the emotions his presence aroused were infuriating and deeply unsettling. As the moon rose, casting a brilliant white light across the garden, she hated him with a vehemence which terrified her. At the school, he had protected them; he had not reported her on the cliffs. She did not want to be in his debt.

VI

The tube was packed with people. Those lucky enough to have a seat were immersed in books and newspapers, the rest hung unsteadily from straps, avoiding eye contact. As the train pulled out of Chalk Farm and hurtled through the dark towards Camden Town, the grey and rust-coloured granite and green seas of Guernsey came vividly to Roz's mind. She thought of the seagulls' cry and the creak of their wings and the taste of the damp wind in her face.

Two weeks had passed since her visit, but she thought about the place frequently: the twisting narrow lanes, the glimpses of sea, the stone cottages and the rows of bungalows with their neat gardens. She went over the details of the disturbing, beautiful visit to Alderney, with its magnificent sunset. Above all, she analysed every nuance of the meeting with Maev and Mrs Blampied. She was becoming obsessed. Her birthday was on 10 April, and she would be forty-nine this year. According to her birth certificate, she had been born in 1946 in Weymouth. But was any of that true? Justin said they had used his name on a replacement birth certificate. Perhaps Weymouth, perhaps 10 April, had been lies also. She could not be sure any more. Her mother had lived through five years of German Occupation, with all its deprivations and fear. She had never struck Roz as courageous, but was there some story of remarkable wartime bravery? If so, why the secrecy? Could Maev and her mother have had any idea of the impact of their comments? Roz remembered Maev's worried concern, and Mrs Blampied's fascination; she felt they knew what they were stirring up.

She had booked another visit to Guernsey, in three weeks. Jim had been intrigued when she spoke to him on the phone about her visit, but Ed had abruptly changed the subject when she had been to his house for supper. He had returned to one of his favourite themes.

'Is there anyone interesting right now? Anyone you might want to settle down with?' he asked, as they sat in his sitting room after dinner. The sound of Roz's niece practising the piano came from the room next door, the same phrase of music again and again. Roz didn't answer.

'You're a very attractive woman; I don't understand why you're on your own.'

'Ed, I'm fine. I don't think I'm cut out for settling down. Too set in my ways.' She had become adept at brushing off her brother's concern, but it irritated her. She changed the subject.

'There is something strange about Mother's past, and her experience of the war. She lied to us about Devon. We were never told anything about her having been brought up in Guernsey. I had the sense that this woman I spoke to was hiding something. She didn't want to explain things to me.'

There was a pause.

'It's digging up old ghosts. It might be better to let them lie. I'm getting used to the idea that you are not Justin's daughter – that you are a half-sister.' She winced at his careful emphasis on this new word, 'half'. 'But to be honest, I don't like it. I'd rather not know any more.'

'Really? You mean if I find out something, I shouldn't talk to you about it?'

'That's right. I have my memories of Mother and I like to think that her marriage to Justin was a very happy one. I like the idea that we were a happy family. I'll leave it at that.'

'Jim seems curious. He said he'll come to Guernsey with me sometime.'

'Well, that's Jim for you.'

She didn't know what he meant by that.

'This is your bag, Roz. I can understand you might want to know who your father is, but leave me out of it. I don't want to sound too brusque, but let's not come back to this. OK?'

Ed's reaction had struck Roz as odd. How can you choose not to know something? It spurred her to make an uncharacteristic decision, which she had already been mulling over: she would piece together her mother's past. In her work, she was methodical and attentive to detail, and she would bring those skills to bear on her mother and her own origins. She talked it over with Jim in long late-night phone calls and, from his house in France, he urged her on, offering suggestions: had she tried the Colindale newspaper library? How about the British Library for histories of the time? He spoke to an historian friend in London, who suggested the Imperial War Museum's collections.

Roz took a couple of days off work and headed out to Colindale on the tube. She skimmed the editions of the *Guernsey Evening Press* for the Occupation period, and in the evenings, she took notes from books she had bought on Guernsey. She became familiar with the key events of the war: the evacuation of many islanders on the eve of Germany's invasion of France; the arrival of the Germans in early July 1940, after an unexpected bombing raid on St Peter Port; the desperate shortage of food after imports from England were cut; the deportation of a couple of thousand English-born islanders in 1943 to German internment camps; and, finally, the Liberation – it was one of the last places in Western Europe to be freed. She tracked some of this in the island newspaper. After 1940, censorship ensured a steady stream of stories extolling the virtues of the Germans, the Third Reich and their occupation of the island. Roz found fascinating the pages of household tips and recipes using the limited ingredients available: parsnips and dandelions for coffee, blackberry leaves for tea, and carrageen moss as a setting agent for milk puddings. Then she moved on to the national newspapers, and found reports of the ecstatic welcome for the liberating force in St Peter Port in May 1945. The swift arrival of the King and Queen in July 1945 as solace for how the islands had been abandoned to their fate. Then the enormous task of clearing the mines and the fortifications around the islands.

A few weeks ago, the Second World War had meant little to her. She had vague memories of London bomb sites, the rubble covered in tall spires of purple willowherb, of grown-ups referring to rationing when she was a child. But by the time she reached her teens, the country seemed to have set the war firmly in the past. A subject for those history books which she had impatiently tossed aside. She had never thought much about the war of the Europe she loved, with its history of murderous states and their ingenious killing technology. She had flinched from learning about the brutal suffering endured in a decade which had cost fifty million lives. She had never thought of how people had lived through it, nor the moral choices many faced when even the simple decisions of every human life – to love or to hate, to judge or to forgive – were loaded with fear. She had thought history was something finished, but she was discovering that it was alive, feeding the memories of people, and capable of springing savage surprises. She found herself trying to imagine Nazis in the rue Saint-Honoré and Fascists at La Scala.

She realized she had relied on an irrational assumption that the war generation was fundamentally different, people who didn't feel pain in the same way. How else could they have endured it, or inflicted so much of it? Instead of the comfortable lives she and her contemporaries lived – the interesting jobs, holidays, restaurants, exhibitions – ruffled only by the small storms of a divorce or an early death, so many lives had been shattered. Now she felt the war all around her, both the perpetrators of its brutality and their victims, dead and alive. They were in her own family; she was a part of it. It was people like her who had travelled to ghettos and camps in their fur coats, and who had pawned their jewellery for bread.

Roz followed Jim's suggestion and arranged a visit to the archives of the Imperial War Museum. She had cleared a few days in her diary, suspecting it would be slow work. A librarian escorted her through the back rooms of the museum, a warren of tatty corridors and offices before they climbed several flights of stairs to reach the reading room. She had requested material on the Occupation of Guernsey, and a kind librarian had reassured her on the phone that she would find plenty.

At the desk they had reserved for her, they had assembled a pile of diaries; on top lay a set of exercise books: a diary from 1940 and 1941. Judging by the ornate, copperplate handwriting, it appeared to be that of an old lady, who found little comfort for her bowel and indigestion problems in St Peter Port's pharmacies, but drew some solace from the church services. Roz put it aside. The next document was an account written in 1959 by a Methodist minister who had travelled to St Peter Port for a pastoral visit in April 1940 and found himself stranded by the arrival of the Germans. The poor man had been lonely without his wife and family, back in Portsmouth, and was consumed with anxiety for their safety as he heard the reports on his illegal wireless of intense bombing of the port. He tried to salve his homesickness by tending to his congregation. Roz found his story poignant, but it offered no insight into her search, so she set it aside too. History was made up of this flotsam, the scraps which had, by chance, survived. It suddenly seemed a haphazard business.

Looking through the catalogues, she saw listed a collection of taped interviews with islanders. She listened to two of them, with their detail of Occupation life: the privations, resource-fulness and monotony. The disembodied voices on the tapes became repetitive. Those interviewed did not mention names, and she sensed that they were editing their accounts carefully. When questioned about people who worked with the Germans, embarrassment crept into their voices, or the question was dismissed outright.

After two days plodding through the material, she had decided this would be her last day in these archives. She wasn't making any headway. Then her eye was caught by a name in the catalogue index – Arthur Brown. She remembered Mrs Blampied had mentioned him. He was a gossip. This might be interesting.

I'm no islander. I'll admit that straight off, but it's not going to stop me from speaking my mind. I was born in Southampton, and lived there until my younger sister Grace was born. So, that would have made me about seven years old when we first came to Guernsey. Of course, these islanders are tight-fisted buggers, and they never forget where you're born. You're labelled by your parish and by your family name – there aren't that many names to go round, which makes for plenty of confusion, with dozens of Fallas and Duquemins, not to mention the fancy French-sounding ones like Le Mouilpied and Jamouneau. Not ordinary surnames like mine – Brown.

Roz felt the thrill of discovery; her detective work might pay off. She felt tantalizingly close to a crucial piece of the puzzle. Here was a man who was blunt and rude. He wasn't going to cover anything up. She just had to be patient as he told his life story.

What with this taste for having tabs on people the minute they've popped out, I've always been down as an incomer. Even now I'm sixty-two, I'm still an incomer. No matter. You takes 'em as you find 'em, and, as for me, I've grown fond of this bit of granite.

I can still remember the boat docking at St Peter Port. My sister Grace had been badly sick on the journey over, and my mother was trying to mop her up before we disembarked. I remember the whitewashed houses and the light. It was different from England. Everything was brighter and the sea was more blue. And I remember the flowers. Lots of them in the front gardens. Things we'd never seen around the docks in Southampton. Big gladioli and hydrangea, dahlias as bright as anything you see on a colour TV nowadays. I suppose that would mean we arrived in the summer. We'd come because my dad wanted a better life for the family. He worked on the docks at Southampton, and one of the crew on the Channel boats had told Dad there was work on Guernsey, what with the new trade in tomatoes getting going – only we called them 'love apples' then – and the flowers really hotting up by then. No pun intended, of course. But the vineries were hot – glasshouses, you call them – and thick with the smell: freesias in one, roses or carnations in another. But I'm getting ahead of myself here.

When we arrived in 1919 after the Great War, I knew nothing about vineries. Later, when I worked on the docks in St Peter Port with Dad, I came across the wooden crates of flowers for the London markets, and I fell in love with the smell. I know that sounds daft, but it's true. I thought, I don't want to work like my dad has done all his life, lugging huge weights around, and working on the pulleys which lowered them onto the ships for England. I saw a man die when a load fell on him. No, early on I decided on something different. Of course, Dad couldn't understand. He thought growing things was daft. Lonely work, he called it. He was right, but I got to like it that way. So I started off doing odd jobs in a big glasshouse at the Bridge. The boss was tough, but he could see I was keen, even though I was only fourteen. I liked watching the way the man worked with the plants. I suppose you'd say it was gentle. These stocky islanders, with big barrel chests, had fingers as nifty as a lady's when grafting roses and planting out the shoots in the soft soil. Their fingers knew what made the *seedlings grow. My fingers got sore, I remember that. Big blisters from the picking I did, morning, noon and night. And back ache. I'm not sure my back has ever recovered. I've spent so much of my life bent over the growing of things that I can't straighten up at all now. But I learned to recognize the first signs of an unhappy freesia or carnation. How to pinch out weedy offshoots so that the full strength went into the blooms. I love a perfect flower. Still do. I know there's some who sniff now at freesias, but to me there's nothing in all God's creation as perfect as a Guernsey freesia. Mind you, I never held with those bright colours they went for some years back. No, I like things plain. White or yellow does nicely, and I still grow them out the back to pick for the lounge. I've often wondered how the island came to be so good at growing things. We've a real knack, though I say it myself. I've seen land which is nothing but rock and sand turned thick with flowers and vegetables within a few years here. Many of my old mates in the vineries did it when they built their bungalows at Vale when the money started coming in. The 1920s were good years for the flower trade. There was a lot to celebrate, what with the end of the war and everyone keen to have a good time.*

When I was a lad, I had a fanciful turn of mind – or so I was often told – and I used to think, as I did the picking, of the fancy lapels where the flowers would end up, or the fine dinner tables. Or perhaps the flowers would be pinned into some young lady's smart hair. I liked thinking that we were growing the finest flowers for big occasions like weddings and funerals. I didn't agree with Dad that flowers were a woman's thing. That was what we rowed about when I left. Funny this, but flowers are powerful. I've seen grown men in tears when they bury their faces in a big bouquet. That's going a bit far, I agree; I've never cried myself, but then I worked with the things for nearly fifty years, so you could hardly expect me to cry over them. I was too businesslike for that; the flowers might be nice, but they were also money.

For a while, when I was a lad, back in the 1920s, I worked up at

The Vicarage at Torteval for the vicar and his wife. I helped out their old gardener, George. He gave me the boot. But I liked the wife. It was sad, what happened to her. She was only young. A lot of people thought she was stuck-up, but she knew a lot about flowers. I haven't been up that way in years.

There! Roz replayed these sentences. The Vicarage at Torteval: he must have been talking about her grandmother. She looked at the date of the tape – 1974. A connection to her own family via a stranger's chance remark twenty-one years ago, recorded on the thin ribbon of a tape machine. She was taken aback by how powerfully the small details registered with her: 'young', 'sad', 'stuck-up', 'knew a lot about flowers' – like her daughter, like her granddaughter. Roz replayed the clip. Then she picked up Arthur Brown's story again.

After the time I did on flowers, I switched to tomatoes. That's what I got my name for. I'm not one to sing my own praises, but I know a thing or two about growing tomatoes. And so I should – I've been at it for a fair while. We started off with just a corner of the glasshouse, but this has been the century of the tomato. The more we've grown, the more people have wanted to eat them. Back in the 1930s, they preferred their food hot – meat and two veg – but then they started on salads after the war. Tomato in sandwiches, tomato salads, tomato in their fancy sauces. I can't deny I've done well on it. We bought our own house with a mortgage in 1952 and we put up a glasshouse on the end wall. I managed two big glasshouses at the other end of the parish here in Vale. I grew everything for our kitchen in the patch we had out the back – peas and beans, cucumbers, lettuce in summer; leeks, parsnips, Brussel sprouts in winter. We'd put the spare in an honesty box out front. I didn't buy a vegetable in a shop for years. Only now it's hard to do the digging, and my son's not interested. I don't think he'd know the difference between a parsnip and a carrot top. He was always bookish.

I had moved up to Dieu Donne, the big house on the edge of Torteval parish, to work in 1937. I was the gardener, but then in 1940 the family all upped sticks to England and left me in charge. Gave me the run of the house too. I had to look after it all, except the silver. They might have been falling over themselves that June morning to get to the boats, but they were canny enough to bury their silver first. The only thing was that I found it all a few weeks after they'd gone. So I made some money, I don't mind admitting. There was a German officer buying up silver on the island. He sold it to people all over Europe, I heard. He must have made a pretty penny.

Dieu Donne. That was a name Mrs Blampied had mentioned. Roz checked in her notebook. It was where the Le Lacheur family had lived. Roz was confused. Her mother's family had lived at The Vicarage, and yet her surname was that of a family who lived nearby. Roz released the pause button and continued, fascinated by this garrulous character.

I learned about vegetables in the war. There was no use for flowers in the Occupation. There were a few German officers who did buy the odd bunch of carnations, for their lady loves, I imagine. I kept one corner for them, for the money. One officer was very regular. But I turned most of the glasshouse over to veg.

I'll say this for the Germans, they paid regularly. Sometimes, they were quicker with their money than shopkeepers in St Peter Port, and they certainly paid a good price during the Occupation. They didn't know much, so I charged on the high side. Potatoes, turnips, swedes, cabbage: they bought the lot. I just kept some back for myself; there was no wife then, she'd gone to England too. I did well, and it set me up for after the war. I changed my Reichsmarks into pounds, no problem, after the war. Mind, during the war I never kept the money under the bed in those Occupation banknotes or anything daft like that; I used it to buy some land, paid in instalments.

They liked my vegetables. I was supplying the officers' mess in St Peter Port by the end, as well as the billet at Dieu Donne. It was quite a business, and I took on a few lads and a couple of women whose men were away in the forces to help me out. My dad would have been surprised to see me as a boss, giving all the orders. Of course, people talked. Some were very down on me, jabbering on about the war effort. But it was all talk. I knew for a fact that they were all in it, one way or another. The ones working for the Germans made the loudest noises. I just kept my trap shut and my head down.

I saw the people coming and going at Dieu Donne after they put the officers in there. I saw everything, believe you me. The people I saw coming to the house, all friendly with those officers, would amaze you. No one on this island – I mean, no one – was too grand to curry favour with the Germans. I've no time for them that wanted to make out they were being patriotic. They were far too sensible, these islanders, to make life difficult for themselves. They just settled down after the first few days and got on with it. There wasn't much between the Germans and the English: they both liked interfering and meddling, and they both liked mucking about on the beaches. Lying in the sun, getting in and out of the water. Still, I was surprised sometimes. The ones with the talk about King and Country, and then they were creeping round of an evening, to drink the Germans' wine and eat their meat. And those young women – some of them weren't much more than children. All tarted up in lipstick and stockings. After the war, I reckoned human nature held no more surprises for me.

There's plenty of things I could tell you about the Occupation. Plenty. Rest assured of that. And most of it would horrify you. That's why I agreed to do this taped interview. I think people should know about the things which went on.

Everyone was out for themselves. That community spirit just fell apart. And the quickness of it. It took my breath away. People who had been neighbours – the kind to say 'Good morning' and lend an egg or a pint of milk before the war – informed on each other. I knew, because Miss Greville at the post office used to tell me that she kept an eye on what was put in the mailbox. Letters for the Feldkommandantur she steamed open, and ripped up the ones which looked suspicious. It was the pettiness of it, with people informing on neighbours for a pig killed on the sly. Or the nasty stuff, like informing on someone for having a wireless. You could get a prison sentence for that. Those informers seemed worse than the girls. Most of them were giddy things, just out for a good time.

Some families invited German officers for meals, and the food they had! I know because my niece did a bit of cleaning in one house. She said their pantry was full of cold joints, whisky, wine and chocolate. There were shelves sagging under the weight of sugar from France and black market butter and milk. Bloody hypocrisy.

Here Brown came to a sudden and surprising stop. Roz went up to the librarian's desk to ask if they had anything more by Arthur Brown. It was nearly closing time. She waited while the man checked a card file. There was a diary by Brown. Roz could have punched the air. It was stored off-site, but they could order it in for her. On her way home that evening, she called work and said she still had a very bad cold.

Brown's diary, the next morning, was another of those cheap exercise books. The green cover had faded and the pages were yellow. The writing was crabbed but clear. Inscribed on the inside cover was the name, Arthur James Brown. Roz skimmed the first pages. He was a bitter character, full of complaints about his neighbours, colleagues, the States and the Germans. His employees at the farm where he worked were the subject of his frequent tirades, accusing them of stealing his vegetables. He described financial transactions, which Roz couldn't follow, in which he sold a portion of his crops on the black market. Then he had illegally slaughtered a pig. Brown also dwelt on his health. He had a lot of back pain, which he attributed to the extra gardening he took on at home in the evenings. He recorded what he had planted, and where, and how much it had yielded. He made notes of growing tips from neighbours, the yields of various types of potatoes, and the medicinal benefits of certain herbs. Roz was disheartened, but then, amongst all this, she began to spot a different subject matter. She read more closely, copying excerpts which interested her into a notebook:

Back at the beginning of the Occupation three officers were billeted in the big house. I had to move back into the cottage. I was pretty unhappy, because I had been asked by the family to look after the place when they left for England. The first lot made a terrible mess, but they got moved on and the next lot were quiet and kept themselves to themselves. They left in late 1940 and the new lot are a very different kettle of fish. It looks like they are on a bloody holiday rather than fighting a war. They've brought a gramophone player, tennis racquets, golf clubs and one of them has a riding hat. As far as I can see, none of them can be much older than twenty-five.

Yesterday, an older officer came to visit me. He speaks good English – there are several who do – and he said a lot of blarney about nice weather and liking the island very much. He apologized for moving me out of the house, and said I could still use the garden for growing vegetables, but he didn't want the tennis court dug up. He even said he would tell one of his orderlies to help me with the vegetable patch if we shared the produce.

The German comes round from time to time with a bar of chocolate or a piece of soap as presents. He told me his name was Heinrich. He lives in town but he is a regular visitor.

  Last night, there were three or four cars. I watched from the window. Several officers arrived, and then about five women. A couple of them I recognized. They aren't from around here. They shrieked and made an awful noise as they piled out, dressed to the nines in fancy dresses, high heels and lipstick. Then the real noise started. The gramophone didn't stop until past two o'clock. It was a warm night, and the French windows at the back must have been open because I could hear it from my bedroom. The same three dance tunes, again and again. It was driving me crazy, and I got up to look out of the window. Those shameless little hussies, mixing like that with Germans. In the light from the windows, it looked like that Heinrich was with them. I went back to bed, but when they left, the noise of the cars on the gravel and the shouting woke me up. The next day I was up late, and a bar of chocolate was on the doorstep. Real chocolate. Must have come from France. I had forgotten just how good it tasted. Heinrich came round a couple of days later to apologize for the noise. I asked him who the girls were, and he looked a bit embarrassed. I began to see why they were so keen to get the house. It is a perfect place for parties. They can make plenty of noise up here and the top brass can come over from St Peter Port for an evening.

Sometimes Heinrich comes over on one of his visits and even gives me a hand in the garden. He is a nice enough man. He seems bored, and rather lonely. He speaks English because his father sent him to study in England before the war. He's very worried about bombing raids on Berlin, where his family live.

Of course, word has got around, and there is gossip about what is going on here. Some girls were named. It causes a lot of hard feeling down in town. The girls are driven up in those nice cars requisitioned from islanders. Their German boyfriends bring the stockings and lipstick back from Paris.

Heinrich came by with a bottle of wine. He said he had been to Alderney, and he seemed very out of sorts. He went on about having studied in Paris for a while before the war, and how his father wanted him to go into the family business when the war was over. After we had finished the wine, he asked me if I'd like to hear the news on the wireless. I was amazed, but it turns out that most of the officers listen to the BBC secretly. I asked him how he thought the war was going, but he didn't say much. He only half trusts me. And me him. But we did listen to the news together.

They have moved some horses into the old stables. Some bloody war – a boys' own camp, more like. From time to time, I see one of them out riding; I think he used to meet up with a young woman, but I only saw her the once. There is plenty of gossip about these officers. I heard that several girls have got themselves a baby. Breeding, class, money: they make no difference. Who would have thought!

Arthur Brown then returned to the detailed lists of vegetable crops and growing techniques. Half the notebook was empty. The staples had rusted through, and Roz thought of the salt-laden air on the island. She wondered how the book had ended up in the museum. Brown was probably dead. Roz sat back in her chair. She had barely looked up, captivated by the possibility that, at any point, the next sentence might let slip something connected to her mother. She let out a long, slow breath. She was surprised to see from the library clock that it was past one o'clock. She had lost track of time, and was hungry.

Downstairs, a school party had arrived and Roz picked her way through a crowd of children armed with clipboards and pencils. The boys stared with fascination at the planes suspended from the ceiling and at the tanks sitting incongruously on the shiny marble floor, their enormous treads gleaming clean. It was hard to think of these toys as weapons of war. There was another school group in the café.

She queued up for a sandwich and coffee, and sat as far from the children as possible. She was thinking about Brown and the parties when she felt someone's eyes on her.

'Could I sit down here?'

She nodded at the man, and returned to her sheaf of notes, but he coughed expectantly. She smiled politely and briefly, hoping to deter further conversation.

'I'm sorry if I'm disturbing you.'

He spoke English with a slight French accent.

'I noticed you in the library.'

He paused, but she gave him no encouragement.

'You have the documents I am waiting for.'

Roz found his manner slightly rude, and offered a chilly apology.

'It is not a problem for me,' he added quickly. 'I have other things to read and I can wait. But perhaps when you have finished, you can pass them to me?'

She looked at him properly for the first time. He was several years younger than her. He had large brown eyes behind his glasses. He was wearing a thick grey sweater and jeans, and he looked like an academic. Obviously French. He met her eye and smiled warmly. She was surprised by his friendliness.

'Antoine,' he announced, and offered his hand, which Roz hesitantly shook. Then he ran it through his thick, wavy brown hair as he leaned back in his chair.

'Roz,' she replied stiffly.

'So what are you researching?'

She couldn't think what to say. She pushed her hair back.

'Just a case,' she mumbled.

Antoine, recognizing his mistake, continued swiftly, 'I'm in London for a few weeks. I work in Paris. I have a research project here and then I return home. I am almost finished.'

She smiled in response. She liked his self-assurance, but she didn't have time to waste chatting with a stranger. She looked away and watched an old lady negotiate the schoolchildren with her tray of food.

'Ah, the food in these British museums. It is always – what can we say? – terrible.' He grimaced as he pushed the plate of uneaten food away.

Roz couldn't help but laugh. He had a point. He sat back and was looking at her so intently she felt confused. He was too young, surely, to be picking her up.

'Perhaps you can help me. I am doing research on the war and I wondered if you had some experience of other archives in London,' he said. 'How do I get to Colindale?'

Roz didn't believe he needed tourism advice, but she pulled out her tube map and explained the route.

'What aspect are you looking at?' she asked at last, uncomfortable in the pause.

'I'm doing research on Second World War art theft,' he said, as he fiddled with a packet of cigarettes. 'I'm looking into what happened to a few private French collections. It's part of a European Union project, with funding from France, Germany and Holland. We're collaborating with the Institute for Art Research in New York to try and trace a number of artworks. I'm an academic – a legal historian.'

Roz smiled blankly, stunned. Either he didn't notice her reaction or he was being polite. Antoine pulled out a cigarette and offered her one. She shook her head. He bent over to use his lighter. She noticed a faint nicotine stain on his long fingers. He was a heavy smoker. He inhaled deeply, then looked at her expectantly, and carefully exhaled away from her. She tried to keep her voice even.

'Why are you interested in the Channel Island diaries?' she asked.

'Why?' he repeated with a careful casualness. 'I think it might give us new clues. '

He got up. 'Now, do I dare try the English coffee? Can I get you another?'

She shook her head. She watched him walk over to the till. He was tall and he walked with confidence. He was laughing with the young cashier. He was charming, flirtatious even – he couldn't help himself. It was quite appealing, in its way, thought Roz, putting away her notebooks.

As he sat down again he teased her: 'You tell me, and I'll tell you.'

Flustered, she didn't reply, and he laughed. She felt unnerved, but forced herself to smile and finished her coffee. His clothes were well made. The scarf was cashmere. He seemed a rather glamorous figure to be digging in obscure archives. Like a television don. She needed to be wary.

Antoine feigned disappointment, but he seemed amused. They walked back upstairs to the library, exchanging pleasantries about the weather and London. He knew the city well and had an abundant supply of opinions on the English; she found him entertaining, despite her misgivings. When they got back to the library, Roz found that his papers and books were set out on the big table opposite her own. She had been so absorbed by Arthur Brown that she hadn't noticed him. She felt embarrassed by the proximity. He must have been watching her long before he turned up in the café.

She turned back to her pile of papers. The afternoon was disappointing. Nothing matched the frankness of Brown's diary, which she had passed on to Antoine as requested. She turned to an account of a doctor who described his struggles to find medications for his patients. She had finished by the time the librarian announced the library was closing. Antoine looked over as he packed up his papers. They walked downstairs together.

'Successful day?'

'Yes, thank you,' she said, feeling irritated now by his intrusiveness.

He was waiting for her when she came out of the cloakroom,

and asked if he could walk with her to the tube. She didn't know how to refuse. In the chilly evening, a few birds were singing as the light faded. The first daffodils were coming into bloom. Antoine explained that he was staying in a hotel near the British Museum. He added that he was meeting friends for dinner, and Roz thought for a moment he was going to invite her to join them. They stood on the tube platform, neither of them sure of what to say next. Roz stared ahead, wondering whether Antoine's research had covered Justin's trial, and thinking of Brown's German lodgers, and his brief reference to her grandmother. When the tube arrived, there were spare seats at either end of the coach. She sat in one, and Antoine moved to the other; several stops later he got off, turning back to nod goodbye.

It suddenly occurred to her that she might be making a mistake. He might have been able to help her search. He made her nervous – there was something too polished about him, but she was spending a lot of time in archives without learning much that was relevant. She jumped up, scrabbling after her bag, and tried to get off the tube. It was too late; the doors closed and she caught a glimpse of Antoine walking through the crowd on the platform to the exit. She had lost him. The only way to meet him again was to go back to the Imperial War Museum tomorrow. With any luck, Antoine's desire to read Arthur Brown would bring him back. She could call the office to say she was still laid low with this cold. She hadn't taken this much time off in years.

The following morning, she was back in the Imperial War Museum, but there was no sign of Antoine. By late morning, he still had not appeared and she was losing heart. She took a break and slipped downstairs to wander round some of the art galleries for a few minutes. When she returned, there was Antoine's dark head bent over Brown's diaries. She scribbled 'Lunch?' on a note and pushed it across the desk. He looked up and nodded.

As they walked down to the café an hour later, she asked how his research was going. Antoine shook his head.

'Slow. But I have an idea and I am hopeful. I'm planning a trip to Guernsey, and I might spend a few days in the Public Records Office before I go back to Paris. And you?'

Roz deflected the question. 'I enjoyed Brown's diary. It's a riveting read.'

In the café, they sat at a table by the window overlooking the bleak, muddy garden.

'What's the idea?' she asked.

'I'm looking for one particular art collection. We know where it was in 1942, and we know where some of it ended up in 1947. If we can trace what happened to it in between, then we might be able to find the rest of the collection.'

She nodded, apprehensive.

'In 1940, one of the largest collections of drawings and prints of post-impressionist and modern art was owned by a rich Parisian family, the Morels, who were Jewish. They also had a few – perhaps no more than four or five – Northern Renaissance paintings, most importantly a painting by Cranach the Elder. They sold a few of their drawings between 1941 and 1943 to a group of German officers for a very low price. Then, sometime in late 1943, they went into hiding and the rest of their collection disappeared. Two of the children survived, but the mother, father and eldest son went on the convoys to Auschwitz-Birkenau. Their names are on the lists for February 1944. The children who survived were smuggled into the *zone libre* and later adopted by a French farmer. They are now in their early sixties, and could benefit from any compensation scheme that the European Union might set up on the basis of our report.'

Roz pushed her plate away. 'Coffee?' she asked, and he nodded.

As she stood at the counter, she thought over Antoine's information, disturbed at how closely it matched the circumstances of her father's trial. She had a deep sense of foreboding; these were pieces of the puzzle that she hadn't expected to stumble upon. An international investigation at her heels. Even worse, the collection had been taken from a Jewish family. The awful possibility had occurred to her, but she had pushed the thought away; now Antoine had voiced it. She felt nauseous and her palms were clammy. She suddenly remembered Ed's firm lack of interest and her irritation at the time. He was nothing if not shrewd – that was why he had managed to make so much money.

'Thank you,' he said as she set his coffee down in front of him.

'And where was this collection in 1947?' she asked as lightly as she could.

'This, you know.'

'What?' Roz stared at him.

'Your name was Rawsthorne before you married, no?' said Antoine.

'How on earth – how did you know?' she stammered.

'I'm sorry, I shouldn't have surprised you like that. I don't want you to think I've been spying on you. I admit I've been working some things out since yesterday, but it wasn't very difficult.'

'You'll have to explain,' said Roz, alarmed.

'I will. Relax, there's nothing to worry about. I'm not going to accuse you of having Picasso prints.' He laughed. 'I was surprised myself.' He took a gulp of coffee and lit a cigarette.

'When I started on this part of the research, I began at the end. In 1964, as you know, Justin Rawsthorne, a distinguished art historian and adviser to the Tate and lecturer at the Courtauld, was arrested for having in his possession a collection of valuable prints and drawings. He was tried in 1965. I looked up the records of the court case at the end of last week. For nearly two years, between 1947 and 1949, Rawsthorne sold other parts of this stolen collection to a dealer in America. When this dealer died, his collection was donated to the Ohio Art Center. The curators tried to establish the provenance of the drawings and that led to Justin Rawsthorne's arrest. Perhaps it would have been better for them if they hadn't. In the end, they had to give up about thirty pieces of work to the French government. The American curators' investigations alerted the French authorities, and eventually Rawsthorne was tracked down.'

Roz still had her eyes fixed on his face, incredulous.

'But how do I come into this?'

'Well, Justin Rawsthorne is your father.'

'That, I know,' said Roz crisply. 'But how did *you* know?'

'I read the newspaper reports in the archive last week. It mentioned a daughter called Rosamund. Because of your father's official position for the Queen, there was a lot of publicity in the newspapers. Then I saw on your library request form the name Rosamund Wardle – your married name, I presume?'

Roz could feel her heart hammering in her rib cage. Her mind was spinning as she tried to make sense of what he was saying. He was watching her closely. She looked away, at a plane tree in the garden.

'The thing we now know about this collection between 1942 and 1947 is that some of it reached Guernsey. A folder of three Picasso drawings – they were very carefully catalogued and numbered – turned up three years ago in the tack room of a stables, where it had been hidden behind panelling.'

'Are you telling me that you deduced I was a Rawsthorne from my Christian name and the fact that I was reading Brown's diary?' asked Roz, her tone heavy with scepticism.

'Yes. It may sound absurd, but it fitted together. I have thought a lot about your father's court case. His explanations of how he got the pictures always seemed –' Antoine hesitated as he searched for the word – 'unconvincing to me, and I've asked myself what might be the real story. This morning I was trying to figure it out. Your mother was a witness in the case, but she claimed she knew nothing, and the prosecution didn't spend much time questioning her. But there was one significant fact which the court records reveal: she was born in Guernsey and only left the island in 1946. She gave her address on the island as The Vicarage, Torteval.'

Roz was looking at her coffee, now cold.

'I went to Guernsey last year and collected information about the discovery of the Picasso drawings. Do you know – they were found in Torteval. No, not at The Vicarage, but at a large house a few miles down the road called, rather curiously, Dieu Donne. This was the house where Arthur Brown was a gardener. I agree that might be a coincidence, but perhaps not. Could your mother be the link between the island and London? If so, how did she get the drawings, and what was she doing with them?'

Roz flinched. The questions were blunt and accurate. His questions were hers too, but she had no inclination to reveal her interest. Fortunately, she had learned in her profession to conceal private responses, and she knew that ability would serve her now. She made a show of moving her chair to allow another visitor to sit down at the neighbouring table. It gave her a moment.

'So sorry,' she murmured as the other visitor also apologized.

She had stumbled into a very awkward situation and things were going to get difficult. Ed would be furious. She thought about phoning Jim.

She smiled smoothly at Antoine.

'What questions, indeed! But there still seem some rather large leaps in your conclusions, don't you think?'

Antoine ignored her question. He leaned forward, his face intent. Excitement evident in his eyes.

'What convinced me was the photo of your parents on their

way to court. Your mother was an elegant woman, and the papers used it on the front page. She was about the age you are now. When I saw you yesterday, you looked familiar, and I couldn't think why. Last night, I looked at my photocopies of the newspaper articles, and looked again at the photo. You are obviously related.

'Finally, I thought about why you had first caught my attention yesterday. You were completely transfixed by Arthur Brown's accounts – the material I have been so keen to read. You did not move for at least two hours. I was watching you. I asked myself, why would you be so interested? You wouldn't tell me, and that seemed further evidence for my theory. There was some family secret you didn't want to talk about. If it was academic research for a book, there would have been no reason to be –' Antoine paused for the right word – 'shy. So there you have it. Do you follow me?'

'Well, I have to admit, I'm impressed by your detective skills,' said Roz. Her tone was light. She didn't want him to know how disturbing she found his information and the possibilities it opened up.

'You're trying to find out how your mother acquired the pictures in the Channel Islands. That's why you are here. Am I right?' Antoine concluded triumphantly.

He leaned back in his chair; he looked pleased with himself.

'Yes . . . very clever,' she said hesitantly.

It was better to leave him with this assumption.

He shrugged his shoulders, and offered her another cigarette. Under his scrutiny, she felt that she needed a legitimate distraction and, for the first time in two decades, she accepted. He was drumming the fingers of his other hand on the table. She could almost hear him thinking. What would he guess next? She inhaled and watched the smoke, and steeled herself for his next question.

'This is what I suggest: we join forces. We want to find the answer to the same question. We will be more effective if we work together. What do you think?'

'We may be interested in the same end, but for very different reasons,' she replied, more sharply than she intended.

'Perhaps you can introduce me to your mother?' Antoine was choosing to ignore her brittle responses. He added blandly, 'This is not a criminal investigation, she wouldn't have anything to worry about.'

That seemed an unlikely claim, Roz thought.

'Both my parents are dead. My mother died last year.' She was clipped.

'I didn't know.' Antoine looked taken aback. 'I'm sorry. I'm being insensitive.'

'This is only a research project for you. For my family, it's personal.'

'But there is something you're looking for. Perhaps I can help you. I can get you access to archives and records. Think about it. Have you been to Guernsey yet? Yes, good. You know how difficult it is getting information out of the islanders. They are closed.' Antoine illustrated his point by clenching his fist tightly so that his knuckles whitened.

'Are you planning to go back?' he asked.

'Yes, next week.'

'You're in a hurry. Good. Listen, I can help. Think about it.' Antoine stood up, picked up his cigarettes, and put them in the pocket of his jacket. 'I can help,' he repeated. 'And now, I must finish Brown's account before the end of today. Especially if I am to come to Guernsey with you next week.'

He was teasing her.

She watched him as he left the café. She felt sick at his story of the Parisian family. Did her mother have any involvement, however indirect? Her instincts warned her against him, but her research efforts were clumsy. She could fumble around for months in these accounts of indigestion and vegetables. If she didn't tell him the real object of her search, perhaps there was no need to worry about not trusting him. He need never know that Justin was not her biological father. She slowly stubbed out the cigarette. In any other circumstances, she would have kept well away from him. He made her feel too uncertain of herself. She had always been intimidated by men who were good-looking, knew it and liked the effect it had on women.

But, she reasoned, as she scribbled her phone number on a note and pushed it across the reading-room desk that afternoon, if Antoine could find out her identity from a few scraps of information, there was a good chance he could help her find her mother's – and so her own – story.

★

It was nearly midnight. Roz couldn't sleep. She waited a long time for Jim to answer the phone. She imagined the sound of the phone echoing through his ramshackle studio in the barn.

'There's an investigation into Nazi art theft going on and the trail has led to Guernsey,' said Roz as soon as Jim picked up.

His house sat on the bank of a wide river; in the long silence which followed her comment, Roz imagined that she could hear the cries of the ducks as they flew over the water.

'Hell,' said Jim finally, with a long sigh. His voice sounded sleepy and distant. 'What time is it?'

'Sorry, did I wake you? I couldn't sleep. It's really disturbing me.'

'No, I wasn't asleep. Just working.'

She knew Jim when he was like this. The hours he spent in his studio were like time under water, the outside world indistinct and muffled. His wife, Françoise, knew to keep the children away. Roz waited a while before continuing.

'The investigation is funded by the EU. I've met this French historian who is doing some research. Three years ago, some Picasso drawings were found in an outbuilding of a house in the parish where Mother probably lived.'

'Hang on a minute.' There was a pause. Jim seemed to be moving – perhaps sitting down. 'We don't know where Mother lived yet. It's a bit of a leap to assume she had anything to do with this find –'

'I don't think so. It can't just be a coincidence. Unless all the garages and stables in Guernsey were full of stolen art – and that's unlikely,' she replied drily.'

Roz felt disorientated and anxious. She had found herself worrying away at the questions Antoine had asked. Jim was the best person to call at this time of night. He often worked into the small hours.

'He's some kind of legal historian on a research project to trace Nazi art theft. He's been reading about the trial.'

'How on earth did you bump into him? That's extraordinary.'

She had Jim's full attention; she could hear the apprehension in his voice. She explained the encounter.

'He guessed who you were!' Jim was astonished.

'Yes.'

Jim was silent for a moment.

'Be careful. He's hoping you have information. We don't want our name dragged through the news. Not again.' He added slowly, 'Ed will be furious.'

'I've thought of that, but he's clever. I don't think we have much choice. Besides, I've been thinking: he can help me. I could waste a lot of time in these archives and only find a few tantalizing scraps.'

'Who does he think smuggled the paintings to Guernsey – and why there?'

'A group of German officers. They were buying them in Paris.'

Roz took a gulp of tea.

'By the way, I found a reference to our grandparents in a diary. It's only a few sentences – our grandmother was "stuck-up" and she knew about flowers. Our grandfather was a vicar. And a comment that "it was sad". That's all. Maybe she did die young, as Mother maintained. It's whetted my appetite.'

Over the past few days since listening to the Brown interview tape and meeting Antoine, Roz had been remembering occasions as a child when her mother had disappeared for a 'rest', as her father described it. The absences were no more than a week, but they had seemed an age to Roz. She recalled her mother returning late one evening. Roz was already in bed but she had heard raised voices, a door shutting loudly, her mother walking quickly upstairs. Now, from some lost depth, the memory arose of her mother's stifled sobs as she passed her bedroom door. How had she forgotten that? Why did she remember it now, all these years later?

'Jim, you were right. We never really knew Mother. I find that so strange. A person I thought I knew has vanished. She was a fiction.'

'She was not the sort of person who wanted to be known,' Jim said patiently. 'All that charm and elegance. She was of a generation who believed that life required the performance of a role. She had no time for personal revelations. Least of all her own.'

'We didn't even know the most rudimentary things, like where she was born, who her family were, what kind of childhood she had. Her life before Justin.'

'Nor her love affairs,' broke in Jim.

'That's the hardest part.'

'You're going to have to keep looking.'

'Why am I doing the looking? She was your mother too,' said Roz bitterly, resentful at how this investigation had landed squarely in her lap. How had Jim cast himself in the role of sympathetic, but passive, supporter? 'Come with me to Guernsey.'

There was a long outbreath. 'Sorry, Roz. I'm in the middle of a series of paintings. I could come later in the year – maybe in a couple of months?'

'I can't wait – we can't wait. I want some more answers before Antoine finds them out for me.'

She was lying on her sofa as she spoke. She had pulled the curtains back and turned off the lamps so she could watch the city's lights beyond the park.

'You're right. But I've got too many other things on. An exhibition coming up. Besides, I suppose I feel I left them both behind a long time ago. I couldn't stand all the silences and evasions, and now they are dead. You're the one with fire in your belly about it all – understandably.'

Roz felt very alone, but she saw his point. Jim had struggled with their parents. He had dropped out of art school and moved to France in his early twenties. They had been disappointed by his chaotic life, although too polite to say so. He kept a careful distance from Ed, Helene's favourite. Edward's success and money were too loud and certain for Jim.

'OK, I suppose I'll call if I have more news,' she said lamely.

'I want to help. Come over here sometime and talk it through – whenever you want. I may not be interested in Helene's past, but I want to help you,' said Jim, adding, 'I think you're brave.'

When she was six, Jim had been placed in her arms as a tiny baby, and ever since, she had adored her little brother. After he left art school, she had sent him money regularly. Now he had his own family, she sent large sums at Christmas. Jim had, touchingly, been in awe of her. Ed had been more complicated, always trying to compete.

Roz recalled walking through their family home last summer after everything had been cleared. The estate agent was waiting downstairs for the keys. Sunshine poured through the curtainless windows, lighting up the dust motes suspended in the air. Patches on the wall revealed where pictures had once been, indentations on the carpet where the furniture had once stood. It was their family home in negative, full of absence.

*

Antoine was over an hour late, and now the tannoy was calling for the last passengers. Roz slowly walked to the desk to show her boarding pass. She explained to the air steward that the passenger with whom she was travelling had still not arrived. The woman behind the desk took in a short breath of exasperation, and began checking the passenger lists.

'We'll have to see whether we can get him on a later flight.'

Roz felt a moment of intense irritation; all she had done was book the flight. She didn't even know what hotel they were booked into. He had offered to organise the hotel and rental car. She had been grateful – she had a big case on at work – but she also suspected that it was his way of ensuring she didn't postpone. He had seemed in a hurry, yet now he couldn't even turn up on time for a flight. It was careless.

She would have to leave a message at the airport for him. She picked up her hand luggage and made her way to the plane. She squeezed past several passengers who were putting their bags away, and scanned the faces of those already seated, hoping that Antoine might have slipped past her.

As she was fastening her seat belt, she saw him making his way down the plane nonchalantly, his bag slung over his shoulder.

'You almost missed the plane,' she exclaimed.

Antoine looked surprised.

'No, no, there was plenty of time. I overslept. Rough night. I needed some coffee.'

He turned to look at her. 'Do you worry when you travel?

Curious. I didn't imagine you would. You have an air of calm efficiency.' He laughed.

With that, he dug out his newspapers and buried himself in the sports pages for the duration of the flight. He seemed to be nursing a hangover. She was irritated with him for his unreliability and with herself for getting muddled up in his research. Why on earth had she allowed him to join her on this trip? she asked herself. He had suggested on the phone that they do their research independently, and then they could swap notes in the evenings. They only had two days.

After the short flight, with its glimpse of the English coast, the Isle of Wight and the freight ships seemingly still in the expanse of the Channel, they landed. They found their way through the small airport to pick up the hire car. Antoine looked at the map to work out the route to their hotel. He was chuckling.

'Imagine, nowhere is more than ten miles away. No wonder they were such sailors – it was the only way to get away from the neighbours.'

As Antoine drove, Roz stared at the narrow lanes and the granite walls and stolid farmhouses with a bitter sense of dread. He was driving faster than the speed limit. He turned on the radio and hummed along. He had booked them into an old farmhouse tastefully restored as a hotel. It was tucked into gardens in the centre of the island. Roz felt miserable as she sat down heavily on her bed with her bag at her feet. The pale green of the decor accentuated the chill of the bedroom. A few minutes later, Antoine knocked. He had the car keys in his hand. He was full of purpose.

'Shall we go?'

She nodded, picking up her handbag and her coat.

'I'm going to the police station,' he said. 'You can't come with me because you don't have security clearance. The police have recovered a large collection of documents which hopefully will include the German billeting records. Why don't you drop me off in St Peter Port, and take the car? You can pick me up later.'

Roz agreed. But after she had dropped him, she felt unsure about what to do. Perhaps a walk on the cliffs would help. The memory of the awkward conversation with Maev and her mother made her apprehensive about asking people questions. She had been hoping that Antoine could help. He seemed so good at starting up conversations with everyone. She drove around the town until she found herself on a road which seemed to be heading south. The leaves were struggling to break out of their sticky buds in this uncertain spring weather, but there were plenty of daffodils. A pretty, delicate variety, she noticed. As she drove, she saw a signpost for Forest and Torteval, and took the turning. She decided she could walk on the cliffs tomorrow, when the weather might be less oppressive; today she would try to find The Vicarage. As she drove, the sense of indecision faded and she could feel her resolve returning. It couldn't be hard; you can't hide a handsome house near a church. She parked in a driveway and pulled out her map. She found Dieu Donne, the house where Brown had lived and where the Picasso drawings had been found, on the edge of the parish as it headed towards La Vallée Les Sages.

First, she would walk along the lane to look at Dieu Donne. After a short while, she came to a high stone wall and the entrance to a big house. Its wrought-iron gates were slightly ajar and she slipped through and walked down the short drive. Between the dark green shrubs, she glimpsed the brilliant green of an immaculate lawn. The drive opened out in front of a large, cream house. To one side, a long low building backed on to a courtyard, where several cars were parked. Perhaps this was where Brown had lived when the Germans had moved in, or perhaps it was the tack room where they had found the drawings. Roz felt self-conscious in front of so many windows. A face could appear at any moment. She turned and walked quickly back up the drive. Back in the car, she pored over her map.

She could see the Torteval church marked just off the St Peter Port road about a mile away. The Vicarage must be somewhere around there. She parked by the handsome stone church. Its spire would help orientate her in the network of small lanes. She folded the map into a pocket of her raincoat and set off again down one lane. On either side of the road were the island's distinctive banks made up of stones and earth, scattered with primroses and wild daffodils.

She had in her pocket the newspaper clipping that Jim had sent her, with the grainy photo. She found one house called The Vicarage, but it was a modern bungalow from the 1970s. It was not the house she was looking for. She began to check each of the lanes between Torteval and the neighbouring parish of St Peter's. She methodically marked a small cross on the map for each house she dismissed. Those which could conceivably match the clipping she marked with a question mark. She had noticed from her drives on the island that a stone arch was a feature of several houses. It was not as singular as Jim had hoped.

It began to rain, but she didn't notice, nor did she feel hungry, although it was past lunchtime. The lethargy of the morning had left her and she felt invigorated, almost happy. She enjoyed meandering down these lanes, peering over the banks into the small fields where the occasional pony was grazing. Down several turnings, she spotted dilapidated glasshouses with panes of glass smashed and sagging wooden frames. The only people she came across were workmen, intent on some aspect or another of house maintenance: window-cleaning, gardening, fixing, renovating, repairing and building. House-proud islanders seemed to make their homes a life project. Every last detail lovingly painted, cleaned, repointed. Everyone offered a cheery 'Good morning'.

After an hour, she had explored most of the lanes near the old church and was heading towards a hamlet called Les Jehans. Her damp map was covered in small crosses, and a few question marks. She headed back to the car for an umbrella. Then she resumed work, taking a path out of the car park which led down the steep slope through a copse into a small valley. It was sheltered from the wind and the rain had finally eased. An intense chorus of birdsong greeted her. Roz caught sight of chaffinches, tits and wagtails amongst the dense shrubs. The place was a haven for birds, after that wild desert of ocean beyond the cliffs. Their chests were puffed out to issue their sharp repetitive cries. At the bottom of the valley was a stream which wound through the gardens of a cluster of houses, before gushing down into a conduit under the road and then re-emerging. The sound of water – pouring, gurgling, babbling over stones – came from different directions and, with the song of the birds, reverberated in the steep-sided valley. It was noisy – there was no other word for this orchestra of water and birds.

Several old houses down here were tucked away from the main roads and the sea. The place felt hemmed in. The sun in winter would rarely reach these houses and their damp gardens. The low stone walls were studded with tiny green plants and ferns, and topped with mats of luxuriant moss, glowing a brilliant new green with the spring growth. As the lane began to lead up the other side of the valley, Roz spotted an old gate in a wall under the trees. Looking at the map, she could see a house at the end. She pressed on. Branches from the trees on either side almost met overhead on the narrow lane, and the tarmac gave way to gravel pitted with puddles. At the gate, she paused to admire a garden with a stand of bamboo, tall spires of echium and a spiky palm tree suddenly splashed with an unexpected shaft of sun. She couldn't see the house; it was obscured by shrubs.

Just past the gate she came to the driveway. She could see a solid granite house the colour of pale honey, with large windows.

A Virginia creeper, already coming into leaf, climbed up one side. On the doorstep a pair of green wellingtons lay tossed to one side beside a tray of garden plants. The door was ajar. Over the door was a handsome stone arch. It was the house in the newspaper clipping – Roz recognized the delicate fanlight. Looking around her, she then saw the name carved into a gate pillar: Les Bois Verts.

To the side of the house was a large magnolia tree in the middle of the lawn, the last of its petals lying brown and sodden around the base. Alongside the house was a stone terrace with a bench, and on the wall above roses had been trained round the window. From the terrace, a lawn sloped gently down the wooded valley. Roz tentatively took a few steps towards the lawn, looking beyond the woods to where the sea might be on a clear day. She was standing with her back to the house when she heard a voice.

'Hello, can I help you?' A woman stood on the doorstep. 'Can I help?' she repeated, her voice proprietorial.

Roz stood awkwardly in the garden; she must look absurd, she thought instantly. Her hair and her raincoat were wet and here she was, staring at this stranger's garden. She walked towards the woman.

'I'm so sorry. I didn't mean to disturb you –'

The woman was trying to hold back two Labradors, who were barking. She looked up expectantly.

'I – rather my mother – used to live around here. I'm trying to find her family home. I was curious. I am visiting from London.'

The woman's face softened. A man appeared behind her.

'What is it, Jill? Who is it?'

The two of them looked inquiringly at Roz standing in the rain.

'Your mother used to live here?' asked the woman encouragingly. 'When was that?'

'I'm not sure. It was somewhere round here. During the war, I think.'

'Ask her in, Jill. We can't stand in the rain talking.'

'Yes, of course. We can dig out the house documents and see if we can help. Perhaps you'd like to look round? It might bring back old memories.'

'I don't have any memories. It was my mother who lived here – I think,' said Roz quickly, as she followed them in.

All three stood in the stone-flagged hall. The couple looked at her, puzzled but interested. The dogs were still barking and the man shouted at them to be quiet. The melee of dogs and commands masked the awkwardness of arrival.

'What was your mother's name?' asked the man.

'Le Lacheur,' replied Roz.

He was plump, with a good-natured face. He paused a moment, trying to remember.

'It wasn't a Le Lacheur who sold it to us. We've been here about nine years,' he explained to Roz.

'Eight, Tim,' corrected Jill automatically.

'I have some old papers upstairs which might be of help. I know the house used to be a vicarage, then the church sold it and built a smaller modern vicarage,' said Tim.

'The house I am looking for was called The Vicarage, but I think it was renamed. This must be it.'

'The people we bought from were incomers; they had lived in Surrey until they retired here. The old lady went into a home after her husband died. What was her name?' Jill asked her husband.

'Smart, I think. Why don't you offer the lady a coffee, Jill? I'll get the papers out.'

Roz was led through a door into a large, modern kitchen. Beyond was a conservatory. Jill chattered about the task of renovating the house as she made the coffee.

'It was in a terrible state when we arrived. The Smarts hadn't done much to modernize it – there was no central heating and the wiring was a mess. There was only one bathroom, and the kitchen wasn't much better than a poky pantry. This used to be the nursery, apparently. Lovely long windows overlooking the gardens for the children. Fancy –' Jill suddenly paused – 'your mother probably once played in this room.'

The idea had just occurred to Roz. It was hard to imagine this white fitted kitchen with its elaborate technology as a nursery. Only the shape of the windows and their deep windowsills might be original. Roz looked out at the garden in the now driving rain.

Jill warmed to the task of explaining how they had transformed the old house. The coffee was left to go cold as she took Roz off to the dining room. She wanted to show her the photos they had had framed of the house in its original state before their improvements. One was of a library lined with shelves, another of a bathroom with its old-fashioned plumbing. The wooden shelving of the library had been riddled with worm and had to be pulled out, explained Jill. She showed Roz how the library was now a television room. They had turned the stables into an indoor swimming pool with a Grecian theme. The long sitting room still had its original stone fireplace. Its row of windows, half hidden by elaborately draped curtains, looked on to the magnolia tree and the lawn. Upstairs, Jill showed off a brass four-poster bed and a neighbouring bathroom with a Jacuzzi. Suddenly she broke off.

'The photos, I've only just thought – you might know them.'

She turned to Roz, half laughing. 'Here I am, so interested in showing you what we've done to the house that I forgot all about the photos.'

Jill led her to the far end of the landing. One wall was covered in old sepia photos framed in modern gilt frames. Roz looked at a photo of a woman with two small children and then turned to Jill questioningly.

'Your family?' she asked.

'No, but perhaps they're yours?'

Roz peered more closely at the image.

'We found some old albums in the attic when we moved in. There was a lot of junk up there, but I looked through the albums and I liked some of the photos. The women are extraordinarily beautiful and their clothes so elegant. Tim and I had some of the photos enlarged and framed for the wall. It added a sort of "age" to the decor. It was just curiosity value, I suppose.' Her voice had grown unsteady. 'Do you recognize any of them?'

Roz was engrossed. Who was this young bridal couple, the groom in uniform? Hanging on the wall beside it was a photo of a beautiful young woman with a sleek blonde bob and a low-cut beaded dress. Next came a photo of two small children, a girl and a boy.

Jill and Tim had hung the photos in sequence, because, as she moved along the wall, she could see the likeness of mother and daughter as the child grew into a young woman. The young woman, she recognized. It was Helene. This was her family.

Two photos formed a pair of Helene and Edward. The latter she knew well; an identical, although smaller, copy had sat on her mother's bedside table in a simple silver frame until she died. The photo of Helene she had not seen before; it was the first she had seen of her mother as a girl. Helene must have been in her mid-teens, and Edward a little younger. They shared the same fair hair, high cheekbones and full lips. Helene's thick hair was pinned back on both sides of her head with ribbons, and fell, wavy, over her shoulders. They stared directly into the camera with an edge of nervous bravado.

'Beautiful children, aren't they?' said Jill, but her voice trailed away. 'Was that your . . . your mother?' she asked quietly.

Roz didn't hear her.

'I can see the likeness,' said Jill, answering her own question.

Roz moved close to the photo of Helene. She had an unfamiliar expression, full of eager anticipation and trust. Roz looked from one sibling to the other. There was a hint of humour, of a successfully suppressed smile around Edward's mouth. Helene looked a little wistful.

Jill hovered nervously.

'Yes, this is my mother and my uncle, and these must be my grandparents,' said Roz finally.

It felt strange, claiming possession of these strangers, from a stranger. Roz moved back along the row of photos. One of the most striking was of Helene, at perhaps ten, standing with a young woman; the two looked very alike and were clearly related. There might have been ten years or so between them. Roz scrutinized the unfamiliar face. Could Helene have had an older sister whom she had never mentioned? The young woman wore an elegant suit and her hair was beautifully curled.

In another, Helene as a little girl, and Edward, a solemn little boy in velvet breeches, stood either side of their mother. A formal family portrait showed Helene, aged about six, sitting beside her father, who wore a dog collar. He had his arm around her seated mother, and Edward stood next to her. The first photo, of the wedding couple, was of her grandparents. The profile of the beautiful young woman she could now identify was that of her grandmother.

Jill was embarrassed. She was fidgeting with a chain around her neck.

'Did you keep the originals, and the rest of the albums?' asked Roz.

'Don't you have the originals yourself?' Jill had an anxious edge in her voice.

Roz shook her head.

'I'm afraid we threw them out. There wasn't much room in the attic. We had so much stuff of our own to store. After we took the enlargements, we put the rest in the skip. I'm terribly sorry, but we never dreamed anyone would want them. I'm sure we could get all these copied. We'd be delighted to help.'

She paused and turned to Roz. 'Why were they left behind when your family left? Why don't you have copies?'

'It's complicated,' said Roz quickly. 'Yes, I'd be very grateful if you could have copies made – please send me the bill.'

'Would you like to see the rest of the house?' asked Jill, edging away from the photos.

'Thank you, but no, I mustn't trouble you any more. Can I leave my address in London for the photos? In fact, let me give you a cheque now. It will be a lot of trouble to take those photos out of their frames and copy them.'

'I won't hear of it,' said Jill. 'I feel terrible for throwing the others away – there were boxes of them. Lots of horses, dogs, croquet games and small children playing on the beach.'

Roz lingered over the photos of Helene and Edward. Their teenage confidence and self-assurance were haunting. Edward would be killed within a few years – if Helene's story was true. And whatever happened to Helene had destroyed the soft eagerness in her expression.

Jill accompanied her back to the hall and Roz picked up her umbrella to go. Tim reappeared with a clutch of papers in his hand.

'Couldn't find the darned things, but I've got them at last. This is a copy of the church tenancy, which dates back to the 1860s, when the house was built. I thought it might be of interest,' he said as he spread the documents out on the hall table.

They leaned over them together. He moved his thick finger across the paper.

'Here we are. It was a Le Marchant who moved in in 1920, and it was designated as The Vicarage.' He shuffled the papers and pulled out another sheet. 'And it was sold in 1973. He lived here for fifty-three years. Would that be your grandfather, Eustace Le Marchant?' asked Tim, straightening and looking at Roz over the top of his spectacles.

'Eustace Le Marchant,' she repeated.

'Is that your grandfather's name?' pressed Tim.

'Yes, of course,' said Roz firmly, covering up her confusion.

'Did you never come here when your grandfather was alive?' asked Jill, inquisitive.

Roz couldn't think of an easy explanation. 'My mother lost contact,' she said, adding quickly, 'Thank you again for showing me around. It's been most interesting, and you've done a wonderful job on the house.'

She hastily scribbled her address in London on a scrap of paper and handed it to Jill. She needed to get away; she dreaded more questions. She could feel their anxious curiosity.

'Perhaps . . . Tim, what about . . .' Jill's voice trailed off.

There was an awkward pause before Tim quickly moved to open the door.

'So sorry we couldn't help more. The photos will be in the post next week.'

Roz found herself back on the drive. Behind her were several outbuildings. The sky was clearer, and there was a glimpse of the blue sea beyond the trees. For the first time since she had arrived at the house, she realized how wet she was. She slowly walked back down the lane, where a rivulet of water now ran along the ruts. More water was trickling from an opening in a wall above her, where the hillside rose sharply.

Her mother had been born Le Marchant, and yet Justin had assumed her maiden name was Le Lacheur. She must have been married before Justin. Was this part of the confusion at Maev's? She recalled how Mrs Blampied had been muddled about Helene's surname.

A hidden marriage was startling enough, but equally troubling, she felt, was the fact that her grandfather had been alive in 1973 – when she was twenty-seven. Why had she never met him? There must have been a terrible disagreement, but about what, and how could it last so long that he never saw his grandchildren? Where did he go in 1973? Had he lived there alone all that time? Brown's reference to her grandmother seemed to support Helene's story that her mother had died when she was a teenager. It was strange to have images of a grandmother and grandfather she had never known. She didn't even have a first name for her grandmother. There were no anecdotes, no family stories and no details about their lives. There was nothing except those beautiful photographs – in Jill and Tim's heavy gilt frames.

Back at the hotel, Roz lay down on the bed and pulled a quilt over herself. It was the only way to get warm, and she felt exhausted. She had planned to phone Jim to explain this new discovery of a first marriage, but she found herself drifting off into a fitful sleep. She was woken by a knock, and Antoine calling her name. It took a few moments to remember where she was.

'Dinner in half an hour? I'll take you out, Roz. I've news!' Antoine sounded excited.

She had been in the middle of an intense dream. A family were sitting round a dining table, the glasses and silver glittering in the candlelight. The beautiful grandmother had turned towards her, gesturing to an empty place. They were looking at her expectantly. Then in a strange disjuncture, Jill and Tim were dragging their leather armchairs into the room, and trampling the fragile, ghostly figures. Only her grandmother held her eye, still smiling, her hand stretched out.

★

The restaurant Antoine had chosen was a small French bistro in a backstreet of St Peter Port. The walls were covered in framed

French adverts from between the wars, the time of her mother's childhood. It added to Roz's persistent confusion about the island: English in some ways, and French in others. Was she at home or abroad? Who was the foreigner here – herself or Antoine? Or both?

He didn't seem to be troubled by such matters. He was in an exuberant mood as he talked at length to the French waiter about a recent football match. After this exchange, and a close scrutiny of the menu, he turned his attention to Roz.

'Now, we must talk,' he announced as he poured her a large glass of red wine.

Roz buttered a roll, wondering how and what she should tell Antoine about The Vicarage.

'You want me to start? Dear reserved Roz. So English,' he said slowly, leaning back in his chair and smiling at her. He lightly touched her elbow where it rested on the table. There was affection in the gesture, but also a degree of irritation at her reticence, Roz noticed.

'I found the German billeting records, and I am very hopeful. I think I will find the names of all the officers who were billeted at Dieu Donne throughout the Occupation. Brown mentioned some of them in his diary. I can check the names against the records in Paris.'

Antoine leaned forward over the table, his face animated by the thrill of the chase. His cheeks were flushed with the wine and the warmth of the restaurant. Every now and then, he flung a hand out to emphasize a point, before running his fingers through his hair. He had a restless mobility.

'The officers at Dieu Donne may have formed part of a syndicate of men who smuggled paintings out of occupied France.'

'Do you have names you are looking for?' asked Roz.

'The Heinrich mentioned by Brown is interesting, but Brown never used the surname. The first name is not enough.'

'What was the motive?' She took a gulp of wine.

'Too early to say. Money, probably.' Abruptly, he stopped eating and put down his knife and fork.

'What I need to know is how your mother came by some of these drawings.' He fixed his eyes on her.

'I don't know.'

'But you have some clues that I don't have?'

Roz shook her head.

Antoine leaned back. She felt acutely uncomfortable under his steady gaze.

'Really. I don't.'

'Do you know where you were born?'

'Weymouth. That's what the birth certificate says. April 1946,' she said defensively.

'Do you still have family here? Did you come here to visit grandparents? And your father? Was he from Guernsey?'

'All these questions, Antoine. Tell me, if you find names of German officers, will there be prosecutions?'

'Perhaps – who knows? Justice needs to be done. But my questions, Roz,' he persisted, 'do you have any answers?'

'I know very little about my mother's background. I suppose that's what I'm looking for,' she said slowly, and explained how she had found the house where her mother lived as a child. Hesitantly, she described the photos. When she appeared to have come to the end, Antoine filled their wine glasses.

'There's more?' he asked.

Roz looked at him. 'No, not really. Bits of gossip,' she said in a level voice.

'Bits of gossip?' he repeated.

There was a strained silence.

'You look lovely,' he said suddenly. 'Walking in the rain must be good for you.'

He had switched tack, in a way that Roz was beginning to

recognize in conversations with him. The handbrake turns in the choice of subject caught her off guard. He was flirting with her. She looked away, tears in her eyes. She felt oddly vulnerable. Through a blur, she picked up her glass and took another gulp of wine.

'This is ridiculous. I haven't cried for years. This afternoon I felt like crying, and now . . . I can't really explain. I don't feel myself,' she mumbled, embarrassed.

'Sorry for asking, but are you sure Justin Rawsthorne was your father?'

'Why on earth would you ask that?'

'I'm sorry. I was just checking.'

Neither of them said anything. Roz weighed up the advantages of explaining her search. He was looking at the dessert menu, but she knew he was waiting for her answer. She remembered Jim's warning.

'He was not my father,' she said, in a rush. 'And, before you ask, I don't know who was. It turns out my mother was married before Justin. None of us knew. Presumably, I come from this first marriage,' she said finally.

'There is a chance your father was German, no?'

'Absolutely none, knowing my mother. This first marriage was to a Le Lacheur – the family who lived at Dieu Donne before the war,' said Roz, with as much certainty as she could muster. 'He must have come back to the island after Liberation. My mother is the last person who would ever have had an affair with a German. We always knew she was devoted to her brother, and he was killed fighting in the war. She was a very old-fashioned kind of English patriot, with a deep suspicion of Germany. Adamantly opposed to reunification. Very prejudiced against Germans – a generational thing.'

'If the Weymouth birth certificate is accurate, nine months back from April takes you to July 1945, and there were still

Germans on the island then. They were in POW camps, but some island girls managed to visit them,' he said, 'according to interviews with islanders.'

He was intent on his own train of thought. 'Your father might be the missing link in the puzzle of the Morel collection. He may have given the drawings to your mother. He may have given her the Cranach painting, which has been missing for over fifty years – *The Virgin and Child Under an Apple Tree.*'

'Hang on, Antoine. These are huge assumptions.' It was Roz's turn to be irritated now. 'I knew it was a bad idea to talk to you. You're leaping to your own conclusions.'

'I've only ever seen a rather bad black–and–white reproduction, but it's a beautiful painting,' continued Antoine, ignoring her last comment.

Seeing Roz frown, he added, 'I want to find this painting, and I want it given back to its rightful owners. To achieve that, I have to keep an open mind to every possibility. You should know that – you're a lawyer.'

A waiter came and cleared away their plates. Roz waited a moment before she replied icily, 'There is more to the story. According to an islander I met on my last visit, my mother hid an escaped Russian slave labourer in outbuildings at The Vicarage. My father might be Russian.'

Now it was Antoine's turn to look surprised. 'I have to admit, that thought had never occurred to me.' He went on, excited, 'There are lots of things for us to research. Birth registers for 1945 and 1946, for a start. We need to check you were not born on the island. Also, I know someone who was involved in the network of safe houses for escaped slave labourers. He might have heard about Helene's Russian.'

'That would be helpful.'

Antoine might be irritating occasionally, but his determination was endearing. They were alike in some ways, she saw, both capable of being single-minded. The difference was that, for her, this was a goal unlike any other, with a dizzying array of complications. But her instinct had been right. He was going to be useful.

She smiled at him. 'Thank you.'

Antoine accepted her thanks, inclining his head. As they left the restaurant, he put his hand on the small of her back for a fraction longer than was necessary to usher her through the door, and Roz felt a jolt of anticipation. Time with Antoine was charged with an unfamiliar volatility.

He offered to drive. It was a clear night and stars were scattered across the sky. A rich smell of the recent rain, the sea and new spring leaves filled the air of the quiet backstreet. They got into the car and Antoine put the key in the ignition, and then, impulsively, quickly turned towards her and put his hand round the back of her neck, pulling her towards him. Cupping her face in his hands, he kissed her.

His lips were full and warm and she felt a surge of intense desire. But she knew: not here, not now. Not yet, perhaps never.

'Antoine, no . . .'

He let go, but kept his hand on her arm.

'I wanted to do that many times this evening. You're very beautiful.'

'Things are complicated enough right now,' said Roz. She didn't speak for a few moments. 'This is just work for you; for me, it's family.'

'It's also personal for me,' he said sulkily.

They sat in the car, and she waited for him to explain. The street lights were glinting in the raindrops on the windscreen. The road gleamed in the orange light.

'I'm Jewish. My mother escaped to Switzerland, but many of my relatives were not so lucky. This is my way of reckoning with my people's history. Only a matter of time saved me from the atrocity of a concentration camp. If I'd been born fifteen years earlier . . .'

His voice trailed away. Roz put a hand on his arm. He cleared his throat. 'None of them had a choice. I don't think you do either. There has to be justice, however long it takes.'

He started the engine, and turned the car round to pull away. Neither of them said anything as he drove. He was still breaking the speed limit – either he hadn't noticed the island's signs or he was not in the mood to abide by them.

'My mistake,' he said, as she got out of the car, her bedroom key already in her hand.

Still a little shocked, she said goodnight quickly.

★

At breakfast the next morning, Antoine pretended that nothing had happened between them the previous evening. He had already phoned his friend Mike to arrange a visit that morning, and in the afternoon he proposed going to the registry office to find details about Helene, her birth, her marriage, and perhaps also Roz's birth. He had met Mike on a previous trip and, between long conversations about the Occupation, they had discovered a mutual love of football and jazz. Mike had been a teenager in the war, and he had helped several escaped slave workers. He had recently written a detailed memoir. Antoine explained all of this between mouthfuls of scrambled egg and gulps of coffee.

Roz had slept badly. In the early hours, she had sat in the dark at the window of her room, watching the stars as she considered Antoine's questions. Was the price of his help the public humiliation of her family once again?

To add to her confusion, she was attracted to him. His energy, determination and intelligence were compelling. But it was an absurdly implausible affair: a gap in age, different countries and, most importantly of all, divergent interests. He wanted justice; she wanted something much less clear-cut: a history of her family – or as much of it as she could find. Could she ennoble it and call it the truth? It was a much more humble thing, an approximation of truth: a few facts (she hoped), which she could string together with a bit of imagination. Their two goals were not always compatible. Things were moving fast and it was hard to keep her thoughts clear.

Mike had told Antoine he could only see them in the morning, so they agreed that they would go to the registry office later. His bungalow lay on the outskirts of St Sampson, in a row of what might once have been fishermen's cottages. Through the side gate, they glimpsed washing on the line blowing in the wind. A large, gentle woman answered the door and said Mike was down the garden in the vegetable patch. She ushered them into a sitting room, and went to call him. A few moments later, Mike appeared, his hands dirty with soil. He was a big man with a ruddy complexion and thick eyebrows above kindly eyes.

'What brings you back so soon?' he asked good-humouredly, as he wiped his hand on his overall to shake Antoine's hand.

'Research takes curious turns,' responded Antoine. 'This is Roz, who is helping me at the moment.'

'You're very welcome. Sit down, make yourselves comfortable. I'll clean up and be back. I'll get the wife, Sheila, to make us some tea. You caught me short. It's a busy time of year in the garden, and I thought I'd get some potting done before you got here.'

Mike disappeared and they could hear him talking with his wife in a low voice in the kitchen, then he re-emerged.

'Research been going well, Antoine? Any progress yet?'

Antoine smiled and described his weeks in London in the archives.

'Well, I'd like to think you'll get them – don't want Germans getting away with that kind of crime. Ghastly business. Do you think a Russian could have been mixed up in your picture business, then?'

'No – it's a separate but related inquiry.'

'Ah, here's the tea.' Sheila came in, carrying a tray with cups and saucers on a lace mat and three home-made scones.

Roz noticed how the conversation was between the two men. The wife had returned to the kitchen and Roz was politely ignored. It reminded her of the farmers who were neighbours at the cottage in Dorset: a rural conservatism in which everyone has their place – except a single middle-aged working woman. On this occasion, it suited her; she could hide behind the role of deferential research assistant.

'So you said on the phone you wanted more details about the escaped Russians. Anything in particular?'

'Everything. How many did you know? Where did they hide? Who hid them and why?'

'I can't answer many of those questions. I don't know how many escaped, nor who hid them, nor where. It wasn't the sort of thing people talked about during the war, for obvious reasons. We lived on a need-to-know basis. When the war was over, it sounded like boasting to talk about it, and there was a lot of sensitivity about the Occupation, so everyone kept quiet for a good while. Best not spoken about. But your last question – why people hid them – that's easy to answer.'

Mike stopped for a moment and rubbed his hand across his forehead. When he started again, he spoke heavily.

'It was a pitiful sight watching the Russians march past. They weren't much more than boys and they were skinny, white wretches. Their hair was matted with mud, and the worst thing of all was that many of them had no boots. They put anything on their feet. Sometimes it was nothing more than newspapers bound with twine; if they were lucky, they had rags. Their feet were often bloody and septic, and the stench was awful. We held our breath when they passed. They were covered with cement dust – they used the cement sacks for clothing, held together with bits of wire and string. Islanders looked away, afraid to meet those boys' pleading eyes. They were hungry, the poor sods. They scrabbled like dogs for the smallest scrap. Everywhere their eyes went, they were looking for food. You could tell they were people who thought of only one thing.'

He paused and shifted in his chair. 'When a man is hungry, the pitch of his voice rises. In the evening in their camps, they almost sounded like birds. It was uncanny.

'There's no denying we were scared of them. There were rumours of typhoid, even cholera, amongst some of them in St Peter Port. People crossed to the other side of the street when they saw them coming. Some were worried they would catch their fleas and lice – they were crawling with them. But there were many islanders who put out food or spare items of clothing for them by their gates. They didn't want the Russians in the house, and they didn't want any trouble, but they felt sorry for them. They felt guilty. You couldn't rest easy in your bed, knowing there were boys with aching bellies in the next-door street.

'My mother was always a tender-hearted woman. She left food out – food we couldn't spare – but she was a chapel-goer and she insisted that the Lord would provide. She was right: He did. She gave away food, but we never went too short for long. We missed the odd meal, but we never starved. She left out everything she thought was edible; she boiled up potato peelings, and even they disappeared by morning – we never knew how, but the prisoners must have found a way to get out of the camp at night. Giving away clothes was more difficult, but she did what she could.

'In the spring of 1942, I was collecting kindling, and I came upon a detachment of Russians with their guards. It was too late to run away, so I hid. As they were passing the hedge where I was hiding, one of the Russians stumbled and fell. The guard kicked him in the head, and the Russian howled like an animal; that incensed the German, and he hit him with his rifle butt. He might have killed him if another guard hadn't intervened. Two other Russians picked up the fallen man, covered in blood.

'I was a young lad of fourteen and I was so shocked I vomited. I told my ma about it. A few months later, I came back from work one evening to find a Russian sitting at our kitchen table. He was not much older than me – in his late teens.

'We got to know him well. He was very good at setting traps for rabbits. Brought them in from time to time for my mother to stew, and it was the only taste of meat we had throughout the war. He stayed on and off in our house for the rest of the Occupation. We called him Vladimir, but I don't think that was his real name. Sometimes he went off for a few months to stay in other houses, but we never asked where he went. It was too dangerous to know. We knew there were other Russians who had escaped. Once he brought one back, a young man called Alexei, who was hiding in a country parish somewhere. In the 1950s, a man from the Soviet embassy came round asking lots of questions. We found out then about the other islanders who had hidden slave workers. My mother was given a gold watch from the Soviet government for what she did. She was a good woman. She always said that what she did had nothing to do with politics.'

Mike brought down a box from a bookshelf. Inside was a gold watch, with his mother's name beneath a hammer and sickle. On the back was engraved: 'For Muriel Le Lievre, with the gratitude of the Soviet people'.

'She was very proud of it,' said Mike. 'She left it to me, because I did odd things here and there to help her look after Vladimir.'

They admired the watch, and a framed photo of his mother receiving it at an official ceremony in the late 1960s. The plump, ageing woman stood in her hat and gloves beside the Soviet officials, beaming with pride.

'Did you know anything about a girl called Helene Le Lacheur hiding a Russian?' asked Antoine.

Mike looked uncomfortable. 'I wouldn't know anything about that.'

'Are you sure?'

'Well, there was a lot of talk about her.'

'Do you know why?' asked Antoine.

'It was all very odd, that business. Nobody got to the bottom of it. Some called her a tart,' Mike went on unhappily. 'But I don't want to speak ill of her, and I'm not going to repeat ignorant gossip. After the war, people who were in no position to judge were very free and easy with their condemnation; I didn't hold with it then, and I don't now. No, I don't know anything about that. If that's what you're after, I'm no help.'

There was an awkward silence.

Antoine thanked him for the information. They stayed a while longer to listen to Mike's reminiscences about the Occupation and his mother. Antoine hoped something might emerge about Helene, but it didn't. Mike was a good man, and the Occupation had been the most dramatic event of a quiet life: he enjoyed his memories. After repeating their thanks for the tea, and admiring his large collection of cacti in the conservatory, they left.

'Registry office next?' asked Antoine as they got back in the car.

Roz felt nauseous. What were Mike and Maev hiding from her? She nodded, and braced herself. But on their arrival, an official wouldn't even listen to their request. He explained that they were in the process of reorganizing and they would have to return at the end of the week. Frustrated, they found a café for lunch and discussed their plans for the afternoon.

'You OK?' asked Antoine, concerned by Roz's silence.

'Not really. It's the "tart" comment. I get the sense that a lot of people on this island know something, but they won't tell me. They're holding back.'

Antoine nodded. 'It's unlike Mike to even repeat a word like "tart". Listen, I'll stay on and wait for the registry office reorganization. By the end of the week, I should be able to get in, and I'll call you.'

Roz needed to get back to London for work. She would have to trust Antoine. It was public information, after all. She couldn't stop him finding out dates.

'Small rural communities are judgemental,' said Antoine. 'It's how gossip works in a place. You must know that. It was war. We had plenty of this in France, as did every occupied country. After the war, judgement was a way to ease the guilt. You must learn to ignore it. This is how a tight community copes with its past. Only the British didn't learn this. Instead their war is a very simple story – one of great heroism. A delusion born of geography. 1940 has become your defining identity; it will be a burden for your country – an absurd myth of exceptionalism. The last consolation for a lost empire. Ah, Albion!'

He was laughing.

Roz was quiet for a moment. 'I'm thinking of what you're saying – it's what Justin believed. It's what he fought in the war for – if it's a delusion, as you say, it's one which gave meaning to his whole life.'

'Well, it's not a useful delusion any more,' he replied briskly, adding, 'judgement is a very different thing from justice.'

'You're right. I don't like judgementalism. I've seen enough of it at work. Wives or husbands who develop it into an art form. They feed off it and it puffs them up. I can see how it gives them energy. I suppose I sense the same thing here – that my mother's complicated history, whatever it was, has been the fodder for smug self-aggrandizement.'

Antoine put his hand on her arm. 'Yes, I see that. Justice without judgementalism. That's our challenge.'

'I'll toast that,' said Roz, raising her coffee cup. Antoine smiled.

He suggested a walk along the cliffs. After looking at the map, they chose Pleinmont. Patches of blue were visible between the clouds, and when the sun did break through, there was warmth in its rays. For the first time, there was a hint of the summer to come.

'We will find someone eventually who can explain,' said Antoine as they drove.

'It's the unfinished sentences, hints, brief references – whether in museums or from islanders – I keep feeling I am on the point of a discovery and then it slips away. Like a fisherman who sits on the riverbank for hours and the fish keep getting away. Nibbles on the fly, but nothing more.'

'You fish?' asked Antoine, surprised.

'No – but the analogy seemed to fit,' laughed Roz.

'You never know – the English have all these outdoor habits. They even seem to like their rain.' This time, they were both laughing.

'But seriously, you will catch plenty of fish. All you need is patience. In the end, someone will always tell you what you want to know. Gossip is like that – knowledge only has value if it's repeated. The pleasure of gossip is in the telling. That brief moment of importance it provides: knowing that you have something to say which is of immense interest to another. It's a power thing.'

Roz glanced at Antoine's profile as he drove. The slope of his forehead and the line of his jaw. More than clever – he had a way of seeing through the makeshift constructs people used to give their lives importance. She found his insight impressive, but unnerving.

They took a small lane through the fields and parked the car on the headland. The cliffs tumbled down to the rocky shore, where the waves crashed in flourishes of white spray. At frequent intervals, benches had been placed thoughtfully for visitors more interested in contemplating the magnificent view of the sea than in walking the cliffs. Heavy grey clouds had closed in and the sea was an uncanny dark turquoise, but Roz watched as the light opened up on the horizon and patches of silver appeared on the sea's surface where the sun pierced the cloud. As she set off at a brisk pace along the path, she watched the splashes of light shift. Antoine had fallen behind. His cigarette-smoking was catching up on him, she thought.

Up here, the wind was bracing, and the breadth of sea to the north, west and south was exhilarating. It was like being on the prow of a ship. Ahead crouched a German watchtower. Its rounded, stocky form was silhouetted against the sky. Antoine eventually caught up with her and they walked, single file, along the narrow path. The roar of the sea on the rocks came and went as they followed the contours. The cliffs were a tapestry of plants: primroses on sheltered banks, mats of succulents, and a dense scrub of salt-stunted hawthorn, crouching close to the land. Given the wind and the roar of the waves, it was hard to talk until they arrived at the tower. Here, they paused in the lee of its thick concrete wall for Antoine to light a cigarette. Roz could see the tiny indentations in the concrete left by the wooden shuttering used in its construction. She thought of Mike's story of Vladimir working on a site like this, high up on the cliffs in rain and shine, with no shoes and an empty stomach. Further along the cliffs was another tower, several storeys high. Its profile was as brooding as an Easter Island statue.

The tower was open, the entrance strewn with pebbles and puddles. The walls were marked with graffiti and Roz could smell urine. The wooden doorframe had weathered and its grain had been split by the wind and salt. The iron bolts and reinforcing had blossomed into thick flakes of brilliant orange rust. Apprehensive, Roz followed Antoine inside. It was dank and oppressive. He had disappeared down a spiral staircase, the noise of his footsteps reverberating in the confined space, and Roz had no appetite to follow. She looked out of the narrow slit in the concrete wall across the ocean. She sensed the enormous weight of concrete and iron above her head. The tower was a sturdy shield from all weathers, and almost as durable as the granite cliffs on which it had been built. The materials and labour poured into this building were testimony to the belief in a Reich that would last a thousand years. The Reich had not, but the building might last that long, serving now as a hang-out for rebellious teenagers. She imagined German sentries as they sat out here on the cliffs, waiting for the invading British, eyes trained on the sea. She watched the clouds suddenly blown open and a setting sun cast a red glitter on the now grey sea. The fragments of glowing colour rearranged themselves continually as the restless ocean moved under its skin of patterned light.

*

That evening, Roz and Antoine were the first customers at a little fish restaurant overlooking Cobo Bay. From the window by their table, they watched darkness gather and the tide recede. The sea spray had left a residue of salt smeared on the glass. They drank strong Martinis, and Roz felt the warmth of the alcohol and food after the walk.

After their silent walk on the cliffs, they talked about Mike's account of the slave labourers. Antoine outlined the scale of the vast Organisation Todt, which had moved millions of workers to German factories and occupied territories to complete its engineering projects.

'If Hitler hadn't diverted so many men and materials to these islands, northern France could have been better defended. A ratio on Guernsey of one German soldier to two islanders – it was an insane concentration of troops.'

'I was cycling in France once, on a holiday in Burgundy,' said Roz. 'Lovely summer day, delicious picnic. It was an area of huge forests rich with the smell of pine needles. Suddenly, we come to a small crossroads, a long way from the nearest hamlet. Beside the road was a large war memorial to dozens of men who had been ambushed by the Germans and killed. They were resistance fighters. Someone had betrayed them.'

Antoine nodded. 'There are many places like that in France – in the south, in particular. Occupation is a savage business. Fear and distrust creep into every relationship. There are many villages in France still divided by that history, struggling to "put the past behind them", as you say in English. Such an odd phrase – how can it be behind?' With a flourish of his hands, he added, 'The great mistake of the Western imagination is that time is linear. But history is more like . . .' He seemed to be searching for the right metaphor. 'Like radio waves. At times, the reception is good, and other times it is muffled or lost entirely, but the music is still being played – if you understand my meaning?'

Roz looked confused.

'We are always using history – we choose to forget bits, we choose other stories to remember. Always for a reason. The next generation chooses another set of stories, and so it goes on. Like a jukebox! Sorry, I'm going on.'

He was laughing at himself. She wasn't sure she quite followed him, but she smiled. Antoine changed the subject.

'I'm talking to a couple of American universities about jobs. The salaries are good. I want a family. It's time.' He smiled ruefully.

Roz managed to laugh. Of course he does. It is indeed *about time*, she thought bitterly for a brief moment. It didn't occur to Antoine that the comment could hurt. He was asking about her work.

Their knees were touching under the narrow table, and, from time to time, Antoine took her hand to emphasize a point. He used his hands almost continuously, waving his fork as he spoke or playing with his cigarette before he lit up. Thin and full of his nervous energy, they were the hands of a thinker. Not a practical man, she thought, but she liked their fluid movement. Almost like those of a dancer.

She was unexpectedly enjoying herself, and it had been several years since she could say that without hesitation. It would pass too quickly, she thought. She was almost ten years older than him; he wanted a family, and, above all, he was intent on establishing her mother's role in a war crime. Yet, despite her tidy, sensible life, she didn't care. She found her new recklessness exhilarating.

At the hotel, the receptionist greeted Roz with a note. Jim had asked her to call. She kissed Antoine goodnight on the cheek, lingering a fraction of a second longer than usual. She could smell his faded aftershave.

★

'Jim?'

'Sorry, Roz, love. I had this feeling that I needed to know what you were finding out. I felt something was happening.'

'I should have called before. You're right. I've found the house. Mother's family house. More important, it looks like Mother was married before. To a man called Le Lacheur. She was born Le Marchant. And, really odd, we had a grandfather who was alive until at least 1973.'

Jim was taken aback. 'Hang on . . . What? . . . Another marriage?'

It had all come out in a rush. Roz took a breath and started again, explaining how she had found the house and the photos.

Jim gave a long quiet whistle. 'Who would ever have guessed

168

she had all this up her sleeve? What bothers me is the grandfather. How come we never met him?'

His tone shifted, suddenly practical. 'There must be a registry in Guernsey that would give more information about all this – the marriage, our grandfather, and when he died?'

'Yes, we tried the registry. It's closed for reorganization but we should be able to get in later in the week. '

'Who is this "we"?'

'Antoine, the French historian I told you about. He's helping.'

Jim groaned. 'I told you, Roz. It'll make things more complicated. You do know that this may get out of control? You won't be able to tidy this one up now, big sister.'

Roz was silent, then she said, 'Jim, the photo of Helene as a teenager was so beautiful. She looked a different person. I don't know how to describe it . . . there was an openness, a softness. I never saw her look like that. There were many more photos but they're lost – they threw them out.'

'I want to see them. I'll be back in London soon. Show me the copies then,' said Jim, and then his voice became sharper: 'You're not falling for this Antoine, are you, Roz?'

'Oh, Jim, don't be daft. He has too much Gallic charm, I don't trust him.' Roz thought she sounded quite convincing.

Jim was doubtful.

'My advice is to keep well away.'

VII

The next few days were terrifying. They expected the arrival of the German officers at any moment. The house was ready for the billet: the beds made, the towels neatly folded in the clean bathroom. The covers had been taken off the furniture in the sitting room and the dining table had been polished for the first time in years.

Helene and George made a plan for Alexei. George was trying to find someone who would take in the sick Russian boy. But there were not many people he trusted enough even to ask. In the meantime, they found food for him and smuggled it to where he lay in the dark back room in George's cottage. As soon as he was strong enough, they could ask him to move on. Sometimes his leg caused him pain and he would moan in his language.

It was early July and the long days seemed to last forever. At nine o'clock, when the birds were still singing and the sunset coloured the sky pink, it was still possible that the Germans could arrive. Their nerves were stretched to breaking point. Only when the shadows from the wood finally swallowed the lawn and shrouded the house in dark did Helene breathe more easily. They had survived another day, and that seemed a miracle each time.

When the captain did come, Helene was alone in the garden. Her father was out visiting, and Nanna had gone to help a sick neighbour. She was kneeling, weeding the vegetable bed, and didn't hear the car. It was only when he coughed that she looked up to see his brightly polished boots on the verge a few feet away.

'Mrs Le Lacheur. Good morning.'

She scrambled to her feet. Her hands were filthy and strands of hair had fallen from her scarf. She was wearing a coarse stained apron over her faded summer dress. She couldn't bring herself to speak. Alexei was in the outhouse, only a few feet from where they were standing.

'Good morning,' he repeated.

Helene's mouth was so dry that she didn't recognize the sound of her strained reply.

He looked across the garden to the glimpse of sea in the distance, shading his eyes in the bright sunlight. He smiled with satisfaction.

'This is a beautiful garden. Here, I can almost feel happy.'

He seemed to be directing his comments at the view.

'I have brought a basket of food for this Sunday,' he said, turning back to her. 'It's in the kitchen. I would like to take lunch here again. I would have discussed this with your father, but no one is here except yourself. Perhaps you would convey this request to him?'

Helene could not manage more than a murmur.

'And we will forget the war, won't we? I would like that very much, Mrs Le Lacheur – for us to forget the war for a few hours. Do you think that might be possible?'

She nodded, mute with fear. He strolled across the lawn to the flower bed by the window and pulled down a rose to smell its fragrance. She didn't move.

After what seemed like a long time, she heard her father calling from the house.

'Good morning, captain. I saw the car.' He came striding across the lawn still in his cassock.

The captain walked to meet him, and Helene saw that he had picked a lily from the flower bed beside the glasshouse.

'Ah, Reverend, I apologize for the intrusion.'

The two men slipped out of earshot as they made their way back to the house.

She went through the back door to the kitchen. He was in the hall with her father, talking about the vintage of a red wine he had bought in Paris. Her father's responses were stilted. Then she heard the front door close and a car engine start in the drive. He had gone.

That evening at tea, Father was in a sombre mood. He explained to Helene and Nanna that the house would not be used as a billet. Captain Schulze had managed to get them off the list. The captain had also said that he wanted to make Sunday lunch a regular appointment. He planned to attend Father's church and then join them for lunch. Occasionally he might bring a compatriot, he had told her father, but for the most part he imagined it would be just the three of them. It would be a time to forget the war, he had repeated several times. He had been very particular about the requirements for these Sunday lunches. He wanted to start with sherry on the terrace. He wanted white tablecloths and flowers on the table. He wanted the meal served in the dining room. He would help with the choice of menu, and this Sunday, for dessert, he wanted strawberries from the garden with cream. Finally, and on this he had been emphatic: Helene should attend the lunch as the lady of the house, and as such, be appropriately attired. Her father, embarrassed, admitted that the captain had referred to her dirty fingernails and boys' clothes. As Father spoke, he stumbled over his words. Helene sensed that there had been more, which he was holding back. She had never seen her father look so distraught, not since her mother had been ill.

'Helene, we live in very dangerous times. I do not know if this captain is –' he struggled with a word – 'honourable. I will do everything I can to protect us, but my powers are limited.' He paused. 'We were not given a *choice*. War is a terrible thing, it destroys us all in the end, in one way or another. I have heard things said in town about the captain.'

His hands were shaking.

'Although charming, he has another side which we have not yet encountered. We have to be on guard at all times.'

Nanna was so angry at the announcement of the arrangements that it fell to Helene to open up the dining room. On the previous occasion, the captain had eaten with them in the kitchen. The dining room had been used just the once since her mother's death, for Helene's wedding breakfast, before Edward and Tom left. As she opened the shutters wide, the sun streamed into the room from the large windows. She gathered up the dust sheets from the chairs. She fetched the white damask tablecloth from the linen room in the attic and spread it out, as requested. Finally, she gathered roses from the garden, and arranged the full yellow and pink blooms in a glass vase. That they should be making these preparations for a German, rather than for the return of Edward and Tom, filled her with painful confusion.

On the Sunday morning, she picked strawberries from the beds at the bottom of the lawn. They were ripe and plump with the recent rain. She whipped the cream that the captain had had delivered with the meat. When everything was ready, she waited until both Father and the captain were seated at the table before she joined them. She had cleaned her fingernails and put on a clean dress.

As she sat down, she noticed several leather boxes by her father's napkin. Her father said grace as usual and then he paused.

'Captain, I would like to trouble you with one other matter before we begin the meal.'

He opened the boxes and arranged them in front of him. They were Great War medals – his own and those of his brother, killed at Ypres. Helene had only seen them once before, when he had shown them to her and Edward.

'If this is to be a regular occurrence, I would like to make one thing clear. I fought in the Great War. I had hoped it was the war which would end all wars. Many great friends fell in the trenches – and indeed my older brother.' There was a catch in his voice and he had to stop to clear his throat. 'I always hoped that I served my country with honour and did all I could to alleviate the suffering of those fighting alongside me.

'Now, through unforeseen circumstances, our countries are again at war. Nothing grieves me more deeply than this madness of violence descending on Europe again. I cannot pretend that your presence and that of your compatriots on this dear island of ours is welcome, but I can recognize our common humanity. I am grateful for your polite request for friendship and, in that spirit, I would ask that you respect those dear to me, and the good order of our home.'

Helene glanced at the captain. She could see he was moved and he answered gravely, 'My dear Reverend, I would be honoured to be of assistance to your family in these trying times.'

He left promptly after lunch, saying he had urgent business to attend to. From the kitchen, where she was washing up, Helene heard the car and let out a deep breath of relief. The meal had been a sequence of awkward silences. The captain had tried to make conversation, but her father had been reluctant to talk. Helene hadn't said a word. But the captain, it seemed, was pleased. Her father even came into the kitchen to thank Nanna and to relay the message that the captain had enjoyed his meal and wanted to express his appreciation to those who had been responsible for its preparation. He hoped it would not be long before he was able to come again, he had told Father.

After Nanna had gone to her room for a rest, Helene crept back into the kitchen, heaped a bowl with strawberries, and, covering it with a cloth, made her way to George's cottage.

Alexei was sitting up, whittling a stick. When she put the bowl of berries on the blanket in front of him, he looked at her questioningly.

She gestured to the fruit. 'Eat, very good'.

He smiled and gingerly picked one up, examining it before putting it in his mouth.

Helene watched a smile spread across his thin face. His eyes shone. He picked another and another.

'Very good!' he cried. 'Good!'

Helene laughed at his amazed delight. He looked as if he had never eaten a strawberry before.

★

Alexei was changing. The regular food and rest were transforming the terrified boy into a young man. He sat upright and his shoulders had broadened. Colour was creeping back into his face, a pink flush beneath the freckles and pale skin, especially after he caught some sun sitting in the glasshouse in the afternoon. George had made it clear it was not safe to go into the garden, so he remained indoors. Helene had selected clothes of Edward's which would not be missed – his rugby kit, a set of cricket whites, and a thick Guernsey jumper. Alexei needed to look like an islander in case a neighbour spotted him. The cuts on one side of his face had healed, leaving a barely perceptible network of pale pink scars below his left eye. Helene cut his thatch of pale blond hair, and George lent him a razor to trim the wispy stubble on his chin. He had a pronounced limp, but Helene would hardly have recognized him as the same person. Sometimes when she watched him engrossed in his whittling, or looking at one of the illustrated children's books she had lent him, she felt a deep flush of satisfaction that she had brought this man back to life. This was her reward for the anxious, sleepless nights.

Both she and George attempted to engage him in simple conversation. He was trying to learn English, and she would find him in George's sitting room, hunched over some magazines she had found in the attic. One evening they worked out the alphabet together: matching up the sounds of the Cyrillic and the Latin alphabets as best they could. Using the pictures, he was beginning to sound out simple words such as 'tree', 'cat', 'dog' and 'horse'. He kept notes in the back of George's Bible, until Helene found an old notebook in Edward's desk for him to use.

After a couple of months, he began to help in the garden early in the mornings, when he was unlikely to be spotted. One vegetable bed was hidden from the house by shrubs, and they directed him to the tasks needed there. George showed him where the tools were kept. He didn't much like the rain – it made his bad leg ache – but whenever it was dry, he would be hoeing or looking after the hens. He began clearing out the stable regularly and watering in the glasshouse. He was becoming useful. He was a hard worker, and seemed to know a lot about growing vegetables already – he must have come from a farm, Helene concluded.

He had an endearing smile, which split his face, revealing the two broken teeth. It spread to his eyes, which crinkled with delight. Despite his suffering, to Helene's amazement, his appetite for life was undiminished. At the end of her day at school, she found herself looking forward to his bright face and boyish exuberance. She even found herself smiling at his eager gallantry around the garden as he carried her tools and insisted on pushing the wheelbarrow. Once, he tenderly dressed a bad cut on her hand.

By the autumn, he was strong enough to be in the garden most days. George and Helene no longer hid him from Nanna. They told her he was a mute boy who had come from St Saviour's to help out in exchange for lunch. Helene added that he was a bit simple, and that he would always eat in the glasshouse. Nanna was astute enough not to ask questions, and piled the hot floury potatoes onto his plate. She even gathered up some old clothes of Father's to give him. With Father, it was even easier, since he was in the house so little these days. He had been assigned a welfare job by the States, which required him to visit the sick and elderly of three parishes. Every evening, he came back on his bicycle, grey with exhaustion and pain from his bad knee, but he refused to resign his post. In the evenings, he compiled reports on the worst cases and their urgent need for medicines, a handout of food, fuel or clothing.

Alexei packed up his bed every day so that there was no evidence of his presence if they were caught unawares by a search. He had a place to hide under the floorboards in George's storeroom. Helene could see he was clever, and knew when to make himself scarce. One Saturday afternoon in late November, Captain Schulze had arrived unexpectedly. As he walked down the path to the front door, Alexei was raking up leaves for a bonfire. Helene was in the kitchen and watched, in horror, as the captain spoke to him as he passed. But when the captain arrived at the front door, he asked her where the mute boy had come from. Helene struggled to keep her voice level. He didn't pursue it any further.

It was the first time the captain had visited since the lunches in the summer. He had been posted to Alderney for a few months to replace a sick colleague, and had then been sent to France, he explained, standing in the hall. He had to sort out supply problems in Normandy. He made vague references to building equipment – concrete and steel. Helene wondered what was happening on Alderney, but knew better than to ask. She thought bitterly of the gun emplacement being built on the cliffs at Pleinmont. The captain switched the conversation swiftly to the presents he had brought for everyone. He handed her a series of packages. Brandy and a small bag of real coffee beans for her father; lipstick and stockings for Helene; and, miraculously, a box of tea and insulin for Nanna. Helene, astonished, asked him how he had known of Nanna's condition. Felicity's father, the doctor, had drawn up a list of diabetics on the island, he said. Despite her acute embarrassment at the useless gifts he had given her, Helene felt some softening towards the man. He promised more insulin when Nanna ran out. She offered to make tea with his gift, but he said he had no time; he had to return to France in the morning. Instead, Nanna and Helene sat down in the kitchen with a precious pot to savour the taste. It had been nearly two years since they had had real tea – rather than the herbal brews which Nanna concocted as a substitute.

On 31 December Father opened the brandy to mark the New Year of 1943. Father, Helene and Nanna sat together around the wireless in the evenings, taking it out from its hiding place under the floorboards in the study. Nanna was usually darning or mending by the light from a lamp that used precious diesel and a shoelace for a wick. Father and Helene sat in the shadows. Wood supplies were running low, and they used blankets to keep warm. Through the winter of 1942–3, they listened to reports of the battles in North Africa and on the Eastern Front in the Soviet Union. Across the yard in George's cottage, she knew he and Alexei were also listening to the wireless. Alexei had a mother and sisters in a village south of Moscow. Sometimes, in the morning, he would make brief comments. 'Stalingrad, bad, very bad.' They would nod in agreement and shake their heads. Every night, before she fell asleep, Helene would repeat her prayer that England would forget the islands. She knew George and other islanders worried that the Allies might try an assault, using one of the small bays in the parish. There had been a raid on Sark back in October, and two Germans had been killed. George believed it could be a prelude for a bigger attack on Guernsey, and he feared they would pick an out-of-the-way place like Torteval. A daring attack, a few dead Germans, just to make a point, he muttered as he dug over the potato patch. The reprisals could be calamitous for the island. It made Helene nervous at night. She strained her ear for unfamiliar sounds but, so far, God seemed to be listening to her prayers. On the wireless, the Home Service never mentioned the Channel Islands. It was as if they didn't exist; they had been erased from Prime Minister Churchill's war maps. It was better that way – to be forgotten.

★

Over the winter months, Alexei's English developed rapidly. He had taken to smoking George's herbal cigarettes and sometimes, when Father was busy with his paperwork and his sermon, Helene would slip across to spend the long dark evenings with Alexei and George. Alexei told them in his halting English how he had grown up with his brothers and sisters on a smallholding. They had had a herd of cows, a few horses, geese and chickens. They suffered in the 1930s during collectivization. He was only a boy of eight when they lost their land, and his younger brother died of malnutrition in the hungry years which followed.

Whenever Alexei talked about his village, his face softened. It had been a few miles from a wide river, and as a small boy he had played on its banks and in the neighbouring marshes. His older brothers taught him to fish and set traps for birds. In the 1930s they had been moved to a commune. A roughly built barn accommodated thirty families; there was little to eat except what they could find in the wild: berries and rabbits, if they were lucky. To make the place habitable for the winter was backbreaking work, and Alexei was expected to fetch water from a well every day for his mother, who cooked on an open fire. His younger sister, who was often left in Alexei's care, was frequently ill with bouts of fever and dysentery. She died in 1936. Despite the hardship, his mother managed to get him a few years of schooling in the commune.

Alexei was sixteen when Hitler invaded Russia, too young to be conscripted for the Red Army, unlike his brothers. He stayed with his parents in the commune. Some neighbours fled east beyond the Urals, but Alexei's father believed they would be no better off as refugees, so they stayed put and waited. Alexei was one of the oldest boys in the village when the Germans arrived in the autumn of 1941. A Wehrmacht detachment swung into the commune by jeep, firing their guns at random into the buildings. They used the commune's flock of geese for target practice, leaving their corpses scattered in the orchards. Alexei was hiding in an outhouse and watched the massacre with horror – white feathers and spattered blood, a senseless slaughter of precious food.

In the following weeks, the Germans pillaged everything of value. They harassed the women and two of the commune leaders were shot for protesting. Many of the teenage boys – and girls – melted away. Alexei did not know whether they had run away or been killed. The village was slowly emptying. Then the remaining boys were rounded up, along with a few of the sturdier young women, and they were loaded onto trucks. He didn't have time to say goodbye to his mother and sisters; men took him from the field where he had been working and ordered him onto the truck without even giving him time to put his boots or his jacket back on. Over the next few days, the truck moved from commune to commune, filling up with boys. Eventually, they arrived at a station, where they lined up in a long queue to wait for thin cabbage soup. It was his first food in two days. The men who were in charge were Polish and Ukrainian. They were brutal, shoving their rifles into the stomachs of any who dared protest. One boy tried to escape from the station. He was shot dead. A few German officers appeared to be in command of the huge operation. Thousands of young people waited at the station for several days. Rumours ran through the crowded camp: that they were going to Germany to work in the factories; that they would be well fed and paid; that they would be able to send money back to their families. That they were now part of Organisation Todt. Only this last detail proved to be true.

Alexei had never been on a train in his life and he was terrified of the great metal beast, juddering and clanking as it crawled across Russia and Europe. He lost all sense of time and place; the names of the stations meant nothing to him once they had left the Cyrillic alphabet behind. The boys were packed so tightly into the cattle trucks that there was no room to sit down, and they had to defecate through cracks in the wagon floor. At one station, they were let out onto the platform and hosed down with cold water, but it didn't check the proliferation of lice and fleas.

Alexei's story emerged in fragments. Helene and Alexei sometimes worked side by side in the glasshouse, sowing seeds and pricking out seedlings for the spring planting. Helene was astonished by his lack of self-pity, as if the suffering he had endured was to be expected. After recounting an instance of terrifying violence, he would revert to his cheerful self.

The Russian prisoners arrived at Granville on the Normandy coast sometime in March 1942, and were unloaded from the railway trucks onto the docks in heavy rain. They spent most of the day in the open, waiting for the ship which would take them to Guernsey. When they finally embarked, the real shock came after they left the harbour. The vast moving slab of grey water made many hysterical with fear, Alexei said. They vomited over the ship's side and wept. He was lucky – those times as a boy with his brother on the river had given him a steady stomach.

It was a slow crossing, lasting most of the night, but then Alexei saw what he described as 'a miracle'. Homesick men were all around him, and the air was full of their moaning as they scratched their sores in fitful sleep on the deck, but when the skies cleared, the dawn broke with a creeping glow of pink in the pale blue sky. A gold sun emerged on the horizon. As they came into port, he watched the whitewashed houses catch the first rays of sunshine. He said he had never seen anywhere as beautiful as St Peter Port on that spring morning. He marvelled at the flowers and the palm trees in the gardens. He thought he had died after all and arrived in heaven.

It proved a brief moment of hope. He was put to work immediately on the tunnels they were excavating in the centre of the island. The men lived in a camp of wooden huts near the site. Alexei didn't talk about this much. They had very little to eat: a scrap of bread and a bowl of weak soup for breakfast and lunch. Because he was younger, they assigned him to the wheel-barrows rather than hacking the rock. He had to push dozens of loads of rubble a day from the tunnels. If he stumbled or fell, he would feel the butt of a rifle in his back. Sometimes there were rockfalls and men were killed. He inherited a pair of boots after one died. In another, he was caught, a leg pinned by rubble, gasping for breath while his lungs choked with dust. After a long, silent hour, he was rescued and hauled out, more dead than alive. That time, one of his work gang bandaged his leg up with a scrap of shirt.

From the time he landed on Guernsey, he was determined to escape, and looked for an opportunity on every occasion. Once he slipped out of the line on a march back to the camp but was caught and brought back and beaten. He was left out for the night, tied to a post, his leg broken. Alexei managed to loosen the ties and inched under the wire fence, into a ditch. He lay in the ditch for a day, miraculously he was not found; he could even hear his work gang's voices a few hundred metres away on the other side of the fence in the morning and evening. On the second night, he crawled along the ditch and under the hedge into a copse of trees. For several days he was out in the open, moving every night across the fields, until he stumbled upon the barn at The Vicarage and took shelter there, exhausted and delirious.

When he reached the conclusion of his tale, he was overcome with emotion. He held Helene's hands, tears streaming down his cheeks. 'An angel, an angel. You save the life in me,' he said in his broken English. Embarrassed, Helene pulled her hands away, insisting that he had George to thank just as much.

★

An implausible equilibrium was established in The Vicarage. Captain Schulze came for lunch every few weeks or so. After his initial attempts to draw Helene into conversation, he gave up and talked to her father. They discussed literature and art, and sometimes he talked of his family in Berlin, his younger sister, Beatrice, and of his mother's anxiety for her sons. He had a brother fighting on the Eastern Front. As a routine part of his conversation, he would refer with admiration to the Führer and his achievements in making Germany great again. The comments made Helene flinch, but the references were not triumphant. He spoke of the Führer in the same tone as he might mention the weather. Perhaps such nods to the regime had become habitual, essential to allay suspicion, Helene thought. She found it disturbing that a man of his intelligence and authority had to be so careful – even with a country vicar and his daughter. It terrified her that a culture of fear had such a grip amongst these troops stationed so far from home.

She knew he sometimes watched her closely. She could feel his eyes on her, and when she got up to clear the plates, she was aware that his gaze followed her. He was always polite, and made a point of thanking Nanna for the food as he discreetly gave her the parcels of insulin. Helene noticed that even Nanna's implacable hostility had been tempered, and she gave the officer a brief smile.

Often he brought medicine or small gifts for Father's parishioners. She knew there were others who had come to depend on the captain's supplies. She couldn't trust him, but she did recognize there was kindness. At the same time, she was growing less anxious about Alexei. She was confident that, before long, he would be able to pass himself off as an islander, if they could find him identity papers. Then he might move to another part of the island. The terrible anxiety of the winter was beginning to ease.

One cool evening after heavy rain, in early February, she heard her father come in and slam the door. He never slammed the door. Something was wrong.

'Helene,' he shouted.

She ran to the hall, where he was standing, his coat still on, his hat in his hand. His face was wild. He was breathing heavily.

'Father, sit yourself down. You need water. What's happened?'

He grasped her hands. 'I'm on a deportation list,' he said at last. 'I am to be sent to a German internment camp.' He sat down heavily on a chair. 'As head of the household, I've been informed that . . .' He took a deep breath. 'That m-my family are expected to accompany me.'

Helene sank to her knees beside him. She put her hands on his. They were shaking. They had been assured he would not be deported. He was a Guernseyman, they had explained to the officials drawing up the lists of English-born islanders. He had been born in a Southampton hospital because his mother had had complications, but it had just been a stay of a couple of months. When there had been deportations last year of hundreds of English-born islanders, her father's name had not been included. They had believed they were safe. He was too useful, too busy and too old.

'They have drawn up a new list in retaliation for the raid on Sark. The Germans asked for people in positions of authority, people who might spread anti-German feeling. I've spoken to the States. They can't help. I saw Captain Schulze. He is trying to get our names off, but I don't think he can help. Hundreds must leave. You must prepare, Helene. Departure could be in a week. One small suitcase each is allowed.'

Helene felt sick with terror. An internment camp. She struggled to grasp the idea. Travelling hundreds of miles amongst enemies to Germany. She got to her feet. Her thoughts seemed chaotic and slow. She looked around the familiar hallway, the passage to the kitchen, and tried to imagine leaving it all behind. She forced herself to be practical. She had to work out the most useful things to take: a warm coat, her strongest shoes, the last soap, seeds. She had heard accounts of the dignified departure of deportees last autumn. She would match their bravery, she resolved. But that night, she couldn't swallow food and pushed her supper plate away. As she tried to take off her shoes before going to bed, her hands fumbled clumsily with the laces. They were still shaking.

A few days later, she was sitting in the kitchen with Nanna. She couldn't settle. She was expecting their embarkation summons any day. They were unravelling a jumper of Edward's so that Nanna could knit a new one for Helene to take with her. The island had long since run out of new wool. They heard the sound of the captain's feet on the path. She recognized his tread by now. Her father answered the front door, and she and Nanna strained their ears to catch the murmured conversation. Then they heard them move into the study and shut the door. They waited.

A few moments later, she heard her father's heavy slow step as he came across the hall to the kitchen.

'Would you join us for a moment, Helene?'

His voice was tense. Nanna looked alarmed.

Captain Schulze was seated in an armchair by the window, where the last of the afternoon light was fading on the cold spring day. He rose and bowed briefly before retaking his chair.

'Helene –' her father paused – 'the captain is offering to have your name removed from the lists if we wish. He cannot help me, but he believes he can argue that, as a married woman, you should not be counted as part of my household, and that you are also usefully employed in the school. He has gone to great lengths, I understand, to make your case. Of course, we are deeply appreciative of his help.'

Father gave Captain Schulze a brief glance. He took a deep breath. 'You have a choice, Helene: to stay here, or leave with me.'

Helene looked at her father, his face full of anxiety, and she looked at the captain watching her. Distractedly, she rubbed her hands, feeling her rough palms, squeezing the pads of her fingers, again and again, until it hurt. She was beside herself.

'Father, I can't make such a choice. It's unbearable.' Her voice cracked. It was almost a wail. She was staring at her father.

'You are old enough to make a decision – and, I think, it must be yours,' her father slowly replied, his voice wavering.

There was a long silence as they all listened to the clock in the hall and the creaks of the old house. Helene sat down, still rubbing her hands and pinching the skin. She was barely aware of the pain she was inflicting on herself.

'I can offer my advice . . . if it is needed,' her father whispered.

Captain Schulze shifted in his chair.

'Stay, Helene. You will be s-safer . . .' His voice stumbled on the word and, as he cleared his throat, he looked up at the captain. 'Safer here. Both Nanna and George can help you. The garden ensures a good diet. An internment camp is a harsh life – we know that already.' Helene felt both relief and pity. Her father wanted to protect her from the internment camp, but that meant he would be alone without her help. They had both read the bravely cheerful Red Cross messages from the deportees who left last autumn. They had guessed what they could not say.

She saw his eyes filling with tears. She had never seen him cry before. Not even at Mother's death.

'What about you? What will you eat?'

'I will manage,' he said, adding, 'you can look after Nanna. George couldn't manage without you. You will help me by looking after both of them.'

'But you?' repeated Helene, as the tears ran down her cheeks. He looked old; he had lost weight – they all had – but it had left him shrunken, his shoulders bowed.

'Helene, I want you to be safe. If you are sensible, you can be safe here. Will you remember all the things I have told you? Avoid town, avoid the roads, keep your identity papers with you at all times.' He was listing the advice that he had repeated so often. His voice trailed away into a whispered question – as much to himself as to Helene: 'Will you be safe here?'

He glanced, again, at Captain Schulze.

The man who had survived the Great War, the death of his wife, and sending his own son off to fight in another war, seemed defeated. He crumpled in Helene's arms. She found herself stroking his head as they knelt on the floor. At some point she was aware that Captain Schulze had left the darkening room.

They sat for nearly an hour, unable to move. Fear and grief had brought them closer than they had ever been.

'Helene, you are all I have left.'

'That's not true, Father. Edward is alive. I know it in my heart. He will come back,' cried Helene. 'We will be a family together again, after the war. With Tom. You must have hope. This war will end.'

The tables had turned. He leaned heavily on her as she helped him get up and led him to his study. She brought him some real tea – from their carefully guarded supply – in his favourite teacup and saucer.

He had only five days before the boat sailed.

The night before Father left, they selected seeds for him to take. Helene then sewed them into his overcoat, tucking small quantities into the hems and lining: carrots, turnips, swedes, Brussels sprouts, and a handful of small seed potatoes. She wrote out instructions. Bravely, they exchanged bleak jokes about a vegetable plot in the internment camp. Father had never had much interest in gardening; he had left it to Mother and, in recent years, to Helene.

The morning of his departure, they rose early. His suitcase was standing in the hall, ready. He blessed and prayed over Helene. Then he left, walking down the drive without looking back. She watched his receding figure, bulky with extra clothes, a pitiful figure. She squeezed the tears from her eyes with balled-up fists. She was alone. The last of the family. The house echoed with their silences.

VIII

Roz let herself into her dark flat. A note lay on the floor – a neighbour had taken in a parcel for her. Perhaps the photos had arrived. Without taking off her coat, she went across the landing and knocked. Her neighbour, an elderly lady whom she barely knew, gave her a large box, which she carried back into her flat and put down on her dining table. The stamps were Guernsey, and the address was Les Bois Verts. Impatiently, she tore the brown paper. Inside was an envelope. She ripped it open.

Dear Roz (if I may),

 Here are the copies of the photos and I hope they meet with your approval. Once again, we're sorry for having thrown out the original albums.

 There is one other matter I also wish to apologize for. When you came round the other afternoon, I almost mentioned it, but we were both a little confused that you didn't seem to know much about your family. Since then, I've heard some rumours about your mother and her tragic circumstances. I now understand much more about the difficult position you are in, so I decided – I would prefer to keep my husband out of this – to send you the enclosed. It was found along with an old-fashioned wireless under the floorboards in one of the downstairs rooms when we did the renovation work. I looked over it briefly when we found it eight years ago. I now realize that it might make difficult reading for you. I would hasten to add that we have not mentioned it to anyone in the last eight years.

With all best wishes,
Jill

At the top of the box lay a thick sheaf of photos. Roz spread them out over her dining table. They were as beautiful as she remembered. She stared closely at the one of her seventeen-year-old mother. She looked into the fresh, unwrinkled sepia face of Helene as a young woman, trying to imagine her personality and her life. What would she make of this young woman if she met her now? She glimpsed the painful youthfulness, that combination of edgy self-consciousness and boundless hope. A passing fancy led her to wonder what that smooth-faced seventeen-year-old would make of her – her daughter.

Beneath the photos was a cardboard folder. This must be what Jill had referred to in her note. Inside was a bound book, tied with a strap and buckle. The soft brown leather was tooled in gilt. It was a beautiful thing. Roz carefully undid the buckle and loosened the strap. On the inside cover, in a bolder version of her mother's handwriting than she was used to, were the words: 'Helene Le Marchant, The Vicarage, Torteval, 18 July 1937'. It was a scrapbook and diary, with cuttings from magazines, notes and letters. At the back were some sketches in pencil. Half the book was empty, and these blank pages were tightly compressed, coming apart with a slight resistance, as if they had never been opened. Roz turned the pages carefully – the cuttings were in danger of falling out as the glue had long since dried. On some pages, her mother had written notes in her large looped handwriting. The entries were sporadic, and of variable length: some no more than a sentence, others a couple of paragraphs, one or two longer ones. Roz resisted the temptation to read bits. She would look through it methodically from beginning to end. In its pages, she glimpsed how she might grasp something of how that girl became her mother. Between the cuttings from *Vogue*, postcards, cards and cinema tickets were a couple of pages of dried flowers; they held a trace of their colour still, the faded blue of forget-me-nots and the soft brown of old rose petals.

As she turned to the last pages, first one photo, then another fell out. They were small prints in black and white. Roz stared at the first one of Helene and a man sitting on a wrought-iron white bench. She recognized the tall windows on either side of the bench. It was Les Bois Verts. It seemed to be summer – a climbing rose around the windows was in bloom, heavy with white flowers. She stared at the man. He had short smooth dark hair and deep-set eyes under thick eyebrows. He was wearing a pale open-necked shirt and braces. His head was thrown back, laughing, and one hand was resting on the back of the bench behind Helene. She had turned to look at him and was smiling. Her profile was perfectly delineated against the dark foliage of the rose. Roz turned the photo over and found a date in faded ink: 'August 1943'. The handwriting was not her mother's.

The man had an air of easy confidence, leaning on the arm of the bench, with his free hand dangling, a cigarette between his fingers. He might be in his early thirties. Beside him, Helene looked very slight and young. She was wearing a thin floral dress with a low neckline, showing the line of her collarbone and long neck. Her lips were bright with lipstick and round her neck was an elegant necklace. With her dark arched eyebrows and long straight nose, she had the elegance of a ballet dancer.

Helene's expression stirred Roz. She held herself stiffly away from this man – she was wary, but Roz could also detect an eager curiosity.

Roz turned her attention to the other photo. It had been taken in the same place and perhaps at the same time, because Helene was in the same dress. But beside her on the bench was a younger, fair-haired man. On the back of this photo, Roz found the same handwriting and date, and again no names. The young man was dressed in an open-necked white shirt and white cricket trousers, as if he had just strolled off a cricket pitch. Did they still play cricket during the Occupation? Might there be a club? A list of team members? Roz was already thinking how she might put names to these faces. The man had prominent cheekbones and short blond hair. He had turned his head to look with evident affection at Helene, while she stared straight into the camera, smiling. She had tilted her chin, and had a look full of bravado and challenge. Was the other man taking this photo?

Roz put them side by side on the table in front of her. Was one of these men her father? She scrutinized their faces for familiar characteristics; could she spot the slant of an eyebrow, the shape of a jaw, the line of a nose which she might have inherited? She could see the likeness between herself and her mother very clearly – although she was not the beauty her mother had been – but neither of these men offered any obvious clue to her paternity. She stared at the photos, chewing her lip. They stirred her; they offered so much. In those black-and-white images, she could smell the roses, hear the laughter of these beautiful young people as they played with the camera. All three were clearly enjoying each other's company, whatever Roz's conjectures of rivalry and attraction. Who were these men? It was bewildering. Instead of one possible father, there were two, here in front of her. Helene's gaze into the camera seemed directed at her, all these decades later. She was still defiantly keeping her secrets, even in these improbable chance encounters on film. She seemed to be taunting her. It was exasperating.

Roz put down the photos and went into the kitchen. She pulled a bottle of white wine out of the fridge and poured herself a large glass. As she took a gulp, standing in the kitchen, it came to her. She could sense in the photos Helene's excitement, and the exhilaration of a love affair. The photos captured that moment, early on, when love can be equal parts terrifying and thrilling.

The kind of love that transforms the world into a place of wonder, but also of new dangers.

While she was sipping her wine thoughtfully at the dining room table, the phone rang. It was Antoine. They had not spoken for over a week. He had been searching the Guernsey registries. He came straight to the point, the excitement evident in his voice: a Rosamund Le Lacheur had been born in January 1946 to Helene, registered in the parish of Vale. The father and husband's name was Thomas Le Lacheur.

'This is your father. His occupation is given as soldier. The address is in Vale. Have you ever heard of him?' asked Antoine.

'No, never,' said Roz. She had her father's name. She had one piece − a big piece − of the puzzle in place. But why lose this birth certificate? Why erase Thomas in the substitute? Why lie about her date of birth and move it to April, and the place of birth to Weymouth?

'Could it be another Rosamund?' said Roz, clutching at a way to make sense of the information.

'It's unlikely, Roz. Your mother must have altered the date of birth in a later certificate. There is more,' said Antoine. Evidently reading from notes, he went on, 'Your grandfather, Eustace Le Marchant, died in 1974 in a nursing home in St Peter Port. He was born in 1880. He died at the grand age of ninety-four. And lastly, your grandmother, Elizabeth Le Marchant, died in 1936, aged thirty-seven.'

Roz sighed deeply. The diary she was holding began in 1937. It made the clippings from *Vogue* and the adverts painfully poignant. A motherless girl was trying to grow up.

'I'll keep going. I want to find out more about this Thomas Le Lacheur. I'm staying here in Guernsey for a few more days. I will call if I find anything. Meanwhile, there are a few Le Marchants listed in the telephone directory − they may be relatives of your grandfather.' Antoine sounded brisk and detached. This was work for him, Roz was reminded.

She hesitated a moment, then said, 'I found an Edith Le Lacheur in the phone book. I tried calling her when I first visited Guernsey, but she was too ill to come to the phone. You could try again. She might know something.'

Roz wandered back into the sitting room with the phone cupped to her ear. She was distracted – Antoine was explaining the opening hours of the registry office – as she stared at the two photos again. Could one of these men on the bench be Thomas?

'If he was a "soldier", it's hard to imagine how he was on the island during the Occupation, no?' Roz asked Antoine as she tried to work out the dates.

'I agree, but there were British soldiers on the island by early May 1945. The dates fit.'

Roz didn't reply. She had suddenly noticed a new detail in one of the photos. She had been too preoccupied with the faces.

'If you come across anything, let me know,' Antoine was saying.

Behind the dark-haired man, thrown over the corner of the bench, was a jacket. A uniform. She caught the glint of what could be an insignia on the collar. She felt a cold heaviness in the pit of her stomach.

'Of course,' she replied, and hung up.

In the bottom drawer of the desk in her study she thought she had a magnifying glass; an old one which Justin had used to examine pictures. Hurriedly she pulled out piles of old papers, scattering them on the floor in her search. The magnifying glass was scratched and chipped but useable. Peering through it at the photograph, she could clearly see the details of the jacket, and the corner of a peaked hat on the edge of a table beside the man. He was wearing knee-length black polished boots, which almost merged with the shadow under the bench. He was a German soldier.

★

Jim was visiting London to talk to a gallery about a new exhibition. He was staying with Roz, and, as usual, he had spread his belongings around her meticulous flat. Over dinner, she showed him the family photos that Jill had had copied.

'Beautiful women, all of them. Our grandmother, Mother, and then this mysterious woman. Who is she?'

'I don't know for sure, but I think she might have been a young aunt to Helene,' Roz replied.

'You're very like Helene's mother,' said Jim, adding softly, as if it had just dawned on him, 'Our grandmother.'

'Elizabeth, that's her name. She died in 1936, aged thirty-seven. Very sad. I can see the likeness in Ed's boys too. It's uncanny, isn't it, suddenly discovering these ancestors? Eustace was much older than her.'

'Strange how we never met him. He looks rather severe.'

'He died in 1974.'

'When did you find all this out? I thought the registry office was closed when you were there.'

'Antoine looked it up.'

'Oh God, not him,' Jim groaned. 'Why is he still involved?'

'He found my birth details, too. Registered in January 1946 in the parish of Vale – that's in the north of the island. The opposite end from The Vicarage in Torteval.'

'So she had left home.'

'And I had a father in the register: a Thomas Le Lacheur.'

Jim took a deep breath and smiled broadly.

'You've finally got there. You have your answer!' Jim slapped Roz on the back. 'Well done, girl!'

'I hope so. Thomas Le Lacheur's occupation was given as "soldier". The dates are tight. He must have reached the island in May 1945 after Liberation.'

Roz didn't want to show Jim the photos of Helene and her mysterious friends yet – not until after they had read the diary together. The photos filled her with a sense of dread. She wanted to see Jim's reactions to each new piece of information clearly. It helped her measure up her own responses. She had grown to respect Jim's more intuitive way of thinking. He sometimes saw things she was blind to.

Jim rubbed his hand over his forehead. 'It's still odd. Why move your birth date to April and to Weymouth? It would have been only a few months later that she arrived in London and met Justin. What happened to the first husband? It's not making much sense I'm afraid, Roz.'

She smiled grimly and nodded.

The following morning, after they had cleared breakfast, they sat down with the book beside them. It had lain on Roz's desk for nearly a week. Handle with care, Roz had thought, like one of the Second World War bombs discovered occasionally on London building sites. She felt apprehensive about discovering more of her mother's deception and had not been able to face reading it on her own.

Jim picked up one of the copied photos, one of Helene and the unknown woman.

'She has an arm round her and they look as if they were close. Perhaps she could still be alive? I don't understand why we only met her once – if she is the aunt,' said Jim, his forehead creased. 'Remember Meg?'

'Yes.' Roz was absorbed, looking over Jim's shoulder at the two women.

'The carer who looked after Mother in the last few months? The kind Irishwoman?'

'Yes, of course. Fair-haired? Glasses?'

'I remember you saying that Meg had seen Helene crying – that Helene was crying, or she was, I can't remember. Meg mentioned

Helene saying things towards the end which shocked her.'

'You're right. Meg said some very odd things. I should find her. She might have something. I'll call the agency, they'll have her details.'

Roz undid the buckle and strap, and opened the book. The first page was blank except for a verse written in the centre in bold, childish writing:

> *If this book should dare to roam,*
> *Box its ears and send it home.*

On the left-hand side was written: 'This book is the private property of Helene Le Marchant. You read it at your peril!!' Underneath was the date: 18 July 1937.

On the next page was a photo of a beautiful woman. They recognized it as Elizabeth, Helene's mother. Helene had drawn a single flower under the photo and written:

Dearest Mummy,
  May you rest in peace.
  I miss you.

Roz turned the page. The writing was childish and marred by the occasional ink blot and crossing out. The punctuation was erratic, but the sense clear.

18th July. I'm seventeen today. Daddy can't treat me as a child any longer. I've decided I'm going to write here every day to record my feelings and thoughts. E. can't say I never think of anything but horses. I'm going to be a different person now – much more grown up and thoughtful. This book was a present from E. Daddy has given me the new saddle I asked for. I put it on Sandy this evening for the first time after I had waxed it. We had tea on the terrace and Lily brought her new boyfriend. L. had a lovely dress on – she told me she had got the material from a shop in London. But everybody talked about politics and Germany. It got very boring.

'Another bit of the puzzle falling into place,' said Jim. 'Lily is here in the 1930s and she must be the "L" from the newspaper clipping I found. She was still in touch with Helene in the 1970s. "E" will be Edward. At least her abbreviations are easy to understand.'

The next page was a set of images cut out of a fashion magazine. Underneath the last one, Helene had written:

Cut these out when staying with Felicity. We were planning wardrobes. We even smoked one of Margaret's cigarettes. It made me feel a bit sick, but Margaret says you just have to keep trying. She says all the best film stars smoke because it shows off the natural elegance of your hands and wrists. That's true of Margaret – she's very beautiful, but I bite my nails and all the grooming of Sandy makes my hands look red.

When I'm twenty-two, I want to look like Margaret. She has a lovely curvy figure. E. says she wears nail varnish and that's cheap, but I think it looks lovely. She has a set of pearls which her fiancé gave her and she let us try them on. She says I could be very pretty but that I need more colour. She lent us her rouge and lipstick. She says I should stop wearing plaits, because it makes me look younger than I am.

The next entry was 28 August 1937, with three postcards of St Malo – one of the cathedral and two of the seafront. Underneath Helene had written:

We stayed in a nice hotel where someone played the piano all the way through dinner. Daddy said I had to dress smartly for dinner. E. and I looked like adults. We couldn't argue in a place like that, so even E. had to try to be nice to me.

A small photo showed Helene sitting with Edward and her father on the beach. Roz peered at them through her magnifying glass: Eustace Le Marchant, in a raincoat, looked rather awkward sitting on the sand, his children leaning against him, one on either side. Then there was a ticket for a concert in the hotel, and a photo of a hotel dining room. Roz wondered if the hotel still existed.

12th September. E. went back to school this morning. In a few years he will be going to England to university. I will be very lonely. I really love my little brother. I know he irritates me a bit, but he's clever and interesting and I suppose I can be a bit annoying.

The next two pages were covered in unfinished sketches of flowers and doodles along the margins of dress designs. One was of a lady in a large wide-brimmed hat. Roz was impressed; she had never known her mother had an interest in drawing. She was surprisingly good.

14th September. Daddy has been very nice to me. We drove over to see Uncle Geoffrey for dinner the other day and I was treated like a grown-up. Aunt Cordelia said all these things about if I ever needed a mother. She seems a bit old to me. She's even older than Father. But she wants me to come to her whenever I need to confide in someone. She told me I was like a daughter and she has decided to leave her set of pearls to me. (They are very nice, two strings with a pearl-studded clasp and the earrings are studs.) She let me try the necklace on and I begged her to persuade Daddy to let me have my ears pierced.

15th October. It's getting cold and there's no more swimming at the beach. I've been riding a lot. Felicity is gloating. She has a stack of letters from Harry (he's in England). Daddy was really kind to me the other day. He went into this long speech, which I didn't quite understand, about looking after myself because I didn't have a mother.

L. and Aunt Cordelia do their best, but nothing could really replace a mother. He said I looked very like Mother. Then he stopped for a long time, and I wondered whether I could get down from the table or whether I had to wait until he started again. Eventually he coughed and said Mother had been very beautiful and a lot of men had always been drawn to her, but that she also had a very beautiful soul. I think he was telling me I was beautiful and that I must keep my soul beautiful, but it was hard to know. I gave him a kiss at the end, because he had been trying so hard, and he hugged me very tight and I could hardly breathe.

29th November. There's no point putting anything in here when nothing happens. It's very dark at teatime now. Felicity has been allowed to drop piano, but Daddy says I can't. Lily says she is going to have a Christmas drinks party. She has even promised to lend me one of her dresses to wear. But I haven't got any shoes. I want a pair with proper heels and thin straps. I begged Daddy to give me 15 shillings, which would mean that, with my savings, I would be able to buy the pair I saw in St Peter Port.

The page had a cut-out magazine advert for shoes, and another for lipstick. Underneath the latter, Helene had written a comment: *I like the hairstyle.*

20th December. L.'s party was wonderful. Even E. said I looked very pretty. I wore L.'s pale yellow silk, and Daddy lent me the money for the shoes, so I felt like a princess. F. looked nice too. There were two very nice friends of E.'s there: Tom Le Lacheur is rather handsome!!! His parents bought Dieu Donne, the big house over towards St Peter's, but they have been in India and he's at school in England, so he doesn't know many people on the island. He said that we should all come over and play tennis in the summer, and his parents are building a swimming pool!!!

2nd January 1938. I haven't written for ages, and too much has happened to put it all down. We've had a lovely Christmas, better than last year, when everyone was so sad. Even Daddy looked a bit more cheerful. L., Aunt Cordelia and Uncle Geoffrey came over to us and Aunt C. helped Nanna with the food. Not sure that Aunt C. approves of L., and L. complained to me that C. never approved of her brother's marriage to Mother. She thought Mother was too young, and she was worried that she didn't have enough faith.

'Cordelia and Geoffrey must be dead by now,' said Roz. 'And I don't see how we can find their descendants. They wouldn't be Le Marchant. She will have changed her name when she married.'

'If they had any children – Helene's cousins – they might still be alive. We could track them down through the registry if we find Cordelia Le Marchant's marriage. Can't be many women with a name like that,' said Jim. He added, laughing, 'You could get your friend Antoine to do some research. Keep him busy on family history.'

Then on Boxing Day we all went to the beach for a long walk. It was a lovely sunny day. Daddy took us to the cinema to see Marlene Dietrich. She was wonderful, and so sophisticated.

Tom came up on New Year's Day. We had a great game of hide-and-seek in the orchard. I know it was a bit childish, but it was fun, and then we had tea in the nursery with Nanna making piles of toasted teacakes. There were five of us altogether and we ate TWENTY teacakes. Nanna pretended to be cross, but you could see she wasn't really.

Then followed a couple of pages of unfinished doodles, an advert for a sports car, and a postcard of Big Ben inserted into corners like those used in old photo albums. Roz slipped it out and read the back. It was signed 'Tom':

Have been staying in London with my aunt for a few days. Had a very jolly time at the theatre. Hope you are well.

14th January. E. has gone back to school and Tom is in England. It feels dull without them. The weather is horrible. L. came to see Daddy again today about the typing course. I think of Mother all the time. L. says I would be better off learning to type than moping about in the house.

31st March. It's been a long, horrible winter. I told E. how miserable I had been, and he said he will try to persuade Daddy to let me do a typing course next term, just to keep me busy. Tom is back and he and Harry are coming up tomorrow and we're going to play rounders on the lawn. Daddy has been helping make the stumps. The croquet lawn is in much better condition this year – I think Daddy said something to George about it. Poor old George has a lot of work to do. I offered to muck out Sandy's stables but he won't hear of it.

18th July. I'm eighteen today. E. gave me a set of Charlotte Brontë books and Daddy gave me a dress that L. had chosen, and L. gave me the most beautiful silk petticoat, which she had embroidered with little roses. There is still no date for her wedding. We had a birthday supper with candles, just like when Mother was alive.

Two birthday cards were stuck into the book: one from 'Aunt Lily', and one from Tom.

'An aunt, as we thought,' said Roz, 'but no surname to trace her by.'

28th July. Tom is very kind to me and talks a lot about the studies he is going to do in England at university. We sat in the orchard for ages this afternoon talking about Wuthering Heights and Hitler. He says there will be war soon. It makes me very afraid. He had come over for croquet, but it was so hot we all sat in the shade, until E. suggested we went down to the beach at Le Jaonnet.

15th September. It's been a lovely summer. E. and I sailed to Sark with Tom's family. We stayed in a hotel, and then we went on to Herm and Alderney. I'm quite a good sailor, Tom says. Now it's the beginning of term, and I start on the typing course. I can't wait. I'll go into St Peter Port on the bus every day. I will learn all sorts of useful things, like bookkeeping and administration. Daddy has very old-fashioned ideas about girls and how they must get married young, but I want to have a job and earn my own income for a while first. Then I will stop and be a wife and mother, I suppose. Tom and I talk about our future a lot. We want to travel. To places like Paris and Florence and the South of France, and even further afield – the Pyramids and the Parthenon, and Venice. We have so many plans. Maybe we will just set sail one day and get all the way to South America!

19th December. I can't believe how fast the autumn has gone. It's been so busy, what with helping Nanna in the house here and getting all my homework at college done. I see Felicity most days in town, and sometimes Annie. I've made new friends – Dotty and Alice. We have been invited to Tom's family for Christmas. There are going to be twenty of us sitting down for lunch. Lily is away in London with her fiancé – the wedding date has finally been set for June, and I am to be the flower girl. Lily has said that I may need to come to London for the dress-fitting.

12th May 1939. I leave for London tomorrow to see Lily. I will travel on my own to Weymouth and then take the train. She is staying in South Kensington, and it all sounds lovely. We will choose our dresses for the wedding, which is to be 15th June, here in Torteval, at Father's church.

18th June. It's been a wonderful few days. Lily's wedding was just how I imagined the perfect wedding would be. She looked lovely. I caught the bouquet when she threw it and then I went bright red – Tom was watching me. We danced all evening. I'll write more later but the house is still full of guests and we have a picnic on the beach planned for tomorrow – and a trip on Tom's boat next week! I actually feel happy – for the first time in ages!

The next page was edged in black and, framed in the centre, was the following:

3rd September. War has been declared. We listened to the wireless together. Father was so sad. I could see tears in his eyes. Edward wants to enlist as soon as he is old enough. Father said that would be out of the question. He says we will be safe in Guernsey from the bombing.

The following page had a card:

> *Roses are red, violets are blue*
> *Sugar is sweet and so are you.*

The card was creased but had been carefully spread out and stuck down with glue.

8th September. I am in love. Tom came and we went to sit at the end of the orchard and he kissed me – on the lips. My first kiss!! It felt very lovely, and he put his arm round me. We ended up lying there in the long grass, where we were quite hidden all afternoon. We kissed several times. Tom says he wants to marry me when we are older. I said we are very young and should wait and see, but we've promised to write to each other when he goes to university, and we'll see each other at Christmas. Everyone talks about the war.

On the following few pages were recipes for biscuits cut out from a newspaper, and the announcement of a new film in St Peter Port.

1st November. Every evening we sit around the wireless to listen to the news. Daddy barely speaks. E. is planning to join the navy as soon as he has finished school – he is in the cadets and they've told him he would probably do his training in Portsmouth. Or he says he might join military intelligence and become a spy, because of his French. Tom writes to me every week. He says he is going to join the army. He hopes he will come back before he enlists.

'More coffee?' Roz got up to stretch and stood staring out of the window across the park. She was smiling. 'This Tom must be my father, Jim. We are making headway. Things are starting to make sense. Tom presumably got back from the war in time to conceive me. They sound like they were teenage sweethearts.'

Relieved, she hummed as she headed to the kitchen with the mugs. After a moment, she came back.

'The person I want to find is Lily.' She was standing at the doorway, a spoon in her hand. 'She would have known the whole story. Say she was ten years older than Helene – that would mean she is in her eighties. We just need a surname.'

'Or this Felicity. She's another person who would know the story. How Helene married Tom, and then how he managed to get back so quickly in 1945. How they set up house in Vale after the war, and why she left Guernsey. Perhaps even why she got you a new birth certificate.'

'Maybe we shouldn't read too much into the birth certificates. Justin said they got a new certificate much later. All that kind of documentation must have been very muddled in the war,' said Roz as she came back with the coffee.

'I've just remembered something,' mused Jim. 'Remember how good Mother was at singing?'

'Yes.' Roz smiled. 'She always knew all the words of hymns at weddings and carol concerts. She didn't need to look at the hymn books. I suppose that was the vicarage background.'

'About eight years ago, when Anaïs was born, Mother came to France to visit us with Justin. It was a lovely few days and I have a memory of Mother holding Anaïs in her arms – she was very good with my babies. She was sitting on the bench outside the house, by the river. She was singing to her. I was doing the washing-up, but I could hear her through the open window. I didn't catch all the words, but I remember the chorus was something about "home of my childhood, my heart longs for thee . . . island of beauty . . ." It was very pretty and I asked her what the song was. She laughed and said it was some-thing she'd learned as a girl, and I pressed her to sing it again. I jotted a few words of it down on a shopping list at the time. I meant to look it up, but forgot. It had a line something like, "Thy voice calls me . . . in waking or sleep", and then a bit about "coming home".'

Jim was looking wistful. 'I liked that side of her – the softness you could glimpse sometimes. Perhaps it was a Guernsey song.'

Roz was thoughtful. She was wondering who on Guernsey would know. Mike seemed an approachable, kindly man. She scribbled a note of Jim's words; it didn't give Mike a lot to go on.

'There is such a vivid sense of Helene,' said Jim. 'It's as if she is in the room with us. She feels so young – less than half the age we are now. And so many names we know nothing about – Margaret, Felicity, and so forth. We must be able to find someone.'

'If Edward was killed in 1944 – as mother always said – then he was just twenty-two when he died,' Roz said, finishing her coffee. 'You know the most surprising thing of all?' She looked at him, her eyebrows arched, as she flicked through the pages.

'Mother was good at drawing – really good. With a bit of encouragement and support, she could have gone to art school.'

'I suppose you're right. Perhaps that's where I get it from.
In those days, I don't imagine a vicar's daughter went to art
school.'

Roz looked at some of the drawings at the back of the book
– sketches of the Guernsey coastline. On the inside of the
back cover was a neat pocket that she hadn't noticed before. She
pulled out a collection of notes. The first was a small card
decorated with roses:

*My dearest H., I will be thinking of you, always. This is a little
something to remember me by. Wear them often, with fondest
love, T.*

'Love letters.'

'T. must be Tom,' Roz said.

The second was on tissue-thin paper.

*My sweet Helene, you must believe me. I love you in a way I
have never loved another woman. I will wait to hear word. Until
then, I am dreaming of you every moment and longing for when
we will be together again. With all my love.*

There was no signature.

'The handwriting is different from the first,' said Roz.

'Here's a third.' Jim leant down to pick up a scrap of paper
which had fallen out as Roz unfolded the second letter. He read
it out.

*H., I understand your concerns. I have many of my own. I would
never want to put you in any danger, but you cannot argue with
love. When I was away, I tried to accept what you told me. But I*

*can't. We are destined to be together. I believe that now. I will
keep you safe, I promise. In haste.*

Again, it was unsigned. Roz was fiddling with a paperweight.
They exchanged a glance which both of them understood: it was
not as straightforward as Roz had been hoping. Tom may have
been her father, but there was someone else.

'There is another thing to show you, Jim,' Roz said slowly.
She had been bracing herself for this.

She took an envelope out of her desk and pulled out the two
small black-and-white photos. She put them down on the table.
'They fell out of the scrapbook.'

Jim picked up first one, then the other, and looked at them.

'She's in love,' he said slowly. He looked up at Roz and back
at the photos. He was comparing them with Roz.

'One of them might be Thomas. I can't see a likeness to you in
either of them.'

'No, it can't be Thomas. If this book is right, he joined up in
1940. But the date on the back is August 1943, in Guernsey.'

Roz was waiting. Jim had picked up the magnifying glass to
examine the photos.

'He's a German soldier,' said Jim, and there was a slight whistle
between his teeth as he breathed out. He looked up at her.

'The other one in those cricket whites looks like an English
public school boy.'

'So which one is she in love with?' asked Roz.

Jim didn't reply. He had turned the photos over and put the
notes alongside them. He was comparing the handwriting.

'It's the same. Whoever dated these photos was the lover of the
unsigned notes.'

'"You cannot argue with love",' quoted Roz. She was chewing
her bottom lip. Jim knew the habit. 'It couldn't have been the
German,' she said firmly. She stood up and paced the room. 'I

absolutely refuse to believe it. Mother hated Germans. So much so, it was embarrassing. A German friend from university who came to visit once – Mother was icy.'

Jim nodded in agreement. 'I remember a fierce argument she and Justin once had about Germany. She didn't normally show much interest in politics, but on this occasion, she said Germany could never be trusted.'

They turned back to the book.

28th March 1940. E.'s papers arrived today. He's been accepted for officer training in the navy. He's quite excited, I think, but a little frightened. I have a horrible feeling, but Edward says to stop being silly and that he will be back for leave to see us. He bought me the entire collection of Dickens as a leaving present – he emptied his savings account to do it. He should be leaving in a few weeks. L. has come back to see me – her husband has gone on a tour for several months. She says she will stay for the summer. She says she's a Guernsey girl – she misses the island!

Tom is leaving with E. He says he'll be able to sign up more quickly on the mainland. Tom wants us to get married before he goes. Daddy has said, if we are serious, he can speed up the banns for this kind of emergency. It may mean we marry only a few days before Tom leaves. I want to marry him and I've told him that, if we are separated, I will wait for him. We are in love. We walked along the cliffs yesterday and talked of how we will have lots of children after all our travels. Tom wants to work in London, so we decided we will have a big house in the country and he can travel on the train every day. I want a big garden and lots of horses. We were so happy. We sat on the cliffs with the sea below, laughing and talking of how we will one day be old and bent and surrounded by grandchildren. We kissed again. We had our pictures taken together in town the other day. On the cliffs, he told me that he'll put the photo in his breast pocket. If a bullet goes in his heart, it will have to go through the photo first. I will protect him, he said. I hope so. He has the loveliest fair hair, and it curls when it's been raining. I teased him about his curls and he let me cut one for a keepsake. Here is the wrapper from the chocolate we ate on the walk.

Glued into the book was a chocolate paper and on the back Tom had written:

Pledged on this day, 27th March 1940, Tom and Helene will have lots of children and will love each other forever.

Next to it was a curl stuck with glue which had gone a dark brown. The glue had made the paper wrinkle.

One of the following pages was delicately painted with a border of roses and violets in watercolour. In the centre were the elaborately entwined initials of H. Le M. and T. Le L., and the date, 20 April 1940.

The diary resumed.

29th April 1940. Tom and Edward left yesterday on the boat. I have been very upset, crying in my room. Tom and I were married nine days ago. It was a beautiful day which I will never forget. The service in the morning followed by a wedding breakfast in the dining room, and afterwards Tom and I went in his father's car to Cobo, to stay in a hotel. We were very happy and for a few days we forgot the war. We talked and ate and slept and walked, and there was no one to interrupt us. I might even be pregnant!! Yes, IT happened. If there is a baby, I will move to England to be near Tom's training camp – we agreed that. I can't have a baby without him being near. If it's a boy, we agreed it will be called after him; if it's a girl, we will call her Elizabeth Lily. It was so exciting to think that Tom and I are now married and will have our own family. I like the idea of a baby all our own.

But it came to an end so quickly. When we got home, Tom had to pack and those last few days flew by. Now he has gone. We clung to each other so tightly on the quayside. Then I waved them off. I will miss them both so much. I don't believe in prayers, but I prayed. I prayed God would keep them safe.

Then a few blank pages and a page of pencilled lists: leeks 3L; potatoes 10L; carrots 5L, with dates from the spring of 1940.

'It must be some kind of code for planting,' commented Roz.

10th June 1940. The Germans have conquered France. I might have to leave for England, and abandon Sandy. Or the Germans might arrive. Daddy seems confused these days. Perhaps he is in shock; he keeps talking about 1916 and his time in the Great War. He is sixty. I have to look after Daddy and poor old Nanna. E. wrote yesterday from his training camp to say that he will be assigned to a ship soon and might even go to the Far East; his French won't be much use there. I worry now that we might not get to see him before he goes.

15th June. Lots of people are leaving for England. There are long queues in St Peter Port, with people waiting to get on the boats. L. said you are more likely to be bombed going across the Channel than staying put. Daddy says the States have decided that all officials have to set an example and remain. He will stay – no German will scare him from his home, he says, and he cannot desert his parishioners. I can't leave Sandy, but I don't want to be here with the Germans.

16th June L. announced she is going back to Plymouth, and she says I can go with her. I would really like to go, but I'm very worried about Daddy, Nanna and Sandy. I think they need me. I think I will have to stay with Daddy.

20th June. It's been an awful time. I decided last week to go with L., but when I got down to the harbour, it was so crowded I couldn't get through to the gangway. I could see Lily on the deck, frantically trying to get them to let me on, but there were lots of families separated in the rush, and the ship's crew were telling people to stand back and wait for the next boat, and that it would be dangerous to take any more passengers. It was horrible – people were pushing and shoving. I was shouting to Lily that I would get the next boat, but I don't know if she heard me. Down at the harbour they say there are no more boats for the time being. It is too dangerous. We still don't know if Lily is safe – the post is not getting through every day.

Felicity's father said the island would need doctors, so he wouldn't leave, and her mother wouldn't go without him, so in the end all the family decided to stay. But Tom's parents and sisters have gone. The problem will be food. No one knows how we will find food once shipping from England stops. Father's church looked empty on Sunday because so many have left. It is strange, with everything at home like it has always been.

29th June. The Germans bombed St Peter Port yesterday. I'd gone into town to get some shopping. I was nearly killed. It was terrifying.

15th August. After all the rush and panic of June, it's been very quiet. Lots of the houses round here are empty. We've seen Germans in the lane twice. Daddy and I agreed that I wouldn't go to St Peter Port any more. Either he or George will do the shopping. Occasionally German soldiers go along the main road in their trucks, singing their horrible songs, but you can hear them coming, so there is time to hide.

The following pages included a few drawings and some loose dried flowers. Then a series of Red Cross postcards with typed messages, each stuck onto a different page. Around them, Helene had sketched a design of flowers:

12th November 1940. All fine. Missing you all very much. Learning lots. Edward.

15th December 1940. Thinking of you all every day. Am safely settled in Sidmouth, Love Lily.

21st December 1940. Hoping this reaches you, dear wife. Will love you always. Tom.

The next few pages were long lists of vegetables. Some of the numbers seemed to indicate yields. Roz put the book down.

Jim stood up and stretched, arching his back. 'What on earth happened to make her leave all that behind? Why did she break off all contact with her father?'

'Or did she? Perhaps she visited him but never took us.'

'Why did we never meet or hear of him, when on these pages she is devoted to him? I don't recognize this version of Mother. It's a very odd business,' he muttered.

'Well, we have some answers,' said Roz, brightening. 'At least I know a little about the marriage with my father.'

'But we don't know anything about these two men in the photos in 1943,' Jim pointed out. 'We must be able to trace at least some of the names she mentioned. Put adverts in local papers. Ask around. That sort of thing.'

'You sound interested, Jim. I thought you said you were too busy.' She smiled at him.

'Well, reading something like that gets you interested . . . Do you think we should tell Edward?'

'Who knows?' Roz shrugged her shoulders. 'He was pretty clear before. When we have something more concrete, we can talk to him. Let's see if we find any of these people – Lily, Cordelia, Felicity, and, above all, Tom. He might still be alive.'

IX

Helene was on the landing, folding and sorting laundry, when she heard the car coming down the lane. The only person who drove to the house was the captain. She stood at the landing window and watched him get out of the car and walk up to the front door. He looked harassed. That infuriating air of arrogance had given way to anxiety. The bell rang urgently. She reluctantly made her way downstairs. This would be her first conversation with him since Father had left. They had not spoken more than a brief exchange of pleasantries at the lunches.

He was standing on the doorstep, his hat in his hands.

'I did everything I could. I am sorry. I kept trying to get his name off the lists too.'

Helene could see that he was genuinely upset.

'Your father is a good man. I saw him at the harbour last week. He was waiting to embark, and I was on my way to Alderney. When I arrived back in Guernsey, I came straight here. I wanted to offer you my apologies.'

Taken aback by his intensity, she said nothing.

'I promised him that no harm would come to you. He asked me several times to look after you and your housekeeper, Nanna, and I will keep that promise. If there is anything you need, you must come to me.'

Helene murmured that it would not be necessary, but she knew it was a lie. Nanna could not survive without the medicines he brought.

As if reading her mind, he continued, 'I will bring the medicines as before.'

She whispered a brief thank you and glanced up at him. He seemed to be deeply distressed. Her surprise must have been evident.

'I'm sorry. Truly sorry –' he grabbed her hand; there was none of his usual poise – 'sorry for what my country has inflicted on you. It is the madness of war. You should never have had to make the choice between your father and your home. I saw that – the other day. Your poor father. You are good and courageous people, and . . . I am . . . ashamed.'

Helene pulled her hand away, but she looked at him, astonished. His eyes were wet and a tear escaped which he brushed angrily away with his hand.

'I am ashamed to be . . . German. It has been a time of great crisis for me. No, no, I don't expect your pity. We none of us can ever expect pity, no matter what our suffering will be. But I see now, clearly, that the war will end and Germany will pay a terrible price. Too many of us were deluded by brutal fools, and they will take us all down with them.'

Helene was speechless.

'There is little I can do – a few gestures of kindness here or there, but I am as guilty as the next man. We are all implicated.'

He was breathing heavily, trying to regain his composure. Helene stood there awkwardly.

'One thing is clear to me. I imposed myself on your family. I have enjoyed the times I spent here more than you can ever know – or understand. They were a reminder of the sanity that might one day return: of the decency of ordinary people's lives. But they should not have been imposed on you. I have taken advantage of you and your father and . . . want to apologize.'

He paused and took a breath and looked straight at Helene.

'I want to give you the choice as to whether you offer any

more hospitality. I will accept your decision — whatever it is — without any consequences for you, or those you love. You have a choice.'

Helene stepped back. She looked down; she couldn't bear the searching intensity of his eyes. She did not understand him, nor the implications of the choice he was offering her. He was making her very nervous.

'Must I make it now? Right now?' asked Helene.

He placed a hand on her arm. 'No, you decide, in your own time.'

He smiled at her tentatively, and she reciprocated briefly. She saw relief flood across his face. It surprised her. She held his gaze for a moment. He was not a bad man, she realized. He nodded his head and turned back to the car. After she had shut the front door, she leaned against it, and found herself sobbing uncontrollably. She heard the engine start up outside and the sound of the wheels on the lane. He had gone.

★

Over the next few days, she was on edge. She snapped at Nanna, and then burst into tears, full of apologies. Nanna sat her down by the stove, and wiped her tears with her apron. She knew more than she let on. She quietly stroked Helene's hair for a few moments while the tears rolled down her cheeks.

The anxiety and fear continued; Helene could feel it in her body — a dull ache in the muscles of her heart, which accompanied her every moment of the day and night. She woke often at night, and then tossed this way and that, trying to sleep. Sometimes she got up and paced the hall, trying to calm the fears that crowded her mind. Once, she crept into the garden and sat on the bench, her dressing gown and an extra blanket tightly wrapped around her in the chill air. She watched ragged clouds being blown across the dark sky. They caught the gleam of moonlight. She thought about the night of a party before the war, when they had filled this garden with their laughter – Tom and Edward and Felicity – as they played games in the thick shadows cast by the moon until Father had finally called them in and sent Tom home. She and Felicity had stayed up late in her room, discussing love and the futures they saw for themselves.

She turned over in her mind the captain's extraordinary outburst. She tried to imagine what kind of a man he was. Four times he had stepped in to help her, since she had first encountered him on the cliffs eighteen months before, either choosing to overlook the fact that she had flouted regulations, or protecting her from some aspect of the Occupation. Why? she asked herself. She knew what Father had feared, but the captain's behaviour towards her had been polite and distant. He watched her, and that was awkward, but apart from the time when he gave her a lily after the first Sunday lunch, there had been no other advances, and no grounds for Father's anxiety. They depended on him for Nanna's medicine. The insulin sent by the Red Cross to the island was not enough for all those who needed it.

But this did not mean he could be trusted. He was German. The choice she had to make was impossible. Say no and they might lose his help – and who knew what circumstances they might face in the future? Say yes and face the weekly ordeal of a lunch with stilted conversation and the fear that one day he could discover the truth about Alexei.

Over the next couple of days, another aspect of her predicament became clearer to her. His astonishing outburst had shifted her perception of him. She had seen a side of him full of confusion and anxiety – in short, feelings which she herself knew well. She might not understand this puzzling man, but she had seen beyond the poise and arrogance to someone as uncertain as herself. She became curious about him. Was he married? Did he have children? He had never referred to a wife, but there must at least be a girlfriend back in Berlin. To her consternation, she found her mind frequently returning to the thought of him.

She tried to keep that realization at bay. Every night, before she slept, she looked at the photo of Tom which she kept by her bed. Tom, who had been gone nearly three years. She felt a different person from the girl who had married him. She had no idea where he was or what had happened to him; the last Red Cross message had been more than two years ago. She remembered their kisses in the hotel in Cobo and the hopes in the weeks that followed that she might be pregnant. She had dreamed of joining him in England. But there was no baby, and the few nights together had been quickly followed by almost three years of absence and longing. It would be years before she heard of him again, let alone saw him. He could have fallen in love with someone in London on leave. She felt dread at the thought that he could be dead.

One night, she dreamed that Schulze was amongst the guests at Lily's wedding. She dreamed that she was dancing with him, and that people were watching them, admiring the handsome couple. She woke with a start in the morning as the alarm clock went off, and was horrified at the memory of the dream: she had enjoyed dancing with him, she had *liked* the feel of his hand on her back, pressing her body against his. She had felt desire. All that day while she was at school with the children, she burned with shame. She wished there was someone in whom she could confide.

She knew the captain was expecting an answer from her. He could arrive at any time. She started at any sound that could be a car. She warned Alexei to keep well away from the front of the house, and to stay alert at all times – the less the captain saw of him the better. Alexei tried to reassure her, but no matter how careful he was, they both knew the risks; he was putting them in too much danger. He told her he would try to find somewhere else to live, and Helene knew it was necessary but hated the thought of it. She would miss his help and steady affection.

★

After a week, a parcel arrived, with a note from Schulze. He said that while he was waiting for her decision, he wanted them to continue to benefit from his gifts of food. He also asked if he could visit her. He had something he urgently needed to discuss with her, a matter of great importance to the household's safety. The delivery boy had been instructed to wait for a reply. Helene stood in the hall with the note in her hand, uncertain how to respond – invite him for lunch, as he seemed to be suggesting, or eat the food without him and agree to a visit another time? She had no way of knowing how significant this choice might be. Perhaps the outburst of shame had been a passing whim – the product of overwrought nerves – which he would disown. She couldn't read him: the arrogance, the entitlement, the presents, the kindness to Nanna. His character seemed inconsistent, which made it difficult to predict his behaviour. She resolved to err on the side of caution. She would follow the example of her father, and offer a meticulous but formal hospitality. She sent a reply inviting him for lunch. She then went through to the kitchen to explain that the captain was coming as usual. Nanna was furious.

'Who is going to eat with him in the dining room?' Nanna demanded, as she untied the parcel Helene had put on the kitchen table. 'This is not right. Not for a young married woman.' She compressed her lips; she was worried.

Helene put her hand on Nanna's arm.

'What else can I do?'

There was silence. Nanna shrugged her shoulders and turned away. They each knew what the other was thinking: Nanna needed the insulin and other medicines.

'The lunch will be as swift as possible. I will conduct it with the same dignity as Father. The captain says he has something he needs to discuss with me.'

On the Sunday, Helene dressed with care. She wore a dress of Lily's and dabbed her lips lightly with lipstick. She planned to be as reserved as possible and, for that, she needed to look grown up.

He arrived at the usual time. It was a day of chilly May sunshine, but he asked if he could sit in the garden for a while with a book from her father's study. She brought his sherry on a tray and left him there, busying herself in the kitchen until it was time for lunch. Helene had taken over most of the cooking from Nanna, who tired easily these days. They were all suffering from the limited diet. They had plenty of potatoes and a few eggs, but no meat, cheese or fish. Most of the milk and butter on the island was bought by the Germans. The stock Helene would make from the captain's joint would flavour meals for over a week.

She had laid the table in the dining room, but this time there were only two settings, one at either end of the long table. She would sit in her father's place.

Schulze rose from his seat when she came into the dining room. Nanna brought in another dish and made her disapproval evident, moving the plates and serving dishes with uncharacteristic clumsiness. Helene wondered if he noticed, and if he did, whether he minded.

Nanna retreated to the kitchen. Except for the sounds of cutlery and crockery, they ate in silence. Schulze began his meal with relish, but Helene found it hard to eat, cutting the meat into small portions. Her mouth was dry.

'So how long has the Russian boy been here?' he asked suddenly.

Stunned, she stared at him.

'I noticed a while ago,' he resumed calmly, as if he were talking about the weather, 'but I wasn't sure that your father knew. I presumed you did. I've seen you in the garden together. Is he sensible? Can you trust him to be careful?'

Helene's mind was racing with the fabrications she could invent to explain Alexei's presence, but there was a disconnect between these thoughts and her voice. She couldn't trust herself to say a word. Her voice would reveal her fear.

'I wouldn't want him to invite any of his compatriots to join him here. That would make it even more dangerous. Have you explained that to him?'

Helene stared at her plate.

'I gather that there are escaped labourers in various parts of the island. They know each other. This was why I was anxious to see you. If one is captured and reveals the Russian here, there will be very serious consequences. I presume I don't need to explain that?'

Helene nodded.

'You must eat. You don't want it to go cold,' he urged, noticing that most of Helene's food was still on her plate, uneaten.

They didn't speak again of Alexei. They finished the meal in silence and Helene rose to prepare the coffee Schulze had brought from Paris. He had always taken coffee with Father in his study or, if the weather was fine, out on the terrace. There was a stiff breeze, but he wanted his coffee outside with a small glass of cognac. Helene brought the tray out and placed it on the table. As she turned to leave he took hold of her arm.

'I won't betray you. You are safe with me. Please believe me.' Then, more gently, he added, almost pleading, 'Please join me. Sit here a while.'

Slowly she sat down on the bench next to him. She hadn't set two cups on the tray, but Schulze handed her the cup with the coffee he had poured. 'It's good, try it.'

She refused.

'I bought it in a shop in Paris that I always used to visit before the war. It has the best coffee. Have you visited Paris?'

Helene shook her head.

'It is the most elegant of Europe's beautiful cities. I used to love sitting in the cafés to watch the people pass. There is much life and love on the streets. I visited quite often before the war, and always I would look for presents to take back for my mother and sister – a scarf, a hat, a length of material or a piece of jewellery.'

He smiled at the memory. Helene glanced at him. He was looking across the lawn at the sea again.

'I would like one day to visit Paris,' she said. 'I used to dream of it when I was younger.'

The captain turned to face her. It was the first time she had volunteered information in a conversation with him.

'I'm sure that dream will come true,' he said. 'I think you would like it. You have visited London?'

'Once – for a few days before my aunt's wedding in 1939. It was wonderful. Apart from that, I've had holidays in St Malo and Rennes, but no further. Never Paris.'

'A country girl,' he said, smiling, and Helene nodded.

He changed the subject suddenly.

'I miss my sister Beatrice. I had two letters from her this week – the first time I have heard from home in several months. The mail from Berlin is very uncertain. One of the letters was sent before Christmas. She is a little older than you. She is clever and wants to be an artist. She tells me that life in Berlin now is very hard. There are many raids and they have to spend the nights in the shelter – we have a way of writing this which can get through the censors.'

'Does Beatrice speak English also?'

'Yes, but not well. I was the only one in my family to study in England after *Gymnasium*. My grandmother came to Germany to marry my grandfather in the last century, and lived in Berlin for over forty years. She used to travel back to visit family and friends. Even after the war, she visited England. She died in 1935. I'm glad she missed all this – she suffered one war, another would have killed her.'

Helene watched him as he sipped the coffee.

'For my family, this war has been very difficult. My father is clever – he joined the Party early. He knew it was the way to protect his business and the family, but my mother was very angry. It is dangerous to talk of these things with anyone – even you – but my family has been pulled apart, limb from limb. We were always both German and English, and both were equally important to us. You see me as German – but it is only half of me. Like many others – many of my friends in Berlin – we have buried ourselves alive, you could say. We have lived a lie now for so long that we forget where the lying starts or ends. That is part of why I have enjoyed coming here: it reminds me that the lies are lies. It is always painful to return to my compatriots, but better that pain than to forget that we breathe untruth every minute of the day. When it is all over, we will need to dismantle the lies and speak honestly and courageously again.'

He turned to face Helene. She looked away quickly. There was a question in his eyes.

'I have not been courageous, I will admit. I have seen too many courageous people killed. Even the smallest acts of courage earn the same brutal response. We had a housemaid – her fiancé was a communist, and she gave him a place to sleep. She disappeared. Her mother came to tell us, beside herself with grief. My city has been destroyed by fear. Every neighbour is watchful, every friendship has become a place of suspicion. Here, in this garden, for an hour or so, I remember the time before the war, before the National Socialists – it reminds me of the holidays I had in Devon with my grandmother and my great-aunt. I know it is absurd escapism, but it reminds me of what it feels like to live without fear and to trust strangers – as I trusted your father and you. Honest people with good, even courageous, intentions.'

Helene put the coffee cup back on the tray. She was struggling to assimilate what he was telling her. She could see a vulnerability in his face which was in sharp contrast to the impression he had made on her in the past.

As she stood up to take the tray away, he held her arm.

'You have enough information to have me executed for treason. That's how my country now works. You have no reason to fear me. Fear should have no part in our relationship.'

She nodded. She didn't know whether it was in agreement. She couldn't say. She took the tray back to the kitchen and heard him leave. She had not given an answer to his question about future visits, and he had not asked for one.

★

Helene's dilemma preyed on her mind over the next few days. Despite Schulze's revelations, she was still frightened of him. They only added to the sense of his contradictory character. He had been reckless. She didn't need to know all the things he had told her. That was disturbing, but even worse was the realization that she *wanted* to know him. At night, she guiltily reasoned with herself: he was a distraction from the tedium and loneliness; what harm was an occasional meal and some conversation? They all benefited from the food he brought – Nanna, George and Alexei. Besides, their safety rested in his hands – surely it was only wise to ensure the relationship was cordial? She was ashamed to confess this bewildering confusion to Felicity or even Alexei. She said nothing to anyone as she swung back and forth in her mind, between pragmatism and recognition of the attraction she felt for him. She wanted to hear more of Paris and Berlin. His words were an echo of the glamour of the *Vogue* magazines which she and Felicity had read together before the war. She had once imagined a future life with Tom in a city, attending parties and balls, visiting arcades of shops and arranging meetings in cafés, perhaps in London. A life like Mother had described when she had lived in London for a few months before she married Father.

After more than a month of fruitless deliberations, a new worry surfaced. There had been no word from the captain. She was alarmed at the possibility that he was offended by her lack of a response. She was anxious on Nanna's account. Her supply of medicines was running low. She resolved on a course of action and carefully wrote a short note inviting him to lunch the following Sunday.

A few days later, she was in the garden. She had been picking the first of the summer's fruit with Alexei, and bowls of strawberries and gooseberries were lined up on the table on the terrace, ready to be preserved. There was no sugar for jam but the bottled fruit would be invaluable through the winter. They had paused for a rest and had sat down to nibble some of the fruit while they talked.

Alexei saw Schulze first as he came round the corner of the house past the magnolia tree. Helene had her back to him and continued talking, unaware, until she heard his voice. She spun round.

He greeted them, and then pulled up another chair. He took off his cap and placed it beside the bowls of fruit. He took a few strawberries, and popped one in his mouth as he leaned back to enjoy the sun.

'Delicious. Just as I remember them. My grandmother loved these English berries.'

He talked easily, as if they were friends at a tea party.

'I'm sorry if I have disturbed you,' he said, turning to Helene. 'On getting your note, I decided to bring the lunch supplies, and a few other things, since I happened to be passing. I am most grateful for the invitation and accept with pleasure.'

He bowed his head to Helene before turning to Alexei.

'We haven't been introduced before, I believe?' he said, smiling. He reached out to shake Alexei's hand. Helene watched, astonished. Alexei looked uncertain and fearful. He hesitated, but, finally, he shook the captain's hand. He was sitting on the edge of his seat, ready to get to his feet. He looked questioningly at Helene.

Helene struggled to speak. Her voice sounded thin and high-pitched.

'It's all right,' she assured Alexei. 'He has promised me —' she looked up at the captain — 'that no harm will come to us . . . any of us.'

Alexei's eyes widened in amazement as he looked from Helene to the captain and back again.

'Your English is good, but there were telltale signs — the age, the limp, the scar. I have given my word — as Helene says. But I have also asked her to warn you to keep well away from other escapees. No one can know where you are; I presume you understand that?'

Alexei nodded.

There was an awkward silence as the captain waited. He clearly hoped Alexei would leave. Finally, Helene offered tea and he accepted, suggesting the tea he had brought as a present after his last visit to Paris. As she got up, she looked at Alexei.

'Perhaps you could help me?' she asked him.

'In a moment, perhaps. I'd like to talk to him,' Schulze said firmly.

Helene left them reluctantly. As she headed to the kitchen, she could hear the captain's confident voice and Alexei's quiet replies.

When she returned with the tray, they were still in conversation. It seemed Schulze knew a city, Kursk, near to where

Alexei had been born. Schulze had travelled in Russia and Ukraine for his father's business, he explained as Helene slowly poured the tea. Alexei began to ask the captain questions about his home in Berlin and his life before the war. Schulze didn't seem perturbed by the strangeness of the situation, but Helene could barely believe what was unfolding in front of her, as the two men exchanged comments and questions about the Europe they knew – places in Russia and Ukraine which Helene had never heard of.

'I love the music in Berlin. I miss it. I went to concerts most weekends – Beethoven, Chopin – and I also loved the jazz cafés. When I am in Paris, I try to go to some performances of the opera. I am not used to the quiet life of your island,' Schulze said, turning to Helene with a smile. 'I grew up in a city, one of the world's great cities – Berlin.'

After half an hour of conversation, Alexei rose to his feet and excused himself; he needed to get back to work in the green-house.

Helene turned to the captain. 'I have something to say.'

She sounded clipped and faintly absurd. She drew herself up and continued with the careful emphasis she had planned.

'Over the last few weeks I have given much thought to the propriety of your visits. I am a married woman and I ask you to respect that fact. We live in very dangerous times and fate has thrown us into circumstances which are not of our choosing. I would like to think that a friendship – of sorts – is possible, but you must understand that my first loyalty must always be to my husband.'

She came to the end of her speech and, to her intense embarrassment, she had flushed a deep red.

'Thank you,' he said simply. 'I am grateful.'

The lunches would resume as before, they agreed. After finishing his tea, the captain stood up. 'One more thing: please call me Heinrich. I would like to be known as someone with a name, not just an army rank.'

Helene nodded reluctantly. He smiled at her.

'I've left parcels by the front door – I brought butter and even some sugar,' he said as he left.

That evening as Helene and Alexei cleaned and sorted tools in the greenhouse, they shared their astonishment at the risk the captain was taking.

'Maybe he hates the war too. Like us,' reflected Alexei. 'I thought all Germans were evil. But perhaps I am wrong? But I don't understand him. What does he want? Why protect us?'

Helene shrugged her shoulders. 'I don't know.'

They continued working in silence for a while before Alexei said softly, 'I don't like the way he looks at you.'

Helene felt her cheeks burning with embarrassment.

'You must be very careful. For now he is our friend. Don't make him angry.'

She nodded.

'If he is in danger, or angry about something – then he could change. For now, he likes it here,' said Alexei. He was looking at her. He could see her fear. He touched her arm. 'Don't be afraid, Helene – fear makes no difference to fate in the end. It is only a poison in the time you have. I have known so much fear in my life. I don't want to live in fear any more. That's a choice we still have. They cannot take that from me.'

They carried the last bowls of fruit into the kitchen. She had already washed and prepared the jars which were ready on the kitchen table for bottling the berries in the morning.

He was the enemy; could he also be a friend? Was such a thing possible?

★

It had been nearly four months since her father's departure.

Helene drew some satisfaction from her management of the household. Father had explained how to draw on their modest savings in the bank for emergencies, and she had her small income as a teacher. With careful budgeting, the garden and the captain's gifts, there was food for the four of them. Thanks to George and Alexei's help, they were expecting a good harvest. Alexei's English had a Guernsey accent and he had even managed to find some identity papers from somewhere. He occasionally disappeared for a few days, but would always reappear – he never left the garden for too long – and usually he brought back something useful, like a ball of string, a piece of the heavy Occupation soap, or a bundle of carrageen moss to set the milk for a pudding. She had come to depend on him – and even found herself laughing, for the first time in years, at the funny things he asked about England. Did they send little children down the mines? Were the capitalists cruel to their workers? Was it true that most people had electricity and running water in their houses? His head was a jumble of information culled from Soviet propaganda and old English magazines.

She felt a new confidence, even pride, in her ability to meet the complicated needs of the three people dependent on her. Nanna still did not fully understand Alexei's presence, but he was careful to keep away from the house. She did not press Helene with questions.

The captain was an awkward addition to these delicate arrangements. His visits prompted silent fury from Nanna, while George made a point of his disapproval. To both of them, he was simply the enemy. Alexei was more open-minded. He was curious about the captain and, from time to time, Helene would find them in conversation in the garden or the greenhouse. She understood that Schulze sought out Alexei. She discovered they compared notes on the progress of the Eastern Front and the battle around the city of Kursk. The captain listened to the BBC on a secret wireless, he told Alexei. It was not uncommon amongst the German officers – some no longer believed the German broadcasts.

Schulze and Helene spoke little during their Sunday lunches. Both were aware of the coming and going of Nanna. But after lunch, when they sat on the terrace, the captain talked more easily. She didn't say very much, but she listened closely as he explained parts of his life. On one occasion, he talked of his childhood.

'I was eight when the war ended in 1918. I remember the hunger of the war and, when it ended, the shock and confusion and the unrest on the streets. It was an anxious time for all of us. We couldn't understand why we had been defeated. It was a terrible war for every country. Two million Germans died – my uncle and many fathers of friends amongst that number. The suffering of my country was terrible – and for what?

'Later, when I studied in England, I heard many people explain the Treaty of Versailles to me, but it was a disastrous miscalculation to humiliate a proud country like Germany. We should never have been blamed for the war. We should have been treated with respect. We didn't even know the terms which were being imposed on us until after the treaty was agreed, and the scale of the reparations was terrible. Vengeance drove that treaty and so much of the madness which has followed. On both sides.'

That sunny afternoon, the breeze was strong and cool. It brought the scent of the philadelphus. Helene was wearing a thin summer dress and she hugged her arms tight to keep warm. The captain noticed, and, without saying anything, took off his jacket and put it around Helene's shoulders. She protested but he insisted. The thick wool of his uniform sat heavily on her shoulders. She could smell his tobacco and the faint scent of aftershave.

'I must have been about twelve when I started travelling to my *Gymnasium* – secondary school – on the tram. Many men who had been in the army were begging on the streets. Some had had amputations and they would wave their stumps at me, begging for coins. Their hunger and bitterness were very disturbing, and my mama often gave me money or food to give to them. That was the time when my father was worried about his business. I learned the word "inflation". As a child, these things are not understandable, but we see the anxiety on every face. We had a neighbour – an old lady – who used occasionally to give me a sweet or a small coin when I was little. Her life savings were reduced to nothing. I remember my parents discussing what could be done for her. She was evicted and we lost contact. So many lives were destroyed in those years. I had an aunt – on my father's side – whose husband and son were killed, and she had no way to support herself but to take in lodgers. My father helped those he could.'

He sighed and pulled out his cigarette case, offering it to Helene. She took one and leant forward as he lit it. She inhaled and had to cough. She had not smoked a real cigarette in several years.

'Your country has been very lucky. Yes, the war was a tragedy and you lost many lives, but you didn't lose your dignity. We lost everything – and then we were blamed for the whole catastrophe.'

Helene flinched at the sharp tone of his voice. He noticed and fell silent.

'Tell me about your city – about Berlin,' she said quietly.

He leant back against the bench and half closed his eyes.

'Ah, which Berlin do you want to know about? I have lived in many Berlins . . .' He seemed lost in his thoughts. 'There was the Berlin when I was a small child – of five or six. I remember the hunger of those years. The turnips. Then there was the Berlin when the war ended. Fights in the streets, the sound of gunfire and explosions coming from the Kurfürstendamm. The rumours of revolution and putsch. Afterwards came years of upheaval. I remember a rare occasion when my mother took me into the city for my birthday. We went to the Zoological Gardens and then my mother wanted to take me for cake in the Café Josty. She was horrified – the cakes were made of frostbitten potato. I must have been ten or eleven. I didn't understand, but my mother did. I saw her fear. We always had a sense of foreboding that even worse chaos was imminent. I remember seeing the crowds gather on the day of Rathenau's funeral. All of Berlin knew something utterly disastrous had happened.'

Helene looked puzzled. 'Rathenau?'

'One of the finest Germans of this century. A man of great intelligence and skill, who served his country with immense dedication. Shot in Grunewald, near to where we lived. Assassinated. I was only twelve. If it had happened to him, it could happen to anyone. My mother insisted on my father having a bodyguard for several years after.

'Berlin was not a safe place. That much I knew as a boy, but there were places which were even worse. We had a piano teacher who was Russian. I understood she had come from a very grand family in St Petersburg. Now she was grateful for anything my mother could spare – a reel of cotton, an old dress. Her cuffs were fraying. She had the softest hands.'

Helene was listening intently, her eyes on his face. He put his hand briefly on hers.

'But there was another Berlin as I grew older – one I came to explore as a boy of fifteen. The currency was stronger and we were no longer taking notes in a wheelbarrow to buy a train ticket. Around where we lived, there are many forests and lakes. In the summer, we swam and sunbathed. I was in a diving club. I cycled there in the early morning. It is a city of parks and forests and everywhere the birds sing. On occasions, my mother would take us to the department stores – such as Wertheim on the Leipziger Platz. I remember that on my first visit, my brother and

I played on the escalators – the first in Germany. The store had crystal chandeliers and marble walls and more than eighty lifts. It was a palace. Even if my mother was only buying essentials, we could still feast our eyes on the finery.'

Helene laughed. 'I can't imagine such a place. Did you ever see Marlene Dietrich?'

Heinrich smiled. 'It's a big city – one of the biggest in Europe – so no, I didn't; she must have been in Hollywood. But we heard from friends how they once saw Anna Pavlova. She was in a bar and the rest of the clientele rose spontaneously to their feet to honour her, and she, in turn, danced for them briefly. And a boy told me that his brother had seen Einstein in the university. But in truth the city was full of so many people – of such energy and brilliance – that these things did not seem remarkable to us. Many Russians had taken refuge in the city. Berlin was a place of invention.'

'So when did you leave for England? Did you want to go?'

'It was my parents' decision. My mother wanted me to be at least half English, and my father was worried because there was still a lot of fighting in the streets – and especially at the university. I was twenty when I left. I was miserable at Oxford. The food was terrible and the English people there were insufferable. I missed the imagination of Berlin. Oxford seemed smug and nostalgic in comparison. I couldn't wait for the holidays, and each time I took my English friends back with me, I watched them fall in love with a city where you could spend the afternoon yachting on the Wannsee and the evening at the Philharmonic or at the opera at the Kroll. You could finish the evening at the Romanische Café – big enough to seat a thousand customers – or one of the other cafés, such as the Schiller or the Monopol. The bars and cafés seemed to stay open all night. That was the Berlin I really came to love. The city was imagining a bright future, not just for Europe, but for the world.'

His eyes were alight and his face full of enthusiasm.

'Berlin was inventing the twentieth century – the cars, the trains, the new roads, the architecture and music. The city was in tumult and, all the time, thousands were pouring in from all over Europe in search of this future, wanting to be a part of it – Jews from Russia, the Baltics, Ukraine and Poland, as well as Germans, Poles, Romanians and Czechs. It was vibrant with possibility and debate. The cafés and bars teemed with political argument. The newspapers, magazines, books poured off the presses. Every week there was an exhibition, film or play to see, a concert to attend, a new jazz bar to visit. New names to remember – Klee, Kandinsky, Gropius, Mies van der Rohe, Schoenberg, Brecht. Buildings were going up on all sides, and our only rivals were New York or Chicago. We were a new city – only a few decades before it had been a provincial Prussian capital. Berlin was being built as one of the world's greatest cities.'

Helene couldn't follow all the names – they meant little to her – but she grasped his intense excitement. She was captivated.

'It is full of museums. One day after this war, I will invite you and your father to visit my family. I will show you the lakes and woods of my Berlin. In summer, we swim and picnic, and in winter, we skate. Then perhaps I could take you for a good Berlin coffee and cake.'

His voice was soft. He was smiling with pleasure at the idea.

'And you could meet my sister Beatrice. Then I would take you to our holiday house in the forests outside Berlin. In winter, the snow is deep and we have races in the sleighs at night. Flaming torches are fixed to the sleigh to light our way on the tracks through the forest. In summer, we gather mushrooms and blueberries for pies. Perhaps we might even take a boat on the lake.'

For a moment, Helene was seduced by this fantasy. After a pause, Heinrich began again, more quietly. The enthusiasm had drained from his voice.

'That Berlin has been destroyed. I returned from my studies in England in 1933 and, within a year, the National Socialists were pulling apart my city. Closing down the newspapers, intimidating the owners of the bars and cafés. Burning books, smashing paintings. Thousands of people disappeared. You didn't dare ask where. People were bullied into joining the Party – into talking nonsense about Hitler, competing in their speeches of meaningless loyalty.

'It felt as if the noose was slowly tightening. I began working for my father's company. I travelled a bit – to Russia and Poland. My father was an engineer. He told me I had a head for figures. But my passion was art and film. I dreamed of being a film producer or an art dealer. Collecting art was still possible in those years. Gradually the artists I admired left Berlin – for London or America. The dealers closed up or left.

'I am no hero, I admit. I wanted to live – how did that become a crime? I have kept my mouth shut and my head down. I looked away. I joined the Wehrmacht in 1938. Better to be in the army than to be hustled into the Party. But enough of all this politics – we are an unlucky generation, and the best we can hope for is survival. I would like to believe that my country will be a happier place at some point in the future. What is the line from William Shakespeare?

> *"As flies to wanton boys are we to th'gods,*
> *They kill us for their sport."*

'My grandmother used to read Shakespeare with me. We are flies – and we will die in our millions before this war has finally exhausted the lust for blood.'

He had become increasingly angry as he spoke. His fists were clenched and his knuckles white. He rubbed his forehead and, sighing, he turned to her.

'So quiet, Helene. I wonder what goes through your mind when I talk?'

'Terror . . .' Helene said slowly. 'I can't bear hearing all this. I worry that Father might never return . . . That the war could kill all the people I most love – my husband and my brother, my aunt.'

'I'm sorry, I'm distressing you.' Heinrich put a hand on her arm. 'I know I am bitter. I feel my country and my city have been destroyed several times in my life already, and this time the very bones will be ground to dust by the Russians in revenge.'

He took a deep breath. Helene had picked a rose and was slowly pulling the velvety petals out and folding them between her fingers.

'And I am bitter because I once loved a woman, and I believed our love was strong enough to withstand this violence and brutality – this "sport of the gods". She was a film actress. She was – perhaps is – clever, beautiful and ambitious. I was twenty-six and we planned to marry. We shared a passion for film, art and music. We talked of a life together and planned our careers. At that time, I dreamed of leaving my father's business. Berlin was at the heart of this new film industry, and we wanted to be a part of it. But as the National Socialists tightened their grip, I could see there would be no future in film unless it was to meet their requirements. Christa would not give up. She joined the Party, and we argued. I couldn't trust her. She was taken up by a senior Party official, who promised to promote her career. I warned her that she would be destroyed, but she told me I was wrong. She believed the lies they told her. She told me that Hitler would make Germany great.

'Everything I had loved in her – her impulsiveness, her love of life – was corrupted. I don't know where she is now. That was seven years ago. I haven't loved a woman since. I knew many others like us, who lost their love – through death, through politics or fear – and I saw the grief.'

★

Sometimes Heinrich would come late in the evening to visit, when the summer light was fading. Nanna was in bed by then and perhaps he had understood this. He didn't come into the house. They sat on the bench, watching the dusk gather, and when it was clear, they would watch the stars come out in the light summer night sky. If it was raining, they sat in the conservatory amongst the lilies and the tomatoes. Alexei joined them on one occasion and Heinrich pulled a pack of cards out of his pocket – he said cards were as essential as a pistol in war – and the three of them played. They were all lonely, in their different ways.

One hot evening in late July, Heinrich arrived with a record he wanted Helene to hear. He put it on Edward's gramophone in the drawing room, and opened the windows wide so that the sound drifted out into the garden. Only the light colour of Helene's dress and her fair hair were visible in the thick dusk.

'Let's dance!' He held out his hand. She hesitated, but he gently pulled her to her feet.

She took off her heavy boots and stood in bare feet on the damp grass. She came up to his shoulder. He placed one hand on the small of her back, and as the music began to play, he slowly guided her around the garden in the summer night. She could feel his warm breath on her bare neck. She turned her face towards him, and their lips briefly met, soft, warm and expectant.

★

It was a Saturday morning of heavy warm rain. Nanna had been away for several days. She had been anxious about leaving Helene alone, but her sister was ill. Helene was in the kitchen ironing when she heard a sharp knocking on the front door. She had not seen Heinrich since the evening of their dance and the kiss. She had left him standing there in the garden, in the dusk, as the music finished. She had fled to her room, and heard him leave, shutting the front door and starting up his car. She felt bitterly torn between a man she could hardly remember – more a sweet boy, whom she had known for less time than they had now spent apart – and a man she could not put out of her thoughts. The fate of too many people lay in his hands. She had taken Alexei's words to heart. The more she saw of Heinrich, the deeper and more helplessly entangled she felt herself to be in his unspoken desire. In the exhausting uncertainty, she felt a numbing passivity take hold. She was drifting into something she couldn't see a way to avert.

As she made her way through the hall, she wiped her hands on her apron. It could not be Heinrich – she had not heard a car. But there he stood on the doorstep. His eyes were red and he was dishevelled and damp. His voice was shaking. Helene was shocked; she had never seen him like this, but she didn't ask any questions. She took him through to the drawing room. She opened the shutters and pulled the dust sheets off a sofa. He sat down, his breath coming unevenly as he tried to suppress sobs which shook his body. She sat opposite him, her hands twisting the tie of her apron, alarmed by his distress, and un-certain how to respond.

'My brother. He is missing. My . . . b-brother.' He stumbled over the words. 'My parents wrote to tell me they had finally received a letter. They had had no word from him for several months.'

He was overcome by anguish. 'Just a few lines in a letter.'

After a while, haltingly, he began to talk about him. 'He was five years younger, the pride of my father, and he wanted to work with him in the business. He fell in love very young, and married when he was twenty-five. His wife, Lise, and their two little girls live near my parents. He is a very good father – so gentle and playful with my nieces.'

Helene listened to his tender description of a man who could have killed her husband or brother. Was she to mourn or celebrate this unknown German man's death? Such questions were unanswerable; she put them out of her mind and focused on Heinrich's grief. She placed her arm around his shoulders, feeling his body shaking under the thick wool of his uniform. They sat together on the sofa in the chilly room, and Helene listened to the rain as it beat against the window panes. After a while, he leant his head back, and she stroked his hair, feeling its unfamiliar softness, as he wept silently. His eyes were closed and she looked at the line of his brow and the curve of his jaw. It was the first time she had been able to look at him closely, unobserved. She saw how, in another life, he might have been the film-maker he had once dreamed of. She imagined what it might have been like to meet him in Paris before the war – then she could have fallen in love with him, without betrayal, guilt and shame.

Beyond his head, she could see the tops of the trees tossing in the wind. It would be very rough at sea and the waves would be crashing against the cliffs. It was the sort of weather she used to love. Before the war, she would stand on top of the cliffs to listen to the roar of the ocean, facing into the warm wind to feel the rain on her face. That was a time which now seemed so full of ease, despite its tragedies. The thoughtless abandon of those pre-war years was an unaffordable luxury. She hadn't been on the cliffs for almost two years, even though they were less than a mile away. She felt a weight of sadness as unbounded as that beloved horizon of sea.

This could be her, weeping for her brother. As she held Heinrich's hand, she thought of Edward and wondered, as she so often did, where he might be. She thought of the bitter irony of bringing comfort to a German soldier for the loss of his brother while she considered the possible loss of her own.

'Tell me of your brother,' asked Heinrich, reading her thoughts.

Helene took a deep breath. 'He is clever, handsome, and Father is very proud of him. He is kind. We were very close as children – despite our childish squabbles – but he left in 1940, three years ago, and I am beginning to forget things about him. I look at his photo every day to pray for him, but it's not the Edward I knew on the beach or on the cliffs. He left on the same day as Tom – my husband.'

Heinrich nodded in understanding. The intimate feel of a person fades with time, they both knew. Helene explained how her mother had died in 1936, and how her Aunt Lily had left for the mainland at the start of the war. He listened carefully and then he leaned over to kiss her.

This time, Helene sprang up as if stung.

'I can't do this. Edward . . . Tom . . . this can't be.' She stood in the centre of the room. Her eyes had filled with tears. She blinked them back.

Heinrich stood up abruptly and walked over to the window. He had his back to her, and he spoke with a soft insistence.

'We can't control love – neither of us can. I've tried, believe me, for almost two years. From the time I met you on the cliffs. I loved you for things I knew were too precious to risk – your innocence – as well as your absurd beauty. You are the most beautiful creature I have come across – and here, on this muddy island, of all places. Not in Berlin or Paris.'

He turned to look at Helene, still standing, her head in her hands. He came over and sat down, murmuring as much to himself as to her:

> '*What, Helene, say, the vortex that can draw*
> *Body to body in its strong control;*
> *Beloved Helene, what the charmed law*
> *That to the soul attracting plucks the soul?*

> *It is the charm that rolls the stars on high,*
> *For ever round the sun's majestic blaze —'*

He broke off.

'It's Schiller — for his great love, Laura. I add your name. Your father has a translation of his poems, and I've been re-reading them. They are better in German. But still . . . they help. Some of the last lines help.'

Helene had to lean forward slightly to catch the words as he began again:

> '*The very Future to the Past but flies*
> *Upon the wings of Love — as I to thee . . .*
>
> '*When Saturn once shall clasp that bride sublime,*
> *Wide-blazing worlds shall light his nuptials there —*
> '*T is thus Eternity shall wed with Time.*
> *In those shall be our nuptials! Ours to share*
> *That bridenight, waken'd by no jealous sun;*
> *Since Time, Creation, Nature, but declare*
> *Love, — in our love rejoice, Beloved One!'*

Helene was looking at him, confused by the unfamiliar words, moved by his emotion.

'My mother loved Schiller. She encouraged me to learn his poems when I was a boy. She says that we are living in the time of the "wide-blazing worlds".'

Heinrich got up and walked to the door. As he opened it, he looked back at Helene.

'I can't,' she said, her voice hoarse from her tears. He nodded.

*

Heinrich returned two weeks later. He said he had some presents.

He had been away in France and Alderney, he explained to Helene, as he handed over parcels of flour and oatmeal from Normandy. He had a package for Nanna, which she received with her usual formal politeness.

When they were alone in the kitchen, he pulled out of his pocket a leather box and gave it to Helene. 'Think of this as a late birthday present – or a parting gift – as you like.'

The box was tooled with gilt and inside, lying on the blue velvet, was a necklace and earrings of amethyst, pearl and gold. Helene gasped at their beauty.

'It's a small gift in appreciation of your family's friendship.'

Despite the resolutions she had repeated to herself since his last visit, Helene couldn't help but smile.

'Try them on, now. I can help you.'

In front of the hall mirror, Heinrich lifted her hair and fastened the gold clasp on the necklace as she fixed the earrings in her ears. The pearls gleamed against her thick hair, which she had loosely plaited and pinned back to keep out of the way while she worked. He leaned forward to push a loose strand of hair aside. She could feel his breath on her cheek.

'My beautiful English rose,' he murmured, and he leant forward to kiss her at the place where neck and shoulder met. Helene moved away quickly; she could hear Nanna in the kitchen. Glancing in the mirror, she could see his eyes fixed on her. She looked away. He was wrong: you can control love. You have to, no matter what the cost.

*

Heinrich didn't knock. It was evening. Helene heard neither a car nor the front door opening. When she came downstairs, she was startled to find him sitting at the table in the kitchen. She didn't know how long he had been there. Nanna was away. He had even helped himself to the sherry he had given Father before his departure. Without a word, he poured another glass for Helene and pushed it towards her. He barely spoke. He was in a strange mood, preoccupied with his own anxieties. They sat in the quiet of the kitchen, listening to the ticking of the mantelpiece clock.

Suddenly, he stretched over and began to unplait Helene's hair. He loosened the long wavy locks, running his fingers through them. She flinched. He seemed very upset, even angry, but when she asked what the matter was, he said he couldn't tell her. She had come to recognize the dark moods following his visits to Alderney. The only time he spoke of the island, he had been terse: 'Hell on earth. Too much building, too many men.'

In a sudden shift of mood, he jumped up. He wanted to see Helene in a dress, a beautiful dress, he declared. The most beautiful one in the house. Where were her mother's dresses? He came alive with enthusiasm for this new project. Where was Helene's mother's make-up? Her scent? Her stockings? Her shoes?

'I want to see my wild beautiful Helene as the elegant woman she should be. The woman who could dazzle the audience at the Kroll or the crowds on Unter den Linden.'

He was pacing the kitchen floor in his impatience.

'So much ugliness everywhere in war. Even here. I want to see beauty.'

Helene was startled by his feverish excitement.

He took her hand and she allowed herself to be pulled behind him as he ran up the stairs, flinging open the doors of bedrooms.

'Which is your mother's room? Where are her wardrobes?' he cried out.

The floral bedspread, the large dressing table and the rows of scent bottles had not been touched since her death. No one had been able to bring themselves to pack the heavy silver hairbrushes away or to empty the drawers of her underwear and stockings.

Every week, Nanna still dusted the china ornaments and polished the wooden furniture. She smoothed down the unused bed and plumped the cushions. On the dressing table were even hairpins, strands of her Mother's fair hair still clinging to them.

Heinrich flung open the cupboard doors and pulled out dresses. Long pale silk evening gowns and short summer tea dresses. He was laying them out on the bed in a riot of colour and pattern. Her mother had loved rich colours, and the reds and pinks, yellows and oranges lay strewn across the room, draped over the bed and chairs. The dresses had not been worn for seven years, bar the one Helene had chosen for the journey to Cobo with Tom. Her going-away outfit. There had been no occasion for such finery since the Occupation began.

'Choose! Choose!' he cried to Helene, who was transfixed by the sacrilege of this stranger, rummaging through her mother's belongings, but also fascinated by his exhilaration.

'This one?' he demanded, holding up a long green evening dress against Helene. She wriggled away. He pulled out another.

'Ah, yes, this one.'

It was a soft red silk, splashed with a pattern of flowers, made from fabric her mother had ordered from London. One of Helene's favourites. She remembered the summer party of 1935 when her mother had worn it for the first time.

'Put it on,' he urged. Helene hesitated. Did he mean her to undress in front of him? He read her mind, and turned away to look out of the window at the view of the woods and the thin sliver of sea beyond. He urged her again to hurry up and put it on.

She fingered the fabric. It was a long time since she had worn anything better than cotton. Impulsively, she untied her apron, pulled her dress off, and felt the cool of the silk as it slipped over her petticoat and across her skin. It fitted her well, and she smoothed it down over her waist and narrow hips. She twisted to catch the buttons down the back to do them up. She felt his hands over hers as he swiftly fastened the long line of small buttons. He spun her round.

'We need jewellery – and make-up.'

She sat down in front of the dressing table and looked at the image in front of her. The low scoop of the neck and the gathering of the fabric on her shoulders were flattering. She smiled. She looked like her mother. Meanwhile Heinrich was urgent, pulling open the little drawers, looking for the things she might need. He was tipping the contents – boxes and small cases – onto the table. She grabbed his hand to remonstrate, and he gave up, throwing himself on a low chair to watch. She found some lipstick and rouge. She used her mother's hairpins to sweep her hair up onto the top of her head.

'Now shoes.'

She found a delicate pair of patent-leather heeled shoes in the wardrobe. They were slightly too big. Helene had not worn heels for several years and she was unsteady on her feet. She leant on his arm for a moment.

Helene fetched the present he had given her from her room.

She sat back down at the dressing table, and he took the necklace and fastened it round her neck. His hands rested lightly on her shoulders as they both looked in the mirror.

Finally, Heinrich seemed satisfied. He stood back to look at her, and smiled.

'My English rose,' he said triumphantly, and he kissed her very lightly on her cheek.

'Guernsey rose– not English,' she corrected him, laughing. He shrugged his shoulders. 'We need a photograph. I don't want ever to forget what I see now before me, the beautiful Helene. Never. No matter what happens. I can go to my grave with this memory.'

He had suddenly become very serious, but Helene, blushing, was shyly giggling. She had never been flattered like this: it made her giddy. She looked at herself in the mirror and stopped suddenly. She saw someone she had never seen before. She could see that she was beautiful.

Heinrich smiled, entranced.

'Where's Alexei? We need a photograph,' he cried exuberantly.

He led Helene downstairs and out into the garden, in the last of the evening sunshine, and looked around to choose the right background for his photograph. He stopped at the bench and declared that here the light was right. He settled Helene, arranged her dress and tucked back a long tendril of rose so that it was just behind her head.

'Don't move. Stay still. I'll be back.'

He ran off down the drive to the car to collect his camera. She sat still, as requested, enjoying the feel of the beautiful fabric in her calloused fingers. Before long, Heinrich was back and Alexei was running across the lawn, roused by the urgency of Heinrich's calls. When he realized the errand, he laughed. When he saw Helene, he was overcome with emotion.

'Beautiful,' he exclaimed, his eyes filling with tears. 'You look so beautiful, my dearest, sweet Helene.' He picked up her hand and grazed her fingertips with a kiss.

She laughed at his Russian gallantry, and Heinrich was smiling. 'A photo with Alexei too,' she cried.

'Yes, yes,' agreed Heinrich, like a child with a much-awaited present at Christmas.

In the rich evening light, wood pigeons cried from the woods at the bottom of the garden, and their laughter echoed against the stone walls of the old house as they swapped back and forth to take the photos. For a short while, they all forgot the war.

X

Roz and Meg finally met several weeks after Roz contacted her. Meg had been busy with work, and Roz had had to wait impatiently until they found a convenient date. They sat in a busy café in Mayfair.

'Your mother was a lovely woman. Very kind and always grateful for everything I did for her,' said Meg thoughtfully, as Roz poured the tea.

'But I was left disturbed by what I heard. Over those last few months, she was distressed and she kept repeating things. It's almost a year ago now, but I still think about it. I try to work out what she was saying.'

'It turns out her life was rather more complicated than I understood,' said Roz grimly. 'Anything you can remember might help me. I would appreciate any detail, however small.'

Meg took a sip of her tea.

'She kept talking about children. Children in Paris. I didn't know what that was about, but she mentioned one girl in particular, who had brown eyes. Helene kept saying that she knew she was terrified. She knew it, or she should have known it. Something like that. It was muddled – knew, should have known. It wasn't clear.'

Roz felt a deep foreboding as she made a few notes. It didn't make sense.

'Then, there was something else. She kept crying out, "Sorry. I'm so sorry." A name – Lara – came up. I didn't know who she was, but Helene kept saying the name. She would plead with me, "What could I have done differently?" I tried to soothe her. She was so agitated that the doctors increased the medication to calm her. Those were the last words she spoke to me before she went into hospital. Over and over. It upset me to see her so distressed.'

Meg had tears in her eyes as she took a sip of tea.

'Do you know who Lara was?'

'It's my second name,' said Roz, blinking back her tears as she smiled. 'Rosamund Lara. Sometimes she called me that as a child – at night when she was putting me to bed. Goodnight, Rosamund, goodnight, Lara, she would say, as if there were two of me, and I would giggle at our private joke.'

'One night – it would have been in the early hours – I was dozing in the room next door. She woke screaming. She said they were chasing her, that they would kill her. She was sobbing, and said they were pulling her hair, that she was safer in prison. She kept asking me: "Am I back in prison now? Am I in prison?" I didn't know what to say. There was another occasion when she was screaming. It was very upsetting. She repeatedly asked, "Who are you to judge? Who are you to demand I give it up?" I think I caught the word "father" that time, but I couldn't be sure.

'A few days later she was calmer and more lucid, and I asked if there was anything she wanted to talk about. She said it was too late. I said perhaps she would like to talk to a priest or a minister, but she gave a small smile and said, "Meg, priests never did me much good."'

'Her father was a priest,' interjected Roz sadly, and sighed heavily. 'Poor Mother – she was so alone with all her secrets, right to the end.'

'Only once did she seem to want to talk. She asked me if I thought there was anything after death. Was there judgement, she asked? She was anxious and she said that she had done what she could in difficult circumstances. She had saved Alexei and she had saved Nanna.' She repeated that a few times. I asked her who Alexei was, but she wouldn't tell me.

'I tried to reassure her that she had brought up three fine children, and that she had been a good wife and grandmother. But she waved all that away. "I destroyed Justin," she said, and began to sob.

'I didn't know what she was talking about, but I know a soul in anguish. She seemed so full of guilt. I held her hand and told her that she should forgive herself. I don't think she understood or believed me, but she gripped my hand very tightly. That was the last conversation we had. Shortly after that she went into hospital. You were the last to see her – did she say any of this to you?'

Roz was touched by this stranger's kindness to her mother, and she placed a hand on her arm. 'Thank you for the comfort you were able to bring. She didn't talk in this way at the end. Perhaps the anguish had passed – I hope so. She just said something about coming a long way – my career, I suppose. It didn't mean much.'

'Does any of what I remember make sense to you?' asked Meg.

'Some of it is beginning to. I had a hunch that this Alexei was important, and now I have a name. Thank you. Other bits are puzzling. The brown-eyed child in Paris is odd. We had a holiday in Paris in about 1955 – it was the first time Mother had visited. I remember because Justin showed us all his favourite places. I can't understand why that might cause distress. But I'm hoping that more pieces of the puzzle will slowly fall into place.'

'I think it was to do with the war. I think your mother was in France or something.' Meg added delicately, 'She mentioned the name Heinrich once.'

'Heinrich? No, she wasn't in France – I don't understand that.

But Heinrich – I've heard that name before,' Roz said, troubled. The name had been in Brown's diary. She called the waiter for the bill. 'Thank you so much for meeting, and if anything else comes back to you, please call.' Roz put the notebook in her briefcase, and repeated, 'Anything, however small.'

The conversation turned briefly to Ed and Jim, and Meg's grandchildren, and then Meg left to return to work. Roz looked over the notes she had jotted down: Paris. Children. Terrified. A chase. Saving Alexei. Heinrich. Prison. Judgement. It was a strange sequence of memories. Was Alexei the Russian she looked after? And how did she know this Heinrich? Was he the same one as Brown mentioned? Could this be the man in the photograph – the German soldier? What hope had she of ever making sense of this?

★

Antoine called the flat late one evening. He came straight to the point. 'Thomas Le Lacheur was killed in 1943. He can't be your father.'

'What?' Roz sat down at the table where she had spread out her notes.

'He was killed in 1943 in Burma. There's a plaque in his memory in the St Peter's parish church. I went to Guernsey to do more research, and chanced on the church – it has a sloping aisle, I was curious. I had a look around and there it was, on the wall, big and bold.

'Then I found out why he is on your birth certificate: children born to married Guernsey women during the war were automatically registered under the husband's name, even if they had left the island. You're back to the start, I'm afraid.'

Roz's heart sank. She realized now how relieved she had been to think the pieces could fit neatly together with this Tom. She was bitterly disappointed, but she told herself she wasn't back at the start. She had photos. She had names – Alexei and Lily. She had Meg's memories. She had a list of puzzling clues – but not much idea how to discover what they meant. There was a pause at the end of the phone.

'Have you found out anything more?' asked Antoine.

'Bits and pieces. A diary and some photos have turned up. I spoke to the woman who cared for my mother in her last months. She said my mother was very distressed and incoherent. She talked about children in Paris. That seemed to bother her a lot. Can you make anything of that?'

Antoine was silent. She could hear him tapping on a computer.

'What is it?'

'Is there any way your mother could have gone to Paris in the war?'

'During the Occupation? I hardly think so,' Roz replied crisply.

'Think carefully. Does she mention it in the diary or leave any gaps?'

'There are lots of gaps; she wasn't a very good diarist. It stops after only a couple of years of the Occupation.'

'I'll check the dates on something. There might be a connection to my research in Paris.'

'Antoine, to be honest, I don't know if I want to carry on with all of this.'

'We're close. I can feel it. I have more to tell you.'

'Like what?'

'Roz, there is no need to get irritated. I'm helping.'

Roz was silent. She could see that he was right. The history was painful, but that wasn't his fault.

'You could come to Paris and look over my files. I can explain how it might fit.'

'I'm busy at work.'

'I'm serious, Roz. I know this is difficult, but you're the sort of person who needs answers. I can tell. You cannot give up now. Think about it – a day in Paris, and we can look at some of my research.'

He was helping because it suited him, and his own career, but at any moment their interests could diverge, and that moment would be painful, thought Roz.

'I appreciate the help. I'll give it some thought. You're right, it's difficult.'

It took a few days to reach a decision. She wanted to visit Jim, and she could stop in Paris on the way. She remembered Justin's comments about the truth, and his metaphor of champagne. Bubbles rising to the surface. She didn't want to be like her mother and live with secrets. If Antoine's research findings were painful, a couple of days by the river with Jim would put her back on her feet. She usually found his household – full of children and animals – reassuring.

Besides, she needed Antoine's help. She had fixed on finding Alexei. She wanted to see if Antoine could trace him. Mike, and now Meg, had mentioned the name. Mike said an Alexei had been hidden in a country parish. Maev's mother had made a reference to Helene hiding a Russian. Helene could have taken him in, or he might know another Russian who remembered Helene. She had a crazy idea that he could even be the man in cricket whites in the photo.

She booked a week's holiday, and Antoine gave her the name of a place to meet in Paris.

*

Antoine was already at the restaurant when she arrived. He had chosen a table at the back, well away from the sunlight beating down on the pavement outside. The city was hot and dusty. The cool dark of the small bistro was a relief. He had his head down over a newspaper and was smoking, but looked up as she walked towards him, his face breaking into a broad smile. He stood up and stretched out both arms to greet her as she walked through the restaurant. He kissed her on both cheeks, and put his hands on her shoulders.

'Well done, Roz.' He looked genuinely pleased to see her. 'I'm really glad you decided to come. I think it's important for you –' he sat down again – 'and also for our history, that we fully account, to the best of our ability, for this past.'

'That kind of comment makes me nervous,' said Roz with a grimace.

Antoine laughed and called the waiter to order the wine.

'You look very lovely, Roz – Rosamund. Does anyone ever call you that? It's such a beautiful name. Shakespearean.'

'Thank you, Antoine,' said Roz, smiling. She was surprised by how pleased she was to see him. She had forgotten his warmth. 'I've always felt Rosamund is a bit pretty. Roz felt more like me, I suppose. Pretty is a drawback in a career like law – you don't get taken seriously.'

They laughed, and then talked about a new exhibition of Miró. Roz realized it was good to be in Paris again; she had vivid memories of the summer she had spent here studying French before university. She had fallen briefly in love with a fellow student. They had little money, so they spent their time walking around the city or lying in parks, sharing embraces and picnics of camembert, wine and baguettes.

After they had ordered, Antoine asked, full of eager enthusiasm, 'You want to know about Kapitän Heinrich Schulze?'

'I'm not sure I do,' she said wryly. 'It depends. Is this the Heinrich that Brown writes about?'

Antoine nodded. 'I think so. The research is working – we are making progress.'

Roz thought about Helene's ramblings to Meg and the reference to Heinrich. She rummaged in her bag and pulled out her notebook. Inside were the small photos she had found in Helene's diary. 'I brought these to show you.'

He studied them carefully, turning them over to read the handwritten dates.

'They're fascinating.'

He continued to examine them, side by side on the table. He had pushed the cutlery and crockery aside to make space.

'Helene was in love.'

'I'm not so sure. She looks slightly wary.'

'Yes, but that can be part of love too. Look at her expression in this one. The excitement, the eagerness.'

Antoine picked up the photo of Helene and the young man in cricket clothes. 'He has his arm around her waist.'

'Does he?' Roz craned her neck to see the photo. She was leaning against Antoine's thigh and could feel its warmth through the silk of her skirt. She put her hand lightly on his arm as she looked at the photo. He looked up briefly, surprised, and caught her eye. They looked at each other steadily. She leaned over and kissed him very lightly.

A waiter arrived with their food. In their smiles there was now an unspoken agreement. The two photos were on the table between them and as they began eating, they looked from one to the other.

'Here, can you see his fingertips on her waist?' Antoine gestured with his fork.

'I hadn't noticed them before. I've spent hours looking at the photo, but I missed them in the pattern of her dress. You seem more interested in this photo, not the one with the German.'

'I'm interested in both. She is about to embark on an affair with the German – that is obvious. But I don't know what role the other man plays – or who he is.'

'He looks very adoring.'

'Indeed. Helene was very beautiful,' said Antoine softly.

Roz raised her eyebrows.

'There's something about the line of her mouth and the tilt of her nose which is very appealing. And she had a good figure – you can see that. Long, slim legs . . .'

Roz found Antoine's survey of her mother disconcerting.

'They make a handsome trio.'

Roz had brought the notes from the back of the diary, but she hesitated to show them. Perhaps later; perhaps not at all. Antoine had a way of using information that unsettled her.

Antoine paused a moment and looked at her. 'Do you want to hear about Schulze?'

She took a gulp of wine.

'Are you ready for this?' Antoine was suddenly serious. He leaned forward so that she could smell the cigarettes on his breath.

'Schulze is the name which has haunted me at every point of my research since I first started looking into this subject, three and a half years ago. First, let me tell you that I have tried to trace him in Germany, and I've failed. His family address – on his German war records – no longer exists. Perhaps he is dead, or perhaps he went to South America. We know parts of the Morel collection reached Brazil and Argentina. I have contacts in both countries trying to trace him.'

Roz nodded.

'I know from army records that he had an execution order for desertion in late April 1945, but it's not clear if the order was fulfilled. It was the last days of the war and chaotic, I imagine. From the beginning of the war, Kapitän Schulze was something of an entrepreneur. His name began to appear in the account books of several art dealers in Paris in 1941 and 1942. At first I thought he was a collector, but the regularity and scale of his acquisitions began to make me curious. There were three other names that appeared a number of times in the ledgers, and I began to research all four. Between 1941 and 1944 the four of them had spent a small fortune in Reichsmarks on a collection which would now be worth many millions. Most of the art they bought was modern – the art described by the Nazis as degenerate – but they bought a few old masters too. Their taste was impeccable, and they only bought the very finest. They were very well organized. Schulze and a man called Rigner seem to have been the art experts; they knew the value of what they were buying. They pursued particular works in French collections, public and private. The trade in art in Paris in those years was intense, and there were various smuggling syndicates. A huge quantity of work was taken back to Germany, and many masterpieces ended up with Nazi leaders. Both Göring and Hitler were insatiable. Investigators after the war managed to repatriate a substantial amount, but some of the smaller operations, such as that of Schulze, seem to have slipped through the net.

'Theiss was the financier. He borrowed the capital from banks in Switzerland, France and Germany. Some of the collateral was an associate's property in Geneva; they set up a company registered in Geneva and there were several shareholders. At least four of them were Germans: Schulze, Rigner, Theiss and Heiner. We are still looking for other shareholders.

'Heiner was responsible, I believe, for hiding their purchases. He managed to get them out of the Occupied Zone into the *zone libre*. We think they had storehouses in Paris, Toulouse and Bilbao; from Bilbao, they sent some work to the US and Brazil. Heiner, and possibly Theiss, reached Brazil after the war; I haven't established all the details yet, but Heiner died there in 1989, aged eighty-two, the owner of considerable property. Various works from French collections reappeared on the art market via a Brazilian dealer in New York in the early 1960s; maybe they were some of those "bought" by Heiner and Theiss. I still haven't managed to trace Theiss in Brazil. Perhaps he changed his name.

'A large number of paintings were recovered in Toulouse after the war, and Rigner was put on trial. He hired good lawyers and they made a strong defence, arguing that he was protecting the artworks from destruction by the Nazis. He insisted that their plan was to return them to France after the war. He did hand over several works, including some by Picasso, and four paintings by Klee. The court was sympathetic to his story and his sentence was light. He ended up serving a few months. He died in Germany in 1993; he was a very rich man. They seemed to have been very clever – they got away with it.'

'Were they all posted to Guernsey?'

'No, only Schulze. Heiner and Rigner were in Paris for most of the war, with a brief time in Nantes.

'Now we come to the most difficult part.' Antoine paused and took a large gulp of his wine before hurriedly finishing his food. Roz had eaten a small amount while he talked. She waited for him to resume.

'The Morel collection was one of the private Jewish collections which the four men bought. Six families appeared to have sold paintings to them. Some were from Paris, another family came from Dijon, and two other collections were from Amiens.'

'When did you find all of this out?' Roz's voice was unsteady.

'I knew some of this before I went to Guernsey. What I discovered about Schulze in Guernsey was different. Not so much his business, but his relationships with islanders. I spoke to two sources who remembered him. He appears in two islanders' diaries. You'll remember that he was one of the officers who visited Arthur Brown. There are several references in his diary. Remember – he brought presents? He was known for being good-looking, and speaking perfect English. I know it's not much, but it's useful. I am hoping to find more. I'm curious about his English – where did he learn it? Could that be significant? Perhaps he had English relatives?'

Antoine shrugged his shoulders and smiled. 'He seems to have made a point of getting on well with the islanders. One described him as 'a very civilized Anglophile'. In fact, he comes across as an interesting man, if unscrupulous. In one diary reference, he seems to have intervened to protect a prominent farmer from being prosecuted for the possession of a wireless. On another occasion, he helped remove a family's names from the deportation lists for Germany. He is still remembered with affection in some quarters. Not so in others. There are other rumours about him. He had a reputation with women, and his name is linked with a French lady who ran a club in St Peter Port. One islander remembers Schulze driving this woman in a smart car through the town. She was still bitter at the memory of the woman's lipstick and fine clothes. There were stories of parties at Dieu Donne, which you already know about from Brown's diary.'

He paused as the waiter cleared their plates. He ordered another bottle of wine.

'Schulze is awful. I'm not sure I could face a man like that – if he was my father,' Roz said, fiddling with the stem of her wine glass.

'He intrigues me – he was certainly an opportunist. There are occasions when his behaviour is disturbing, I agree, but it's very hard to get a clear picture of the man, or to understand his motives. He clearly loved art and was knowledgeable, so perhaps he was trying to protect the artworks. He knew that these collections would have been confiscated – perhaps destroyed – by the Nazis. Besides, the Jewish families would have been desperate for cash – to plan their escape or for bribes to avoid deportation.'

Roz grimaced.

'I know what you are thinking. That these are the easy justifications of evil actions. Perhaps you're right – he was no hero, for sure – but it's too easy for our generation to have such moral clarity. Self-righteousness is deeply satisfying – and cheap. How many of us can be sure that we wouldn't have tried to find a way to manage in the war? He saw an opportunity to make money at the expense of a regime he probably hated.'

Antoine leaned forward as he spoke, cigarette in one hand, wine glass in the other. Roz could see how much he enjoyed this – the slow piecing together of Schulze's character.

'Not that that lessens my determination to ensure that the Morels get their art collection back,' he continued, waving his cigarette for added emphasis. 'It's not just for the Morels. Pursuing justice is how democracy keeps faith with a set of ideals. I see myself as offering a service of reminder. Persistence is everything.' He sat back and was half mocking his own grandiose statement. He added wryly, 'A country must not be allowed to treat its history like a flea market – rummaging through and choosing what to forget and what to remember.'

'I just don't want to find out that this man was my father,' Roz burst out. 'I find it hard to believe that Mother would want to associate with him – not least if she was one of several island women he had affairs with. Could she do that?'

'*Ma chère* Roz,' Antoine remonstrated. 'It's not going to help if you climb on this high horse. You're in no position to judge your mother. She was a young woman, without a mother, on an island full of German soldiers. It would have been terrifying. A soldier's kindness could have been vital to ensuring she survived.

'Another thing – I was going to tell you, but I almost forgot – I found the name of Eustace Le Marchant on the deportation list for February 1943. He went to a German internment camp. So your mother was on her own in that house. A twenty-three-year-old woman surrounded by soldiers.'

Roz was shocked.

'Deported? You're sure?'

Antoine nodded.

'How awful. He would have been sixty-three by then . . .' Tears came to her eyes, and she spoke slowly. 'But he survived.

He came back and he lived another thirty-odd years. It's so strange we never met him, I keep coming back to that. What grandfather doesn't want to see his grandchildren? What daughter loses touch with her father?'

'That's very odd. I don't understand it either. Perhaps he made the judgements you're making now?'

Roz frowned. 'That hits home.' She was cross with him.

'Sorry.' He shifted the subject. 'If it's any comfort, as far as I could establish, the dalliance with the Frenchwoman seems to date from 1941. In a couple of interviews, islanders told me that he had some sort of relationship with your family, and there were suggestions that Helene had a baby – you. But no one seemed clear about dates or names. I couldn't tell whether they were being discreet or whether they didn't know. I suspected the latter.'

Roz was looking down at her empty coffee cup. When she didn't respond, he continued, increasingly excited, 'What I'm really hoping is that your mother's story will lead us to the missing painting by Cranach the Elder, from the Morel collection. It hasn't been seen since a man bought it from the Morel family in late 1943. It was the most valuable painting they owned, and it was part of a desperate attempt to avoid deportation. What makes this purchase so intriguing is that we know Cranach's work was highly prized by the Nazi leadership – they wouldn't have destroyed this one. The *Virgin and Child Under an Apple Tree* is a lovely work. But why buy this one? To spite the Nazi collectors? Or to make a fortune by selling it on to a Nazi leader like Göring? I suspect it went to Germany, but we still need to rule out the possibility that it went to Guernsey.

'All the works traced to Schulze in Guernsey – the cache found three years ago and all the works your mother took to London – were prints, etchings or lithographs. No oil paintings. Was this a matter of taste, or of convenience, because the works on paper were easier to transport? But the bigger questions are, why take the works to Guernsey, and why give some to your mother?'

'You think my mother might have been recruited as a sort of courier for the syndicate?' Roz was alarmed.

'Perhaps,' he said, before adding more softly, 'Or perhaps this was Schulze's way of ensuring that she had money to look after herself and her child. Or he was just hiding them there for the war —'

'Hang on,' interrupted Roz. 'Slow down . . . we still don't know if Schulze is my father. There is too much conjecture.'

'Agreed. But we do have some information we can be sure of. We have a detailed statement from one of the Morel children, who remembers the purchaser of the Cranach *Virgin*, and her description bears a resemblance to Schulze — heavy eyebrows, dark hair, slim. But we have to keep guessing because, despite everything we have learned, we are still no nearer discovering the whereabouts of the painting.'

'You think Schulze might be still alive under another name?'

Antoine shrugged his shoulders.

'I don't believe the execution story. Some on the island believe it, but Schulze could have told friends to tell that story. I think it's more likely that he escaped. He was clever.

'In the mid-1960s, some pictures from the Morel collection were sold in Switzerland. I spoke to that dealer, who has now retired, and he remembers that the owner was a Berliner in his mid-fifties. According to German records, Schulze was thirty-four in 1944. That would make him eighty-five this year, if he's alive. He could still have the Cranach.'

'How are you going to find him?'

'We could try using the press.'

Roz flinched at 'we'.

He added, 'I have to warn you that, if we find him, he could be prosecuted.'

Roz was shocked. She shrugged off the hand Antoine had placed on her arm. 'It was never a good idea us collaborating,' she said, her voice suddenly hard. 'I don't want to find this alleged father only for you to announce criminal charges on behalf of the French government.'

'I'm sorry, I forget that we have rather different objectives. Don't worry, it's unlikely to come to that.'

'Why?' said Roz sharply, irritated by the assurance.

'If he helped with inquiries, it would be a suspended sentence – that sort of thing,' he said smoothly, unruffled by her tone.

Roz asked for the bill. Only when the waiter had gone did she speak again.

'There's something I want your help with. I want to find the Russian called Alexei. It's a hunch, but he might know – or even be – the Russian my mother hid. Mike said he was in a country parish.'

'It's difficult. No surname. I'll speak to Mike. He has Russian contacts, and perhaps one of them will know something. Since *glasnost*, a few of the former slave labourers have made contact with each other. If you like, I can find a researcher in Moscow to help speed the process up.'

Roz reached out for the bill lying on the table between them and there was a brief tussle with the piece of paper, but she insisted. 'It's the least I can do,' she said heavily. 'Your work is important – however distressing it is for me personally.'

'Would you like to come back to my apartment and read through the Morel statements on my computer? They have been translated by our American researchers. I think they'll solve the "children of Paris" riddle.' He said this with a peculiar emphasis. Roz had a feeling that he was holding something back.

'It's only a short walk.'

The heat of the Paris street was intense. Antoine took them on a route through narrow side streets in the 13th arrondissement.

They stopped at an unprepossessing door between two shop fronts. He explained that his apartment was in the attic as they climbed several flights of dark and dirty stairs. When he opened the door for Roz to enter, she saw a large high-ceilinged room full of sunlight. It contained little apart from a bed, a free-standing bath, and a long table covered with neat piles of books and papers. On the white-painted floorboards stood a huge vase of lilies. Everything was white, except for the stems of the flowers and the files on the table. All along one side were large windows, with a view over rooftops and chimneys. The room was meticulously tidy.

Roz was taken aback – it was not how she had imagined his flat. This was both more austere and more glamorous. She looked at the extraordinary bath. He followed her eye.

'I have my best ideas in the bath. Crazy indulgence, but when my grandmother died, she left me a little money. I spent it on a bath!'

'And the white?'

'The only way to see sunlight properly.' Antoine was laughing – he was enjoying her surprise.

He sat down at his desk and turned on his computer.

'This might be disturbing,' he said suddenly, glancing anxiously at her. She leaned out of the open window to look at the narrow street below, where two cars were trying to squeeze past each other. They were sounding their horns and a shopkeeper had come out to watch. She turned around and met his gaze.

'Here it is. Sit here – it's the only chair.'

How odd, an apartment with one chair, she thought, momentarily distracted. Did he never eat here with anyone?

He paced the room as she read Naomi Morel's recollections of her parents' negotiations over the Cranach *Virgin*. Roz found it hard to concentrate until she came to the description of an officer who could be Schulze.

There was one officer whose visits we enjoyed, despite the anxiety of Mama and Papa. He was handsome and very polite. He spoke quite good French, and he always brought Mama something useful, such as tins of food or some clothing. Once he came with a pretty blonde woman and they brought dragées – *sugared almonds – for us children. I remember he spoke to her in English, which we thought very strange. The young woman patted my head. We savoured those almonds, sucking them for hours on our tongue until the sugar had melted and the almond itself was dissolving. He drove a hard bargain with Papa. Behind the doors of the salon, we heard Papa remonstrating with him that the pictures were worth many times what this officer offered. Then the voices would fall again. Papa looked upset after the German left. He must have come three or four times during 1942 and 1943, but the woman only came once. I know Papa was trying to get us all off the deportation lists.*

Roz felt sick. Those almonds. Her mother had loved them. Taking almonds as a present for the children was exactly what she would do. How had she managed to get to Paris in the middle of the war? It was extraordinary. Couldn't she have done something to save those children? If she remembered how frightened they were, she must have guessed they were in danger. Surely she could have done something more than give them sugared almonds?

She drummed her fingers on the desk, saying to herself, as much as to Antoine, 'Are these people my parents? My mother? My father? Couldn't they have rescued the family?'

'That's why we want to find him. To hear his account. Perhaps he did help them. The children survived; their names came off the list and they were spirited away to the *zone libre*. That's something.'

'Not enough,' she replied emphatically. Her cheeks were wet with tears.

Antoine put a hand on her shoulder, and his voice softened. 'For now, enough of the war. You are in Paris and you need to enjoy yourself. What shall we do?'

Roz shrugged her shoulders. She was angrily wiping away her tears with the back of her hand.

'How about a boat trip on the Seine? Along with thousands of Japanese and American tourists. I've never done it before.'

He was smiling at her, and she managed to smile bleakly in return. She needed fresh air.

It was past four o'clock as they left the apartment, and Antoine promised cool breezes on the river. He held her arm as they wove through the tourists on the banks of the Seine. It took a while to reach the boats, but they were lucky and secured two of the last seats on a boat about to depart. Up on the top deck, the view of the Île de la Cité and Notre-Dame was magnificent in the late-afternoon sun. Antoine put his arm around her shoulders. The sun on the white stone of the quayside was dazzling, but the rhythm of the boat's engine and the slap of water on the keel was soothing. Roz felt calmer. Nothing had been proved, she told herself. Antoine pointed out places along the riverbank, describing how he fell in love with Paris on childhood visits with his parents. His father, a distinguished lawyer in Tours, had been keen to impress on his son the French republican tradition; they visited the Arc de Triomphe and the Louvre, and his father described to his children the events of the fevered days of 1789.

'My mother would get very bored. She would insist we went to the cinema. She loved the films of *la Nouvelle Vague*. It was the perfect combination of art and politics – don't forget, this was a time full of politics in Paris – even if I understood only half of it. We were visiting just after 1968.'

Afterwards Antoine and Roz wandered back though Saint-Germain-des-Prés and the 6th arrondissement as smart Parisians headed home for dinner. In the Jardin du Luxembourg, they sat down in the shade of the pollarded lime trees, and watched the children playing. Roz leant her head back against the bench and looked up at the glimpses of fading blue between the dense foliage.

Antoine leaned over and put his finger on her lips.

'You're beautiful. You inherited your mother's looks.'

She couldn't see his eyes behind his dark glasses, but he smiled. Then he kissed her. His lips warm and dry.

After a few minutes, she stood, pulling him up. They kissed again, this time with more urgency. He ran a hand down her spine as she leaned into him. The moment had finally arrived. They left the gardens hand in hand, and hailed a cab. Streets spun past in the warm evening as they kissed.

Inside his apartment, he put his hands on her shoulders and leant over to cover her neck and shoulders with slow, deliberate kisses. She undid the buttons on his shirt and led him to the bed.

★

When Roz woke, the light in the flat was dim. For a moment she was confused, then she saw Antoine's head next to her and she moved over to kiss his brown shoulder. He was still sleeping, so she carefully lifted his arm from where he had flung it across her belly. She looked at him, lying spread across the bed, his dark hair on the pillow, and was filled with tenderness. She reached for her watch – it was nearly ten o'clock. She felt hungry and wanted a shower. She got up and gathered her clothes.

In the shower, she lingered, enjoying the cool water against her skin. She felt exhilarated. She was drying herself when she noticed with a start a bottle of perfume in a corner of the bathroom shelf: a discreet staking of territory. But of course, why wouldn't he? She hadn't wanted to ask. When she came out of the bathroom, already dressed, Antoine was up and sitting, naked, typing at his computer. He turned round and smiled.

'I'm going,' she said, more abruptly than she had intended.

He looked hurt. 'Don't you want some supper? Where are you staying?'

'You live with her?' asked Roz.

Antoine looked baffled, then he realized.

'No, she visits. You didn't remember?' He teased her, 'Is that some jealousy I see?'

'Remember? I didn't know – you never mentioned her,' Roz replied.

'Really? Perhaps you didn't ask. What does it matter? I thought you didn't want to know – that we both wanted to keep these things separate.'

Antoine stood in front of her, and tucked a strand of hair behind her ear. He stroked her cheek.

'Separate?' Roz repeated.

'Roz, stay for supper,' Antoine pleaded. 'Don't leave like this.'

'And your girlfriend?'

'I love her. She wants to marry.' He shrugged his shoulders.

'Will you?'

'Probably. I love her.' He added, 'We want children.'

Roz nodded. 'Of course.' She tried to keep her voice calm. It hurt.

'I am hoping to get a position at the university in Montpellier. We could marry then, and find a big enough apartment for children. Paris is no place for families – unless you have a lot of money. Or we'll go to America.'

Roz realized that she knew little about his life. He had once mentioned children, she remembered now. She had been so preoccupied with her own search that she hadn't given much thought as to why Antoine was committed to his research, beyond his evident ambition. As if following the train of her thoughts, he continued, 'The job appointment depends on a successful out-come to this research project. It would certainly help if I could uncover an old master buried in Germany or Guernsey; even a minor Italian Renaissance work would be enough.' He laughed, adding, 'Bureaucrats always need results for their grants.'

She felt a wrench. Perhaps for a few moments today she had allowed herself to believe that they were starting an affair. She had glimpsed her own suppressed longing. She still felt desire. She didn't want him to see that.

'I've enjoyed my visit to Paris. Thank you.'

'Ah, my English lady. So polite. Always remembering to say please and thank you,' said Antoine. His tone had a sharp edge.

'You give with one hand and take away with the other, no?' retorted Roz.

He smiled and walked over to the bath to turn the taps on. Roz watched his long legs and broad back.

As he stood up he said thoughtfully, 'That's what my last girlfriend used to say to me. Power is very important to me in love. Yvette – my girlfriend – is the only woman to have understood that.'

'I see,' said Roz icily, maddened with herself as much as with Antoine. 'I'm going.'

Roz picked up her earrings and watch from the table, and stuffed them in her bag.

'Rosamund,' he remonstrated, frowning, his hands in the air.

She looked back at him as she opened the door.

'I'll be in touch,' she said, with as much casualness as she could muster.

★

It was a relief to see Jim at the sleepy provincial station, standing waiting for her, arms open.

'You look tired, sweet.'

'I didn't sleep much in Paris last night. A noisy hotel. Antoine has dug up stuff I need to talk to you about.'

Jim put her bag in the back of the car while Roz cleared the clutter of rubbish on the front passenger seat. Jim and his wife Françoise lived in a state of comfortable chaos. As each child arrived, the mess became more pronounced. Roz squeezed her feet between children's toys, old crisp packets and a forgotten shoe.

As they drove, she recounted some of what Antoine had told her.

'I was angry at first. Now I feel disgust. If it *was* Mother, how could she?' Roz asked unhappily.

'Wait a minute – it's Antoine who is making the connections. It might not have been Mother who was in Paris. He says this Schulze had other women. We still don't have any evidence that it was Schulze she had an affair with. It could have been the other man, whoever he was.'

Jim was driving in his characteristic style – fast and erratic. Roz found it hard to take her eyes off the road. There was a pause as they pulled out onto the motorway.

'We can't leap to conclusions, even if Antoine is keen to do so,' Jim concluded.

'You're right. Alexei is important. I want to find him. Someone on Guernsey must know of him. Antoine is asking an islander called Mike, who has contacts in Russia. Perhaps Alexei was the man that Mother sheltered.'

After leaving the motorway, Jim braked sharply to pull into the narrow lane which led to his house. He slowed down on the rough track, and Roz wound down the window to breathe in the smell of the vines in the heat and the sound of the crickets. She leant her head on the window frame. She was feeling less bruised already. Sleeping with Antoine had been a mistake, but she couldn't say she regretted it. All the same, there was no point telling Jim. He would be cross; he had warned her.

'So complicated,' said Jim, rubbing his forehead. The car had come to a stop in the yard. Roz agreed with unusual energy, and he looked at her quizzically.

'If Schulze is my father, how do I face him if he's still alive?' she asked. Jim nodded sympathetically.

At the sound of the car doors slamming, animals and children tumbled out of the house. Two dogs raced across the yard to bark at Roz, and chickens in the orchard looked up. Jim's two oldest children, Isabelle and Anaïs, arrived in their swimming costumes from the river. Françoise emerged from the kitchen, wiping her hands on her apron.

'*Ma chérie!*' she exclaimed warmly, throwing her arms around Roz, and kissing her vigorously on both cheeks. 'You must need *le déjeuner. Tout de suite. Viens, viens.* Let us sit . . .'

Even after twelve years with Jim, Françoise jumbled the two languages together, and the children followed suit. Sometimes it seemed that everyone lost track of which language a word originated in. The cacophony around the table could be hard to follow – and often Jim gave up, retreating into an amiable silence.

The table was laid with cheeses, bread and salad. A jar of wild flowers sat in the centre – grasses, vetch and buttercups. Roz liked visiting. The old barn was full of the interesting things Jim or Françoise picked up in antique shops: curious engravings, odd pieces of china, and old farm utensils. Each time she visited, another layer had accumulated.

Anaïs wanted to introduce the new guinea pig to her aunt, and Isabelle wanted to show her English homework. The baby was sleeping. After Roz had been on a tour of the new animals and inspected the homework, Françoise insisted the siblings take their coffee outside alone.

'I know when a sister and brother have *les choses* to discuss.' She waved away their offers of help.

Just outside the kitchen door was Jim's favourite seat: a long low bench, usually piled with old cushions, newspapers and used coffee cups. He cleared a space and they sat down. On the riverbank below, Anaïs and Isabelle were playing with a dog, throwing a stick into the shallows in the hope of tempting the elderly creature into the water. Roz and Jim watched them for a while.

'If we can track down an address for this Russian, if he is still alive, I want to go and speak to him,' Roz said.

'What about Schulze?'

'I have a feeling that Alexei can help. He will tell the truth.'

The river was wide, but at this time of year the water was quite shallow here. You could almost walk across to the far bank, where families came down with their picnics from a neighbouring village. Roz and Jim watched the swallows swoop down to take sips from the surface. The branches of the willows dabbled in the dark water at the river's edge. Occasionally, a fisherman waded out to the rocks in the middle and cast his line over the rapids. The quiet murmuring of the water was soothing. Both sat with their own ruminations.

'What was it Mother said to you right at the end – that evening in hospital?' said Jim suddenly.

Roz was surprised. 'I can't remember. Why did you think of that?'

'Just wondering if it was relevant – if there was any hint of all this.'

Roz thought for a moment.

'I'm trying to remember. It was something like, "You've come a long way." I assumed she was talking about my career.'

'Could it have been "we" rather than "you"?'

'I suppose it could have been. Turns out that was true. We did come a long way – from Guernsey.' Roz's laugh sounded a little harsh.

'Anything else?'

'Actually, there was,' said Roz thoughtfully. 'Something about "never wanting to give me up". I'd never thought of that before. Could that be important?'

Jim leaned forward. 'Of course that's important. If she was having an illegitimate child, she would have come under pressure to give the baby up. Tightly knit community, and all that gossip. Perhaps that's what she argued with her father about when he came back from Germany.'

Roz was looking at Jim with admiration. 'That's a good point.'

'That puts Mother in a very different light.' Jim was stroking his top lip meditatively.

'Maybe Antoine was right. He said I shouldn't judge her. She was trying to manage as best she could and we would probably never know the full story.' She added, sighing. 'I am beginning to feel I was recruited long ago for Mother's project, for keeping her improbable life on track, keeping all this hidden. She needed me to be organized and efficient. Now that it's all falling apart, it feels odd, but also something of a relief. I don't have to do any of that for her any more.'

Jim leaned back and put his feet up on an old stone trough in front of them. It was full of weeds and wild flowers. He had picked a stem of grass and was chewing it absent-mindedly.

'The thing which bothers me is how evil was done by an accumulation of seemingly small things,' said Roz. 'Schulze and Mother – if she was in Paris – were tiny parts in a sequence of events in which Jews were robbed, persecuted and killed. Thousands of individuals, even millions, obeying Nazi laws. They didn't buy from Jewish businesses; they looked the other way; they didn't ask questions; they drove the buses and trains. All those people who were just trying to get by and survive. Evil is not a tidy business – it corrupts and sucks in so many ordinary people.'

Jim nodded. 'It uses fear to spread. It's contagious.'

Roz shivered and Jim put his rough hand over hers. Peals of

laughter echoed from the river, where Isabelle and Anaïs were splashing with the dog.

'One day, I'd like to see some of the etchings and prints Mother brought to England and sold to Justin. Just to see them. As if they might offer a clue. Justin said they were exquisite. Schulze – if it was him that chose them – had a very good eye, Antoine said. Some might be in galleries somewhere.'

Jim agreed. 'After you have found your father, you can use your new research skills to track them down. I'll come and see Picasso's *La mère* with you – I'm interested in his Blue Period at the moment.'

He put an arm around his sister. 'Antoine was OK with you? No tricks?'

'All fine. I think he's told me everything he can. I'm just hoping that he can give me a lead to find Alexei. After that, I doubt we'll meet again.'

As she said it, she felt unexpectedly sad. Despite the moments of irritation, she had liked him. Liked talking with him. Liked sleeping with him. He was clever and charming and the time they had spent together had always entailed an element of the unexpected. He had never been predictable.

'He's doing important work,' she said brightly, relieved that Anaïs chose that moment to arrive, dripping wet, with an old piece of pottery she had found in the river. Jim was distracted as he carefully examined the find. They passed it back and forth between them, as first her small brown fingers and then his rough paint-stained fingers stroked and rubbed the ceramic indentations.

Later, Roz would look at Jim's new work and then they would all have supper around the kitchen table. Tomorrow, Jim wanted to take her to a concert in the old ruined chapel in the forest. Roz sighed with contentment. She had spent much of the previous night in tears. She hadn't been quite certain who or what she was crying for: the Morel family, her mother or herself. Here she felt safe, even if only for a few days. She could rest for a while. The warmth of Jim's family and the beauty of this place would help her keep at bay that sense of contagious evil.

PART II

XI

Helene heard the back door shut. She rolled over on her side and tried to make out the time. From what she could tell on her alarm clock, it was about midnight. Heinrich didn't usually come this late. She pulled herself out of bed and wrapped a dressing gown around herself. He would need food. Since France had been liberated last August, the German garrison was running out of supplies, and Helene held back a portion of supper for him. The soldiers were forced to rest for hours every day, weak with hunger. The islands had been left behind to starve as the Allies pressed on through Belgium and Holland to reach Germany. Almost every day now, the wireless gave news of progress towards Berlin from both the east and the west. The end of the war was only a matter of weeks, a month or two at most.

Nanna usually retired to her room early and only then would Heinrich slip in through the back door to the kitchen. That way they could maintain the fiction that she didn't know about his continued visits. There had been fierce arguments back in the autumn of 1943 between Helene and Nanna over Heinrich. Helene shuddered at the painful memories, at the secrets she now kept. Nanna had said that she had betrayed her husband, her brother and her country. That she would not – could not – escape judgement for what she was doing. Nanna wept and lamented that Helene's reputation would be ruined and insisted on complete discretion: everything had to be hidden – there was no alternative. Helene, overcome with shame and confusion, knew Nanna was right, but what choice had she had? They were all dependent on Heinrich. His money had supported the household after she lost her job in January 1944. Nanna was only alive because of his supplies of insulin and painkillers. But Nanna was stubborn and fierce in her judgements; tight-lipped, she said she only stayed at The Vicarage out of duty and loyalty to the memory of her beloved Elizabeth. At the mention of her mother, Helene was stung. For several months, they did not speak, moving around each other in the house without a word between them until finally they settled into an uneasy truce.

Neither Helene nor Heinrich found it easy to sleep on the nights when they lay in each other's arms. Each was overwhelmed with their own private anxieties, on top of the gnawing hunger. His whispered comfort failed to ease her distress and, in turn, when she tried to soothe him, they both knew that any reassurances she offered were meaningless. The Soviet armies would show little mercy to any Germans as they arrived in Berlin.

Alexei had moved to a farm in Castel in the late summer of 1943. Helene had suspected that Heinrich had had a part in the move, fearing that Alexei put them all at too great a risk. Recently, Alexei had moved again to a nearby farm in St Saviour's, and sometimes came to visit Helene, always careful to avoid Heinrich. She had feared his condemnation or criticism, but he showed only his usual warmth and appreciation. On one of his recent visits, Helene had never seen Alexei so exuberant.

'My people, my people – they are true warriors! We have liberated our brothers in Warsaw and Krakow. Berlin is in our sights,' he exclaimed, and swung Helene around in an impromptu waltz. She had laughed until there were tears running down her cheeks. She didn't know if they were tears of anxiety about what the future might bring, or tears of grief for what her past now held. She longed for the war to be over with an intensity which overwhelmed every question as to what peace would mean for her. Occasionally, she wondered what it would be like to be married again, but those days after the wedding with Tom were like an overexposed photograph, with only the ghost of an outline.

Heinrich, on the other hand, was all too real: demanding, intense and full of longing. He clung to her like a drowning man grabs a life raft. How did one provide solace to a soldier whose country was being destroyed, for the second time in his lifetime? Whose cities were being reduced to piles of rubble, whose children and old men were the only ones left to fight? How could she live alongside someone consumed by this suffering, and yet recognize how she greeted each Allied advance with eager anticipation? Bomb, bomb, she urged the Allies on. She wondered at how she could celebrate the violence which caused him such heartache. She lived the sharp contradictions, with no way of reconciling them. They were yet another layer of painful confusion over wounds that refused to heal, snagging her heart with a bitter anguish that made her feel like a woman twice her age, exhausted and wretched. She longed for it all to be over: the bombs, of course, but also the inner war of loyalties.

It was chilly and Helene wrapped the gown tightly around her. She found Heinrich in the kitchen, sitting by the stove, his head in his hands. His usually immaculate uniform was muddy and the fabric was ripped. He had cut himself and his leg was bleeding. He hadn't shaved for several days. He had a long narrow wooden box on his lap. Helene was aghast.

'What's happened? What have you done? How did this happen?'

In the dim light she saw that his white face was smudged with dirt, his eyes wide. He stood up to put his arms around her. He had grown so thin she could feel his ribs. The islanders were getting Red Cross parcels, and they had supplies of potatoes, swedes and carrots from hidden vegetable patches, unlike the starving German soldiers.

'I've deserted,' he said, making an effort to keep his voice steady. 'A few of us are trying to organize the peaceful hand-over of the island to the Allies. We are trying to make contact with Allied intelligence in France. Berlin will fall in a matter of weeks. It is madness for us not to surrender this island. We cannot bring the battle here. I know my beautiful city will be destroyed, but not here. Not for a few more days of the rule of that madman.'

Heinrich's fists were clenched and Helene wasn't sure if it was anger or fear, or both, which made them shake.

'My country will pay the price for decades to come,' he said, full of bitter anger. 'I saw the destruction as we arrived in France. I stood in the Louvre . . . they ripped paintings from their frames, the barbarians slashed them with knives, burned them in piles in the courtyards.'

His eyes were glittering. Perhaps he had a fever. She was struggling to follow him. Pictures ripped? The Louvre? She didn't know what he was talking about. But deserted? She was astonished. It was reckless and futile.

'I didn't want to come here – it puts you in too much danger – but I needed to give you something – this.' He gestured to the box. 'If I can spend the night here, then I will move on, and hide for a few days – perhaps two weeks at most. The Allies will be here very soon.'

He was chewing his fingernails. Helene had never seen him do that before. His charm and authority had evaporated, leaving behind an edgy, skinny man. One hand kept stroking the rough wood of the awkwardly shaped box. She felt sorry for him. Of all the many powerful emotions she had felt for Heinrich over the last three and half years, protective pity had not been one of them.

'You will have to stay here,' said Helene, trying to work out what to do. 'If we managed to hide a Russian for the best part of two years, we can do the same for a German.'

She smoothed back his hair, matted with blood and mud, trying to calm his agitation.

'You're a brave, good woman,' whispered Heinrich. He was covering her face in kisses. He was feverish. His face felt clammy with sweat. She pulled away.

'The outhouse has a basement. There is a trap door under the mat. George built it. You can move in the morning,' she said briskly. 'Alexei is due tomorrow and he will know somewhere better for you to hide. For now, you need to eat and rest.'

Heinrich was pacing the room. 'There are too many people who know about us. If they are looking, this is the first place they'll come. I have only a short time – they think I am on duty at one of the batteries, but in two or three days, perhaps sooner, my absence will be noticed.'

Helene didn't reply. She knew the truth of what he was saying, but it was a risk they had to take for one night. She gathered a dish of cold potatoes and turnip from the pantry and put it down on the table in front of him. He ate hurriedly, with grubby fingers. Between mouthfuls, he muttered that he hadn't eaten for two days.

'We need to dress the wound and then you can sleep.'

Helene made him tea from Nanna's dried herbs, and as he gulped the warming drink, she knelt to bathe his leg. There was a deep rip in the flesh, made, she guessed, by barbed wire. She bound the wound with strips of old sheets. She brought down an old pair of Edward's trousers. A little colour had come back into his face. As she gathered up the bowl of water and dirty swabs, he grabbed her hand.

'Helene, after . . . after the war. I want us to be together. I will come back for you.'

She looked at him. 'Don't ask this of me, Heinrich. You know it isn't possible. Not now.'

'If not now, then when? Get divorced.' His voice was a hoarse whisper. 'Come to Berlin.'

'Heinrich,' she remonstrated softly. 'How can you ask such things?'

Heinrich began to sob silently. His shoulders were shaking. 'My country is ruined. There have been so many mistakes. I did what I could here on this island – I loved its people. But it was not enough. Nothing will ever be enough. I have a past now which will kill me . . . a future I can't face.'

'Sh, sh . . .' Helene tried to soothe him, as she would a child.

'Whatever happens . . .' He stumbled. 'Whatever happens, believe me, I have loved you . . . not well . . . but it was love.'

'Was it?' murmured Helene, but she wasn't looking at him for an answer. With liberation imminent and Heinrich a fugitive at her mercy, she felt that suddenly she could release her tongue – she could finally speak her mind.

'Perhaps you did, but there were so many of you – so many different versions jostling within you. I don't think I ever knew who you were – who you really were. Arrogant, overbearing, gentle, loving, generous; I have never known who would arrive when I heard your steps.'

There was no reproach in her voice; it was just a puzzled statement. Heinrich looked at her, but she wouldn't return his gaze. She was staring at the worn tiles of the kitchen floor.

Later, when neither could sleep, Heinrich said quietly, 'In the kitchen. What you said was right. I have had – I have – several lives. The pieces don't fit together. Nothing has held steady in my life, ever. My preoccupation has been survival, and that distorts many things.'

He was whispering into her ear as they lay side by side, which gave a strange intensity to his words. Helene listened silently.

'When I was seven or eight, my father took me to see the gigantic wooden statue of Hindenburg, which stood outside the Reichstag in the Königsplatz. It was 1917 or 1918, during the Great War. We were living off a diet of turnips. This trip was a treat for my birthday. You were allowed to bang a nail in the figure if you donated one mark to the Red Cross. Between us, my father and I banged in ten nails. I was so proud as I stood there, holding my father's hand – of my country, of the service and sacrifice of millions of our soldiers.

'Within less than a year, the whole thing meant nothing – when we heard that the Kaiser had fled, my father was in tears. The war was lost and the country on the edge of communist revolution. All that sacrifice. Nothing has been what it seemed, nothing has lasted or proved true.'

His voice was cracked with bitterness, and he held Helene's arm so tightly it hurt. She prised his fingers off.

'I grew up assuming that, like many of my forebears, I would die in war – it was simply a matter of when and where. Germany has been extravagant with the lives of its sons. I found consolation for this brutal randomness in beauty and pleasure – I admit it. Along the way there were some acts of generosity – but I know well that they were nothing compared to the atrocities I have witnessed. I'm glad I lost my Christian faith, or I would fear judgement.'

He propped himself up and looked at Helene. She turned away from him; if this was a confession, she could not give him absolution. He lay back, finally silent.

Just as she was drifting off to sleep, he put his hand on her shoulder.

'The folders I gave you last month – they will be useful, if you need anything, before I can get back for you. If anything happens to me . . .' He faltered. 'Look after them. They are very precious. I couldn't risk them falling into the hands of people who could never appreciate them. The box I brought today is the most important of all. You need to look after it for me. It's here.'

Helene pulled herself up onto one arm. In the dim light of the March dawn, she could see the box on the table beside the bed. It was fastened with many nails.

'Look later. After the war. Until then, it needs to be well hidden. It's very precious and must be kept safe. I have done that for eighteen months, but I can't any more. It was my small victory – to keep it out of the hands of men like Göring.'

'We can hide it in the morning,' mumbled Helene. 'Alexei can help. Now sleep. You will need it.'

Exhausted, he eventually slept, his head on her shoulder. But Helene's sleepiness had passed and she was wide awake. She watched the grey light strengthen to day. She slipped out of bed quietly, so as to not wake him, and dressed. She needed to talk to George as soon as possible. Heinrich was right; he was putting all of them at risk.

By the time he woke late in the morning, Alexei had arrived and, with George, they devised a plan. There was a derelict fisherman's hut at the top of the cliffs, beyond the barbed wire. Heinrich could hide there for a few days at least.

After his sleep, Heinrich was much calmer. Helene could see that Alexei was sceptical of Heinrich's talk of a plot to hand over the islands to the Allies. The three of them sat in the kitchen as he ate bread with a small portion of milk for breakfast. Helene packed a bag of food – all she could spare. They would bring him more supplies if they could. Water was a problem, but Alexei thought there was a rain butt. He would lead Heinrich out beyond the parish and then he could make his own way. Alexei drew a map of how to reach the hut over the fields. Then they tore the map into small pieces and fed the fragments of paper into the embers of the stove. Heinrich had borrowed a coat of

Helene's father and some old boots. They would wait until dark in George's basement and then set off.

Helene paused a moment by the sink, looking at the two of them sitting at the table, leaning over the map: Alexei's fair head close to Heinrich's dark one, almost touching. She felt her heart tense with now familiar pain. These two men had shared evenings of music, conversation and cards over the last two years, and now each of them had saved the other's life. They had made a strange household – full of contradictions and the unspoken. Theirs had been a fragile place: a make-believe world of forgetting the war. That had always been Heinrich's story. Alexei and Helene had indulged him. Neither of them had forgotten the war for a moment. Their war had included Heinrich, with his generosity, yes, but also his sense of entitlement and calculating self-interest. Now the precarious tale was ending and Heinrich would never be able to forget the war again. As he waited for its end, shivering in the damp hut on the cliffs, he would be facing a future full of memories of this war. As they all would.

Heinrich hurriedly said goodbye to Helene. They would slip away that night. In the morning Alexei would return early to help Helene hide the box and then she would go to Felicity's to stay for a few days. The Vicarage was too dangerous. It was not how they had thought the parting of ways would come; they had hoped for the celebrations of liberation. Helene knew the three of them would never be together again. History would fling them back to their corners of Europe, putting thousands of miles between their different lives.

It was a tense day. Helene tried to keep herself busy, but her mind kept straying to the outhouse. George had taken himself off to his brother's. Helene picked up some mending in the kitchen. Nanna had guessed something was up, because when she came into the kitchen after the men had left, she was restless, moving from task to task and nervously rubbing her stiff fingers. They didn't speak.

When dusk began to gather, Helene sensed the possibility of relief. It came with an intense, unexpected grief. Within a few hours, Heinrich would have left, with no knowing when, if ever, they would see each other again.

Later that evening, from the dark drawing room, she watched the garden. She thought she glimpsed the two men disappearing at the end of the lawn into the wood, but her tired mind might have been playing tricks on her. She listened to the soft sound of the rain falling on the stone path below her window and tried to imagine what the end of the war might mean for Edward, Father and Tom. She wondered where Edward might be. She hadn't heard from him in over four years. At least Father was alive and cheerful, despite the severe conditions of the camp, according to his brief Red Cross message six months ago. But there was no knowing how he would survive the battles being fought across that godforsaken country.

She must have drifted off, because she was woken by banging on the front door. She could hear men shouting outside and the sound of boots on the path. They had come for Heinrich. She could hardly tie the cord of her dressing gown for the shaking of her fingers. Her heart was thumping inside her ribs like a wild animal. Keep calm, she told herself. Keep calm.

She slipped on her shoes and went downstairs, holding the banister tightly to steady herself. She undid the bolts on the front door. Three German police pushed her aside, issuing orders. They needed to search the house. A few minutes later, Nanna appeared downstairs in her dressing gown. She looked afraid, but she did not meet Helene's eye. They were told to sit in the cold hall and wait.

More police arrived with dogs. Helene could hear them moving upstairs through the house. They were searching the gardens. The slamming doors, the running, the shouting, the sound of furniture being thrown on the floor, drawers emptied: it seemed interminable as she sat waiting, her knee jigging up and down uncontrollably. She held out a hand to Nanna. There was a moment of hesitation, and then Nanna took it and held it tightly. Helene's heart filled with sadness; she had brought dear Nanna so much pain – as had she to Helene.

At one point, a gun went off. Helene gave a start, her hand clammy. But the noises calmed down and one vehicle drove off down the lane. An officer returned to the hall.

'Mrs Le Lacheur, we believe that you have been hiding a deserter and an escaped Russian. You are under arrest.'

Nanna held tight to Helene's hand. Helene had to prise herself loose.

Questioningly, she gestured to Nanna.

'We will leave the old woman.'

Helene was allowed to put a coat on and was bundled into the back of a van. It was the first time she had been in a vehicle since Heinrich had taken her to the Vale the previous year. The memory made her feel sick. She found herself praying desperately to a God she had sworn she no longer believed in.

XII

'Is that Rosamund Rawsthorne?' asked a smooth young female voice.

Roz stiffened instantly. 'That was my name . . . before I married, yes. Who is this?'

She was standing in the kitchen of her flat, preparing her supper. Vegetables were on the cooker. She had been nibbling on some cheese.

'I was wondering if I could ask you a few questions.'

'What about?'

'It will only take a few moments. Are you the daughter of Helene Le Lacheur?'

'Who is this? How did you get my number?'

There was a pause and a rustle of papers at the other end of the phone. The voice resumed, 'I'm calling from a national newspaper. We're very interested in the story of you and your mother . . .'

'What story?' interrupted Roz.

'It's very romantic, isn't it? How your mother and father fell in love at the height of the war between their two countries. We thought it would make a wonderful feature to celebrate the peace between Britain and Germany over the last fifty years.'

Roz was furious. Her voice was hard.

'I don't know what you're talking about. Where on earth did you get my name?'

'I wouldn't want to reveal my sources, but I was on the island recently and a number of people mentioned you. They said you had been visiting. We believe there is a link to your father's trial in 1965.'

'It is complete nonsense. I have nothing to say,' she replied sharply, and put the phone down.

Roz was shaking with fury. The phone rang again. She let it ring, echoing in the flat, until the answerphone finally clicked on. She hadn't thought to turn it off.

'I'm very sorry if I upset you,' said the journalist with practised ease. 'Perhaps I caught you off guard. If either you or your mother would like to talk, please give me a call. I'm sure we could come to an arrangement which you would find financially rewarding, and I think the issues that the article would cover are very important. I will call again in the hope we can have a quick word. Many thanks.'

She left her name and her direct number, her pager and her home number.

Did Antoine give this woman her details? How dare he give her name to a newspaper without permission?

It was four weeks since she had been in Paris and they hadn't spoken. Antoine had called and left messages, but she hadn't responded. He promised he would contact her if they found Alexei, and she was waiting and hoping. She presumed he was still trying to find Heinrich Schulze, and she dreaded hearing news on that score. In the meantime, she had been busy at work. Every evening she had brought home a stack of papers to read. On the few occasions when she thought about her mother's past, she winced. Sometimes when she woke in the early hours of the morning, she found herself imagining her mother's visit to the Morel family – if it had, indeed, been her. How she might have bought the *dragées* and carried them in her handbag. Did she know there were children, or was it just chance? Why was she accompanying Schulze? If it was a business transaction, why didn't she wait in the hotel? Did she ask to come, or were they on their way out to dinner? They were banal details, but they mattered to her. They were part of the picture she needed to help her understand this encounter. How much did Helene know of the Morels' circumstances or what was threatening them? There were no answers, only the knowledge that the visit had probably lain on her mother's conscience for over half a century. After the decades of silence, as she was dying, the memory had punctured her sleep, and left her inconsolable.

Reluctantly, Roz was coming to accept the idea that Antoine's research had explained Meg's story of her mother. But still, she hoped that it could be proved wrong. She was furious with her mother for her lack of courage in facing up to the past, and her lack of honesty with Justin and her children. At other times, she reasoned that it would have been impossible to tell Justin. He would have been horrified. He had fought in the war. He had seen the atrocities of the concentration camps as his battalion pushed through Germany to Berlin. She swung between condemnation and pity. Even her own volatility provoked irritation. She wanted clarity, and there was none.

Could Jim be right that Helene had managed to prevent Roz being adopted, and had arrived in London as a single mother? Was she a heroine or a villain? She pinned all her hopes on finding Alexei. Perhaps he would be able to fix the image – like the chemical in a photographer's dark room; without that, Roz found herself deeply unsettled. 'We need to know where we come from – even if we only ever end up with myths. Without a story of origins, we're at sea.' That's what Antoine had said on the boat in Paris.

Antoine. It still hurt when she thought of him. She wanted to be angry with him. But he had never promised anything, and he was right that she had never asked him about his life. She didn't want a complicated triangle – if that had been on offer. But she was surprised by what he had stirred in her. Something had been reawakened; something she had not known since she was much younger. For the first time in years, she felt lonely in the evenings, working in the quiet flat. The bed seemed too big.

★

A few days after the reporter's call, Antoine phoned.

'I have good news. I've tracked down Alexei in Russia. He is alive and eager to meet you.'

'Are you sure? Where?' In her excitement, Roz even forgot to ask him about the journalist.

'He lives in a town called Orel. It's south of Moscow, near Kursk. He invites you to visit him any time. He says it would be an honour to meet you, Helene's daughter.'

'So he did know Helene?'

'You were right. I think he lived on and off at The Vicarage for a few years. He was vague about the details on the phone, but he wants to explain everything.'

Russia. Roz felt a surge of excitement. She would go to meet Alexei, and he would be able to give her answers. He would know who her father was, she was sure of it. He had known Helene and Schulze. He would tell her the truth, finally. He could explain their relationship.

'This is wonderful. Thank you, Antoine. How did you find him?'

'Mike's contacts found him. They knew him well. And I've spoken to a researcher who can meet you in Moscow. She's called Olga. She can help you with the travel arrangements and translation.'

Roz smiled with delight.

Antoine continued, 'Still nothing on Heinrich Schulze. I have been checking through contacts in Brazil with no luck. Roz, the simplest way of concluding this business would be a newspaper article about your search in the hope that it is picked up in the German media. Someone might know of Schulze and contact us.'

'I don't want to talk to a journalist,' she said doggedly. 'I told you that. But someone did call me – did you give her my details?'

'If not a national paper, what about a small anonymous advert in the Guernsey press?' he replied, ducking her question. 'What harm could that do? It would get all those rumours out into the open. At least you would know then what all the gossip was about. Come on, Roz, you don't need to put your name on it.'

'I'll think about it.'

'And for the record, Roz, it wasn't me who tipped off the journalist. Our visits on Guernsey have been noted. Nothing stays hidden on that island. Various people have put things together. She picked up your name quite easily.'

Roz felt guilty for being distrustful.

'The journalists won't give up. Not now. Once one journalist has a name, it's only a matter of time before others get it. If you give the information, you have more control of the story. Think about it – but not for too long.'

Roz was struck. There was a harshness in his voice. He was angry about something.

He added with a flourish, 'We're looking for justice, don't forget. The people who deserve it are dying. They've waited long enough.'

'You sound angry.'

There was a pause on the line.

'I suppose I am. I've been through files in Guernsey. Documents on the registration of "aliens" – Jews left stranded on the island in 1940. They were refugees from Germany, who must have thought themselves lucky to have reached Britain. But instead they found themselves trapped on the island, unable to return to the mainland after they were declared "enemy aliens" by London. The Germans deported them, and several died in the camps. The island authorities made no attempt to help or hide them. No one since has acknowledged it. It's been quietly forgotten. One of them worked on a farm, and they showed me her signature in the visitor's book.'

'I've never heard about any of this,' said Roz, wondering how much more of the history was waiting to be uncovered.

'Plenty of history goes this way – a discreet forgetting. It's a mixture of embarrassment and indifference. It's put me in a bad mood.'

Roz promised to call from Moscow with any news. It was only after she had put the phone down that she wondered how Antoine knew the journalist had found her name on the island.

★

A few days later, Roz had booked her flights for Russia, and had spoken at length several times to Olga, who understood very quickly the sensitivity of this meeting. Olga made the arrangements with Alexei. Everything was fixed. Roz called Jim and talked over her plans. He urged her to take plenty of presents for the people she would meet – useful things like nice soap. It was good advice, and she tried to guess what Alexei might want. She would visit Jim again on her return.

'I'll need some time beside the river to recover,' she laughed.

'Any time, sister,' Jim replied. 'I'll be wanting to hear everything as soon as you get back.' Then he added, 'You've changed, you know. In the last year or so.'

'How so?'

'It's hard to put a finger on it – less certain of everything all the time. It's a good change,' he reassured her.

They had not said anything to Edward. They agreed there was nothing definite to tell him, and Edward wouldn't want conjecture and gossip. Neither voiced it, but they both knew they were avoiding that particular complication.

In the days leading up to her departure, Antoine had called a few times, leaving messages, but she ignored them. Then, on her way into the office one morning, she found him sitting in reception.

'What on earth are you doing here?' hissed Roz in a whisper. She was very cross.

'I want to finish this project. I want to talk to you. You don't return my calls.'

'Not here.' Her tone was acid. 'I don't want my company tangled up in this. I'm busy today.'

'Roz,' he remonstrated. He was angry. 'You're doing what your mother did – pushing it away. Don't you have a responsibility to help the Morel family get the Cranach back?'

She was furious. 'So your motives are purely altruistic, are they?' she whispered sarcastically.

'Of course they're not. But my father didn't extort the pictures from this family. Doesn't this family deserve justice? Should your father get away with it?'

'My father? How dare you? Neither of us knows who my father is, so you have no right to make assumptions. I can hardly be expected to take on responsibility for a stranger and his sins. Can I?'

'I think you can,' replied Antoine aggressively. 'And if he is your father, you must.'

They stared angrily at each other in the centre of the lobby. Colleagues of Roz hurried past, casting curious looks at Antoine.

'We can't have this argument here,' she said, trying to control her fury. 'I have a meeting now. I can join you in the café around the corner in half an hour.'

She was late and almost missed him. He was just leaving as she arrived, breathless from hurrying. He was still angry. They sat down at a small table.

'OK, I agree to an advert,' said Roz reluctantly. She had

found it hard to concentrate in her meeting as she struggled with the dilemma: was the sacrifice of her privacy the down payment on a reckoning with her alleged father's deeds? That was not a question she would put to Antoine. She knew his answer would be unhesitating.

'We can put a small advert in the local paper and see what turns up,' she added.

'We'll need a PO box number,' Antoine added swiftly.

Together they drafted the advert:

Does anyone have information about the life of the late Helene Le Lacheur, née Le Marchant, born in 1920 in Torteval? All information will be treated with the strictest confidentiality.

Antoine said he'd organize getting it into the island paper as soon as possible. One column wide, two inches high, Roz specified. Antoine wanted it bigger, but was overruled.

'We could add something about the EU research project,' she suggested.

'Better to leave it. We can explain if anyone is prepared to be interviewed,' said Antoine, adding, 'It would look better if we were offering a reward.' He was only half joking.

Roz could barely suppress her irritation. Justin's motto after the trial had been never to meddle with journalists. She felt uneasy.

There was no response for a week after the advert appeared. Roz began to think that she wouldn't hear anything until she was back from Russia. Then two letters arrived a few days before her departure. She sat down over supper to read them:

I am very curious as to who is trying to find out about Helene. Is it her daughter? I am now too old and frail to be able to write, so my grandson is kindly taking this down in dictation. A woman rang about six months ago asking after Helene, and I presume you are the same person.

I am Edith Le Lacheur, and was married to an uncle of Thomas Le Lacheur. Tom married Helene shortly before he left Guernsey to join the Forces. He was killed in the Far East in January 1943. I cannot say it gave me pleasure to be reminded of Helene. I do not wish to be rude to you, but our family was very angry that Tom's name appeared on the birth certificate. I saw Helene only occasionally during the war, and became increasingly concerned by the rumours.

Tom's parents were in England for the duration of the war. When they returned, they were still heartbroken at the death of their son, and deeply shocked by what they heard of their daughter-in-law. She left for England not long after the war ended, and I wasn't surprised. It would have been impossible for her to stay on the island after what had happened.

Tom corresponded regularly with his parents until shortly before his death, and I gathered from them that he was deeply in love with Helene to the end. Tom's father told me once that Tom always had her photo in his breast pocket. On his leave home to his parents in England, he talked frequently of 'Hel', as he called her. In the early summer of 1943 they were told he was missing in action, but didn't have confirmation of his death until June 1945. It was very hard for them.

I heard the rumours that Helene had been with a German officer. At first, I wouldn't believe it. After the war, I went to visit her father, and he denied it all. He said it was lies. But the rumours persisted. They said she went to visit him at Dieu Donne, the home of my brother-in-law. They said she had several German lovers. Despicably, she met them in the childhood home of her husband. It doesn't bear thinking about. I find it hard to forgive her, even though she is dead. She took a German lover when her own husband was risking his life as a soldier for his country. It's incomprehensible to me. I still find it difficult to be civil to Germans. The tourists who come here are all very nice, but I always wonder what they did in the war.

Edith Le Lacheur

Roz groaned aloud, and quickly turned to the second letter.

I knew Helene very well. We were very close friends before the war and friends through the Occupation, although there were periods when I lost touch. I corresponded with Helene intermittently after she left Guernsey in 1946 with a small baby. We met in Devon once, at the house of her aunt, Lily, when my children were young.

I do not know everything that happened to her during the war. She became a very private woman. After the early part of the Occupation, we were no longer so close as we had been and we rarely saw each other. I know she suffered greatly. Not many know, but my own sister also had a relationship with a German soldier. When her fiancé came back from the war, he forgave her. It has always been kept quiet. He was a good man. The Occupation was a very difficult time for us all, and those who didn't live through it have often found it easy to judge and condemn.

As for Heinrich Schulze. In my opinion, he was a scoundrel. He spotted a lovely, lonely girl and if he did seduce her – if – what choice did she have? I know they depended on him for her nanna's medicine. Of course, he was handsome and charming – I met him once in town – but I could tell he was a bounder. Helene was desperate for affection after her mother died. Her father was a very reserved man. In the last two years of the war, I didn't see her and there were rumours and people jumped to conclusions, but none of us knew the full story. I believe there were Russians hidden at The Vicarage as well, but I didn't know about that. It was a tragedy.

*Heinrich deserted in the last days of the war and was executed,
I heard. He jumped a sinking ship and got caught. He was from a
wealthy family in Berlin. He was used to the good things in life.
Even during the worst moments of the Occupation, he knew where
to find good food and wine. I heard that the parties at Dieu
Donne were extraordinary. The war was a holiday for some of
those German officers.*

*Perhaps I shouldn't say all this about someone who might be
your father, but I have always felt so angry about what happened
to Helene. She was more sinned against than sinning, whatever
they say around here. May she rest in peace.*

Best wishes,

Felicity Durand

Roz was grateful for her comments, but neither of these
women knew about her mother's lost years. They were both
relying on gossip. Her focus had narrowed to one question now:
who was her father? She feared that it was probably Schulze, but
she still didn't have the proof she needed and she clung to that
sliver of doubt. The letters didn't tell her more than she had
already managed to piece together, but she conceded that Antoine
had a point: some islanders knew more than she had been able to
glean from random interviews, and adverts seemed the best way
to reach them.

The one new thing was Felicity's reference to Lily, Helene's
aunt, living in Devon. Roz's childhood memory of a visit to an
aunt in Devon was right. Helene had kept in touch with Lily.
Perhaps Felicity Durand would know the name of the town
where Lily had lived, or have an address for her. After all, Lily had
had no reason to break all contact with Guernsey. She would
write to her.

Roz called Antoine and they agreed on another advert, bigger
this time, with the same wording. She would be back from Russia

in a fortnight and by then, someone else might have been in touch. Meanwhile, a local journalist had written, asking who wanted the information and why. Roz and Antoine had a heated discussion about the advantages of responding.

'She could do an article on your research,' said Roz.

'My research is too delicate. I can't reveal anything at this stage.'

Antoine tried to persuade her to do an interview. It could be under a pseudonym, he said, and they could do photographs in silhouette so that she couldn't be identified. She didn't have to acknowledge Helene was her mother. Reluctantly, she agreed.

The journalist was full of polished enthusiasm when Roz called. It would be a 'marvellous feature', 'really strong', with 'lots of human interest'. Roz suppressed her dislike of the facile comments, and asked her to promise to show her the article before it went to print. Roz recorded the phone interview, and a photographer came round the following day. The journalist came to her office to show her the layout of the article, and it was a shock to see the headline of the double-page spread: 'Woman's Quest for Lost Wartime History'. Underneath was a moody shot of her on the balcony of her flat. The prose had a grating sentimentality: 'A woman wronged by history . . . did she have a German lover? Time to set the record straight. Heroine or victim?'

Antoine was delighted. 'Wonderful exposure,' he declared when he called.

Another letter came through the morning Roz set off for the airport. After months of struggling to find information, she had suddenly tapped into a rich seam. There were plenty with opinions about her mother. She put the letter in her bag as she picked up her suitcase. She would read this one in the departure lounge.

At the gate for the Moscow flight, cup of coffee in her hand, she sat down to open the envelope. She smiled with amazement – even pleasure: it was from Arthur Brown, the author of the extraordinary account of Dieu Donne. The garrulous raconteur was still alive.

I know a fair bit about Helene Le Lacheur and her lovers. I didn't put any of it in the diary I gave to the Imperial War Museum twenty years ago. At the time, it was all very secret. They taped an interview too. But there's plenty more. I'm not much of a letter writer, but I'm happy to talk to someone if they come to Guernsey.
    A. Brown

Roz used the call box in the departure lounge and rang the number he had given at the top of his letter. She could hear her flight being called. After a couple of rings, he answered and she breathlessly explained who was calling.

'Why do you want to know about the Le Lacheur girl?' he asked, cutting to the chase.

Roz hesitated. She looked at the planes on the runway through the window. 'I'm her daughter.'

Brown let out a loud laugh. 'I thought that might be the case. Are you the one someone said was in the paper? Well, you've got your homework cut out trying to sort out the Le Lacheur business. I doubt the family was of much help to you. They wouldn't hear of Helene after the war. Don't get me wrong, she was a nice enough girl in her way. But she got herself in a right muddle during the war, there's no mistake. I can tell you all about that. And about Heinrich. Have you heard about him? He's a clever man, that's for sure. Sent me Christmas cards for a long time. Don't know why. Waste of money, in my view. Don't you think so?'

'Ye-es, I agree . . . waste of money,' stammered Roz, bewildered. 'Is Heinrich alive, then?'

'I don't know. He stopped sending the cards, but then I never replied, so maybe he gave up. He'd be getting on.'

It was the final call for the flight.

'I'm at the airport. I'm just catching a flight to Russia, but can I come and see you when I get back?'

'Russia, you say? Ah, would that be Alexei you're looking for?' Roz could hear him laughing.

'A good worker. Mind, he never sent me Christmas cards.'

XIII

The smell was overpowering. The prison was crowded and the small room accommodated five women in addition to Helene. She didn't know any of them, but they were friendly enough, and they showed her the ropes. None of them had soap, of course, and washing was very difficult, with only brief access to a stand-pipe in the morning. The smell of so many bodies in a confined space accumulated into a thick fug. The toilet bucket in the corner filled during the day; they took turns to empty it in the morning and at night. A lot of time was spent waiting. Queuing for lunch took nearly an hour, and it was a bowl of watery cabbage soup and a tiny portion of hard biscuit. Most of the time Helene lay on her bunk, staring at the ceiling. 'It is a waiting game,' she told herself.

When she first arrived, the others eagerly asked her for the latest news. Had the Russians reached Berlin yet? Were the Allies in Germany? They all knew it was a matter of weeks at most before the war ended. Surely Germany could see the end and would surrender. Why would they drag it out and allow Berlin to be destroyed?

She notched small lines on the wall by her bed to mark each day. It was the only way to tell the passing of time. She reached fifteen and gave up. She lost track of time. She had heard nothing about her case. The German administration was breaking down, and it was rare that a German came to the women's section. The guards were islanders and, although they were rough women, they did their best with small gestures of kindness. They allowed a woman to use the standpipe one night. Another brought in a comb for the women to share. The prisoners couldn't keep themselves clean, but they tried to be neat.

At least the weather was warming. Sometimes they were allowed into an exercise yard, and then they could see the sky. Most of the women had been imprisoned for minor infractions of the German regulations – for having a wireless, hoarding food, or petty black-marketeering. They knew they could no longer be sent to France, so the women were not anxious. They were just waiting. One woman, Sarah, seemed to know something of the prison system. She assured Helene that her case would come up soon. But there was no charge, no paperwork, and nobody knew anything about her.

At night, when she couldn't sleep – some of the women snored – she tried to remember the Russian poems Alexei had translated and taught her, but it was a struggle. Her memory moved in strange fits and starts. Odd memories came back perfectly sharp, unbidden. Her mother dressing for a dinner party, and the delicious smell of her as she leaned over the bed to kiss Helene goodnight. The softness of her cheek, the silk of her dress, and the gleam of her pearls. Or Edward on the beach with his friends, playing cricket, their legs and feet brown from the summer sun, and their white trousers rolled up so that they could run into the surf to catch the ball. Their cries of delight and the sound of the waves breaking, and the seagulls wheeling overhead in the sky. Sandwiches and lemonade in the basket waiting for tea on the beach. Helene passed hours with such memories of another life running through her head. They helped to distract her from the wretchedness of all that had followed.

One morning she woke with a feeling of sharp nausea. She retched over the toilet bucket. Sarah eyed her closely. There had been outbreaks of dysentery in the prison. This was not a place for secrets; everyone wanted to know everyone's business. Helene lay back down on her bed. She was crying silently, the tears squeezing out from beneath her closed eyelids. She tried to return to the scent and touch of her mother.

The first they knew of the Liberation was the banging of the guards on the doors. Cheering erupted from every corner of the prison, and the women hit their spoons on the pipework. A clattering echoed all over the building as everyone joined in the impromptu percussion music. A few women were raucously singing *Sarnia Cherie*, the island song: 'Island of beauty, my heart longs for thee'. The women in Helene's cell were hugging each other. Many wept with relief.

The island government would process prisoners' cases as quickly as possible, they were told. The prison began to empty. Every day, there were fewer people in the soup queue at lunchtime. All the conversation was about release dates, but Helene heard nothing. She was feeling ill, unable to eat, and vomiting repeatedly. She lay exhausted on her bed, waiting. Sarah had left and only one other woman now shared her cell. Her paperwork was being processed, she was told by the last remaining guard.

About two weeks or so after Liberation, Helene was taken to the office of the new prison governor. The Germans had all been removed. He was British. A nervous man, he appeared very embarrassed. Helene stood in front of his desk.

'Mrs Le Lacheur. I'm afraid your case has been held up. We are concerned for your safety. There have been some very unpleasant incidents in the town recently . . .' His voice petered out.

'Is there someone who could come to fetch you and accompany you home to Torteval? There is very little transport at the moment. No petrol on the island. You will have to walk, and we think you need to be accompanied. We also understand you have been ill-disposed.'

'Thank you, but no, that won't be necessary,' said Helene stiffly, relieved to be leaving. 'My father is in Germany and our gardener is too old to walk into town and back. I wouldn't want to put him to that trouble. I can walk home alone.'

He looked unhappy. 'This is for your safety. There has been trouble, with women . . .' He placed a curious emphasis on the word 'women'. As if they were dirty.

Helene wasn't sure what he was talking about.

'I am very anxious to get home as soon as possible. My elderly housekeeper is waiting for me – she needs me. She must be beside herself with anxiety. I have been away almost two months. I would like to leave as soon as possible.'

She said this last with emphasis, looking him in the eye.

He dropped his gaze quickly. 'I've done what I can to warn you, Mrs Le Lacheur. I suggest you leave shortly before dark. With luck, you can get through town without incident.'

Now that she had made the decision, he seemed glad to be rid of her.

A few hours later, she was standing outside the prison, the fresh sea air on her face. She breathed deeply. The walk home couldn't be more than five miles. She felt a bit unsteady on her feet, so she walked slowly. She had lost a lot of weight. It would take her a few hours along the main road, but she didn't mind, she was going home. Her spirits lifted. She would take backstreets, and before long she would be out of town heading towards St Martin, but she was nervous. She thought if she kept her head down and avoided eye contact, she should be all right. British soldiers were on the streets, she had heard.

The prison entrance led on to a quiet street and there was no one around. She was wearing the clothes she had been arrested in, and she had worn them most of the time she had been in prison. She knew she smelled. She dreamed of getting home and finally washing herself properly. A bowl in front of the fire in the kitchen, with perhaps a precious sliver of soap, a sponge and a towel. Such things had seemed like harsh deprivations in the early days of the Occupation, when they had had to adjust to the shortages of fuel for heating water. Now, they were luxuries.

She knew that if she turned left onto the Grange, and took another left turn onto Havilland Street, down Allez Street and then Lower Vauvert, that would lead eventually to Trinity Square and then up the Ruettes Braye out of town. That way she avoided the area around the harbour, where there were likely to be more passers-by. A woman came out of her house with her children. She looked at Helene with the usual islander curiosity. Helene gave her a small nod as she stepped aside to let them pass. She pressed on, heartened by the normality of this brief encounter. She didn't think she knew anyone who lived round here. Her confidence was growing. Perhaps people hadn't heard about her; perhaps Nanna and Heinrich's plan had worked after all.

Then she heard a shout, then another.

'Oi, you.'

She turned round. In that second, she realized the danger. The tone was aggressive. Perhaps someone had seen her leave the prison. Perhaps she had been recognized. She couldn't see anyone. The street still appeared to be empty, and it was eerily quiet after the shout. Seagulls were crying from a nearby rooftop; they seemed to be watching her. She hesitated. Should she continue along the street, or try to shake off whoever had spotted her by turning back? She pressed on, her pace a little quicker, despite knowing that it would exhaust her limited strength. She could slow down when she was out of the town.

Then a stone hit her on the side of her head. She stopped, too shocked to move. She looked up to see where it had come from. A group of teenagers on a corner were looking at her. Their expressions were blank, a kind of hard indifference. She could feel blood beginning to trickle, wet and warm, down the side of her face. Bewildered, she turned to see whether she could return the way she had come, but three people were coming towards her. One of them was a woman who used to work in the fish shop. She wouldn't hurt her. For a fraction of a moment, Helene felt relief. She remembered how the girl had served her many times before the war. She also thought she knew one of the lads – hadn't he been in her class for a while, early in the Occupation? They couldn't mean to harm her. Both groups were now moving towards her. She stood still, uncertain of their intentions. She looked from face to face. It was as if they had a premeditated plan. They knew what they were doing. Perhaps they had seen her come out of the prison, and followed her.

She glanced up at the windows of the houses which lined the street, silently begging a door to open. She caught sight of a face behind a net curtain, but it swiftly vanished. She looked at the group coming up the street towards her and turned to face those coming down. She edged back against the wall of a house.

They were closing in around her now, their stares hostile. It was as if they could smell her fear, and it made them bolder. One of the young men had a walking stick and he swirled it around in the air. Helene stared at it and at him. He looked like the brother of an old school friend, but she could be mistaken. They were just a few feet away. She moved her eyes from face to face with an unspoken plea.

Now she was cornered, they were uncertain as to what to do next. They stared with a combination of intense curiosity and malevolence, as if they had glimpsed a way to vent five years of frustration and fear. A cold terror gripped her.

Then someone spat. She heard the sound before she felt the warm wet spittle land on her face. In her eyes and on her lashes. Astonished, she turned; a large young woman stood staring back at her, defiantly.

Someone pulled at her clothing, and then someone else. Several hands were tugging at her coat. The spitting seemed to have unleashed the energy of the crowd. They moved in and she was pushed from one side of the group to the other as they jeered. Her coat had come off, and a cheer went up, then someone grabbed at her skirt. A short rusty knife was thrust in her face, and she was pushed roughly to the cobbles. She heard raucous cries as more people joined the small crowd. She lay on the cold pavement, struggling to breathe; panic had set her heart beating so fast. Someone kicked her hard in the shins.

She tried to scream, but her voice was barely louder than a whisper. 'Please, stop, please help me,' she begged, fixing her eyes on an older woman, who was peering over the shoulders of the teenagers.

'Jerrybag, filthy tart. Your lover kept you well fed, didn't he?' They taunted her as they kicked. Grotesque insults, and their echoes, ricocheted up and down the narrow street.

'Chuck her in the harbour.'

'Tar and feather 'er, like they did in France.'

Helene looked up and caught a glimpse of the horrified faces of an elderly couple at their upstairs window. She saw them stare, motionless. No one was coming to help.

People were pulling her hair now. She felt the wrench and tearing pain. Her head banged down on the cobbles. She saw blood. Her own. Blood on cobbles, again. And clumps of her bloodied fair hair. Someone was using the rusty knife to hack it off.

'Slept with Germans. Kept it all well hidden. No better than a tart, and she a vicar's daughter.' She could hear the murmurs in the crowds as the comments were passed from one to another. A woman moved forward, her feet in heavy men's boots. She kicked Helene. The blows were hard and fast, pummelling her body. She curled into a ball to protect her stomach. She could feel the chill on her legs. Her skirt had been ripped off. Someone was trying to cut off her cardigan with a knife. They were going to strip her. She was screaming uncontrollably. Sobbing. Her voice had returned and she filled her lungs to scream, again and again: 'Mother, Mother. Help, help!' She was hoarse. The words became barely comprehensible.

★

She may have passed out. There was a gap in her memory when she tried later to recall the sequence of events. How long had she been on the ground, how long had they been kicking her? Then a young sergeant with a thick English accent was picking her up. He held the crowd back with an outstretched arm. She couldn't understand what he was saying, but she remembered the sing-song sound of his voice. He carried her in his arms, and pushed through the angry crowd. He yelled at them to leave her alone. They slowly dispersed.

When the street was empty, he sat her down on a doorstep. He offered her a handkerchief and his water bottle. Her teeth were chattering. He had retrieved her coat and put it round her shoulders. She had lost her skirt.

'Home . . . I want t-to get home,' she finally managed to say. 'The Vicarage, Torteval.'

He said something to her, but when he saw she couldn't understand his accent, he gestured to her to walk. He supported her, but she was limping badly. Her foot hurt. They walked down to the end of the street. She noticed several people were still watching her from their windows, half hidden.

A lorry came, full of soldiers chatting and laughing. She was half pulled into the back. They made space for her on a bench, and fell into a sullen silence. She shrank against the canvas side, clinging to a metal upright. The back of the vehicle was open, and she kept her eyes on the road disappearing behind them. She recognized the parishes after a while: St Martin, Forest and, finally, Torteval. No one spoke on the journey back to The Vicarage. Every jolt of the rough road was agony; every time she took a breath, there was a sharp stabbing pain and she realized some ribs must be broken.

When they arrived at the house, the sergeant jumped down, and rang the front doorbell. Nanna appeared. Reluctantly one of the soldiers helped her down. She heard him curse her under his breath, but he half carried her into the house. She couldn't put weight on one foot; it was badly hurt. Nanna, too shocked to speak, gestured them to the kitchen. Helene sat down at the table and put her head in her arms. She felt she was going to vomit and her head was spinning.

Nanna filled a bowl with warm water and her ashen face loomed over Helene as she bathed the blood from her face and cleaned the raw wounds on her head.

She could feel hot tears pouring down her face. Her war was finally ending.

XIV

Roz and Olga arrived at Orel station on the night train from Moscow early in the morning. The air was crisp and the last of the mist still hung over the tracks. The train waited at the station for a long time, as if exhausted by its night's exertions. Only a handful of other passengers got off and on. Roz had not slept much; the clanking metalwork of the train had kept her awake, and she was too excited. She felt the end of her search was now close. She had fixed her hopes on Alexei. He would have answers to all her questions. She still hoped that he might be her father. He might even be able to tell them the whereabouts of Cranach's *Virgin*.

The night before Roz left London, Antoine had rung to tell her that he had booked a flight to Moscow. He wanted to talk to Alexei too. She had only a few weeks' head start. On the train overnight from Moscow, she had raised the blind from time to time, and watched the Russian towns and forests slip past in the dim light of dawn. She saw the rising sun burn through the mist. She remembered Mike's descriptions of the young slave labourers on Guernsey – how they had been packed into train wagons and transported across Europe to reach the Channel Islands. The history felt close, breathing down her neck.

At the station, a group of men waited at the exit. As she and Olga walked down the long platform, a man broke away from the group and came towards them. Was this Alexei? Could this plump, balding man have known her mother more than fifty years ago? He greeted them in Russian, and Olga began talking to him. After a while she turned to Roz to explain that Alexei had waited for them for two days, but after their repeated delays in Moscow, he had now gone to his farm, where he had planting to do. He had left his friend Vladimir with detailed instructions to meet them, take them to his flat in the city and find a taxi to bring them to the farm the following day. Vladimir smiled at Roz and shook her hand. He insisted on picking up her suitcase. Olga and he walked ahead, talking.

Outside the station, on the forecourt of beaten mud, families had placed things for sale on bits of cardboard and on plastic bags, carefully positioned between the ruts and puddles. A few cigarette lighters, cheap toys and the produce from vegetable plots, such as radishes and small cucumbers. Roz and Olga made their way past the makeshift stalls to the bus stop. Vladimir had refused to take a taxi, claiming that they charged too much. People waiting at the stop cast sidelong glances at Roz. She felt more conspicuous here than she had done in Moscow. Her coat, her boots, her suitcase were different: they were relatively new.

'Vladimir was in Alderney,' said Olga. Those standing beside them, hearing her English, turned to stare at Roz.

'Ask him if he ever went to Guernsey, if he ever met my mother.'

Olga relayed the question to Vladimir, and they talked for a long time while Roz waited.

'He asked me to tell you that he remembers your island very well. It was a very difficult time for him,' said Olga, as Vladimir resumed. When he had finished, Olga summarized: 'No, he never met your mother, but he remembers that Alexei spoke of her often after the war. He used to say he was going back to London to live with her. She had saved his life. Vladimir said they laughed at Alexei for his impossible dreams. After a few years, he stopped talking about her and the islands. It became a big problem for them.'

'A big problem? Why?' asked Roz.

Vladimir shrugged his shoulders, but didn't say anything.

'For many of those who had been deported for slave labour, life in the Soviet Union after the war was very difficult,' Olga explained under her breath. 'They were treated as traitors. They struggled to get jobs, flats, even televisions. Their children suffered.'

Vladimir was looking away. He seemed embarrassed. Olga added quietly, 'I think he is a communist. He doesn't like what is happening now in Russia. People are losing their jobs, and the factories are closing. Others are making money. He says it was better in the Soviet Union.'

The bus arrived. The windows were coated with grey dirt, so the people inside could barely be seen. The three of them squeezed in, pushed by others behind them. Roz hung from a strap, pressed against a man with vodka-laden breath and a young woman in thick make-up. She craned her neck to see out of the grimy window at the streets. At her feet, a woman had put down her bag, full of bunches of fragrant coriander and dill.

Vladimir, Olga and Roz got off at a housing estate on the outskirts of the town, where the wide, virtually empty road was bordered by tower blocks. They passed a run-down children's playground, with broken swings and climbing frames. Under some small trees a group of men were drinking from vodka bottles. The two women followed Vladimir across open wasteland, where the grass was growing tall after the summer rain.

Alexei and Vladimir lived with their families in the last block. The lift had broken, so they climbed three flights of stairs. The stairwell reeked of urine and cooking fat. As they passed each landing, they heard the muffled sounds of family life – a child singing, a television drama and, once, a couple shouting. Outside several flats were large chained dogs, who bared their teeth and glowered at them. Alexei and Vladimir lived in adjoining flats.

Both doors had been padded and covered in leatherette to insulate them. From one came the warm smell of baking. Vladimir rang the bell. The door was opened immediately by Alexei's wife, Irina, almost as broad as she was high, an enormous gold-toothed smile on her face.

Roz was ushered in with great excitement and was hugged, kissed on both cheeks several times, and offered a chair at a table in the small living room. From the sofa opposite, a small girl watched her with huge eyes. Irina and her daughter then disappeared into the kitchen. Roz looked around the small sitting room; on every available surface were piles of books. *Paris for Art Lovers* read one spine in English, *Plato* read another. The shelves of a glass cabinet were laden with photos of weddings, factory parades and grandchildren. On the wall was a framed photo of the Eiffel Tower, and another of a Renoir painting. The warmth and atmosphere of the little flat was in sharp contrast to the bleak streets outside. Irina bustled between the kitchen and the sitting room, bringing trays laden with teacups and plates. She kept up a stream of chatter in Russian to Olga, full of questions about the journey, what they ate last night and how had they slept. She brought out her best linen from a drawer in the sideboard, and polished her glasses. It was only nine in the morning, but, despite Roz's translated protestations, the small decorated glasses were filled with vodka. Vladimir swiftly drank his.

As Roz sipped her tea, Irina carried through plates heaped with slices of sausage, potatoes, cucumbers and radishes. Roz was pressed to try some of Irina's pickled gherkins. Later in the autumn, there would be the harvest on Alexei's farm, Irina told Olga. Then, with a great fanfare, Irina produced sweet cheese pastries straight from the oven. The little girl overcame her shyness in her eagerness to take one. It was so hot it burned her tongue, and she and Roz smiled at each other as she blew on the pastry to cool it. Irina was finally satisfied that she had done her duty by her honoured guest. Roz explained, through Olga, that she was tired after her train journey. A bed was already made up for her in a narrow bedroom, where she gratefully fell asleep under a photo of the Île de la Cité, faded and yellow with age.

Making the arrangements to leave for Alexei's farm thirty miles away required all of Olga's considerable diplomatic skills. Vladimir wanted to show them the sights of Orel – a memorial to the unknown soldier, a museum of science and the old town centre. Irina wanted to feed them. Both protested at the thought of Roz and Olga setting off again in the morning. Irina warned that the farm was not comfortable: the roof leaked, it had mice and was dirty. She said that Alexei lived like a dog there. But Roz was impatient, and told Olga to find transport, adding in a whisper that she didn't care what it cost. Several times, Vladimir disappeared to negotiate with possible taxi drivers, only to return, shocked at the prices they were asking. Roz tried to explain that money was not a problem; she showed him a fifty-dollar note, but his face showed no recognition – he didn't know what it was. By 9 p.m. it was settled, and a couple arrived to finalize travel arrangements over several glasses of vodka. They were planning to visit relatives at a nearby collective, and they agreed to drop Olga and Roz at Alexei's farm, and pick them up again the following day.

Early next morning Roz and Olga set off with boxes of food prepared by Irina, and a bag of seed Alexei had not been able to carry when he had left two days before. The road surface was poor, and the aged car was so laden with supplies and suitcases that Roz worried it might break down, but no such anxiety crossed the minds of the jovial driver and his wife. Exuberant to have such lucrative passengers, they chatted to Olga, barely pausing to let her translate. As they drove out of Orel, they passed a huge plinth with a flame burning in its centre. They proudly pointed it out as the war memorial, and recounted their terrifying experiences as children in the German Occupation, and their escape from the huge battles fought around Orel in 1943.

'For shelter, they scraped holes in the near-frozen ground and covered themselves with leaves after every house had been razed to the ground,' explained Olga to Roz.

It was hard to imagine that these huge rolling fields, now covered with ripening wheat, had once been the scene of such devastation. Roz felt exhausted by the horror of their stories. The disorientation and unfamiliarity of the last few days' experiences had drained her. She stared out of the window. The big skies of this open country were a relief after the confined spaces of Irina's flat in Orel and Olga's flat in Moscow. She wound down the window to feel the light summer breeze and to smell the freshness of the country air. The driver was skilled and knew the road well, swerving around the frequent potholes, but he could rarely get above 30 mph. They crossed a wide river on a concrete bridge. Roz glimpsed a massive body of brown water between marshy banks. Not long after, they turned off the road down a deeply pitted track. The axles creaked and groaned and the driver drove up onto the verge to navigate the deepest ruts. It had not rained for several days or it would have been impassable, Olga explained. The road was only useable at the height of summer. Roz watched the sunlight filtering through a copse of poplar trees, the pale green leaves glittering in the brightness. Then the track dipped into a shallow valley. They had arrived.

A few wooden buildings were scattered on either side of the track; their thatched roofs were rotting in places and covered in moss. In front of several of these shacks were neat vegetable gardens. Unlike the houses, they were immaculate, with rows of onions, potatoes and carrots. Runner beans climbed a line of stakes made from branches, and their first scarlet flowers had appeared. The car stopped outside one of the most run-down houses. Plastic sacks had been tied over parts of the thatch. A

couple of broken-down vehicles were in the yard in front –
a rusty tractor and an old trailer with no wheels – and a dog
was barking fiercely. Outside the front door was a pile of rusty
tin cans.

A man appeared on the porch and stared at the car. Then his
face broke into a grin and he came down the steps, walking with
a pronounced limp.

'Roz! Welcome!' he cried, and flung out his arms to greet her.

She got out of the car, straightening up after the long bumpy
journey. They looked each other up and down with delight.

'Let me look at you. Yes, yes, just like your mother.' His voice
was choking with tears. He wrapped his arms around her to
embrace her. He released her eventually, but he wouldn't let go
of her hand, and his eyes were fixed on her. He was beaming.
Roz smiled and blinked back her own tears.

'This is wonderful. Dear Helene's child has come to see me.'
The tears were pouring down his creased cheeks, and he kept
wiping them away with his handkerchief.

Roz felt a sudden, inexpressible surge of joy. This warm-
hearted man had used the word 'dear'. He had loved Helene, she
knew it instantly. She was filled with gratitude. He picked up her
suitcase and, still holding her hand, led her up the path between
the vegetable beds to the porch.

'My English is still here with me. I listen to your BBC World
Service so that I don't forget,' he laughed.

Olga made arrangements with the couple who would pick
them up the next day, and the car turned and slowly lumbered off
up the track. After its engine died away, all that could be heard in
the sudden quiet was the song of larks hovering over the open
fields. Alexei seated Roz and Olga on a bench on his veranda and
brought out a tray with black tea and a bowl of sugar cubes.

'We have much to talk about, Roz. Are we sure that just one
day is enough? A life to fit into a few hours.'

Roz stared at him. He was unmistakeably the young man of the other photo – the one in cricket whites. In the face in front of her she could see the features she had studied so carefully in the small black-and-white print. He was still a handsome man, but now his face was scored with deep lines. It looked as if life had been hard for him. He was shabbily dressed in baggy, patched clothes.

'It's not like The Vicarage,' he said, gesturing at his home, and smiling at her. He spoke English with a strange accent. Something of the Guernsey intonations had lasted the decades.

Roz finally had the confirmation she had wanted. The photo was of Alexei, but that only made the questions more pressing: how could Heinrich have been the photographer? How could the German officer have been willing to be photographed by the Russian escapee? Arthur Brown had been right: her mother had got herself into an extraordinary tangle. Alexei, here beside her, would be able to explain. She felt so grateful that she had come, and that she had found him in time. That he was still alive to tell her story. Alexei sat down on a broken wooden chair. His eyes had not left her face. The warmth of his smile transformed the rugged face.

'I've dreamed of The Vicarage all my life. It was –' he paused – 'what is the word? M . . . magnificent.' Pleased with his ability to recollect the word, he smiled. 'There are few houses in Russia like The Vicarage – I have never seen them. Carpets, china, pictures on the wall! In Guernsey, I slept under light, warm quilts and the linen was like . . . silk. And Helene lent me her brother's clothes – soft cotton shirts and fine woollen trousers.'

'The cricket trousers!' exclaimed Roz, laughing.

He looked puzzled by the interruption, but she didn't explain. That could come later.

'Well, well, I paid for this war of luxury. Many times.' He lifted up his hands – calloused and ingrained with earth – and shrugged his shoulders. He paused to drink his tea, leaning back against the timber wall of the house.

'I loved the flowers – I've never seen these flowers again. Big bushes, flowers as big as a dinner plate, and palm trees. And everywhere, the sea. It was a small place. I was surprised how, when I walked, I always bumped into the sea. Many houses and many lanes! It was like the place had been shrunk. I could walk from north to south in a day with ease. These things were extraordinary to me. Here, you can see, the land is big – in every direction. I felt the island was like living in a doll's house.'

Behind the house was a line of poplar trees and, every now and then, a breeze would stir their leaves to a soft rattling; it was the first moments of quiet since Roz had come to Russia. As if he read her thoughts, Alexei leaned forward.

'Listen. Listen to my motherland. Listen to the quiet. All my life I wait to live in that quiet.' He breathed deeply, as if he was smelling a sweet perfume. 'We will eat and then we will talk. My hospitality is simple. You must forgive me.'

Olga and Roz brought out the packages which Irina had given them and together they laid out the picnic of sausage, gherkins and bread on the low table. They helped Alexei bring plates from the kitchen. The interior was austere: a bed against the wall, an old sofa, a stove and a table with a pile of books.

'Irina is a kind woman,' said Alexei, tucking into the food hungrily. 'You are very like your mother,' he repeated to Roz.

'Is it strange after all these years for me to have contacted you?'

'Strange, and not strange. I felt sure that there was a final part to my story with Helene, and now we write it. I'm glad. Thank you for coming.' He paused as he wiped more tears away.

'I remember when I met you, you were only a few weeks old. Helene gave you to me to hold. You had been screaming and I took you out – it was a clear night – and when you saw the moon, you stopped crying and gazed at it. I saw the moonlight in your eyes. I was very moved. Helene was in the Vale at the time. She went there to have the baby – to have you.'

He stopped and cleared his throat uneasily.

'You met me?' said Roz, incredulous. 'You were in Guernsey after Liberation?'

'Yes, yes, I will explain everything.' He smiled at the memory. 'You were born in a cottage in the Vale, and I visited once. My memory is not good these days and I do get things wrong, but I don't think you were Roz then.'

'Well, I was christened Rosamund, and called Rosie when I was little.'

'Mmm . . . perhaps that was it. Rosie, Rosie.' He repeated the name slowly to help his memory. 'Yes, Rosie,' he continued. 'At that time I only saw Helene once or twice. When I could, I went to where Helene was staying with an elderly couple – relatives of her nanna. It had been arranged by Nanna. That's what I understood, but Helene didn't want to talk about it. She was very upset. It was a bad time. I understood Nanna was trying to protect her name. I am so glad you went with her to London.'

He rubbed the stubble of his chin with his big hand.

'I had a letter in 1947 from Helene to say she was in London and she had her baby with her, but after that, there were no more letters. Perhaps they were lost. I wrote several times but I feared the address was out of date – and my written English was not good. Perhaps Helene did not want such letters.'

'I think she wanted to forget the war.'

'Yes, well, there are many of us who have tried,' he said, and added more quietly, 'but I never wanted to forget your mother. I loved her very much. Many times I have asked myself why I didn't stay with her and you. She needed me, and I left her – I made a mistake. I was young and wanted to find my family again. I was homesick for my motherland. I came back to a country which accused me of treason. A country broken by war, a place of terrible poverty and suffering. My mother and sisters were dead. I came back to nothing, and left you and Helene behind. I was stupid; I thought I could return to Helene if my family were dead, but it was never possible.'

'Tell me about how you met Helene,' said Roz eagerly.

Alexei laughed. A cat had jumped onto his lap and he stroked its head, scratching between its ears. 'Loving Helene was easy to understand – she saved my life, she taught me English, and she sheltered me when I thought I was dying. I had escaped and she found me and nursed me back to life. She was very brave.

'She taught me English with children's books. And George taught me how to garden. Do you know of this George? He was also a very good man. He was the gardener at The Vicarage. He must have died. He was already old during the war. He had fought in a war in Africa, and it had left him with terrible pain. I helped him with the heavy work.

'But your mother was more than kind. She was an angel to me. She was beautiful, shy and loving, and full of laughter. Some of the happiest times of my life I spent with her, reading or listening to the wireless we kept throughout the war.

'She was lonely and scared – as we all were at that time – and we talked. Guernsey was a small island and every way you turned, there were soldiers. It was never safe to move from one place to another. We were trapped in a soldiers' garrison. She spoke to me of her brother; she was worried about him, and she spoke of the sadness of having lost her mother before the war.'

His descriptions brought tears to Roz's eyes. She had never heard anyone talk about her mother with such loving tenderness. She tried to imagine the mother she had known as that young woman.

There was a pause. He looked uncomfortable.

'You've heard of Heinrich?' he asked anxiously, looking straight at Roz. 'This is the difficult part. Many judged her.'

He abruptly got up to take the plates back into the house. When he reappeared, he cleared his throat before sitting down again. He was looking at his worn boots.

'She talked to me about him. She didn't try to hide it. She was charmed and fascinated by him. Was she in love? Was she caught in a cruel choice? I think it was both. I knew he helped her in many ways during the Occupation. I couldn't judge her for it. We talked about the right and wrong. Could one love the enemy that a husband and brother were fighting? I hated Heinrich for how he hurt her . . . and I hated him for winning her love . . . and in the end I hated him for putting her in danger. When I left her, I stopped hating him and remembered how I loved him.'

'Loved him?' exclaimed Roz, astonished.

'Yes, in a way. You have a likeness to your father – something about the set of your eyebrows and forehead. He was a handsome man, as I think you have seen from photos. A wonderful man in his way, whatever people have said. Full of generosity, enthusiasm and intelligence. Yes, he was also – how did Helene say it? – overbearing. He was a German, a soldier in an invading army. He took things which did not belong to him – that's what they do. He was determined and knew what he wanted. I couldn't completely trust him, and after a while, I avoided him when I could, but I cannot forget that he did not betray me. I could not help liking him – even admiring him. He was complicated; it made me see German history in a way that no history book could.'

Roz had her answer. She felt sick. Olga looked over at her anxiously. A German father. He might still be alive, according to Arthur Brown. She was filled with sadness for her young, confused mother. Alexei continued, oblivious that the question could have had any other answer.

'Heinrich had a manner which always surprised you. He was amusing. He taught me some German – which was very useful for me – and he even read me poetry – he loved Schiller. I am lucky, I learn languages well, and in the war it saved my life. He had great insight into art and poetry. He explained to me why Picasso, Léger and Braque were great artists. The few conversations we had in the summer of 1943 made a big impression on me.

'For a simple Russian peasant boy, he opened up worlds, and I learned much. Looking back, I wonder that he talked to me. He was in his early thirties, and I was nearly fifteen years younger. He was an intellectual – he knew much about music, film and theatre – and I was an escaped forced labourer.

'I grew up in my time in Guernsey. When I first arrived on the island, I was terrified of the beatings and brutality of the Germans. It was a time of terror, but after I escaped, I met people from many countries. In the escape network, the Russians talked more freely than we had ever done before – or could when we came home. We discussed Stalin, the collectivization programme, which had left my family homeless in 1933, and we talked about the famine. When we met the Spanish republicans in the labour camps on Guernsey, we argued at night in our bunks over communism, capitalism and fascism. I made friends with Felipe, a Spanish republican doctor who treated a wound on my foot, and he taught me what I understand of politics. He was a very clever man from Barcelona.

'When I talked about my conversations with Felipe to Heinrich, he was very interested. In Berlin before the Nazis, several of his friends had been socialists, but he hated communism, and the Weimar Republic had left him bitter with capitalist democracy. I think his love of pleasure came from the disappointments – is that the word? He had never been a Nazi. But he did tell me that his father had joined the Party and had been able to help the family. He said his father had known how to keep safe. He had an engineering business which won contracts from the government, I think. Heinrich was vague – it was probably arms.'

Roz found this description of her father and his family deeply confusing. It felt so – there was no other word – foreign. She knew nothing of Germany, she realized, neither its language or its history. She had never visited, and now she was listening to someone describe her German grandfather. She was British; Justin, with his old-fashioned patriotism, had taught her that. What identity would she now make for herself from this muddled history? She didn't even know where to start – she had never had to give the subject a thought. She thought of that sturdy British passport embossed with its lion and mythical unicorn.

Alexei paused for a moment, but resumed before anyone said anything. He had their rapt attention. 'He loved his fine wines, and somehow he managed to find them throughout the Occupation. He visited Paris several times during the war, and once, in late 1943, he took Helene.'

'Oh, God,' whispered Roz. 'You're sure? Of the dates?' she asked quickly, insistent.

Alexei looked alarmed.

'Why? Is there some significance to this?'

Roz nodded.

'I don't want to cause problems for you. I think that was the date, but I am an old man. I remember a brief conversation with Helene – she seemed nervous but excited. You must forgive me if I cannot be certain. It is more than fifty years ago. Some things about Guernsey are clear – the layout of places and the land, but dates less so. I had no watch or calendar, no way to keep the time.'

'I'm not doubting. Just trying to fit everything together,' said Roz, apologetic. Schulze was her father. Helene had visited the Morels in Paris. She felt shabby; she had been conceived with the guilt of both her parents.

Alexei hesitated and then continued, 'Food became scarce towards the end, after the liberation of France. Heinrich lost

324

weight and was tired, but, even then, he had access to good brandy and cigars. My favourite memories are from earlier in the war – the evenings in the summer of 1943, when the three of us were together, talking or playing cards. It may have happened only a few times, but it is a very vivid memory. Strange to think that, in the midst of such misery, we were happy. It must be rare that two men and the woman they both love can enjoy each other's company. But there was something about all our stories which made our friendship a relief from loneliness and fear, from the war and the future. From everything that had made that – how shall we call it? – triangle of friendship possible.'

'It's an extraordinary story,' broke in Olga, moved by his account.

Alexei nodded thoughtfully. He resumed, his tone sharper, 'Heinrich loved women. There was gossip on the island during the war; George was worried about it. He heard that people were talking about your mother. But be sure of one thing, Roz: Heinrich did love your mother. He was the kind of man who might not have been faithful. He was with a French prostitute at one point, but that was before Helene. I have no doubt that, if Heinrich had lived, Helene and he would have married, and he would have been devoted to her.'

'Lived? You think he died?'

'Yes, he was executed. Shot in the prison at St Peter Port, I was told after the war. In the last days of the war, he deserted.'

'But an islander has told me that he was alive – living in Germany – until quite recently,' Roz interrupted.

Now it was Alexei's turn to look shocked. He rubbed his hands as he repeated Heinrich's name. 'Are you sure? Well . . . well. This is good. I am glad he survived. How did he manage to escape his death sentence? Could we find him alive today?'

'I don't know how he escaped execution, but yes, perhaps he is still alive. Someone is looking for him.'

'I see – well, I don't see, but that is your English expression,' he said quietly, frowning. 'Ha, Heinrich, clever to the last. I would like to meet him again – to talk about those times.' He picked up a piece of sausage but held it in his fingers, absent-minded, for a moment.

'When he deserted, I remember he came to The Vicarage and I took him to the cliffs to a place where he could hide. He said he couldn't face a prisoner-of-war camp. He was close to a fellow officer, a socialist, who had some secret plan to surrender the island to the Allies. I couldn't understand why he was taking such a risk when the island was so close to liberation. But they found him, I was told.'

He broke off to eat the sausage.

Roz was staring vacantly at the poplar trees. She looked disconsolate, shaken by Alexei's revelations. 'I wish Mother had told me – perhaps I could have helped her. She didn't need to die with that guilt,' she whispered.

Alexei put a hand on her shoulder. 'Let me find something for you.'

He went inside and re-emerged with a battered book of poetry. 'Years ago, a friend sent me this book from Moscow. I had told him that I had read these poems on Guernsey. The words are not the same – it is a different translation.' He thumbed through the pages hurriedly. 'Heinrich used to read Schiller to us. He had found a copy of an English translation in the study of Helene's father. Here . . . this is it. Helene was to him what Laura was to Friedrich Schiller, he told me. He read the poem to both of us. I can read it for you – I would like to . . . to their daughter.'

In his rich deep voice, he slowly read aloud,

> '"*On the wings of Love the future hastens*
> *In the arms of ages past to lie;*
> *And Saturnus, as he onward speeds him,*
> *Long hath sought his bride – Eternity!*

Soon Saturnus will his bride discover –
So the mighty oracle hath said;
Blazing worlds will turn to marriage torches
When Eternity with Time shall wed!

Then a fairer, far more beauteous morning,
Laura, on our love shall also shine,
Long as their blest bridal-night enduring –
So rejoice thee, Laura – Laura mine!"'

Alexei looked up at them. 'He told us that he dreamed of the "blazing worlds" turning to "marriage torches".' Roz and Olga were smiling with appreciation of his halting voice, heavy with emotion. He put the book down on the table.

'I think Helene knew that Heinrich was dangerous, and it frightened her. She was young and innocent. She had led a very sheltered country life on Guernsey before the war. When she felt fearful, she came to me. My love was straightforward. I loved her like I could never love another woman, not then and not since.

'Your mother was very lovable. Heinrich and I once spoke about it. He said it was the mix of three things, I remember. There was the sadness of her situation, alone, the guardian of the family house. She was keeping alive the memory of her mother, her brother and her husband. Her father left in 1943, deported to an internment camp in Germany. Then there was her beauty – she had little knowledge of it, but it shone despite her shabby wartime clothes. Finally, there was her shy wish for intimacy.'

Alexei paused and ran his hand through his thick white hair.

'Poor Helene, it must have been frightening to have been left alone,' commented Roz softly.

'Yes, she was not safe on that island. For the last two years of the war, only the two old servants – George and Nanna – were at The Vicarage with her. I left in the autumn of 1943. I found a farm in Castel where I could work. I knew my presence put Helene in danger. By the late summer of 1944, I was able to visit occasionally.'

He took a deep breath. 'In April 1945, I arrived at The Vicarage to find Heinrich there, on the run. I was very angry with him. I told him when we were alone – he was putting Helene in huge danger, as he well knew. But my anger didn't last. For the first time, I saw him frightened. He was worried that his French lover was trying to take revenge for his relationship with Helene and was spreading malicious rumours. He asked me to hide a box he had brought for Helene – something that could be sold in London. I knew he had already given her other works of art. He had told me about his dealing in France – he said the Nazis wanted to destroy the art he loved – and he described the horror of paintings being burned in bonfires at the Louvre.'

'A box?' asked Roz, but Alexei held up his hand, intent on telling his story.

'He was worried about Helene's future. He knew there were rumours on the island about her. I suppose he was also thinking of you. That was the last time we were together. Soon after Liberation, I walked to The Vicarage, and found George and Nanna very worried for Helene. I knew she had been arrested by the Germans the night after we left – I went back a few days afterwards and the house was empty.'

'Arrested?' asked Roz, horrified. 'Poor, poor Mother.'

'At the time, I hoped that at least Helene had managed to say goodbye to Heinrich before he was shot – after all they had been through. But there are things I don't know. Perhaps he escaped, or his sentence was delayed. Those last days, things were beginning to break down. A few weeks after Liberation, I was arrested by the British on a charge of spying. After I was cleared, I was sent to Alderney as an interpreter on a Soviet war crimes investigation. My English and Russian were useful. I couldn't write either well, but I was a fluent speaker. I stayed on until the spring of 1946, until I was finally repatriated. Before I left, I tried to find Helene – I wanted to say goodbye – but she had left The Vicarage.

'I saw her a few times after Liberation. I was horrified. She was almost silent. I didn't quite understand what had happened. She had lost a lot of weight – and she had always been thin. Her hair was short, like a boy. All her long fair hair was gone. Perhaps it had been cut in prison. She was shocked – no, there is a better word but I can't think of it . . . She was ill in the mind . . .'

'How long was Mother in prison?' interrupted Roz.

'You didn't know?' Alexei looked worried.

Roz had fixed her eyes on his face. 'No, she never told us any of this.'

'She was in the prison for about two months. It took them a few weeks after Liberation to process the paperwork to release her. It was hard for her, but it was harder when she came out.'

'Harder when she came out?' echoed Roz, shocked.

Alexei waited a moment as Roz struggled to absorb what he was telling her.

'She was ill in the mind. Nanna and I talked about her needing a doctor, but neither of us knew how to find one with the right skill, let alone pay for it. Nanna was hoping that time would heal her. Then her father came back from Germany, I heard. Later, she was staying in the Vale, but I couldn't find out where. I didn't understand why. To be honest, I had other things on my mind. My memories of that time are very painful. The suffering of my countrymen on Alderney filled me with anger. I grew to hate Alderney – that rock surrounded by a savage sea – and I had terrible nightmares about the island.'

He shifted uncomfortably in his chair.

'Ach, what sad times . . . The most frightening thing about Heinrich was that he was able to close himself off from imagining the consequences of his actions when he chose. It made him childlike – it was both compelling and very dangerous.'

Alexei stood up to pour another cup of tea for everyone. Long stewed, it tasted strong and bitter, and Roz put hers down, but he drank his quickly. She found the reference to Helene's boyish haircut very painful. Was it possible? She remembered reading accounts of trouble in St Peter Port after Liberation.

'When I saw Helene, I suggested I stayed and looked after her,' said Alexei. 'I asked her to get a divorce, but she didn't reply. She seemed lost. She said only one thing to me: she had to leave Guernsey, and she had to leave soon. I remember walking away after my last visit, and the tears were pouring down my cheeks. I was a young man, only twenty-one, and my heart was broken. But I longed to see my mother again, and I dreamed of speaking Russian and of coming back to my family.'

'But you met me?'

Alexei looked a little taken aback, then smiled. 'Oh, yes, I met you – such a content, pretty baby, with your father's dark eyes.'

Roz saw his eyes fill with tears again. She got up and went over to him and took one of his hands. Slowly, he raised her hand to his lips and kissed it. 'I'm sorry I left Helene.'

They sat in silence. A wood pigeon called from the copse. Olga put a hand on Roz's arm in sympathy. She was blinking back tears also.

'Come,' Alexei said to Roz, rousing himself. 'Come and see my vegetables.'

He coughed to clear his throat and wiped his eyes with the back of his hand. He led her down the side of the house, to a large orchard of old apple trees. Their boughs hung heavy with bunches of small fruit skimming the lush meadow grass. Some branches were balanced on props. Ox-eye daisies were mixed in with the grass. Alexei explained how his father had kept the orchard. When the village was abandoned during collectivization, his family had come back to prune the trees and gather the apples. Next to the orchard, Alexei had planted rows of onions, carrots and beans. At each row, he knelt down to inspect the new growth, feeling the tender green leaves with his large worn hands.

He wanted to show her everything. He explained how the irrigation system worked when it was dry in the summer heat; he showed her the tool shed, where he kept his hoes, rakes and forks carefully cleaned and ordered, and the shed where he was growing tomatoes.

'I learned a lot from George in Guernsey. He was a very good gardener. He was also a kind man. He didn't talk much, and he never judged Helene. Everyone else did. He said she had had a hard war. Nanna was a good woman too, but she judged Helene. She thought Helene should have kept away from Heinrich.' He broke off to pull up some weeds, and then added, 'George would have been amazed to hear that I carried his advice back to this garden here in Russia. I am nearly the age he was then, and I still remember things he told me about collecting seeds, storing vegetables and even –' he hesitated as he searched his mind for the right word – 'propagation!' He smiled and patted Roz's arm.

They returned to the porch and for the rest of the mild evening they sat out, nibbling slices of sausage, bread and gherkins. Alexei poured them small glasses of vodka.

'We need a toast!' he declared. 'History has brought us together again. For decades, my life in Guernsey was a strange memory. Now, I sit here with you and memories come back, so clear they shake my heart. It was the other life that I could have lived. Helene needed to be looked after, and I could have done that. But I made a hard choice.'

They drank the toast.

'Tell me of Helene's life. Was she happy?'

Roz took a deep breath. 'Happy? I think so, perhaps,' she said slowly. 'She died last year. The man she had married just before the war, Thomas Le Lacheur, was killed fighting. She married the man I knew as my father, Justin Rawsthorne, in 1949 in London. They had two sons – my brothers. He loved her very much. He never knew what had happened to her in the war, nor who my father was. After her death, I received a letter he had written, explaining how he met her when I was a small child. He was a kind man, an art dealer. They met when Helene took him some of Heinrich's prints to sell. The prints supported us, when we first arrived in London. Justin sold them to an American dealer. They ended up destroying his career – he was put on trial in the 1960s and he lost his job.'

She described Helene's life: her love of gardening and their beautiful house in London. 'But to be honest, I don't know if she was happy. Justin told me that she never really loved him. She was a very reserved, private woman. None of us knew about her past in Guernsey, or her experience of the Occupation. I grew up believing Justin was my father.'

Alexei listened carefully. 'Poor Helene. I heard some gossip before I left. Women were attacked in the streets of St Peter Port.'

Roz watched him closely. 'You think she was caught up in that?'

Alexei shrugged his shoulders. 'Perhaps.'

A deep frown creased Roz's forehead. She rubbed her eyes. 'That is a terrible thought,' she whispered.

They continued to sit on the porch and watched the stars come out. Alexei passed the vodka bottle around.

'This is dangerous stuff. I have seen so many friends waste their life through drink, but I open it in your honour. I have had it in my cupboard for over five years waiting for the right occasion, and this is it,' he said. He gave Roz a broad grin, and the gold of two teeth caught the light briefly.

'I don't want visitors here, I don't want my family. I live like a monk, and that is how I like it. I have the BBC, a few books, and my garden. I have lived all my life surrounded by people; for the first time, I am alone, and it is precious. What I grow I give to Irina and she is a good cook. She makes preserves. We eat better than most in these difficult times. I want my granddaughter to grow up strong and clever. In the winter, I live with the family, and in the summers, I am here.

'For years when I worked in the din of the factory, I dreamed of one day returning here. But it was not possible. This village did not officially exist. The people who once lived here were removed to the collective over sixty years ago. A few people too old to move, like my grandmother, stayed on for another decade or so. I remember coming here to visit her. The house was falling down around her, but she was a stubborn woman, half mad with the grief of what she had suffered.'

'The old apple trees are all that remain of the farm my grandparents once had, and this house was the cowhand's home. After the war, I came back to this place, but no one was left; there were great battles not far from here. Everyone had fled or been killed, either by Nazis or by partisans. My mother and sisters were killed; only my grandmother survived. She had gone to Kursk, where I found her after the war. She insisted on returning here, where her husband had been killed before the war.'

He shook himself.

'What am I thinking? I can see you are tired, and I must make up a bed for you and for Olga. We can talk more in the morning before I take you back to the road.'

They helped Alexei spread blankets over the divan by the stove. Olga and Roz lay, side by side, in the dark. Alexei slept on the other side of the room behind the curtain. Before long Roz could hear Olga's soft breathing, but she couldn't sleep. She lay listening to the unfamiliar sounds of the night – the ducks from the nearby marsh and, occasionally, an owl. She looked out of the curtainless window at the stars which crowded the dark sky.

She must have eventually dropped off, but she woke early and slipped out of bed without disturbing Olga. On the porch was a thermos. Alexei had already prepared tea. He must be at work, because there was no sign of him. Roz sat down with a cup of black tea to watch the first rays of pale sunlight glitter in the dew. She was filled with sadness for her mother and this account of her parents' affair, riddled with ambiguity and anguish. She picked up the book of Schiller, still on the table from the night before, and flicked through the pages:

> *On the wings of love, the future hastens . . .*
> *Blazing worlds will turn to marriage torches . . .*

She tried to imagine the man who might choose those words.

Alexei appeared a short while later, carrying a spade. He stopped and sat down on the porch step, looking down the lane. 'Now that I know she has died, and that I have met you, I feel my life is complete,' he said. 'I loved Helene, and I love my wife. She is a good woman, and I work hard to provide food for her. My pension is little enough, so, all these decades later, we depend on this earth again. Just as my grandparents did.'

He looked up at Roz and smiled, putting his scarred hand over hers.

'One thing troubles me in particular, Alexei,' said Roz. 'I've learned that Heinrich bought art collections from Jewish families in Paris. I don't know how many. It upsets me that he was taking advantage of their persecution.' She took a gulp of tea. 'What did he tell you about the prints and paintings? You mentioned a box?'

Alexei was thoughtful. 'Heinrich never told me where the art came from. The Jewish people suffered much. I know my countrymen have persecuted the Jews, but what the Germans arranged was so big it was hard for anyone to comprehend – after the war when the atrocities were revealed. Even now, we learn new things about how they killed the Jews round here.

'I met a Jewish woman in Guernsey once. She was working on a farm, hidden by a good family. She had escaped to London from Germany, and had taken a job with a family as a nanny. When the family decided to leave London for Guernsey in 1939, she went with them. But they had run in the wrong direction. The family managed to get back to London before the Germans arrived, but she was trapped on the island. She knew she was in terrible danger. I don't know what happened to her. She disappeared.'

'I think I've heard about her,' said Roz. 'Such a terrible story of crossing borders, thinking you're safe, and then the borders move and you are caught.' She pressed her question. 'What did Heinrich tell you?'

'He didn't tell me about any Jewish families. He said that he was buying art that the Nazis wouldn't understand. He said if they got their hands on it, they would burn it. It went either to him or to the Nazis, and he claimed that he was saving the art. He told me that he had seen trucks filled with the contents of the Louvre, destined for Germany. I didn't know if I believed him. Perhaps he also saw that it was a way to make money after the war. He was a sharp negotiator. That was why he was managing supplies for the islands.'

Roz tried to imagine this strange, contradictory man. If he was alive, how could she greet him – shake his hand?

He turned to her. 'Come, I want to show you one more thing.'

They set off down a mud track which led between the houses. Alexei explained that several of his generation had returned to the abandoned village. A boy with whom he had grown up had come back after half a century to live in a house opposite him. Most of the houses were in a similar state of collapse. Any available money went into equipment and fertilizers. Many of the occupants were supplementing their pensions by selling surplus produce at the market. The houses petered out, and they continued walking along the track, only just discernible in the overgrown grass. Alexei turned off onto a narrow path which passed through a copse. The ground was covered in ivy. After a while, they came to a small clearing. The ground was uneven here, and under the vegetation were pieces of masonry. The path wound its way across the clearing between briars.

'This was where the village church once was,' he said.

They had reached a stone pillar, half covered with ivy. 'And this is all that remains of the gates which once surrounded the cemetery. My ancestors are buried here.'

A rook sounded up noisily from its nest, prompting a cacophony of cawing. Roz felt a little uneasy.

'This is where my grandmother insisted on being buried, and this is where I hope to be buried.'

Looking at Roz, he added, 'This is by way of explanation, for leaving you and Helène.'

She nodded. 'I understand. I do.' She could see how even Alexei – surely the most innocent of the three of them – had his burden of guilt.

They stood listening to the rooks.

'Our war here in my motherland was terrible – terrible in a way that foreigners cannot understand,' said Alexei quietly. 'We were fighting for our survival, and it cost us nearly everything – twenty million dead. But we won, and we destroyed Nazism. I think of Guernsey's war and I think the islanders knew nothing – their war was easy in comparison. Islands are strange, enclosed places – your country. Their edges never move.'

Alexei was almost talking to himself as he poked a ruined wall with the toe of his boot. Roz nodded. He looked up at the tree trunks rising high above their heads and the pattern of branches and leaves.

'I'm grateful for what you have done,' she said softly, putting her hand on his arm. 'You have explained so much about my mother and father to me. There are still parts which are not clear – gaps which I cannot imagine, dates I'm not sure of, and so forth – but I have the outline, and that's what I needed. I know now where and who I came from. That's not easy – not by any measure – but it was what I wanted to know.'

As they walked back to the village, he asked her about her brothers. She told him that they differed in their views of her search. He was surprised at Ed's attitude.

'But we must know who our parents are,' he insisted. 'It is sad Helene never told you, but not surprising. We all wanted to put the war far behind us,' he said again.

'I'm not sure I understand why you distrusted Heinrich,' she said. 'Is there something you are holding back?'

Alexei frowned.

'Heinrich was very good to me; he could have informed on me. He knew I was no rival – I was a Russian peasant boy. Helene loved me, but not in that way. To begin with, I think he protected me because it gave him power over Helene. But he came to like me. He said I was clever and needed to get an education. He talked to us both about Paris. After the war, I was in a camp there for a few weeks. I walked all over Paris – wore out my boots – and I visited the places he had talked about. After the war, I tried to give myself the education he would have wanted for me. I collect books – you will have seen – and I read whenever I could. Russian literature, of course, but sometimes English. Once Heinrich knew someone intimately, he couldn't harm them. It was when they were strangers that he could be irresponsible, even cruel.

'I knew that people suspected me of having informed on Heinrich after his desertion, but that was absurd. There were many rumours on that island by the end of the war. I couldn't have done that. I wouldn't have done anything to hurt Helene, and, despite my hatred of the Germans, I liked Heinrich. Well . . . I liked him most of the time.'

Alexei hesitated. 'Perhaps it would be better for me not to tell you what I heard about Heinrich. It might make things more difficult.'

'I need to know everything. I've come all this way,' Roz said quietly.

Alexei stopped in the middle of the path and leaned on a tree stump. 'After the war, when I was working as an interpreter on Alderney, we interviewed the survivors – the boys who had been forced labourers on the island. Most of them had left the island in 1943 and early 1944, but we gathered some information from those who remained. The conditions on Alderney had been terrible, and hundreds of men died of exhaustion, lack of food and the cold. The guards beat them cruelly. Heinrich's name came up. He had a role in the administration there, and every few months he used to come and stay at the commandant's house up on the cliffs. Alderney has its own kind of harsh beauty. Perhaps you know?'

Roz nodded, thinking back to her visit, and the sunset from the commandant's house.

'We were told he had responsibility for ordering supplies from France – concrete, timber and steel, but also flour and vegetables. That's what a German soldier told us. I never understood it all, but there were disturbing stories that – what is the word?' Alexei hesitated, searching his memory. 'That corruption led to deaths on Alderney. The slave workers never received their proper food rations. There was smuggling between Alderney, France and Jersey, and what should have been cabbages and flour on the supply boats for the labour camps often turned out to be brandy, wine and luxuries for the German officers. In our investigations, Heinrich was one of those blamed.

'It might not be true; he was an easy man to blame. He was dead, we believed, and the dead always get the blame. But perhaps it was true; he always had fine things to eat and drink throughout the Occupation. There's no knowing.'

'That's terrible,' gasped Roz. She stood still. 'That's repulsive – people died.'

Alexei roughly patted her arm.

They continued walking back to the house. Roz was too upset to speak.

They found Olga cooking a breakfast of eggs from Alexei's hens in the orchard. She had brewed coffee. Roz pulled up a chair and Alexei came over to her and gently kissed her head.

'Thank you for coming,' he said again. 'You are a brave woman. Few have wanted the truth.' She held his hand.

Over their food, Alexei spoke of seeing the sea for the first time on the French coast before boarding for Guernsey. He had never seen so much water, and it had terrified him. At one point on the crossing to Guernsey, the Normandy coast was only a faint line on the horizon, and he was surrounded by water. He hadn't seen the sea since he left the island in 1946.

Suddenly, he jumped up, explaining that he had something to show Roz. He took several objects off the shelf above his bed. He opened his hand to reveal worked flints.

'I found these around here. This one I found only yesterday. They are many thousands of years old. Made by human hands likes ours. We only borrow our brief time here.'

Roz looked at them lying in the palm of his hand, both flints and palm ingrained with black earth. Alexei gave one to Roz. 'Keep it,' he said, and wrapped her fingers around it.

As they cleared the dishes, Roz asked Alexei whether he had seen any of the artworks Heinrich had given to Helene.

'He showed me a few drawings and prints by Picasso. At the time I thought they were odd but later I understood better,' he said slowly. 'I think there was a drawing by Degas. I forget the details.'

'And the box you mentioned – did you ever know what it contained?'

'It contained a painting. That's why he came to The Vicarage after he deserted. He wanted Helene to have the painting. He said it was very precious.'

'Do you remember the size of the box? Or what you did with it?' interrupted Roz, realizing the possible significance.

He was startled. 'So many questions!'

Roz was watching him intently.

'I hid it exactly as Heinrich told me to.' His forehead creased. 'I left instructions for Helene to find it. She would have taken it to London, surely?'

'She might have done. Think carefully. Tell me whatever you can remember,' said Roz, getting her notebook and a pen out.

'Has it been lost? You think it might still be there?' he asked.

She shrugged her shoulders. 'There are still some paintings bought by Heinrich which are missing.'

Alexei was shaking his head in disbelief. He tried to remember the details.

'I know Heinrich mentioned the box to Helene that last night at The Vicarage. We were going to hide it in the basement but it was too damp, Heinrich said. He wanted it stored in the attic. So we made a plan that I would slip back to The Vicarage and place it under the floorboards in the linen room. He gave me detailed instructions and even provided nails to fix the boards afterwards.

'I returned the following day but there was a German guard at the house – waiting for Heinrich to return, perhaps. After two days he left, and I was able to get into the house. It was empty and I did as Heinrich had asked. I left a note on Helene's dressing table. I was not good at writing English. I wrote something about having tidied the linen room as instructed. I drew a sketch, and I hoped she would see it was a plan of the room. It was vague, but I thought she would understand.

'I saw her a few months later – in August. That was the time when she was ill. Did I mention the box then? I don't know, I can't remember. I thought she would have found the letter, but perhaps she didn't.'

Roz waited in silence. They were waiting on an old man's memory.

'Nanna could have found the note and thrown it away. She had no more time for me than she did for Heinrich. She was fiercely protective of Helene.'

Alexei got up and rummaged in a drawer to find a piece of paper and a pen, and sat down at the table. 'I'll show you where I hid the box in the attic of The Vicarage. I have a clear picture of the linen room – it had cupboards on one side. The door is here, and shelves here. That's where the laundry was stored. I walked from the door along this wall –' he was drawing as he spoke. 'The skirting board, here, was loose. I pulled it away and took up the brown linoleum. A few floorboards in, I cut the boards in two places, to remove a section. I put the box between the joists. It was long and quite narrow.'

'Where in the attic is the linen room?' asked Roz.

'It is on the right, off a landing, I think. It had a small window.'

'And the box? Did you look inside?'

'Yes. We had the whole day to wait until dark, and to pass the time, Heinrich showed me. We had to ease up all the nails. Heinrich told me that of all the paintings he had bought during the war, this was his favourite. I don't remember the artist or if he even told me, but he said it was hundreds of years old. He had hung it above his desk in his billet since he bought it in 1943. He had no time for the baby, but he claimed the Virgin's expression was of a woman who knew unbearable pain, and offered gentle, inexhaustible compassion.

'I saw what he meant. We didn't have much light, but I remember it was a very beautiful painting of rich colours. The Virgin had long strands of wavy hair and it flowed over her shoulders. The expression of the face held you. We both agreed that this woman reminded us of Helene. Her hair, her long nose, her fine eyebrows and red lips.'

'It could be Cranach's *Virgin and Child Under an Apple Tree*,' whispered Roz, overcome with emotion. Antoine had been right all along. She had been right to search for Alexei. 'That's the picture they have been looking for,' she explained to Alexei and Olga.

Alexei was lost in thought for a moment, but then angrily blurted out, 'I still marvel at Heinrich. How could a man with his love of art have been so reckless in his behaviour? You are sure Helene didn't take it? If not, it must still be there. You need to find the box. It had survived hundreds of years before it reached Heinrich's hands. It will be a reason to hate Heinrich if it has been damaged or lost in the last fifty years. The first thing you must do when you get back to England is to go to Guernsey and find it. Then telephone Olga, and she can send me a telegram.'

He had become agitated. His face was flushed. 'I must know it is safe.'

'I will let you know,' she promised him. They studied his plan together to ensure that she understood it.

'Good,' he said, more calmly. 'You will find it.'

'I worry. There have been a lot of renovations at the house. I can't understand why it hasn't been found – or perhaps it was. Perhaps someone has taken it.'

He carefully folded the map and put it in an old envelope and gave it to Roz.

'I spent some time thinking last night. I am sad to think of Helene, troubled by memories. I am sad to hear that Heinrich's prints and etchings brought your family suffering. What would have been different, if I had stayed? I thought about the opportunities I missed – for education and for experiences. I had much to think about.'

'And did you come to any conclusions?' she asked.

'None! Nor will I. I am past the age of – how do you call it? – conclusions. I no longer try to understand anything more than my vegetables and my orchard and occasionally my dear wife.' He laughed and flung his hands in the air with a triumphant flourish. 'Is that a defeat or a victory? Who knows? But it brings me peace.'

. Olga and Roz joined in with his deep laughter.

★

They had agreed to walk to the main road to save the car's axles further strain driving down the track. From there, the car would take them back to Orel. Alexei insisted on accompanying them on the walk, a ten-mile round trip for him. The sky was a bright pale blue. On either side of the track, the fields rolled away towards the distant horizon in the immense landscape. The three figures toiled across the expanse, struggling through the rutted mud. Alexei insisted on carrying both their bags. They felt their smallness in the huge space. Roz thought of the boys growing up here, flung by the randomness of war into the small valleys and tight lanes of an island on the edge of the Atlantic. The bewildering shifts in scale, perspective and horizon.

At the junction with the main road, they sat down on a wooden platform to wait. Olga had made a thermos of coffee, and she and Alexei discussed – in English, out of politeness – the economic reforms. Alexei explained how a lifetime's savings were now worthless, and how, without his farm produce, he and Irina would be entirely dependent on their daughter's salary as a doctor. Roz asked if he would accept some money from her, and he stiffly refused. He seemed offended by her offer. They saw the car from a long way off, slowly crawling along the rough road, finally crossing the bridge over the river.

When it arrived, Roz embraced Alexei. He held her close. He was crying and Roz's eyes, too, were blurred with tears. Once they were in the car, she turned to wave out of the back window. Alexei seemed very old and frail standing in the road. He had a five-mile walk back to his worn books, his vegetables, his orchard, and his radio.

XV

Roz rang Jim as soon as she was back in Moscow and could make an international call. He listened carefully as she told him about her father and that he was perhaps still alive. She picked out some of the details of Alexei's account. Some were too painful – they would have to wait until an evening by the river in France. The urgent issue was the Cranach.

'The painting needs to be found,' agreed Jim. 'You think it's still at the house?'

'I don't know. I have been trying to remember if the owners talked about renovations in the attic.'

'You have to call Antoine, Roz. You know that, don't you?'

'Of course. I just couldn't face it until after I'd spoken to you.'

'And Ed will need an explanation. If the painting is still there, it will lead to press coverage and we might all get pulled into it – again.'

'I suppose so.' Roz grimaced at the thought. 'I can't stop thinking about Heinrich and Helene. The idea that he's my father. I don't like the sound of him, and, if we find him, the thought of meeting him terrifies me. And . . .'

Roz broke off. She still didn't know how to put into words the mixed emotions of revulsion, pity and – she had to admit it – fascination.

'When I look at the photo of Helene, she looks so young and vulnerable – but how could she?' Roz went on, her voice strained with suppressed tears.

'It explains a lot about Mother. That aloofness. She felt so

345

distant,' Jim said. 'I suppose she had so much she was hiding. Nobody could get close.'

'And I'm the result, the child of this disastrous love affair which she was so ashamed of all her life,' said Roz bitterly. She was biting her lip, trying not to cry. She felt that there had been more than enough tears in the conversations with Alexei.

'Was she ashamed? Perhaps she loved him. She could have felt both love and shame,' argued Jim. 'You're telling me that Alexei said she was in love, and that Heinrich loved Mother. Remember that. Even if the love affair was tangled up with the need to secure Heinrich's protection – for herself, for Alexei – it could still have been love. It's too complicated for us to ever know for sure.'

'But imagine having a German lover while your own husband and brother are fighting the Germans, and your father has been interned by them. She must have felt so guilty. And then discovering your brother and husband have been killed at about the same time as you realize you are pregnant. It doesn't bear thinking about. Let alone this business about prison.'

'Do we know what happened between Helene and her father?' asked Jim.

'No,' said Roz, trying to sound calmer. 'I suppose he must have come back sometime in late 1945 or early 1946. Around the time I was born.'

'Before she left the island, then?'

'That must have been a painful encounter. A priest returning to find his son and son-in-law dead and his daughter pregnant.'

'Still, he was a priest. Surely he could do the forgiveness bit?'

Neither of them said anything; they listened to the strange sounds of a long-distance call, the small crackles and whirr, from Moscow to the Loire.

'We need to go to Guernsey. I'm coming this time,' said Jim. 'We can look for the Morel painting together. I'll book the tickets. When do you get back from Moscow?'

Roz was grateful. After the visit to Guernsey, she could get back to her own life. She would leave her father well alone. All that she had learned would take a long time to come to terms with. She would spend some weekends at the cottage, play more tennis. She needed some time also to sort out why the entanglement with Antoine had upset her so much. The disappointment still had a sharp edge. It had revealed a desire for intimacy from which she had successfully distracted herself for many years. She needed to finish this business of her mother's war. She told Jim she would transfer at Heathrow straight onto a Guernsey flight.

'Antoine will be useful . . . I mean, what do we do with a priceless painting if it is there?' Jim added.

'I suppose so,' Roz replied grudgingly.

'He could deal with the police and the authorities,' Jim pointed out. 'And I'll finally meet him. I'm curious. There is something about Antoine that reminds me of Heinrich. The way you talk about them sounds a bit similar.'

'Nonsense,' said Roz briskly. 'What an odd suggestion, Jim. Really.' She was rattled.

Jim laughed. 'Anyway, he has been very useful, whatever else you feel about him. You were right about that. You would never have uncovered all this without his help. You owe him that, at least.'

Roz reluctantly agreed, but she couldn't face talking to Antoine. Jim said he would call him to explain. Jim was planning to drive. Antoine would fly from Paris. They would all converge in Guernsey. But there was one call Roz would have to make – to Jill and Tim at Les Bois Verts – and it would require all her emotional and diplomatic resources. She imagined their astonishment at hearing her strange request to pull up floorboards. On the train back to Moscow, she had been trying to remember her tour of the house. She had seen a staircase next to the photos on the second floor, which presumably went up to an attic. Roz wanted the painting safe. Something as beautiful and precious should never have been a plaything of war. Nor a bargaining chip in the survival of children.

She and Jim rang off, and she braced herself; delaying would only make it worse.

'Jill, it's Roz – Roz Wardle. If you remember, we met a few months ago, in the spring, when I visited your house. You kindly sent me the family photographs.'

It was a clear line. She could hear the dogs barking in the background.

'Oh, yes, of course. Your mother lived here during the war. How are you?'

'Fine, thank you. I hope you and your husband are well. I've been doing some more research into my mother's wartime experiences and some of that has led me to Russia.'

'Was that Russia you said? Goodness. Can you speak up? Was it to do with one of the former forced labourers? I once found some Russian writing on a skirting board in the outbuildings. I always wondered.'

'Yes, that's right. My mother hid a forced labourer. His name was Alexei.'

Roz paused. She realized in that moment, as she said the words, that she was proud of her mother. That she had done something truly remarkable. She had saved a life.

Jill was talking about a signature in Cyrillic. She had had it translated, she said, and it read 'Alexei'. They had cut out the piece of skirting and framed it.

'Yes, that's him. I am in Moscow. I have just been to visit Alexei.'

She could hear Jill's exclamations on the end of the line.

'He believes there is a parcel still stored in the attic,' said Roz, brushing aside Jill's excitement. 'I wondered if you did any renovations up there? Did you come across anything? We think it is under a floorboard. I wondered if I could come to the house to see if we can find it.'

Jill was full of curiosity. 'A parcel? What kind of parcel? In the attic, you say? We didn't do much up there. We had insulation put in and we cleared out all the boxes, but I don't think we touched any floorboards. We could start looking ourselves.'

'No, don't do that. I think it would be best to wait. Alexei has given very detailed instructions.'

'What's in the parcel?' asked Jill.

This was the question Roz was dreading. Should she tell the truth? Would Jill talk about it? Would that bring the journalists? Best to be vague.

'I'm not sure, but it could be important. I can explain more when I get there. I'll be with a French historian.'

'Perhaps the *Guernsey Evening Press* would be interested.'

That was quicker than even Roz had feared.

'Jill, would it be possible to be completely discreet at this stage?' she asked swiftly. 'Not mentioning it to anyone yet? It could be sensitive for *everyone*,' she added, with what she hoped was the right touch of firmness and a hint of threat.

Jill pressed her for more information, but Roz held her ground, explaining that she would be in Guernsey in three days. She dreaded more of Jill's inquisitive questioning. Antoine could deal with that.

★

Roz had two more days in Moscow before her flight home, and Olga, sensing her sadness, invited her to their family dacha. It was a short train ride away, she explained, adding quickly that it was very modest. Touched, Roz accepted the invitation.

The train was full of people heading to their dachas for the day to take advantage of the sunshine. Roz and Olga got off at a suburban station, and, along with several others, made their way past blocks of tenements down a well-used path overhung with shrubs. They came to an area of densely worked gardens, each with its own small hut. It reminded Roz of allotments. She glimpsed rows of vegetables and herbs through the hedges.

Olga's mother greeted them warmly. The hut was sparsely furnished, with a bed in one corner and a cooker in another. On the small table was a bright embroidered tablecloth and a vase with a few marigolds. She had spent the night there. She ushered Roz to a deckchair in the garden under an old plum tree. In the warm sun, Roz lay back, her eyes half closed, looking up through the leaves at the blue sky, while Olga and her mother gardened. She loved listening to their murmured conversation in Russian. She didn't understand it, but she could sense their warm intimacy and ease. Occasionally, she heard the sound of neighbours in their adjoining gardens: the laugh of a child, the call of a woman and, in the other direction, the murmur of a family lunch.

It was a day of rest. Butterflies flew through the branches and one rested on the arm of her chair. She watched it open and close its brilliantly coloured wings. Her mind wandered over her long conversations with Alexei. She wrote the odd detail in a notebook; she wanted to be able to tell Jim everything in Guernsey. But how could she describe to him the weight of sadness in Alexei's story? His own, that of Helene, and even, possibly, of Heinrich.

She struggled to focus her mind on Heinrich, but she seemed to skid past, over, and around him every time. He remained the shadow in the story, yet he belonged to her. She owed half her genetic make-up to this contradictory man. Loving but faithless, generous but corrupt, charming but unscrupulous. She had a disconcerting sense that a shabby string of beads had finally snapped; the structure of family on which she had based her life had disintegrated. The beads had skittered across the floor in every direction. She now realized that her search would bring no finality. There were many questions which could never now be answered.

The three women drank tea as the sun dipped behind the trees. Olga translated for her mother because she didn't speak English. A formidably clever scientist, she was deeply devoted to her one child. She asked why Roz hadn't had any children. Few people asked the question so directly, and Roz found herself explaining that her marriage had ended, and there had never been anyone else she wanted to marry. She was surprised to feel suddenly wistful. In the presence of this mother and daughter, with their easy, affectionate warmth, Roz saw what she had never experienced with her own mother, and would never experience now with a daughter. But she insisted that she enjoyed her career.

Olga's mother smiled. 'Of course. I have worked all my life as a professor, but children bring a particular significance to life.' She had her hand on Olga's knee as they sat together on the bench. An uncomfortable sense of pity hung in the air.

When the last of the sun had left the garden, Olga and her mother packed up the leftover food, and gathered some fresh herbs from the garden to take back to the city. They locked up the hut and headed back to the station.

Roz was on her way home.

★

Roz was in Guernsey in time for afternoon tea, and only that morning she had woken in her Moscow hotel. She thought of Alexei making roughly the same journey over half a century before, travelling in dirty train trucks for several months.

Jim picked her up from the airport. They were in Torteval in a few minutes and parked on the lane leading to Les Bois Verts. Antoine was due in half an hour. Roz wanted to show Jim the house and garden. They walked down the lane which she had found that wet day earlier in the year. The thick green foliage of late August hung over their heads, plunging them into cool green shade. They stood at the gate in silence, looking at the lawn sweeping down to the wood. Beyond the treetops, a line of deep blue sea lay across the horizon. The roses were in bloom and, on either side of the front door, brilliant blue agapanthus spilled out of big pots. Jim was spellbound.

'What a beautiful place to grow up,' he murmured.

They opened the small gate, and the sound of their feet on the stone path alerted the dogs. They began barking and came bounding round the side of the house.

Jill appeared at the door. She had been waiting for their arrival, clearly eager with anticipation for this visit. Roz asked if they could look at the garden for a few minutes. Jill agreed and suggested she make tea for them all before they started work. Roz wanted to see the bench where the photos had been taken, and work out what had been the croquet lawn. By the stone terrace, the two windows evident in the photo were unchanged, and between them still stood a bench. An old rose clambered up the wall giving off a heavy scent. Perhaps it was the same rose. Jim and Roz sat down and looked out over the garden to the woods.

'That stretch at the end of the garden looks flat enough for a croquet lawn,' said Jim, pointing to the bottom of the garden, where the ground levelled off. 'Imagine Edward playing there with his friends, as Helene wrote in her diary.'

'Poor Edward.'

A seagull was flying in the sky above them, the sunlight catching the white feathers of its outstretched wings. Roz stirred herself.

'Enough of reveries and ghosts. We have work to do,' she murmured to Jim, as she heard Antoine's voice.

He appeared round the corner of the house carrying a tray of tea things, followed by Jill. He had just arrived and had been helping her in the kitchen. He was as charming as ever, and Jill could not resist his slightly flirtatious manner. He set the tray down on the table on the terrace, and greeted Roz with warmth, kissing her on both cheeks. Roz awkwardly introduced Jim.

'Let's have a look at the sketch Alexei drew,' said Antoine.

Jim flattened out the crumpled drawing on the table.

'That's the attic room. Nothing much has changed in there. We use it as a storeroom. We'll have to pull some boxes out,' said Jill.

Jim and Antoine offered to help and headed upstairs with Jill while Roz finished her tea. She could hear the dull thuds of furniture being moved. She pulled herself away from the cool freshness of the garden and headed inside, half excited and half dreading what they might find.

Tim had gathered a collection of tools. He and Roz climbed the stairs to the landing. She felt slightly sick, and, without saying anything, he pulled a chair from a bedroom for her to sit on. He had guessed how nervous she felt. Grateful, she sat down for a few moments while the others cleared the room above.

Tim handed over the crowbar and saw, and came back downstairs to wait beside Roz. With the three of them in the attic room, there wasn't enough space for everyone, he explained. Finally, the room was clear enough. Jim called down to Roz and she joined them.

The small room probably hadn't been decorated since before the war and had an old-fashioned wallpaper of roses. Down one side was a set of large cupboards. Tim called the occasional comment or question up from the landing below. Jill watched, eager-eyed, as Antoine counted the paces from the doorway along the wall, following the directions Alexei had written out that evening on the porch in Russia.

Roz sat down on a box in the corner. Jim helped Antoine roll back an old piece of linoleum. It cracked as they moved it.

'It must date from before the war,' commented Jill.

Beneath the linoleum, two floorboards had clearly been cut. Alexei's memory had been accurate. They were in the right place.

The boards had been nailed down, so Jim used the hammer to

pull out the six nails. It had been very securely fastened. Then, with his fingertips, he worked the board loose and lifted it out. They all craned forward to look except for Roz. She was looking out of the small window, where she could just see the sea in the distance. It was clouding over.

'It's there,' cried Jim, excited.

He was kneeling down, leaning over the hole, and he pulled out a long, battered wooden box. It had been tucked between the joists. Thick with dust, it was about a metre long and twenty centimetres wide. Jim rubbed some of it off to reveal a row of nails in the lid. These were much smaller, and there were more than a dozen. Jim patiently worked his way around them, pulling them out, one by one.

Antoine was drumming his fingernails on the floor; he couldn't help himself. Even Jill didn't speak. The small room was packed with bodies and tension. All eyes, even Roz's, were now fixed on Jim's dogged work. Finally, he pulled out the last nail and sat back on his heels.

'Roz, I think you should take the lid off,' said Jim.

Jill and Antoine moved aside, and Roz leaned forward and lifted the lid. It came loose quite easily. Inside was a covering of yellowed French newspaper. She picked it off. Underneath was a long roll wrapped in a linen covering. On top of it was a letter addressed to Helene. She handed it to Jim. They would look at it later – in private. She carefully lifted the roll out, and started to unwrap the covering on her lap. She looked up at Antoine, anxious not to damage what she assumed was a canvas. He leaned forward to help, holding it carefully in his fingertips. As the linen fell away, they could see the rough brown surface of the back of a canvas. It was a painting. They slowly unrolled it. First brilliant golds and greens appeared. Then the feet of a baby, then hands, and thick strands of reddish gold hair, glinting against dark foliage. Finally, the pale face of the Virgin was revealed, gazing askance from her narrow-lidded green eyes. Roz and Antoine held the four corners. Jim supported a side, Jill another. There lay Cranach's *Virgin and Child Under an Apple Tree*. They all stared at the beauty of the painting: the perfect red apples hanging above the Virgin's head, and, in the background, a fairy-tale landscape with buildings clinging precariously to a rocky pinnacle – a magical place of turrets, a spire and a balcony which jutted out over the cliff edge. Below lay a castle beside a lake.

Jill was open-mouthed in astonishment.

'We've found it, at last! Years of work. Finally the Morels have justice.' Antoine was laughing and crying with exhilaration.

Roz stared at it. My father loved this picture; it reminded him of my mother, she thought. My father took advantage of a desperate Jewish family to buy it. It hung above his desk during his years in Guernsey. He left it here. He abandoned it. He never came back for it. Did he ever try to check that Helene had safely received it? This treasure of civilization which had survived for centuries. The grotesque irresponsibility. She found herself shivering with disgust.

Antoine and Jim were talking. Jill was full of questions. Tim, hearing the commotion, called up, impatiently wanting to know what was going on. Jim moved aside so that Antoine could wrap up the picture and close the box. He picked it up, carrying it as carefully as one might a newborn child. Antoine said nothing about the letter.

Roz remained where she was, sitting in the attic room. After a while she could hear sounds in the house. A telephone ringing. Cars arriving. Loud male voices in the hall. She couldn't move. Alexei had been right in every detail. His memory had been flawless. She had to hold on to everything he had said. Heinrich had not been a bad man. Helene had been young and in love. She found herself repeating the two short phrases as she rocked gently, back and forth. She thought of that exquisite background: the castle by the lake and the buildings on the cliff edge. The balcony. A place to dream of, a utopia, beyond reach. For anyone. Above all, for a soldier in war.

She was calmer by the time Jim knocked on the door.

'The picture has gone. The police have it, and Antoine will make the statement.'

Roz nodded.

'He is going to keep us out of it. No one need know.'

'No one need know,' she repeated slowly. '*Need know* . . . an odd phrase.'

But she was relieved; at least she wouldn't have to deal with journalists.

'Jill is very excited. She wanted a photo of herself with the picture.' Jim smiled. 'She and Tim are very understanding. She says she won't mention either of us.'

'Have you looked at the letter?' Roz asked.

Jim shook his head and handed it over. The handwriting on the envelope was similar to that on the photos. It had never been opened. Roz ripped it open. Inside was a short note.

5 April 1945
My dearest Helene,

I am about to do something very dangerous so I wanted to make sure this was secure in your possession. As we discussed, take it to London and sell it, if you need to. What I am about to do is the right thing to end the madness of war on this island. I never expected to find such happiness here. Remember the poem I recited to you that summer night? This is the comfort you have brought me, here by the edge of the ocean.

> *Thy soul – a crystal river passing,*
> *Silver-clear, and sunbeam-glassing,*
> *Mays into bloom sad Autumn by thee;*

Night and desert, if they spy thee,
To gardens laugh – with daylight shine,
Lit by those happy smiles of thine!
Dark with cloud the Future far
Goldens itself beneath thy star.

Schiller will be my motto in the next few months, and all that they
hold. 'The very Future to the Past but flies, Upon the wings of
Love – as I to thee'. One day, I know we will be together again and
will live as a family. It may be several years before that happens, but
I will find my way back to you. Struggles lie ahead for both of us,
but we are young and in good health. We can start again.

When the war is over and Germany is rebuilt after this terrible
destruction, I will travel to London to find you, as we agreed. I
will be in Trafalgar Square at midday on 17th November – the
anniversary of our first meeting – of every year until you come.
Until then, I will remember you as I saw you that first time on
the cliff path, when your hair was wet and your cheeks were
flushed from the chill of the sea breeze, my love. Your hair fell
around your shoulders – like this Virgin – and it glittered with
raindrops.

Every 17th November, I will be there, waiting for you. As soon
as I am able. As soon as I can travel. Now wish me strength for
the dangers and tragedies which await me here and at home.

I send you all my love,
Heinrich

Roz handed it, speechless, to Jim.

'Did he come back? Did he look for her after the war?' he said,
as his eyes quickly scanned the note. He put a hand on her shoulder. 'How could Helene have left the picture here all these years?'

'Alexei said he left a note, but perhaps she never got it. He
wondered if Nanna destroyed it,' said Roz. 'Such a mess.'

She took a deep breath and stood up. It was time to leave the attic room. She rubbed her eyes and pushed back her hair.

Downstairs, Antoine was standing on the doorstep. He was leaving for the police station. He had called the Morels already, and they wanted to hold a press conference to announce that they would donate it to a museum. Antoine would fly back to Paris immediately. The picture would be handed over to the French police. He had a broad smile on his face.

'Thank you, Roz.'

Jim tactfully fell back as they walked up the lane together.

'You know, Roz, this picture is symbolic. The Virgin is the second Eve. She redeems the sin of the first Eve – hence the apples.'

Roz smiled. 'It's a beautiful painting. I'm glad it's safe and will be returned to its rightful owners. I'm really moved that they want to donate it.'

Antoine held out his hand. 'My post at Montpellier will be confirmed after this. I'm grateful. We did important work together. You can be proud of that. It was your courage which made today happen.'

She shook his hand. He put his arm around her and squeezed her shoulder. Then he kissed her on both cheeks and looked straight at her. 'I couldn't have done it – if I had been in your shoes. I admit it. I was asking you to do something I didn't think I could have done. I admire your courage, and determination. Only you could have done this.'

She was touched.

He walked back to his hire car, turning to wave. He called out, 'Goodbye. Come and visit me.' She returned his wave, smiling.

She hadn't told him about the letter from Arthur Brown, or that she was now going to visit him. He didn't need to know any more. She and Jim walked back to their car. Jim had the key in the car door when a thought suddenly occurred to Roz. She remembered the dream of her grandmother and how she had turned to her, and held out her hand in welcome.

'Can we visit the graveyard of the church here? I have an idea that our grandmother might be buried here. It wouldn't take long.'

Jim nodded.

The gate to the church creaked on its rusty hinges as they pushed it open. The graveyard was not large. Jim took one side of the church, Roz the other. They each walked down the lines of stones, many marked with fresh flowers. Before long, Jim gave a shout. The grave was in the corner: 'Elizabeth Le Marchant. Born 1898 and died 1936. Beloved wife of Eustace, adored mother of Edward and Helene.' Roz pulled away the grass which had grown up around the base and read aloud the inscription:

> *'I love thee to the level of every day's*
> *Most quiet need, by sun and candlelight.'*

'Elizabeth Barrett Browning,' said Jim. 'The poet,' he explained, when Roz looked up, puzzled.

Next door, a simple stone was engraved with 'Eustace Le Marchant 1880–1974'. Pale grey lichen was creeping over the granite headstones. The graves looked neglected.

'I keep thinking about Eustace. Imagine. He comes back from being interned in Germany after the war to discover his son has been killed and his daughter has had a baby . . . or is about to have a baby,' said Jim.

'I'm still confused about the dates. Perhaps there is some test I could take which could determine my exact age. Teeth or something.' Roz was weeding round the headstone as she spoke. 'Helene must have had some contact with her father after the war. It seems very hard. Why could they not manage some reconciliation?'

'Perhaps they did, who knows?' suggested Jim. 'I still think it might have been something about him wanting Helene to give you up for adoption.'

'Mmm.' Roz was distracted, pulling up dandelions. 'Did you notice – in Heinrich's note – he used the word "family". He knew about me.'

She sighed as she sat back on her heels. 'It seems so sad that the old man was left alone. And no descendants to visit or keep the graves tidy – until now.'

They headed back to the gate in silence. They were bracing themselves for their visit to Arthur Brown. Roz had described his long interview and gossipy diary. Jim was curious.

★

Brown's house was a large bungalow. A tall, handsome man with a florid complexion, he carried his eighty-odd years with ease, greeting them with enthusiasm, and ushering them into his lounge. It had a magnificent view of the sea from its generous windows.

'It was the picture business that I most admired Heinrich for.'

As soon as they had been settled with tea and biscuits, Brown plunged into his story. He was eager to talk. 'During 1942 and 1943, he came back from France several times with boxes of drawings and a few paintings. He brought me in on it. He offered me a cut after the war if I would help him hide a few, and then keep an eye on them if there was a British invasion. That was the plan. We boxed them up very carefully. He knew the value of what he had, and showed me how to look after them. He wanted somewhere dry to store some, so we settled for a false floor in one of the rooms in Dieu Donne. I didn't look too closely at much of it. It wasn't my kind of thing. I know he hid other artworks elsewhere.

'He told me that he was looking after them to make sure they didn't get damaged in the war. He said Paris was a dangerous place for art and that the Nazis were all peasants. That was in the evenings, when we used to share a glass of two of his French brandy and listen to the wireless. He was no Nazi, that's for sure. I liked him.

'We talked about what was happening in the war, and what might happen afterwards. He said that Russia and America would split Germany. He was right about that. He was a clever man. Said he'd studied in England before the war.

'I don't know when he started seeing Helene Le Marchant – well, she was a Le Lacheur by then. The first time I met him was November 1941 in the lane. I had been watching him through my binoculars – I'd seen him on the cliff path with Helene. I kept my binoculars to hand during the war – there was a lot to keep an eye on. I couldn't believe it. I was shocked. It didn't take Helene long – if you don't mind my saying so – to get going. Mind you, they were discreet. I'll give her that. She didn't come to the parties at Dieu Donne. She came to the door once, but she was looking to get insulin from the German doctor that time, because she told me so.'

'So you met her – my mother?'

'Yes, that time she came to Dieu Donne. And I had seen her around town before the war – she was the kind of girl you noticed. Nice hair.' He paused to pick up the thread of his story. He didn't like interruptions.

'Heinrich used to go over to The Vicarage. They must have hidden, somehow, from the vicar, because people told me that he didn't know. He kept his eyes shut, I always thought. He claimed he didn't know anything about the Russian who was hiding at The Vicarage either. It was a rambling old place, so I suppose it's possible.

'The vicar would get up in the pulpit and talk about "forbear-ance", but no one sitting in the pews listening to his sermons was heading home to the kind of fancy meals I heard he had in the war. The States got him to give a sermon in town. Never had any time for him. A severe man, and his wife was all airs and graces, even though she married beneath her. Never made much of a vicar's wife. He was nothing but a curate when she took up with him. He went into the church after the army and India. It was her family, the Galliennes, who got him the parish and put money into the old vicarage to do it up. She and her sister – Lily was her name – they were chilly types, for all their prettiness, and the daughter took after them. The aunt left for England before the war. I never quite saw what people were talking about, mind you; too thin and pale for my liking – their noses were so far in the air they were in danger of falling over their own feet. People said the girl lost her way, was motherless, and the father never knew what to do with her. He certainly didn't know what to do with her after the war. I heard there was a right ding-dong about adoption. Sorry, that would be you that was the baby, wouldn't it? She took the baby to England. He became a near recluse. Got to the pulpit every Sunday, but otherwise barely spoke to a soul. Stayed on in the house. I heard she came back to visit twenty-five years later. Sad business. The boy was all right. Shame he never came back from the war. Helped me in the glasshouse once, tying up the carnations. Said he wanted to find some butterflies for a school project. A nice polite lad.'

'You mean Edward?'

'Yes, the brother. He was killed – his name is on the memorial in town,' he went on. 'I knew the Russian who was up at The Vicarage – he came over to work for me for a while. I needed workers – I had a big business at that time – and he chipped in and worked hard. He spoke good enough English to pass for an islander. Alex, he was called.

'Sometimes in the evenings, Heinrich talked to me about Helene. He never used her name, but he said he'd fallen in love with an English rose – that sort of stuff. I was always a bit sceptical myself. He'd been such a one for the women before. I didn't know how long it would last, and I was proved right in the end. He never came back for her, did he?

'He took her to Paris once, I heard. A friend saw them boarding down at the harbour. That got around. Later there were rumours that he had taken her to a doctor in Paris because she was in the family way by then, but you never knew what to believe. How would people know something like that? She didn't talk. But Heinrich would have done something like that. A girl died in Guernsey from a backstreet abortion around that time. Girls were that desperate, it was an awful business.'

Roz interrupted: 'Paris? What date would that have been? Do you remember?'

He sat back, rubbing his chin.

'Well, I can't be sure. Dates blur in the memory. I remember it was cold. Maybe late 1943 or early 1944?' He paused. 'My memory is not what it used to be, so don't hold me to it. Could have been earlier. I never saw her myself at the harbour. It was only what I heard.'

Roz was listening intently. 'When did you hear this rumour?'

'Ah, well, that I wouldn't remember now. What difference does it make?'

He was irritated by her close questioning. He resumed his account: 'I heard the gossip about his execution. I can't say I know what happened. By then, all the Germans were starving. Heinrich was miserable. He was very worried about what would happen to his family in Berlin when the Russians arrived. The last time I saw him in the war was about March 1945, and he told me to hang onto the pictures no matter what. He would come back and get them.'

Mr Brown sipped his tea.

'And he did. He came back in 1967. He strolled up the drive

one day without any warning. He looked much the same – less hair, but lean and well dressed. He had a woman with him in the hire car. It was like the twenty-two-year gap had never happened. He was, "Hello, Arthur. How are you?" as if it was the most normal thing in the world. I was in the potting shed and saw him through the glass. I was amazed. I'd thought he was dead, and there he was, as happy as you like.'

He chuckled at the memory.

'He'd brought a bottle of the French brandy we used to drink during the war. I was rather pleased to see him, to tell you the truth. It had always seemed a bit of a shame to me that the man had been executed. He sent his wife back to the hotel, and we sat down to the brandy and talked. He asked about Helene and I said I didn't know anything. Had heard she'd gone off to England after the war and there'd been rumours of a baby. He didn't ask any more.

'Then he asked about the pictures. I had kept them all. Moved them out of Dieu Donne when I left, and carried the boxes around with me until we bought our first house, and then I moved them into the attic. The wife often asked what they were, but I just told her to leave well alone.

'Well, to cut a long story short, Heinrich made it worth my while to hand the boxes over. We went on holiday to Barbados. He was very generous. The wife never knew – I told her I won the money on the pools. We had a good holiday – a month in a top hotel. Cocktails on the beach. That sort of thing. Wonderful. Mind, don't you go telling anyone now. This is between us, isn't it?'

Roz nodded.

'He came back a couple of times in the 1970s. He said he liked the place, and he usually stayed at one of the smart hotels. He did a spot of cliff walking, I gathered. He would drop by with a bottle and some perfume for the wife. Always had presents for us. A nice man. He never came back with his wife – he said he preferred walking the cliffs on his own. Don't blame him. It's pleasant on the cliffs when a good breeze is coming in. You don't want a woman's chatter.

'When they found the paintings at Dieu Donne a few years back, I wrote and told him. I must have missed some. He phoned up that time and said, 'Keep it quiet, Arthur. Don't talk. Easier for everyone that way.' I understood him, and kept my mouth shut. I've always thought that was the right way to go about it anyway. This is the first time I've talked. I saw the adverts you put in the paper and that got me thinking, but I wasn't sure about calling. I guessed you were Helene's daughter. Everyone guessed that. We were all talking about it down the golf club – I don't play much these days, but we like the company.

'But I thought, a person needs to know her parents. So I took the plunge and got in touch. I imagine you wouldn't want to cause any problems for your old father. You must have had more than your share of problems, what with your mother. Your mother had a tough time after the war, there's no mistake.'

'I don't understand – what do you mean? What happened?'

He looked uncomfortable. 'A friend of mine who lived out at Portelet Bay, near Pleinmont, said she used to wander around there after the war. Half out of her mind, she was, he said. She used to go out to a place near the headland. A spooky place, to my mind. Near the old stones at La Table des Pions. She used to sit up there for hours in the dusk, he said. They found witches there in the olden days, and your mother was a bit witch-like. Meaning no disrespect, of course.'

He came to a stop. Roz waited. He knew he hadn't answered her question.

'Well, now, it was that trouble in St Peter Port after she came out of prison. You must have heard about that. Yobs who should have known better . . .' He trailed off. 'She got a bit bashed about in town . . .'

'Bashed about?' whispered Roz.

'Well, you know – cut the hair. Kicked,' he said unhappily, changing the subject quickly. 'You'll be wanting Heinrich's address, won't you? I never bothered with Christmas cards, so I don't know if it's any use still. I hope you won't cause Heinrich trouble. He changed his name – took his mother's name, I believe. He's called Klein now. Said it was easier that way, after the war, to make a clean breast of things. I could see his point.'

Brown had said all he wanted to say. There had barely been a pause, but now he seemed anxious to be rid of them. He wrote out the address in Berlin and handed it over.

'There is just one other thing,' intervened Jim for the first time. 'My mother used to sing a song – something about "Island of beauty, home of my childhood", that sort of thing. Do you know what it might be?'

'Oh, yes,' said Brown cheerfully, glad to be back on firmer ground. 'That's *Sarnia Cherie*.'

Jim and Roz looked blank.

'The island's song – bit like Guernsey's anthem.' He took a breath and began to sing:

> '*Sarnia: dear Homeland, Gem of the Sea*
> *Island of beauty, my heart longs for thee . . .*'

He broke off and began humming. 'I'm not good on all the words . . .

> "*I left thee in anger, I knew not thy worth.*
> *Journeyed afar, to the ends of the earth.*
> *But thy cry always reached me, its pain wrenched my heart.*
> *So I'm coming home . . . da . . . da . . . dear island of rest.*"

'I've missed bits, but you get the gist. They sang it at Liberation in St Peter Port in 1945. We sing it at the Island Games, that sort of thing.'

'An anthem to homesickness.' Jim smiled.

'That's right. You can see why. Guernseymen were sailors and emigrants – whalers, fishermen, privateers . . . until everyone discovered tomatoes, and then the finance thing.'

Roz and Jim stood up, thanking him for his help. As they all headed to the front door, Brown said, suddenly nervous, 'Mind you don't go making any trouble for your old man.'

For a moment, Roz couldn't understand who he was talking about. Then it registered. 'Of course not,' she said automatically.

Brown looked as if there was one more thing he wanted to say. Roz stood in the hall with Jim, waiting. He cleared his throat. 'I'm sorry about the business in town. Hunger turned people odd – plenty of things happened in the war and they shouldn't have – simple as that. Poor girl.'

They got back into the car. Roz suddenly burst out, 'Brown talks about rumours of a pregnancy in late 1943 – perhaps even an abortion.'

'Brown seemed a bit unreliable,' said Jim, his tone revealing his dislike of the man. He was looking at the map. 'Nosey. He was relying on hearsay. Not sure he really knows what he's talking about.'

Roz chewed her lip, reverting to the question which had been preoccupying her. 'Jim, he could be alive.'

He nodded in agreement, and took Roz's hand to squeeze it. He suggested they head to the place Brown had talked about – La Table des Pions. It was a few miles through the middle of the island from Brown's house in St Sampson. Jim drove and Roz read the map, guiding him through the lanes. They got lost several times and ended up on the coast road. At least if they kept to the coast, they would get to Pleinmont eventually, Jim remarked ruefully.

'Strange how you can get lost in such a tiny place,' he mused.

'Alexei said it was like a big place that had been shrunk,' Roz laughed, adding, 'The only signs are at waist height, carved into granite – not easy to find in the dark, I can tell you. The good thing is that you can never be lost for long – the place is too small. So it's a bit like a maze. You just keep going and there may be a few wrong turns, but before long you can put your mistake right.'

They chuckled. The tension of the day was beginning to ease. They drove along Cobo Bay and then Vazon Bay. The tide was going out, leaving behind it glistening blond sand. They had to slow down repeatedly to allow people to cross the road back to the parked cars. They were laden with buckets, spades, deckchairs and picnic bags. They bore all the signs of a satisfying day at the beach: sandy feet in flip-flops, pink cheeks under sunhats, buckets filled with rockpool treasures.

'There's nowhere along here where you can't see German fortifications,' commented Jim, as they paused to allow a large family to cross. A small child trailed behind, dragging a crabbing net. Roz watched the child's steadfast determination with a smile.

Jim was right. The holidaymakers had laid towels out on one German bunker, and people sat on a bench by another, licking their large ice creams. One headland, pockmarked with concrete fortifications, was riddled with small paths and people were perched on the grass, enjoying the late-afternoon sun. As they drove, an observation tower stood out like a giant thumb against the sun. It required a particular kind of effort to avert one's eyes from all these ruins of war, to look instead at the brilliantly coloured rocks which spilled messily into the sea. The scattered outcrops here snagged the waves rolling in from Newfoundland.

When the eye slipped back to the land, it was drawn to the tower's brooding ruin on the hill.

'It's the way they sit side by side,' said Jim, 'the beautiful coast and the ruins. Renoir came here to paint. That's why the rocks and sea look familiar – I've seen it through his eyes for years. That romanticism is an odd contradiction with the ruins and all that they signify.'

'I've come to like this place. It reminds me of an exquisite embroidery, which becomes more admirable the closer you look – the fineness of the stitching, the neatness of the line,' Roz said. 'It works best at walking pace, when you can accompany the granite walls along the lanes, banked up with earth, studded with plant life – ferns, mosses and succulents. It has an odd intensity – crowded not just with people, but with histories. And not just its own stories – those of people like Alexei and Heinrich too. Like a transmitter mast, picking up the frequencies of other countries' history. All squeezed into a few square miles of granite.'

'Roz – you don't sound much like a lawyer any more. Listen to those metaphors!' Jim chortled with laughter and Roz joined in. They were still chuckling, in the way of those who have known, and enjoyed, each other's foibles for decades, as they parked the car in Pleinmont to walk out to the headland.

'I don't think there is anywhere on this island where you can't hear the sound of the sea in the distance when it's rough – at least I haven't found it. The granite may be solid, but you are always at sea here,' said Roz. The sun was dipping towards the horizon beyond the lighthouse and the silhouette of the treacherous rocks out at sea. They walked along a lane through a copse of fir trees. The ground was covered with the soft brown needles and the scent of their resin sweetened the warm sea breeze. On the headland of short cropped grass, paths led off up the steep hill through gorse and bracken. Plenty of other walkers with their dogs were enjoying the fine evening. La Table des Pions was a shallow circular ditch with low stones set in the turf. A sign recounted a story of elves, fairies and witches associated with the spot. They found a bench nearby and sat down, leaning back to gaze out to sea.

Roz described to Jim a standing stone in the church at St Martin which she had passed in the car on one of her previous trips. The stone stood by the churchyard gate, and it caught her eye, so she had parked the car to take a look. It had been smashed in two at one point by a zealous vicar, then cemented back together and was still standing. The Romans had carved a rough form of a head and face in the thick stone. But the breasts were older – round, plump breasts, close together. She looked it up in the guidebook afterwards: La Gran'mère du Chimquière, dated to 2,500 years BCE. There was something about the figure's dogged persistence against all the odds which had moved her deeply, she added. How objects far outlast the humans who create or venerate them, and how these inanimate things carry the burden of histories forward in their stead. Histories which are not always known or intelligible. Jim nodded in agreement.

She suddenly had an acute sense of her mother sitting there between her and Jim. She was enjoying the sun with them, her eyes closed and a smile on her lips.

For half an hour or so, they sat on the bench, listening to the crash of the waves and watching the spray explode over the rocks out at sea. The sun began to slip behind a band of thick cloud on the horizon and Roz turned to Jim; she was feeling chilled. It was time to find somewhere to stay.

'I think I need to give Heinrich's address to Antoine. Let's finish off what I've started,' said Roz.

Jim put an arm round her shoulder. 'I think that's right. There could be more paintings to trace.'

*

Roz got home to her flat in London, exhausted. She had been on three flights in as many days, and had barely slept. But the answerphone was blinking and she knew what that could mean. A message from Antoine. He had been quick.

'I don't know if it's a relief or a disappointment, but Heinrich Klein died two years ago. It was easy to track down his details. He lived at the address Brown gave until his death. I'm glad that at least you have a conclusion to that search.'

She felt relief. Perhaps she'd later feel regret, but, for now, she didn't have to confront Heinrich. There would be no criminal charges. She picked up the mail and sorted through the small pile. A few bills, and a slim package with handwriting she didn't recognize. It had used the PO box address, and had been redirected to her. It had a Devon address on the back. She ripped it open.

I believe you are Rosamund Rawsthorne and that you are the daughter of Helene. I am Helene's cousin. Lily was my mother. I did meet you once, when you were nine or ten, I think, and I was fourteen, but you may not remember. My mother told me that you and Helene were very important to her, but that we could not see you often. I have no memory of any other meeting. I never really understood why there was this family rift, but my mother told me that things had happened on Guernsey during the Occupation and that Helene's father had found it hard to forgive. She said to me that your mother had managed as best she could, whatever anyone else said.

I had the impression that Helene was reconciled with her father at the very end of his life. I was told that he asked for her forgiveness. Eustace had wanted you to be adopted, I believe. She ran away to have the baby and then she left Guernsey.

For a short while, she lived with my mother in London. You were a small baby then. I remember this period a little. I believe there was some possibility of your father coming to find her. But he didn't appear, and by 1948 my mother wanted to join Daddy in Aden. Fortunately Helene had met the man who would become her second husband by then, and, as you know, they married shortly after. Lily was very sorry never to meet him.

Lily ended up spending much of her life in the Far East, where I grew up. She stayed in contact with your mother and they met occasionally.

I would be very pleased to meet you and to learn more about you and your mother. In the meantime, I send you a small parcel my mother kept in her desk. Helene asked her to look after it many years ago. I gather she told my mother that it represented what she had left behind in Guernsey – at least that is what my mother told me before she died. When I was sorting her things, I confess I almost threw it out.

I hope your mother's death was a peaceful one, and I am so sorry that I was not at the funeral. I hope we can heal this old rift now. I know my mother was very fond of Helene, and felt very guilty that she had been alone on the island during the war.

My very best wishes,

Kate

Accompanying the letter was a small bundle wrapped in pale pink tissue paper. Folded inside a silk sachet was a baby's smocked dress, beautifully embroidered by hand with small blue flowers. It was made of soft pink cotton mottled with age. As Roz held it up, a small envelope fell out. She prized the old glue open. There seemed to be nothing inside, and then a soft blonde strand of hair, tied with a faded piece of silk thread, fell onto her lap. Roz fingered the dress. Had this been hers? Was this her hair? Why were these memories Helene wanted to leave behind on the island? Why give them to Lily to keep?

Epilogue
1998

It had been Malcolm's idea. Roz was uncertain, but he said he had always wanted to visit Berlin, and he prevailed. She had told him most of the story since they had met two years ago, and he had been a close listener. She had insisted that she wasn't curious about the city of her father.

They both liked travelling. Every few months, they took a few days off to visit a city somewhere in Europe for a weekend of long lunches, art exhibitions and music. Malcolm had suggested Berlin once or twice, and Roz would counter with another city – Munich, Milan or Bruges. But then she heard that a big exhibition of Picasso's early prints and etchings was opening in Berlin. She was curious to see if any of the works matched Justin's descriptions of Helene's stolen artworks, so she finally agreed to Malcolm's proposal that they make a weekend of it and see Berlin. That's how they found themselves in a hotel off the Kurfürstendamm one weekend in July.

Berlin was hot and dusty, and the city seemed intent on enjoying the long light evenings. The pavement cafés were alive with chatter and laughter, and from every direction came music. They were amongst the first into the exhibition. Roz had Justin's letter in her pocket. He had described two works by Picasso in sufficient detail for her to try to find them. One was a lithograph of a woman's face in semi-profile: a long straight nose, long eyes, a faint smile on her beautiful lips. Nothing matched Justin's description. But, towards the end of the exhibition, Roz saw the second work from the other end of a long gallery. The rich blues of the aquatint *La mère* glowed in the white gallery. The tender affection of the mother leaning over to kiss the child's forehead, and the basket of sewing at her feet.

'A beautiful image of motherhood for a soldier to choose in the midst of a war,' said Malcolm thoughtfully.

Roz nodded in agreement. She was overcome with emotion, standing in front of this mother, an image her father had chosen in wartime Paris, and had then given to her own mother. It had ensured Helene had the freedom to come to England, to keep her baby, and had led her to Justin. The image had also, in the end, destroyed Justin's career. So much of Roz's life history had pivoted around this artwork. All the while, it had been entangled in a much larger public history of conquest, ideology and persecution.

She was overwhelmed by the weight of the family history that the tender picture now represented to her. She watched other visitors in the gallery look at the print, and then move on. They knew nothing of it.

*

That evening, Malcolm found a restaurant by a lake in Wannsee. It was one of the things Roz loved about him – whenever they travelled, he researched with great care the best places to eat. They sat at their table within a few feet of the water. Lights were sparkling on the other side of the lake, and occasionally a phrase of music drifted across. They had finished their meal, but were lingering to enjoy the remainder of a bottle of wine. It was their last evening. They had a flight home the following afternoon. Despite the beauty of the place, they were both subdued. Roz had found Berlin, and the reminders of its brutal history, even more difficult than she had feared. And Picasso's print kept coming back to mind, as if her dead father was saying something to her personally, through his choice.

'Before we leave, you should at least go and see your father's old house,' said Malcolm, leaning forward to put a hand on her arm.

Roz bristled. 'That's not necessary. I've seen the city – and there is no echo of a genetic inheritance; I'm just a tourist here.'

Malcolm shrugged his shoulders. 'Up to you.'

Roz smiled. He knew when to withdraw, but she had learned that it was usually tactical rather than an admission of defeat. The unnecessary emphasis in her voice betrayed the struggle that had been at the back of her mind all weekend. For the first time in years, she was very happy, and she didn't want anything to get in the way of that. The discoveries after her mother's death had been bitter, and she often thought of the hidden pain of her mother's life. It made her love for Malcolm feel all the more precious and unexpected. As if she were carrying a priceless Chinese porcelain on a tightrope. When she had used that image with him, he had laughed.

'Why so delicate?' he asked. 'Why not like an articulated lorry on a motorway?'

They had been lying in bed at the time, and they laughed at inappropriate metaphors and drank his distinctive strong coffee. That's when he had suggested they marry – 'Make it like a motorway, so we know where we are going,' he said. After a moment, he added, 'That vase – why so little trust, Roz? Of love, of life?'

'Perhaps I inherited it – from both my parents. Perhaps such emotions, perceptions, can be passed down. Perhaps it comes from those very early years before Justin, when I was with Mother, alone in London,' said Roz. She added shyly, 'That's a yes, by the way.'

They'd celebrated with an old bottle of champagne that Malcolm retrieved from the back of a dusty cupboard in his studio. By the time its contents were finished, they had planned the wedding. Small – her brothers and their families, Malcolm's two children, and cousin Kate. In the garden at Jim's in France.

It had turned out to be a fiercely hot July day, and they all took to the river to cool down, including Roz, still in her red silk dress. Malcolm carried her, dripping and laughing, out of the water. In her wallet, she kept the slightly blurred snapshot taken by Malcolm's son. She couldn't remember a day so full of love. A year on, Malcolm would occasionally put the 'Chinese porcelain test' to her. They would laugh at their private code, but, yes, she admitted, lorries and motorways were becoming more credible.

They had visited Guernsey together and found a second cousin on her grandfather's side of the family. Over a long dinner in a restaurant in St Peter Port, he had talked of meeting Helene just the once, at Eustace's funeral, when he was a teenager. Roz took Malcolm for a walk on the cliffs, and they spent a couple of days discussing the loose threads of her complicated tale as they walked the coastline of Torteval and the Forest, where she imagined her parents had first met.

On the last morning in Berlin, Roz told Malcolm over breakfast that she had decided to take his advice. He had the good grace not to look surprised. She said she wanted to go on her own. She would just look at the house and the street. He walked her to the S-Bahn and bought her a ticket to Grunewald.

She found the tree-lined street easily from the station. The lawns ran down to the pavement and the houses were handsome, solidly built, without being grandiose. A small boy was cycling down the pavement, and she stepped aside. His mother, walking behind, smiled in acknowledgement. Roz continued, looking for Number 37. She saw the hydrangea bushes in bloom in the front, and, on either side of a front door, two large pots of bright blue agapanthus. She walked halfway up the path and paused; she could hear the sound of classical music coming from an open window. Heinrich had done well for himself, she thought. She was about to turn away when the front door was suddenly opened by a man of about her age, evidently on his way out. He was calling goodbye over his shoulder to the occupants inside. He was plainly surprised to see her, standing awkwardly on the path.

'I'm so sorry to disturb you. Do you speak English?' said Roz hesitantly. 'I'm researching someone who used to live here. Heinrich Klein – or Heinrich Schulze? I was wondering if you knew of him. I believe he lived here until a few years ago.'

'I do not speak good English.' He looked shocked, searching for the words. 'You need my wife.'

He opened the door and gestured for her to come in. 'I get her now. Please stay here.' He moved towards the room from which the music was coming.

Roz waited in the hall. The floor was of polished wood, and a large mirror hung on the wall. She looked through the half-open door to a sitting room. Richly coloured Persian carpets covered the floor, and bookcases lined one wall. At the end of the room were glass doors leading into a garden, where she could see a young woman lying on the grass, surrounded by what looked like textbooks.

A woman of about Roz's age appeared in the doorway to the hall. She seemed familiar somehow. She looked at Roz carefully.

'Hello . . . can I help?' she asked in English.

Then suddenly, before Roz could answer, she said, 'Come and sit down. Perhaps you would like some coffee?'

She led her into the sitting room. Roz was disconcerted.

'Thank you, that's very kind, but really . . . coffee is not necessary.' Roz broke off. The woman was looking intently at her.

'I don't want to take any of your time. I just wondered if you knew anything about the previous owner of the house. A man who lived here until about five years ago,' she added quickly.

The woman's manner unnerved her. She was holding out her hand to shake Roz's.

'I'm Klara.' There was a pause. 'Let me get some coffee.'

Roz felt uncomfortable under her steady scrutiny, but she nodded.

'I'll be back in a moment. Milk?'

She disappeared and Roz could hear an animated exchange with her husband in German in the kitchen over the sound of a coffee machine. He had not gone out after all, she noticed. She checked her watch. Malcolm would be waiting.

Klara returned with a tray. She poured the coffee.

'You are visiting Berlin for a holiday?' she asked, as she handed her a cup.

'Yes . . . visiting an exhibition.'

'The Picasso?' asked Klara.

Roz frowned in surprise.

'My father was very fond of Picasso,' said Klara.

Roz changed the subject. 'I have been trying to find out about Heinrich Klein. I came to see if anyone here might know of him.'

Klara nodded.

'He was my father, but I never knew him,' added Roz.

Klara sat back. This information didn't seem to surprise her.

Roz's eyes shifted under Klara's gaze out into the garden. The young woman had sat up. She had her back to Roz and was wearing a skimpy sundress. Some of her long blonde hair was pinned up on her head. She was gathering up her books. Roz sipped her coffee.

'I was wondering if you knew this man?' Roz repeated.

Klara nodded thoughtfully. 'Yes, I did. I knew him very well.'

In the garden, the young woman stood up, and turned towards the house, walking towards them. Roz watched her with growing astonishment. The woman coming down the garden path was

Helene. The same wide-set eyes, the chin, long nose and the full mouth. The same slight build, long neck and thick, wavy hair.

Roz's hand trembled, and the cup rattled as she put it down in the saucer. Bewildered, she looked at Klara.

'He came back for me,' Klara said softly.

Roz stared at her.

'He came back to Guernsey and found me.' She took a breath. 'He was my father too.'

The young woman appeared on the threshold, and the two spoke rapidly in German.

'This is Helene,' said Klara, introducing her to Roz. 'My daughter.'

Roz looked from one to the other.

'I named her after . . . m-my mother,' Klara stammered. Her eyes filled with tears, and she abruptly stood up and turned away.

Helene came forward to offer her hand to Roz.

'This is your English aunt, Helene,' said Klara, her back still turned.

'Pleased to meet you,' said the young Helene with stiff politeness.

Roz just managed to return the greeting.

Klara turned. 'I know. The resemblance is remarkable. I have one photo of my mother from the war. With my father.'

Roz was speechless.

'You didn't know? I was born in May 1944. I was nearly a year old when the war ended.'

Roz thought of the visit to Paris, of Brown's rumours. He had been right. There had been a pregnancy in late 1943, but no abortion. Roz counted the months slowly on her fingers – twenty. Close enough to confuse everyone – even Alexei. He had not realized there were two babies. Perhaps it was not her he had met but Klara.

She looked up and her eyes met Klara's. She had been watching her count – and she understood why. They were sisters.

The embroidered child's dress, the baby's hair: they didn't belong to Roz. Her mind was racing; they were Helene's mementos of Klara, the baby she had lost. Had anyone else known? She tried to remember the details of Alexei's story. How had her long talks with him not revealed this? All the time they had been at cross purposes. He had assumed Roz was Klara.

Klara went over to a cupboard and picked up a framed photo. She handed it to Roz. It was the photo taken by Alexei of Heinrich and Helene on the bench at The Vicarage.

'He went back to Guernsey in 1949 to fetch me, when I was five. I was fostered, as a small baby, by a niece of Helene's old nanny. At least that is what I've been told. I have memories of Kit – that is what I called my foster mother. She was a very kind lady, and we stayed in touch until she died, when I was fifteen. I remember a few things from those years, such as the beach and the garden of the little cottage where we lived. I remember my father's arrival. When I was older, my father told me that he and my mother's nanny arranged for the foster place soon after my birth. They were worried that Helene's reputation would be ruined. My father kept Nanna alive during the war.'

Roz couldn't bring herself to speak; she was overwhelmed by the pain of her mother's secret.

'My father was a stranger when he first came to see me, but he was kind. He brought presents with him and, a few months later, after the paperwork was completed for adoption, he brought me back to Berlin. I grew up in his family home and became very close to my grandmother, who had survived the war. My father talked a lot to me of my mother. He told me she was a beautiful and good person. Every year we went to London to look for her, although I didn't know it at the time. I thought we were on holiday. Much later he explained why we sat by the lions in

Trafalgar Square on 17 November every year. The visits must have begun in the early 1950s. Then they stopped.'

Klara paused. Her voice became strained. 'I believe he found Helene in the late 1950s, and wrote to her. She replied, just the once, to say that she was married, and had had two more children. She never came to Trafalgar Square. She didn't want to see either of us.'

There was a long tense silence. Helene was staring at the floor, chewing a strand of her hair. She reached over to hold her mother's hand.

'And the Morels? Do you know about the paintings?' asked Roz.

Klara hesitated.

'Yes, I know about that. I saw that the painting had been found in Guernsey a few years ago. My father told me he had given the Cranach to Helene. He would have been devastated to know that it had been lost.

'He was trying to help the Morels. He explained it to me. He saved two of the children. He was a kind father. He was not an evil man, but – how shall I put it? – I think he knew he had made compromises, as many of that generation did. He thought he had managed to get all the Morels off the lists. He told me once that he did not know where the deportees went. He insisted he knew nothing of the gas chambers. The war troubled him, as it did many of his generation. He didn't want to speak about it.'

There was an awkward silence. Klara's voice was tense, and she looked very pale. She was holding her daughter's hand tightly.

'But I know he loved my mother. He didn't marry for over twenty years; he was always hoping that she would join him. He told me much later, when he was old, that he begged her to leave her marriage and join us.'

Klara looked up at Roz.

'And my – our – mother? What was her story? I have always

understood how difficult it must have been, but . . .' Her voice trailed away.

Here was the destination of Roz's search, and it was one she had never imagined, during all the years trying to piece together her mother's life. Not a father but a sister. She was overwhelmed by the aching loss of the sister in front of her, and the anguish of her parents' love affair. The long journey had brought answers, but also new questions: had Helene been waiting for Heinrich in London? Did he know about Roz, his second daughter?

As if reading her mind, Klara said, 'He heard about you, I believe, when he finally found Helene in London. He wanted to meet you. I don't know if he ever did. When I was young, I wrote to my mother, but I never had a reply. I hoped one day I would meet you and my half-siblings – but it was too painful to search for you all. I didn't know if you knew about me. You had to want to know me. I have been waiting – and hoping.'

She looked up, uncertain. 'One day, will you talk to me about Helene? I would like to know something of her through you. I hope she was happy in her marriage and family. You have two brothers, I believe?'

Roz nodded.

'A sister, after all these years. An English sister,' said Klara, and her voice wavered.

Roz was suddenly reminded of Meg's memory. Klara, Lara. Perhaps Meg had misheard.

'When my mother was dying, she continuously repeated a name – Lara,' said Roz. 'Could that have been you?'

'I was named Lara when I was born in May 1944,' said Klara eagerly. 'Father and Mother chose the name together on Guernsey. But after the war, the family here in Berlin felt the name was too Russian, and they wanted me to be German, so it was changed to Klara.'

She was silent for a moment.

'Tell me, what did she say?' she whispered, her voice thick with emotion. 'What did Helene say as she was dying? Did she really speak of me?' Tears were running down her cheeks and she hurriedly brushed them away.

'Did she really speak of me?'

Author's Note

The Virgin and Child Under an Apple Tree by Cranach the Elder safely hangs on the walls of the Hermitage in St Petersburg. This story is built in part around the beauty of this painting and that of two works of Picasso. It is a work of pure fiction and there is no suggestion that any of these artworks were involved in the Nazi plunder of European art collections in the Second World War. Nor does any character in this story have any bearing on real persons, living or dead. Every attempt has been made to ensure historical accuracy, but any resemblance to an individual is coincidental.

Acknowledgements

My thanks to early readers Kate Sebag Montefiore, Kate Rabey, Ellen Farquharson and Natasha Fairweather for their helpful comments. Polly Glynn kindly chased a key detail. As ever, I am deeply grateful to my agent Sarah Chalfant for her encouragement and support, and to the wonderful Bella Lacey and the team at Granta, including the eagle-eyed copy editor Daphne Tagg. Two books proved invaluable: Lynn H. Nicholas's *The Rape of Europa*, and Otto Friederich's *Before the Deluge*.

Thank you, again, to all the islanders who shared their memories and to the remarkable Georgi Kondakov and Galina Chernakova for a very memorable visit to Orel in 1993, when I researched my non-fiction title *The Model Occupation*. All their stories have stayed with me for more than a quarter of a century.

Keep in touch with
Granta Books:

Visit granta.com to discover more.

GRANTA

Also by Madeleine Bunting and available from Granta Books
www.granta.com

THE PLOT

A Biography of My Father's English Acre

WINNER OF THE PORTICO PRIZE
SHORTLISTED FOR THE ONDAATJE PRIZE

'Grippingly readable ... among the very best non-fiction to have been published in a long while about what it means to be English'
Simon Schama

Keen to understand her complex father and the plot of land he loved, Madeleine Bunting makes an extraordinary journey deep into the history of Yorkshire and of England itself. From medieval ruins to ancient droving paths, through to the tiny stone chapel her father built himself, Bunting reveals what a contested, layered place England is, and explores what belonging might mean to any one of us.

'This is a seriously good book: a borehole history of both an acre of England and Bunting's complicated father ... a wonderful excavation of what a "sense of place" might mean – and of the delusions and fulfilments that landscape can inspire'
Robert Macfarlane

'Through the prism of a single acre, she plays witness not only to the moors, but to England and its people – how our lives have transformed over the past thousand years, and how our connection with the land has itself changed' *New Statesman*

Also by Madeleine Bunting and available from Granta Books
www.granta.com

LOVE OF COUNTRY

A Hebridean Journey

For centuries the remote beauty of the Hebrides has attracted saints and sinners, artists and writers. Journeying through these islands, Madeleine Bunting explores their magnetic pull, delving into meanings of home and belonging, and uncovers stories of tragedy, tenacious resistance, and immigration – stories that have shaped the identity of the British Isles.

'A magnificent book, a heroic journey that takes us as far into the heart as into the islands of the north-west'
Richard Holloway

'Excellent ... I cannot think of a more intellectually challenging or rewarding travel book in recent years'
Mark Cocker, *New Statesman*

'Moving and wonderful ... the author and reader of this book end up losing themselves not just in politics and history and the details of nature, but a sense of wonder'
Amy Liptrot, *Guardian*

'A luminous enquiry ... an exquisite and realistic account of life at the edge ... Bunting [is] a shining companion through the tangle of the isles'
Candia McWilliam, 'Best Books of the Year', *Herald*